SKULL ROAD

Also by Keith C. Blackmore

Mountain Man
Mountain Man
Safari
Hellifax
Well Fed
Make Me King
Mindless
Skull Road
Mountain Man Prequel
Mountain Man 2nd Prequel: Them Early Days
The Hospital: A Mountain Man Story
Mountain Man Omnibus: Books 1–3

131 Days
131 Days
House of Pain
Spikes and Edges
About the Blood
To Thunderous Applause
131 Days Omnibus: Books 1–3

Breeds
Breeds
Breeds 2
Breeds 3
Breeds: The Complete Trilogy

Isosceles Moon
Isosceles Moon
Isosceles Moon 2

The Bear That Fell from the Stars
Bones and Needles
Cauldron Gristle
Flight of the Cookie Dough Mansion
The Majestic 311
The Missing Boatman
Private Property
The Troll Hunter
White Sands, Red Steel

MOUNTAIN MAN

BOOK 7

SKULL ROAD

KEITH C. BLACKMORE

Podium

For my mom

All rights reserved. No part of this publication may be reproduced, stored in a retrieval system, or transmitted in any form or by any means electronic, mechanical, photocopying, recording, or otherwise without prior written permission from Podium Publishing.

This is a work of fiction. Names, characters, places, and incidents are either products of the author's imagination or used fictitiously. Any resemblance to actual events, locales, or persons, living, dead, or undead, is entirely coincidental.

Copyright © 2023 Keith C. Blackmore

Cover design by Alexandre Rito

ISBN: 978-1-0394-2869-0

Published in 2023 by Podium Publishing, ULC
www.podiumaudio.com

Podium

SKULL ROAD

1

Westward.

Grey veils blew across an ice field as awesome and empty as anything the Antarctic might possess. A wide, snowy lace snaked across the blacktop of the Trans-Canada Highway, occasionally obscuring the painted lines and residual tire prints stamping the asphalt. Cones of light flared from the solitary pickup creeping along the road, their range diminishing as the storm deepened. The snow blew harder from the shoulders, raging off knee-high crescents and dunes. The gusts became more frequent, lasting long seconds, lifting great white bands that erased everything beyond twenty feet.

Those were the worst, forcing Gus to slow down even more and wait for the wind to subside. The tire prints, his most trusted link to the road, remained visible underneath him. Those prints allowed him to coast through the center, the safest place to drive. To the monotone beat of wipers, he peered over the steering wheel, eyes narrowed, scanning for pitfalls. The pickup could handle a pothole or two, but he didn't want to test it if he could help it.

A mighty blast of powder screamed across the highway, erasing it from sight.

"Je-*sus*," Gus huffed and applied the brakes. The wind rocked his machine, working itself up to shoving the rig off the road entirely. Worse, it was getting darker. Gauges and numbers lit up the pickup's dashboard. The clock said it was twenty-three minutes after twelve. In the afternoon. The doomsday grey beyond his windshield, however, said otherwise. They'd been on the road for all of thirty minutes when dismal clouds banished the sun.

"Something, isn't it?" Uncle Jack asked, puffing on a fresh cigar.

Gus didn't remember him lighting it up. "Yeah," he said, keeping his foot on the brakes and worrying about whiteouts and snow buildup.

"I don't expect this to ease off anytime soon," Uncle Jack said.
"Yeah. I don't expect it, either."
"I imagine this rig will pull us through."
Gus grunted. He was having doubts.
"How's she handling?" Uncle Jack asked.
"Huh?"
"The truck."

A Ford F-350, once dubbed the Vanguard for its next generation of hybrid engine. Gus remembered commercials for the rigs way back when, remembered how fine the machines looked, but damned if he knew anything more about them. The truck certainly had all the features. Top of the line. Super cab. Cameras for nearly every angle. Luxury interior with stitched leather almost everywhere. Built-in game consoles with screens in the back of the headrests. Monstrous stereo system, the woofer situated right under the seat and ready to shake your pudding. Just to name a few creature comforts. There was no radio anymore, no internet, or even phones or memory sticks . . . but there were old-fashioned CDs. Twenty-two of them. All ambient rock. Gus didn't care. It was music, and music was fine, even fitting, considering how the weather was going. The one thing that surprised him the most, however, was the massage option for the seats, which he discovered while flicking through dashboard screens, searching for the tire pressure.

Massage option.

Nothing but the best for the fucking Leather. He smirked, though a touch sadly.
"Something funny?" Uncle Jack asked.
"No. Well, yes. The truck. Gives massages."

Uncle Jack brightened in a *that so?* kinda way. "Feel like having one?"

"No, it's just . . . well . . . the fuckhead Leather. Never expected *that* crowd to be driving rigs like this. Ones that gave massages. Kinda fucked-up when you think about it."

Uncle Jack drew on his cigar, the end flaring red as he considered the interior with greater scrutiny.

"I mean," Gus continued, "I thought they'd be . . . harder. Y'know? *Real* hard. Like, what's the word? *Spartan*. Yeah. Spartan-level hardcore. Like a religion or something. Give each other an openhanded slap in the morning sorta deal. Sleep on beds of sharpened nails. Shit like that."

Uncle Jack's eyebrows flexed in a *suppose so* kinda way.

"Just didn't think they'd be drivin' top-of-the-line rigs, is all I'm sayin'," Gus finished, gripping the steering wheel that much harder.

The Leather... The words flash-burned his craw. Gus could let loose a few curses when angry. Pure chemical combustion when he got real angry. That insane group of mask-wearing killers raised his internal temps to a savage boil. Letting off steam through his nose, Gus checked his side mirrors. Uncle Jack watched him. He could *feel* his eyes on him, which was weird. Not an hour on the highway and Uncle Jack watched him a lot.

Gus didn't really know the guy, but he hoped he didn't start talking crazy shit.

"So . . ." Uncle Jack drew out, right on cue. "This is top of the line?"

"Oh fuck yeah, I mean . . . listen," and he switched off the wipers.

Uncle Jack listened.

"Hear that?" Gus asked.

"Hear what?"

"The engine."

Uncle Jack listened hard. "It's rumbling."

"Barely though, right? I mean I just pumped the gas. Or whatever the hell this thing runs on. Even with the wind blowing. Barely any noise, but the RPM did jumping jacks. The limo was like that, sorta, except the limo had fuckin' sound effects added. And she handled pretty damn good."

The limo.

Memories of Milo and the kids invaded his head.

The kids. He remembered the children the Leather had hoarded in the penthouse, chaperoned by their gruesome nanny. They had been a surprise. Would they make it back to Whitecap? Gus hoped so. They at least had a chance aboard the limo, despite Milo having the living shit kicked out of him by Vampire Joe and his crazies. Still, the soldier said he was good to go, and he knew the way back to the once secret government base. If need be, he'd teach the oldest kid how to drive the monster. Gus already forgot her name, but she could adjust the seat to reach the accelerator. No trouble. He seemed to remember an automatic pilot feature, but Collie never got around to showing that to him.

Collie.

His darkening disposition took a nosedive straight into the shitter.

"Yeah," he whispered, slam-dunked into a cauldron of pain and sadness. *Hurt.* He hurt all over, but inside was the worst. Not since the days of Adam and the farm had he suffered through such pain. He'd had his bell rung more than a few times over the years. Fingers shot off. Heel shot off. Even his own teeth—but he'd done that himself, so that really didn't count. Collie, however . . . she'd left a cannonball-sized hole in his chest, ragged and raw and forever smoking.

The dreary cloud ceiling seemed lower. More flakes slapped against the windshield in a series of great big exploding splats. Gus flicked the wipers back on. Took his foot off the brake. The wind enveloped the pickup with brutal force, leaning into its metallic bulk and nudging it just a little off course. Just a little, but it worried him. The gusts were getting stronger, the clouds meaner.

Westward, he said not too long ago, but with a snowstorm brewing around him, a *prairie* storm no less, and a disappearing road, westward wasn't going to happen. Winter was going to happen. And he'd survived enough of them to know where he wanted to be during a blizzard—*not* on the open highway, without so much as a single tree around for kilometers. Even as the thought raced through his head, another gust hit, testing—fighting him—for control. The snow thickened, exploding against the glass, and the road just ahead of his hood ornament faded a little more, lost in the haze.

Gus stopped the machine. He shifted from one ass cheek to the other. "Say . . . Jack?"

"Yes?"

"Ah, looks like snow."

Uncle Jack puffed. "So it does."

"I mean . . . it's a dick hair away from a blizzard."

"Would seem so."

"You, ah . . . you okay with turnin' back?"

Uncle Jack cocked an eyebrow.

"'Cause I don't know where I'm goin'," Gus admitted. "Not really. And winter's just startin'. I know all about winters. I know. They can kick you in the nuts. Know what I'm sayin'? Strand you out in the open. Just trap you in whatever you're driving. I'll tell you . . . tell you about the one time I got trapped inside a van. If it wasn't for the shovel I had thrown in the back, well, I'd be dead."

Leaning back, Uncle Jack exhaled smoke and the curls filled the cab.

"Anyway," Gus said. "What do you think about headin' back to the hotel?"

"The hotel?"

"Yeah, the Four Towers. With the power. And the heat."

Uncle Jack diverted his gaze outside the windshield, where flakes continued to spatter. "Think we'll make it?"

"If we turn back now. At the very worst, we get to hike it back the last few kliks."

"In a blizzard?"

"If we got to," Gus replied.

"You'll need to do more cleaning of the hotel."

"I know."

"You left it in a mess."

"We'll stay on the cleaner floors."

Uncle Jack didn't look convinced.

"Look," Gus said. "I'm no expert, but I've been around the block. And I'm not flicking your balls when I tell you, you *want* power during the winter. That shit's *useful*. You don't know how useful it is until you don't have any. All right?"

"Sounds like you've already made up your mind," Uncle Jack said.

Gus glanced at his companion. "Guess so."

"Well, you're the captain of this vessel. I'm merely a passenger. An observer, if you will."

"So you're okay with headin' back?"

"I'm okay," Uncle Jack shrugged. "Just know . . . I won't be much good if we get bogged down. Or for cleaning for that matter."

Gus supposed so. He shifted into reverse, causing the cameras to display snowy views of every angle.

"The hotel it is," he announced, backing up the rig.

"If we can make it," Uncle Jack added.

As an answer, Gus put the machine in drive and eased his foot on the gas pedal.

2

The road was gone by the time they reached Regina. Snow smothered the streets in a heavy blanket and crusted over signs, hiding their messages. Abandoned vehicles grew tall whitecaps that spilled over windshields, hoods, and trunks. Gathering drifts tethered themselves to storefronts and extended long sinewy crests into the unmoving traffic. Powder piled up on dead traffic lights. Lightless buildings towered overhead, casting shadows across the urban chasms, darkening the day even more.

The pickup struggled in places on the way back, forcing Gus to shift into low gear in places until he reached the hotel. Roughly two hours after he'd left, he parked before the wreckage of the front door. A huge letter *C* and an *H* hung askew above the opening, poised to drop. Through the sheets of blowing snow, Collie's coffin—that long flower bed converted into a grave—could be seen in the lobby, stark and solemn and untouched by the angry weather.

A depressed Gus stared at the burial site. "How you doin', babe?" he whispered, his throat constricting, while the wipers worked away. "Hope you're good. Yeah. I'm back. You know me. Couldn't stay away. Couldn't *get* away."

He glanced over at Uncle Jack, except Uncle Jack wasn't there anymore. A confused Gus blinked and checked the back seats before scanning the area outside.

No one.

"The fuck you go?" Gus asked and opened the door. Winter shoved back, forcing him to muscle the door open. A blast of freezing wind and snow shocked him, however, and he let the door close.

"Holy shit," he muttered with a shiver. The old guy hadn't gotten out for a leak, anyway. Not in this weather. The cold would have frozen his pecker off in seconds. *So where the hell . . . ?* Gus looked around, craning his neck.

Nothing. No one. Just snow-buried streets and the wind screaming against the window.

"Fine, then," Gus said and regarded the demolished entrance. Snow blew inside, whitening the corpses strewn around the entrance. More corpses filled the lobby, but they weren't covered. Then there was Collie's grave, thankfully away from it all, but the thought of having to wade through all that frozen carnage stuck a fork in his guts and twisted.

Then it occurred to him. *What about the other hotels?*

There were three other towers, all connected by skyways overhead to form an above-street square. Plenty of trucks and tankers around, even a grand-looking RV which he hadn't checked out. Maybe he'd do that later.

The next hotel just down the street seized his attention.

He took his time driving to the entrance, hearing the crunch of snow under his tires and expecting them to spin out at any time. A huge sign on a grand overhang identified the hotel as the MERLOT in noble but lightless letters. Underneath that broad outcropping was a series of closed doors. Gus steered the pickup underneath the overhang designed to protect arriving guests from the elements and parked directly before the first set of doors. He got out, cringing at the drop in temperature, and approached the entrance. The doors did not open. A vicious gust staggered him as he pressed a hand against the glass. He pushed but moved nothing. Another blast of wind forced Gus to turn his back to protect his face. The upper frame of the entrance had a motion sensor. He stretched to wave his hand underneath it, but it failed to do anything.

"Merlot," he grimaced, and considered the truck while flakes blew into his face.

Ramming the pickup through the doors was a distant option, one he didn't like. Onward he trudged, through ankle-deep snow, to the next set of doors. Those didn't open either.

"Well, fuck you," Gus declared softly. It appeared the Merlot was closed for the season. Another freezing burst of wind flayed him, urging him to take cover. Gus returned to the truck, climbed aboard, and soaked in the deep warmth trapped within the cab. He turned the rig around, figuring he'd have to crawl through the hotel lobby with Collie's grave after all. On the way back, a sloping driveway leading to the first hotel's underbelly caught his eye. A white *P* hung over the ramp.

"How the hell I miss that?" he asked himself, slowing to study the underground garage entrance. After some short consideration, he turned onto the ramp. A slight bump rocked him as he steered past an empty booth with a raised toll gate. Blotches of dried matter spattered the glass. He drove onward until the snow slope ended at the bottom. The headlights illuminated a vast unlit subterranean bunker that stretched out before him, with dozens of concrete columns. The light swept over a dozen or so vehicles—mostly pickup trucks—parked in neat yellow slots. Yellow warning strips and lettering marked the cinder block walls and columns. Near the rear and beckoning were the hotel elevators and glass columns containing gleaming brass staircases. Weak daylight glared down from the level above, where the stairs ended in a lobby door.

Gus parked the truck next to one massive pillar with a yellow *A* painted on its side. He switched off the motor and left the key fob in the cup holder. Ahead of him, the elevator controls gleamed. He leaned forward to size up the stairs.

"Home again, home again," he whispered, and got out of the vehicle.

Cold. Even sheltered from the storm as he was, the place felt like a freezer. The snowy slope at the entrance glowed at the far end, and the wind blew down the ramp. The snow fell at such a rate, it was hard to believe it was a storm and not some industrial-sized snowblower employed by the city. The tire tracks would be hidden in short time. Gus closed the door and hefted the Ramfist. There were no shells for the weapon but, as far as he knew, he'd taken care of most, if not all, of the zombie presence.

Still, he felt better with the shotgun in hand.

His boots clicked off the concrete floor, echoing in that immense space. A chill stopped him and he eyed the shadows for movement. Seeing nothing, sniffing, Gus made his way over to the first elevator. There, he examined the controls and selected a button.

Overhead, the elevator kicked into life and descended.

The storm quickened into a blizzard behind him, its winds truly starting to howl. Gus pivoted with his gun raised, making sure nothing got the jump on him. The darker recesses of the lot sparked another shiver, one that spread across his shoulders and tingled his spine. Those lightless places dared him to come closer, to just take a minute to check things out, to ensure all was well.

Gus did no such thing. The elevator's doors opened and he lifted the shotgun.

Empty, just a wooden interior with brass railing and a red carpet. A residual stink of fear and shit and dead bodies hung about the chamber, however, and he suffered with every breath.

"God . . . *damn*," he groaned, taken aback by the released smell. Not wanting to take the stairs, he filled his lungs and stepped aboard, the carpet crunching ever so softly. He turned to face the closing doors, impressed by the quantity of brass. There was a lot. Panels, frames, and railings, highlighting scratched wood surfaces. Gus studied the classy decor, his reflection distorted in the dull sheen. He jammed a thumb into the number five button and his stomach lurched as he ascended. Not too fast, thankfully. The smell was already getting to him. The last thing he needed was to barf.

"Sweet Jesus," he gasped, releasing his breath when the doors opened seconds later. He rushed out, breathing in better air, glad he didn't pass out from the ordeal.

"Take all day to get rid of that stink," he sighed and regarded a wide corridor covered in a brown carpet with a helix-inspired design. More wood paneling, dark and rich, graced the walls, reminding him of where he was. This was no roadside motel. Oh no sir. This was a five-star *dream*. A fairy-tale *palace*. The desired destination for extremely wealthy world travelers. At least at one time. Vague memories of the lavish penthouse teased him, where the Dog Tongue and his henchmen had taken up residence. Gus had no intention of revisiting that room of nightmares anytime soon.

The hallway hinted at what a healthy corporate expense account could provide.

"And only the fifth floor," Gus muttered, glancing around. He wandered to the left without reason, still somewhat in awe of the grandness of the hallway. A somewhat tarnished grandness as some of the chandeliers were smashed, their crystal shards strewn across the carpet, leaving the walkway crunchy underfoot. The shadows bled into opulent blackwood. The thick carpeting reduced his footfalls to dull thuds, and when he slowed his steps, he was damn near soundless.

"Ninja Gus," he whispered, and tried to stay soundless.

All the doors were closed and required keys. He tried each one.

A sharp turn to the left marked the end of the corridor, along with a corner door. A slightly discolored bronze plate read 512. A splash of maroon stained the surrounding wood surface. As he'd been doing, he tried the knob and discovered it already open. The toe of a vacant slipper was jammed in the opening. Shotgun ready, he nudged the slipper inside and pushed open the door.

"Excellent," Gus said under his breath. Kicking the slipper aside, he checked the hallway before easing into the room.

Where he stopped and stared. "Holy shit," he exhaled.

Under soft lighting, a queen-sized bed draped in heavy brown comforters dominated the floor. Three lines of pillows blotted out the headboards, inviting weary travelers to jump right on. Over the bed hung a painting of an ancient forest with a winding pathway, leading off into some fantastical realm where elves or fairies might lurk. High-end furniture surrounded the bed, from night tables to a television stand that seemed too big for the room. There was a gas fireplace with what looked like a oak mantle. A circular table and posh chairs lay at the end of it all, situated before ceiling-high curtains of thick material.

Gawking at all that elegant goodness, Gus eventually realized no one would be inviting him to enter. So he went in, stepping onto the hardwood entry. A posh carpet covered the rest of the room, one so nice Gus didn't want to walk over it with his winter boots on. He did, however, turning left and flicking on a switch. The resulting light froze him, and his mouth dropped open at the second wondrous sight.

A small kitchen, with tasteful cupboards and refrigerator. Marble countertops with surfaces resembling galaxies. Next to that, a short hallway to the bathroom. The bathroom was the juice, however, and it lured him in. High, spotless toilet, with a full roll of crap wrap waiting for someone to give it a spin. More marble countertops, as if the hotel had been built next to a quarry. How much marble could the Anchor Bay have in it? And what was the cost? Even the gleaming porcelain left him speechless. Scented soaps by the half dozen lay in a nearby clay basin, along with a collection of shampoos and conditioners and a razor with a pack of complimentary blades of a quality that was hard to believe was free. There were thick towels and facecloths a plenty, all neatly stacked on a shelf. A glorious hair dryer that still worked. A high-end bathtub two skips away from the toilet, perfectly placed after a messy spray and pray. The shower was a skip beyond that. A clear glass wall partitioned the shower, showing off the space-age luxury of not one, but eight individual heads.

"Jesus, Jesus," Gus whispered. Once again, he felt as if he wasn't worthy enough to use the shitter. It wasn't a penthouse, but it *was* the penthouse equivalent of any lesser hotel or any place he'd previously bunked down for a night. And it was warm. Good Lord above, it was warm, almost convincing him that it wasn't November outside, but rather a sultry day in late July. The Leather had left the heating system on, or perhaps it was like this anyway, regulated by some AI overlord. In any case, he was starting to overheat.

There was no need to check under the bed as there was no exposed space underneath to check. A solid baseboard ringed and supported the box mattress, and Gus checked its stoutness with a couple of toe taps. Eyeing the palatial room, he wandered over to the curtains. Dark and heavy and impenetrable, he pulled one back, allowing grey light inside. Wet snow slapped and pasted the exterior glass in heavy splats. Under angry heavens, the storm continued to rage, obscuring streets and the nearby buildings with every gust. No lights lit up those buildings and the streetlamps remained off. All that dreariness caused Gus to close the curtains. It wasn't his first blizzard and, all things considered, all he needed was champagne.

The carpet cushioned his footfalls until he hit the hardwood. The room's door had locked automatically. There were two interior sliding bolts above and below, which Gus thought almost ridiculous. If a fifth-floor room was this nice, their main lobby security measures must have been top-shelf. Still, he bolted the door, briefly feeling the same sense of safety as his place in Whitecap's residential area.

"See what you're missin', Collie?" he asked the empty room and waited for a reply. When none came, a hot rip of sadness branded his chest, and he lowered his head. Memories then, of times before and presently lost. If she were still here, they would be sharing the bed, snuggling up to each other. Maybe he would spoon her. Maybe she would spoon him. Maybe there would be a fork in there somewhere, and that brought on a wretched smile. They would whisper, so as not to wake any nearby children, and talk about the things they missed about the old world.

The sadness welled up, hot and eye-watering and throat-hitching.

"Jesus," he choked out and wiped his nose with his palm. He smiled in spite of his grief. "All right. All right. Enough of that."

But it wasn't all right. It would never be all right. She was gone, gone forever, and all he had left were the memories.

Dabbing at his eyes and clearing his throat, Gus decided to test the nearby lamps, which worked. Since he had no ammo, he tossed the Ramfist onto the bed and spotted a comfortable set of slippers tucked damn near perfectly into the baseboard.

Gus left them, however, and exited the room. He returned to the garage and his truck. Picked up his cooler and lugged it back to the elevator, where he set it down outside the doors. Next was his spear—a dirty spike, really, atop a six-foot length of wood. Perfect for thrusting, but the thing didn't impress him. Not really. Shells for the Ramfist would have to be a priority, right after food and water. Maybe he'd luck out and find a sport shop nearby. Maybe. This far downtown, chances were most shells would have been found and used. With a contemplative nibble on the inside of his cheek, he walked back to the lift and loaded everything inside. Sweat flowed in earnest by the time he entered room 512 once again and wrestled the cooler over to the table. He stuffed two loaves of bread into the fridge along with the meats. Cold cuts and sandwiches. There was no salad dressing, however. No mayo. Not even a squirt of mustard.

"Cook," he said. "Where's my lunch? Where's my dinnah?"

No answer, which was a good thing.

Deciding he'd put in a fine bit of work, Gus felt thirsty, and not for water.

That urge pulled him back to the window, where he parted the curtains and peeked at the weather. Wind battered the pane. Snow caked the exterior screens and frosted the nearby buildings, glimpsed only in brief lulls before the blizzard flexed and made the downtown depths disappear in a rush of white-water fury.

He thought of ancient televisions, and their off-air patterns from disrupted antennae signals.

Off-air. Yep.

That was him. Here.

Releasing the curtain, Gus faced the room, the suite really, and mentally shrugged. The urge for a drink hit him. Clobbered him, really. And he wondered if the hotel had a bar somewhere. That would require him to look for it, which brought a frown to his shaggy face. Standing there in the empty room, he had no desire to look for anything.

The faucets in the bathroom worked, so he turned one on and let it run. He filled a complimentary glass, did a quick sip test, mouthed it around, and guzzled the rest before gasping at the end. A refill and he gulped that down as well, wiping his wet beard afterward and catching sight of himself in the mirror. Not caring for what he saw, he refilled the glass and retreated to the door. He locked everything and felt a little better doing so.

On impulse, he placed an ear to the door.

Nothing. Not a goddamn thing.

He occupied one room of perhaps hundreds, in one hotel of four, in a city getting buried by the first blizzard of the winter. The sadness returned and he knew from experience that it was going to linger for a long time.

Gus inspected his clothes and started to strip, dropping everything on the carpet. When the Fruit of the Looms came off, he walked into that glorious bathroom, scratching at this and rubbing at that, and eyed the tub. There was hot water, so he got it going and let it run. While the tub filled, he planted his scarred ass on the toilet. Welcome steam drifted across his face. When the tub finished filling up, he eased himself down, right to his chin. Hot water. Near scalding, really, but tolerable. World's best invention. Hands down. Straight from a tap, too. Water breached the rim and spilled onto the floor. Gus ignored it, resting his weary head against the inner curve of moulded porcelain.

The faucet above his feet dripped, slowing to a stop.

Within that dream of steam, he drifted to sleep.

3

Morning.

A soft filament of light outlined the curtains, ruining the pitch-black depths of an otherwise dark room. Ice pellets peppered the glass outside and that harsh sprinkling roused Gus. He winced as if trapped in a bad dream. Truth was, he had no dreams from the night before. At least none he could remember and, for that, he was grateful. Under the blankets, he slid a hand across the mattress, his palm warm against the sheets, and stretched out his whole arm. No one. The absence of another body moved him to look, where he saw no one beside him.

Oh yeah. About that. She's gone. Still *gone. And will* remain *gone.*

Gus lay on his back, blankets pulled up to his chin, and stared at the ceiling. The warmth of the bed tempted him to stay, but there would be no going back to sleep. He rolled over to face the clock on a night table.

7:28, it said.

He sighed. Seven thirty. In the morning. Maybe a half hour into the new day, which meant he only had about ten hours left for shit to happen. He grimaced at that. Some would say he was lucky to be alive, to have made it this far. His tongue probed the gaps from missing teeth, his first and last foray into home dentistry. He clenched a fist that no longer had a full complement of fingers. The missing muscles, tendons, and bones still bothered him at times when he scratched at stumps. All the while, he endured the constant, harsh burn of nerve pain from where he took a bullet to his heel. He didn't even count the scorch marks from his attempt at self-immolation years ago. To add to his permanent wounds, he was also mentally fatigued, which mere rest didn't seem to do much for. The mental weariness was every bit as serious, as it seemed time could never cover up his memories, what with so many triggers to bring them back. Being with Collie had provided him a much-needed sense of positivity going forward, but losing her . . .

Gus rolled his eyes as the nuke dropped. Memories of Collie returning in an unwanted ache that ate his whole heart raw. Somewhere in there were images of Tammy, no longer recent but still painful. Then came everyone else he'd lost along the way, their ghosts parading across his mind.

Lucky to be alive, his mind repeated.

Yeah. He was real lucky.

He also really needed to take a piss. Not once did he have to get up for the toilet, so deep was his sleep. He threw back the blankets and swung his legs over the bed's edge, the air warm to his bare ass. His bladder urged him to hurry, reminding him about the water he'd taken in before bedtime. He mentally informed it to hold on a few seconds more, that it took a little longer to haul his aging ass out of bed in the morning, despite needing to pee. He wasn't a young guy anymore and he was increasingly aware of that fact.

The doorframe cracked his shoulder on the way in, as if telling him to stop such nonsensical thoughts. Once he assumed the position, swaying ever so slightly while he peed, his mind didn't bother him one bit. When he finished, he lumbered back to the bed and regarded the curtains. Was it really still snowing out there? Scratching his nose, he shuffled over to the curtains and pulled them open. The hard glare of daylight penetrated the snow stuck to the window and caused him to squint, but he saw.

Winter.

Massive drifts buried the avenues, tethering their ends to storefronts and snaking away beyond his sight. Whole dunes submerged most of the smaller vehicles, leaving only dark windshields, side windows, and exposed corners of metallic paint. Snowcaps dressed the upper portions of trucks. Powerful gusts continually blew thick streamers of powder across everything, the spray broken by streetlamps.

Gazing down upon all that frigid splendor, he decided he'd made the right choice in coming back to the hotel. Now all he had to do was . . . wait it all out. Wait out the winter. He'd done it before, back on top of his mountain. The fifth floor wasn't nearly as high as the house he'd taken refuge in so long ago, but it was certainly more opulent. Not a great thing, as he preferred something a little more homey, but he would adapt. Sure he would.

Reality struck him then and he released the curtain.

Trapped. He was trapped.

In a hotel. Nay, in a *complex* of hotels.

He slapped that troubling notion away like the unwanted touch of a stranger. *Trapped*. Gus scoffed, reminding himself he had *been there done that* before, back on his mountain. Even when he was on Big Tancook, isolated not only by winter but by waves. Though that time he wasn't alone. Still . . . Isolation was not new to him. He knew what to do. Knew what was important. Just a matter of doing.

The fridge gleamed in the room. He would need more food. One cooler of beef jerky and homemade bread wasn't going to last the winter. As depressed as he was, he would eventually eat and starving wasn't high on his list of things to do. The memory of a certain can of sweet peas came back to him and how it was . . . what was it? Yes . . . *the finish line of side fixings*? The absolute *last* thing you would put on your plate? Something like that.

Which got him thinking.

The cooler he had had come from one truck. There were other trucks, out in the street and down in the garage. Seeing as it was shitty outside, the ones in the garage were more doable. He would search them. Then he remembered the hotel. It had been a base for the Leather. Did those masked wingnuts carry all their food around in coolers, or was he missing something? More memories then, of when he was hunting for leftover zombies in the hotel. Just after Collie died . . .

That familiar ache returned as fizzy as fresh acid, chewing through his chest until his throat hurt and his eyes misted. The corner of the bed was there, so he plopped himself down. Minutes later, after he'd weathered the misery, he looked around in a waking daze.

Christ, he was a wreck. Might be one for a very long time. He could sit in the room and die, remembering Collie and longing for a time that never really transpired the way he wanted . . . or he could make himself useful.

Collie would have wanted him to be useful.

Would have *ordered* him, in fact.

So he rose, wiped his nose with the flat of his hand, sucked back snot, and got moving.

Dry. The sandwich he ate for breakfast was dry. And bland, as if someone was going easy on the condiments. Maybe the meat was a new batch. Maybe the cook was learning as he went. Whatever the case, it was better than nothing. He'd warmed up the food in the kitchen microwave and got it down with some water. After that, he dressed, making a face at the faint but lingering stink of old man piss on his winter coat. A parting gift from Collie, and a reminder that he could do with a new one.

He left the shotgun, picked up the woeful spear, and unlocked the door.

A third of the ceiling lights were on, illuminating a fancy but empty corridor. Gus waited, expecting shapes to step out into the open any second, except nothing of the sort happened. He went for the elevator, the rigs in the hotel garage on his mind.

Daylight glared through the distant entrance, where the wind continued to scream and blaze snow. All that stormy fury framed in concrete held his attention for seconds before he studied the overhead lights. The hotel was enormous, and the spotty lighting made him wonder how all its power needs were being met. Renewable energy was all fine and dandy and the tech had reached a point where whole households could be self-sufficient if you had the cash to invest, but an entire hotel? Four hotels? Without a crew to maintain and service it all? His old place on the mountain had its share of solar panels, but the hotel would have to have a shit ton of those to generate the juice needed to keep its systems working.

Ruminating on the power issue, he approached the first truck, his footsteps loud on the concrete. Some lights flared on as he walked underneath and winked off when he was out of range. Most of the fixtures didn't come on at all.

The first truck was a battered Dodge with a snowplow fixed to the front, offering him the opportunity to do a little downtown clearing if he was ever in the mood. The rig had no food cooler, however. Nothing to drink, either. There were old paperbacks and even a few magazines stashed behind the driver's seat. Gus grabbed the *National Geographic*s, and a ratty copy of a fantasy book called *The Dwarves*.

"Fuck yeah, I'll read about dwarves," Gus said under his breath. "Read about dwarves all day long. Elves, dwarves, fairies. I don't give a shit."

He realized he needed a bag.

"Starting over," he muttered. Then, on impulse, he faced the garage. "I'm fuckin' startin' over here. And makin' startin' over mistakes. C'mon man. It's not that long ago. You're better than this."

He glanced around the vast subterranean lair. "I'm better than this."

The snow-choked ramp at the entrance to the garage caught his attention for a time, where he marveled at the heights piled up there. Then he undid the front of his pissy winter coat—the same grey one taken when he and Milo went shopping a few days earlier. He tucked the ends of his sweater into his jeans and stuffed the book and magazines into the resulting pouch. *Still need that bag though*, he thought as he zipped up. Otherwise, he'd be making a lot of single trips. And stretch out his sweater. Fuck that.

Nine pickup trucks and two cars later, he finished his search and scowled mightily.

Not a goddamn thing. No grub. No drinks. No *nothing*. Plenty of blankets, some of which looked like dogs might've shit on them, judging by the amount of hair and stains. He found some wrenches and screwdrivers, a dozen or so jugs of washer fluid, and even a few air pumps, but nothing else. There were some gas cans with various amounts of fuel, which didn't help while he was marooned by snow. Using the spear as a walking stick, the end clicking on concrete, Gus hiked back to the elevator, eyeing the darker recesses of the garage.

"Nothing down here," he said. "So what does that tell you? That tells me . . . they might've already unloaded everything they had. Maybe brought it all upstairs . . . like I did. Or . . . maybe didn't need to bring anything. Because . . ."

Gus trailed off. The place was big. Mighty big. Probably had a restaurant. Maybe even two or more. He didn't recall seeing any when he was actively clearing out zombies from the hotel, but that didn't mean anything. He'd been in something of a red rage at the time and not overly concerned about restaurants and gift shops. That would change. He would explore the place in greater detail. The other hotels as well, since it might be a couple of months before warmer weather allowed him to leave. Might as well get to know the neighborhood.

While thinking all that, he jammed a thumb into the elevator panel and waited for the doors to open. When they did, he got aboard and rode it to lobby. Gus took a firmer grip on the spear, hating the damn thing. The doors opened and he warily leaned out, holding the elevator doors at bay so that they wouldn't close on him.

"Holy shit," he whispered.

He realized he'd been in shock after Collie died and hadn't really paid much attention to the battleground—the *killing* ground—that was the lobby. Snow had drifted inside the wrecked entrance, covering the red carpeting a quarter of the way to the front desk. Snow had also blown in through the smashed windows, creating small slopes that spilled into the hotel.

Then there were the zombies.

Regular ones and freshly turned Leather. All dead—truly dead—and left to rot. Heads were half blown away or shredded like broken pottery still holding onto their flowers. A few were decapitated entirely. One neck ended in a raw mass of meat and the lower rack of blackened teeth. Ripped bodies lay over furniture that had the unliving shit gunned out of it. All manner of poses, unimaginable twist ties of limbs, and gruesome displays of hyperextended joints. Then there was the seepage from all those carcasses. An oily, congealed slop steeped with fleshy particles no one should ever see. Numb to the show, Gus didn't linger on the clotted puddles of meat and bone. The smell affected him, however, despite the cold, as evidenced by the frosted-over red bits.

He stepped into the lobby, onto blackness. A long-cooled lava flow of gore had pooled at the base of the elevators. Every step left a soft boot print, which he didn't appreciate, and he couldn't help. He watched for movement. Wooden columns highlighted with strips of tarnished brass filled the lobby. Some of the strips hung off, bent like flattened antennas. Others were blown off. More ruined bodies and furniture, entire sofas and chairs exploded right down to their splintery bones. Fallen coffee tables and upended luggage carts, one of which bore the weight of not one but three unmoving corpses, each splayed across the other. Pillows had been blown apart, and their stuffing lay over many things in great red clumps, discolored by soaked-up blood. Bullet holes perforated windows in great spidery designs. In fact, the glass panes to the left and right of the main entrance had taken the brunt of the destruction, being completely shattered.

Jesus, Gus mentally projected, witnessing the smokeless aftermath of extreme violence. Even the artificial plants had suffered, mowed down in a spray of gunfire. He suspected he was responsible for some of the damage done, but not all. Certainly not the destruction of property.

The front desk, perhaps once a long and dignified piece of woodcraft, had been saturated with undead blood, peppered by shells, and now resembled something plague-ridden. A silver bell rested on top of the counter, miraculously untouched and doing quite well, thank you kindly. Gus treaded along the check-in area, resisting the urge to ring that silver dome as he passed. Dozens of the mindless lay underfoot, forcing him to use the spear for balance. He didn't really need to go back there. Not really. He could just leave and go back to his room. Or search another part of the hotel. He'd missed searching the office behind the desk, however, and that was where he intended to go.

But to get there meant climbing over the stiff pile of dead things heaped up before the desk. It was a slow, stumbling trudge, wallowing to the desk over limbs and torsos. Twice he lost his footing and sank up to his shins in arms and legs. When he got close enough, he clutched at the front desk for support and smiled at reaching the finish line. Then he looked behind the front desk.

"Goddamn," Gus released, eyeing the slaughter between him and the open office. A morbid stew of corpses filled the space behind the desk. Upturned boots and knees crisscrossed in an uneven pattern, all forcibly clumped together. Dried gore splashed across and clung to the office clutter of phones, notepads, and smashed computer terminals.

He sighed at the carnage. No way he was going through that, but the desk itself offered a solution. Girding himself, he pulled his aging carcass onto the top of the furniture. He rose with a twinge of light-headedness, cringed at the mass grave below, and spotted an axe.

A shaft, really, but no mistaking the red handle of an emergency fire axe. Gus looked from the axe to his spear and back again. Taking the pain, he got back down on hands and knees again and tried reaching for the thing, teetering for a split-second before hauling himself back.

"Shit," he fired off angrily. He would have to crawl closer to get the axe, and just his luck, it was under a gruesome threesome. Realizing he was without gloves, he decided to leave the axe alone. For the moment, anyway,

"You wait right there," he said and stepped across the top of the desk, bypassing the worst of the mindless clumped together. He then eased himself down where there were fewer bodies. There he teetered, fumbled for balance, and planted a boot heel into a man's spongey face. Grossed out at the contact, Gus yanked his boot away only to step onto a crab-like hand.

The fingers broke with a crunch.

The disturbing crackle froze Gus. Cringing, he stepped off the blue-grey mitt and groaned at the sight. Then he spotted a gun's magazine. Half of one, which he recognized as belonging to the Ramfist. Trouble was, the other half of the magazine lay under the frozen ass of a mindless.

Knowing he wasn't going to enjoy this next bit, he braced himself against the desk, got a boot up, and pushed the corpse. He cringed at the mewling, peeling noise of thick glue coming unstuck. The mindless—a leather-dressed man missing most of his face—only moved halfway, leaving a barcode of nastiness in his wake.

Gus couldn't reach the magazine. He tried hooking it with the spear. Didn't work. There was too much weight on the thing, plus the chilled gore acted as a crude cement. One he didn't want to touch.

"Goddammit," he snarled, and booted the body. Three hard kicks until he mashed it away far enough to toe-drag the magazine free.

"God*dammit*," he swore, and kicked the thing into the office.

The mindless didn't move, the same horrific expression on what remained of its face.

Gus turned around, saw where the magazine had stopped, and went after it. Dewy organic slop the color of motor oil coated the thing. He glanced around the office, searching for something, maybe a pair of gloves. A figure dressed in leather was sprawled facedown across the floor, shot through the chest. Gus didn't spare the corpse another glance.

The desk had brochures on it. A little too thick to use, so he rooted through the furniture's drawers. The first one contained a box of tissues, which he took. A set of regular keys lay in the wider drawer, nearly missed among a tangle of stationery. Moving a clutter of odds and ends uncovered a medium-sized bottle of hand sanitizer, guaranteed to kill off ninety-nine percent of all bacteria. There wasn't much else in the desk, so he picked up the sanitizer and keys.

The keys he hefted. *What do you unlock?* Gus wondered and eyed the brochures again. He pulled the unstained ones apart with a finger, inspected the glossy pics, and then picked one up.

Rest and relax at the Anchor Bay. Luxury at its luxurious best. Living life to its fullest.

Somewhat intrigued, his eyebrows arched at the snapshots of available rooms, from the lowly basic to the celebrity penthouse, where Dog Dick and Vampire Fuck Joe laired. The rooms were stunning. Fit for royalty. And as far as Gus could tell, he was only in a basic single. What was available on the upper floors was even more opulent.

He flipped the brochure over. "Oh my."

Restaurants. Three of them. Huge, stylish eateries just waiting to be experienced. A sports bar; a more family-oriented deal; and third, a more upscale place exclusively for fine eating. Eighth and Tenth floors, right around the skyways. None of the restaurants were any he recognized, but he wondered what might be in their kitchens.

He'd have to take a look.

He'd also have to look at the other amenities of the Anchor Bay. Guest-only gym. Swimming pool. Classic '80s arcade with original video games cabinets and pinball machines. A fucking driving range, of all things, for the golfers, and a neon light lounge area for live shows. Even a nightclub.

All upstairs.

"Where the fuck you hidin' it all up there?" he pondered aloud, searching his memory. There was an elevator to the roof, but he had no idea how many levels up that was. According to the brochure, the place had twenty-five floors, with at least another being developed.

He stuffed the brochure and keys into his pocket.

The office computer had been trashed, whipped off the desk and stomped on in a monster's frenzy. The only thing left of interest was the dead Leather, blasted through the chest. Gus studied the corpse, not wanting any part of that shredded thing, before relenting and yanking out a handful of tissues. Scowling in distaste, he patted down the parts not spattered in gore. Found a fancy brass key with 414 stamped across its end. For a place so high-tech, at least for power, the rather old-fashioned means of security perplexed him. A lather of sanitizing hand gel followed by a quick wipe down and he tucked the key away in his own pocket. He used more gel and tissues to clean up the shotgun magazine and retrieve the fire axe behind the front desk. The magazine was empty, but he took it anyway. Once ready, he left the office and the corpse filled trough behind the front desk. He crawled back over the countertop, cursing and fuming all the way. On the other side, he picked his way through the dead, until he reached the low-grade ski slope flooding the entrance. There, he scooped snow and used a fair amount of tissues to clean off the axe. After a finishing squirt of sanitizing gel and a rubdown, he hefted the new weapon, very much approving of it, and left the spear behind.

"All right," Gus said, gripping his new friend behind its head.

At the other end of the lobby, away from the piled-up dead, was a narrow hallway. Gus eyed that opening before considering the remaining Leather strewn about the floor. His last pair of gloves had been lost somewhere on his journey westward, but a nearby gentleman with his throat chewed away wore a pair of biker gloves. Gus removed and cleaned them with the last bit of gel. A minute later he patted down the same dead gentleman and discovered another brass key, this time with the number 607 stamped on it. He figured each one of these leather-clad morons were probably assigned their own room. The perks of being psychotic asswipes, he supposed.

He could pat down everyone in sight searching for their keys, *or*, and this was a thought, he could hunt for a master key.

A fine, white mist puffed into the lobby, carried on a freezing wind that pierced his clothes and delivered a shiver. *Cold.* Prairie winters were the worst, or so he had once heard from his departed Jerry, before Jerry became the killer calling himself Shovel. Wanting to end his search before his nuts crystalized, Gus treaded back to the desk, spotting a large cubbyhole cabinet made of fine oak where the hotel's keys were kept. Right next to the office doorway. He'd gone right by it.

Unimpressed with himself, he grabbed a chair and used it to get over the desk. He still stumbled over dead things.

A thin layer of dust dulled the lustre of the cabinet. The Anchor Bay apparently boasted two hundred rooms, each with its own cubbyhole, but not all containing a key. And there was nothing to indicate a master to unlock every door.

"The hard way it is, then," Gus scowled and faced the cabinet. "Fuck you muchly."

Then it occurred to him that the master key might very well be with the master.

The Dog Tongue.

The Dog Tongue's dead body, more precisely.

That thought pinched Gus's taint and gave it a rough grind. At the base of the cabinet were a few drawers, and another cabinet beneath that. He opened the drawers and peered inside. Nada. Squat. He shoved them closed and tried the cabinet. A blue plastic bin awaited him, fixed with a LOST AND FOUND label. He pulled out the container, removed the lid, and inspected the contents.

And was pleasantly surprised.

Inside were a couple of Christmas-themed coloring books and a generous pack of crayons. A sketch pad, but no pencils. A couple of pens, pencils, and notebooks. A heavy flashlight. A child's winter hat, along with a smiling stuffed toy lamb with floppy arms and legs. Several pocket novels. A leather belt, the buckle fashioned with a smudged lightning bolt of brass. Keys, tarnished and rattling, all attached to fobs. Even an ancient handheld gaming unit with a dozen games preinstalled.

He heaved the container up onto a counter. One huge intake of air later, he plucked the flashlight free and judged it about two pounds.

"You're heavy," he said and stuffed it into a pocket. The toy lamb stared at him. It had a pleasant little smile, almost sad in a way. Gus gave it no further thought and turned back to the cabinet. He found the cubbyhole with his room number but no key and no replacement. Keys for other rooms were present, so he took them, figuring what the hell. He'd check those rooms later, when he felt like it. Be like a treasure hunt. Considering the amount of snow already down he guessed he would have plenty of time to look around.

Then the Dog Tongue entered his thoughts. The dead bastard was still up in the penthouse, where Collie had infected him. She'd also shot him in both legs, or something to that effect. Gus's memory of the events was a little hazy, but he knew she'd infected him, which was as good as putting him down. Gus considered making it official. And if there was a master key, the Dog Tongue would have it. Get the master key, and that would spare him from rummaging through the pockets of any more dead Leather. Then he could get on with checking out the rest of the hotel.

His newly acquired fire axe in hand, Gus went for the elevator.

4

A pleasant *ding* signaled the end of the line, gently popping Gus out of his moody thoughts. He barely felt the elevator stopping, but then the doors parted to a familiar leather sofa, its puffy guts ripped out and generously spattered with dried blood. Two leather-clad corpses were splayed across the cushions, both killed by gunfire. A third guard lay facedown like a very unwelcoming mat, a pool of dried blood spread far and wide across the white marble floor. Blood spattered the tropical sun wallpaper behind the sofa. An equal amount of fluid spattered the two fake palm trees flanking the furniture. Matter of fact, thick maroon streaks and dollops coated pretty much everything in sight.

"Jesus Christ," Gus whispered, awestruck by the amount. If he didn't know any better, he would've sworn someone had torn through the place with a chainsaw.

The doors started to close so he stopped them with a boot. They retreated. Frowning, Gus concentrated on listening.

Not a peep.

Not that he trusted the peace. He didn't. Not for a fucking second. Zombies had come this way. A lot of zombies. He remembered the mindless rushing by the elevator doors just as they were closing on him and Collie.

Collie.

That familiar god-awful ache gripped him once again, and he figured it would keep on grabbing him for a very long time. *Goddamn*, he thought. She should be with him, leading the way. Not him. *Anyone* but him. And certainly not by himself, all alone.

The doors attempted to close once again. Gus stopped them with a hand and they withdrew.

To his left was the dark entry of the stairwell, the door propped open by a single festering corpse. Gus scanned the other direction. A pair of doors that might have been pulled off a medieval castle marked the penthouse entrance. They were swung open and looked inviting, until you noticed the dried gore sprayed across the wood and fine lines of embossed gold.

The elevator nudged his hand again.

"Sweet fuck, two-tits," he muttered and stepped off the impatient thing. *Two-tits.* The hell did that one come from? He surprised even himself at times.

The hallway lights were on. Probably never went off. Underneath that soft glare lay several ruined bodies, splayed out in checkerboard fashion. Just a handful, but enough for the hairs on his neck to crawl. Just like the old days, but damn if he didn't feel naked. Especially after experiencing the comforting weight of body armor.

Licking his lips, Gus gripped the fire axe and eased toward the stairwell. He checked on that chasm, the only light from some unseen source one floor down.

All empty, however.

A scuffling from the penthouse entrance jerked him around.

There, like a guardian emerging from some defiled temple, stood a charred and oily figure, hands poised and ready as if about to draw six-shooters. The grey-faced thing limped into the light, head bouncing on failing musculature, only to straighten with a pop of rotten vertebrae. One eye stared, while the other was a filth-caked hole of ocular jelly. Lipless jaws flexed, shivering a long sail of skin hanging off its jaw. The rotten stink surrounding the walking corpse reached Gus first, a sinus-melting mix of putrefying fluids that stunned him the moment he got a whiff of it. That noxious odor pushed him back an involuntary step. He faltered, squared up, and checked on how close he was to the wall and the stairwell.

The mindless shambled through the penthouse doorway, where it stubbed a foot into the first corpse draping the floor. The mindless fell, mashing its face into hard marble without so much as a bounce but rather a hollow coconut *clop*. One arm flopped across the nearby pelvis of another carcass and there the face-planted zombie stayed, twitching yet unable to rise.

Gus crept forward, threading his way through the gruesome obstacle course littering the floor, intent on splitting the thing's skull. From within the penthouse, glass crashed onto the floor and two more zombies ambled into view, arms swinging as if they carried some great invisible weight.

Gus closed the distance to the first animated corpse. When he got within range, he deftly split the skull of the fallen Moe. Steel bit marble underneath, the sound crackling loud and the impact thrumming up his arms. Checking his footing, he planted a boot against the cleaved head and yanked the axe free.

The two other mindless entered the hallway.

Gus backed up, daring them to follow.

They dared.

And immediately tripped in the open graveyard that was the floor. Both went down as if shot through the chest.

Gus pounced.

He chopped the first's head, splitting it apart and burying the blade in the spurting neck. The neck refused to give up the killing weapon and when Gus yanked hard to free it, he stumbled. He landed in a broad stance, still on his feet, when the second mindless reached for an ankle—always the ankles. Gus darted a step back and soccer-kicked its head. The boot toe sunk deep into that brittle facial bone, the tongue popping out like an obscene slug.

Which was right about when Gus realized neither of the dead fucks was decked out in leather. He dragged his foot free, ignoring both the squeezebox sensation of nerve pain and the chunky dribble of matter that followed and reared up his axe. Still moving despite having its face kicked in, the zombie clamped a hand around his ankle.

Too close to swing the weapon, Gus pistoned the axe head into the profile of the corpse, squishing an ear. The zombie ceased moving. Gus delivered a second blow, then a skull-shattering third. The mindless quivered and its grip relaxed.

"Yeah, fuck off," Gus panted, freeing himself with one flick of a boot toe. The resulting stink cloud nearly made him puke. Face screwed up and eyes watering, he glanced at the penthouse entrance.

Another zombie. Draped in leather. Its entire abdomen horribly excavated, and everything once held within hanging to its feet and being dragged behind. That purple-black hemline didn't bother the undead, however, whose face had been gnawed down to the grisly bone.

After all those years, it took *a lot* to shock Gus, but the sight before him stopped him cold.

Then he swung the axe, connecting with the monster's neck in a bloodless cut. The head toppled to its neckline while the rest crumpled against the doorway. Gus kicked at a leg and the zombie fell onto its spine, where he smashed the thing right between its unseeing eyes. He struck three times—until the head wasn't a head anymore, but a poorly sliced loaf of broken skin and bone. Even though the mindless had been disemboweled, presumably draining the body of any remaining fluids, a few dark bits speckled the floor.

Movement from within the penthouse caused Gus to glance up.

*Zombie*s. About a dozen of the shitty-assed bastards, all in various stages of decay. All converging on him.

Drawn to the noise, he knew and backed away, wary of tripping. The dead littering the floor had impeded the first wave. No reason it wouldn't do the same for the second.

And he wasn't disappointed.

The first two fell flat, arms flailing like fleshy logs that slapped marble and other bodies. Those two entangled the others and they all went down. In seconds a half dozen deadheads lay flat on their chests and, rather than rising, were crawling for Gus.

Not that he would let them get up.

He bashed the head of the lead Moe with one mighty chop. Then he took out the second crawler, creating a barrier that the others had to slink up and over. From then on it was only a matter of killing them as they slunk within range—usually one strike to the head, sometimes two. Bodies flopped facedown and did not rise again. Oily fluids seeped onto the floor and added a fresh, viscous layer to the mess underfoot.

No sooner did Gus dispatch the initial rush when *another* wave emerged from the depths of the penthouse.

Jesus Christ.

There was no time to rest, not that he needed it. And truthfully, he discovered a part of him *wanted* this. Wanted the action. The danger. The *destruction*.

And, yes, the revenge.

"Come on," he seethed, eyeing the main event—a dozen or so shapes oozing into the light. He squared his shoulders and took a batter's stance. It wasn't his old aluminum bat, but it did the job.

Accepting the invitation, the zombies came on, ignoring the deadly accuracy of the axeman.

And when the last one fell, no others came forth.

Gulping for breath, Gus waited for more of the undead as sweat ran down his face and back. As an afterthought, he checked on what was happening behind him before peering back into the grey-lit interior of the penthouse. No other zombies challenged him, and all was quiet except for his breathing. Feeling perspiration on his face, he dragged a sleeve over his forehead and got a faint whiff of old-man piss.

Well, shit, he thought sourly, sniffing at his wrist and forearm. Each whiff screwed up his face. It was barely there but make no mistake, the arm of his coat smelled like rancid urine.

He dropped his arm. The smell was from Collie, of course. He remembered how she had clutched to him, drenched in the Leather's homemade milkshake that the undead went bonkers for.

"Unbelievable," he remarked.

Then he considered the pile of meat, bone, and cracked skulls at his feet. A quick count informed him he had taken down twenty-six. Twenty-six of the monsters, but a few of those might have been shot by Collie. He wondered how many more of the little devils might be running around the place.

"Good question," he muttered, wondering if it mattered. He decided no, not really.

Gus sighed and climbed over the bodies, meaning to explore the penthouse. "Stay still, you crusty dicksmacks. Stay still. I swear. I'm not cleanin' up your greasy, shit-stained asses. Fuckin' housekeepin' can do that. Oh, they're not around, you say? Not my problem."

Then he was standing just inside the threshold, in a huge room bathed in wintry daylight. Between tall marble columns, blowing snow scratched at floor-length windows that seemed to make up the entire far wall. Beyond the glass, otherworldly buildings faded in and out of sight with every blustery blast, but there was no doubt on a fine day, the majestic downtown quarter could be seen. Right now, however, Gus felt as if he had wandered inside an Antarctic deep freeze.

A pair of chairs lay on their sides before those windows. One in much worse shape than the other. That sight yanked on Gus's memory. His mouth went dry as he recalled images of a brutalized Milo sitting across from him. Worse, he remembered the pink fright called Joe—Vampire Joe—interrogating him, whittling away at Gus's attempted deception, until only the sore truth remained. Just before Collie rushed in and saved both him and Milo.

Gus relived that moment in his head, hearing the sounds of combat over the wind at the windows. He moved further into the room, keeping his back to a wall and the axe close to his chest. The carpet cushioned his every footfall. Dozens of belts lay around the chairs, coiled and discarded, as well as shredded lengths of duct tape. He listened. Watched. Very much aware of the second floor overhead. Bodies littered the place, dead and gone and strewn out in every position. One that caught his attention was the sprawled form of the one wearing a pig's mask. A marble column obscured the corpse as Gus continued to creep toward the windows. Other columns drifted in and out of his line of sight. The floor dropped at the center, becoming an open pit with huge L-shaped sofas, blood soaked and covered in corpses. Gus circled the pit, checked out an empty bathroom, and then moved toward the windows. A piano was set up over there, as well as a bar. The bar interested him, although the bare shelves hinted he should not be too hopeful.

Then he saw him.

The Dog Tongue.

Lying at the bottom of that plush pit, next to a smashed coffee table once made of glass. Facedown and on his chest, but still clinging to some degree of unlife, the Dog Tongue swung his head left then right, perhaps smelling a visitor, but then he faltered and collapsed.

Though Gus had only been in the presence of the warlord for a short time, it was intense enough that he would remember him forever. The wind rising and falling behind him, Gus stood at the edge of the pit and gazed upon the leader of the Leather. Bodies were strewn about down there as well. Far more than he remembered. A gruel of blood and other putrefying slop soaked into the carpet, producing the worst of that stomach-turning stink flowering the air. Only the flies were missing.

Holding his breath and fingers tight around the axe, Gus backed away. Reaching a point where the overhang was above him, he leaned out, eyed the second level for danger, and continued to the windows. Snow peppered the glass. The sun was up there, an indistinct glow trying to punch through the storm clouds and failing. He took a moment to gaze into the white chasm of the streets below, marveling at the heights.

A thump whirled him around.

The Dog Tongue became animated once again, struggling to lift himself but failing to do so. Gus remembered Collie shooting the killer in the legs, but there was something else wrong, so he returned to confront the thing in the pit.

Head hung between sunken shoulders, the Dog Tongue propped himself on his elbows, one of them splayed outward at an impossible angle. The sight didn't bother Gus. He'd seen worse just entering the place. In fact, he hoped that somehow the Dog Dick felt pain—and he meant unbearable agony—from the weight the warlord placed on that warped, broken spear tip of an arm.

The Dog Tongue had pulled himself to the steps, determined to crawl free of the pit. One arm failed to find purchase on the carpet, while the other swung and dragged its forearm like the slab of meat it was. The ravaged face of the warlord rose with every lopsided movement, slowly revealing itself.

Since the beginning of the zombie outbreak, Gus had beheld death in all its guises, to the point where not much shocked him anymore. The zombie he'd killed earlier had done a number on him, but that was the first time in a while.

The Dog Tongue's face would haunt him for a very long time.

Chipped and stained teeth filled a lipless mouth. The jaw slowly flexed, as if chuckling at a morbid anecdote, then hitched in a question. Rivulets of dried jelly caked the cheeks of the executioner's mask, stemming from the dark, smouldering holes of its empty eye sockets. The Dog Tongue propped itself up and then fell, clacking his chin off a carpeted step, only to stubbornly rise again. It reached the floor and swept its arm in a wide, empty search. It fell once more, smashing its face, the mask askew but the lower jaw still happy to apply a bite. The thing paused, gathering its lower self before lurching toward the last living thing in the room.

Gus waited as the thing crawled for him. The head rose and fell with each push, thumping the floor with all the weight of a bowling ball, only to rise again. The Dog Tongue overreached and collapsed. It reached for Gus's boots, black fingernails clicking off the toes. The reanimated warlord lifted its ruined face, sending the unspoken message, *I know you're there.*

"Yeah," Gus whispered, holding the axe across his pelvis. "I know you know."

And in an angry, overheated rush of red, he split the dead thing's skull with one fell cut.

5

Gus exhaled mightily, shaking inky droplets from the blade. "I feel better already."

On impulse he kicked the Dog Tongue's cleaved face, the impact lifting the split melon off the floor. It was petty. Insult to injury, really. But it was also gratifying as all fuck.

"Yeah," Gus yelled. "Feel fuckin' fabulous here! Just fuckin' rinky dink! I'm handin' out free shit-kickins all goddamn *week*. So here I am, sweeties. Right here. Anyone else want some of this? Huh? Last call . . . Anyone? Anyone?"

No one did. At least, no one stepped out from hiding.

"Yeah, didn't think so." With that, Gus examined the dead mass at his feet and remembered what brought him to the penthouse in the first place.

"Goddammit," he muttered with a shake of the head.

He had to pat that corpse down. Check its pockets. To be totally honest, he'd rather just torch it and go back to his room. Not quite ready to do the deed, Gus stepped over to the windows and squinted at the avenues below.

Then he noticed the bar again.

Shattered glass twinkled, covering whole shelves. Spilled alcohol and crystal shards pooled upon the floor. The sight momentarily saddened Gus, summoning a memory of another time, when he was under siege in his house back on the mountain. Still, he carried on, deciding to check out matters. Glass crinkled underfoot as he walked behind the bar where he discovered an extra two shelves below the counter. Two shelves filled with bottles.

"Holy shit," Gus whispered, his spirits spiking.

Weak light poked through a snaky line of bullet holes. The same burst of gunfire had claimed a few bottles on the far end, but the rest were intact. Gus hauled out one by its neck, flipped it over, and gazed upon the label.

Scotch.

He placed the bottle on the countertop and hauled out another.

Then another.

"You're not *all* fuckin' Scotch, are you? I mean, Jesus..."

But they were, except for the very last one.

A bottle of gin.

Gus pulled that out and slowly stood, a pained expression on his face and flaring through his chest. *Good Lord.* He placed the odd bottle out on the bar and studied it, surprised right down to his frizzy nibbles. A dozen bottles of McDonovan's So Very Fine Scotch were lined up beside the solitary English Spring gin. There were other bottles down there, but of the same design as the Scotch. He sifted through the tatters of labeling sticking to the slivers of destroyed glass. As far as he could tell, those were Scotch as well.

"Scotch," he said, inspecting the inventory. And then the gin. "Well, well."

"Eeny meeny..." he intoned while his finger went from the gin to the Scotch, before finally settling on the Scotch. Not overly impressed but needing a smile, he took a bottle of McDonovan's and twisted it open. The sound of a fresh bottle being cracked open was a beautiful thing. Had to be up there with a long and satisfying piss. At least in Gus's mind. Scotch wasn't his favorite, though. No sir. Last time he drank Scotch... he had to think about it. Had he ever? Yes. Yes he had. In fact, it might have been when he was on a drunken rampage and burned down Annapolis. Maybe. In any case, he wanted a drink and Scotch was provided.

And a bottle of gin.

"Any port in a storm, I guess," he said and raised the bottle. "Here's mud in your eye. Shit in your ear." He toasted the very much unanimated corpse of the Dog Tongue and took one cringing sip.

"God," he gasped and then took another drink.

And another.

"Not..." another mouthful. "Not so bad." And shivered violently at the end of his words, placing a hand to his chest. An idea took him, and he glanced under the bar once again, searching for mixed nuts. No go, and it dampened his mood.

There were cabinets behind him, underneath the shelves where all the other bottles had been blasted away. One more shot of Scotch, needed for luck, followed by a shiver that reached his boys, and he opened the cabinets.

And stared.

"No way," he softly let out, and nearly dropped the Scotch bottle while trying to place it on the bar. It had been a few days, granted, but he still recognized the duffel bag. The same one Collie had stuffed full of ammunition and other supplies back when they were heading out to confront the Dog Tongue and his merry band of psychopaths.

The bag wasn't so full anymore, but it still weighed enough to get a grunt out of him, followed by a warning twinge in his lower back. Glass crinkled underfoot as he swung the bag onto the counter where it landed on more broken bits. Wasting no time, he unzipped the thing and pulled it open.

"No *way*," he whispered.

Stuff. A bag full of stuff. In particular, ten cases of shotgun shells for the Ramfist. Ten spare magazines for Collie's HK, and a dozen magazines for his Glock and her Sig Sauer. If the ammunition wasn't surprising enough, the dozen sticks of ocean mist deodorant choked him up until he smiled, because, really, who wants to smell like dead ass and unwashed ball sacks?

Not this boy, Gus thought, his throat tight and achy.

Then the memories. Besides the weapons, Collie had stuffed food in the duffel bag. Not a lot, but some. From Whitecap's considerable stockpile. But that wasn't there anymore.

"Goddammit," he said, checking the ends and finding a gun-cleaning kit but nothing more. "You bastards didn't eat it all, did you? 'Cause if you did . . ."

He shook his head. "Fuck, you did. You . . . fuck knuckles."

Gus sized up all that ammunition. Then the dead bodies. Collie's rifle was down below and he would search for it later, but he remembered the *Pig*. More precisely, the man called Pig. Then he remembered . . . a *gunfight*. The penthouse doors flying open. Shots fired. And that big man called Pig shot in the head before falling. Gus thought very hard about the next part, because didn't the Pig have a *gun*?

Right there, not a dozen strides back from the penthouse door, lay the corpse of the Pig. Sprawled out across white tiles, with a dark, uprooted flower of a wound marking the side of his face.

Gus approached the body. Others lay around the Pig. Leather and regular undead. Most of the regular undead had their heads blown away, but the Leather had been shot while human—at least the ones lying near the fallen Pig.

Who lay on his back, his right arm outstretched, fingers curled like the legs of some humongous dead bug.

But no firearm.

Not that it surprised him, but Gus wouldn't let the thought go. This little pig had a gun. Probably a right-handed shot, which meant . . .

The corpse's outstretched arm pointed toward the pit. Gus walked to the edge where the plush back of the sofa was just beyond his toes. A gap between the furniture and the floor's edge was narrow but doable. A shadowy shape rested at the very bottom.

"No fuckin' way," Gus said in complete disbelief.

He dropped to his knees and peered into that crack.

And spotted his old Glock.

"Holy shit," he said, not believing his eyes. He poked his hand into the gap but couldn't get past the wrist.

"Holy *shit*," he panted. In a flash he stumbled down the stairs, halting on the last step to avoid the witch's broth of spilled guts and gore at the bottom. He grabbed hold of one end and hauled back the sofa. Stumpy legs squealed. Things squeaked. It was a custom fit, so he had to wiggle it out, the joints groaning with every energetic tug. His lower back started singing, warning him of exceeding recommended weight limits.

"Can't believe. You dropped. Your *gun*. Well. *My* fuckin' gun."

But the Pig had.

And there it was.

Gus wrenched the sofa out and shunted it aside. Not going anywhere near the blood-soaked carpet in the pit, he bounded up the steps and dropped onto the floor.

There he stretched out his hand, reaching into that widened crevice.

"Ah-ha," Gus smiled, fingers grazing the gun metal. He leaned into the gap, thinking if there ever was a time for a zombie to bite his ass, *this* would be the time.

"Ah, ah . . ." he strained. "Got you."

He pulled back, held up the Glock, and smiled hugely. "God bless us every one. Holy, holy shit. I thought you were gone. Well, okay, I didn't think of you at all until now, but, yeah, figured you were gone."

Flicking the magazine's release, he saw that the Pig, as big and fearsome as he was, didn't even get off one shot.

"Loser," Gus scoffed and slapped the magazine home. He stood, held the weapon in both hands, and immediately flowed through a couple of action hero poses, ending each one with a manly grunt. Getting that out of his system, he turned the weapon over and marveled at such good fortune.

He'd give it up in a flash if it meant getting Collie back.

That killed his momentary high. Quick as that.

Depressed once again, he dropped the gun at arm's length and stared. The fire axe was on the counter, next to the Scotch. He didn't even remember putting it there.

The corpses around his feet drew his attention.

Especially a pair lying farther back in the hall.

"No . . . *way*," Gus said in disbelief, hopes soaring yet again and in complete awe of the treasures the penthouse held.

For there, sprawled out over the head of a long-deceased zombie entangled with an equally dead Leather, was the barrel of a rifle.

When Collie died, resulting in Gus's alcoholic bender, well, things got blurry. Dreamy, even. In a fucked-up sorta way. He didn't bother coming back up to the penthouse, mostly because he was drunk and half-mad in mourning. At least he didn't *think* he did. He did remember the Leather had captured both him and Collie. They obviously appropriated their guns and their spares. Collie had her main rifle that Gus had laid beside her grave, but here was a *second* rifle. In a hallway of the penthouse, of all places.

And he almost hadn't come up here.

Silly bastard.

Walking over to the two bodies, he stopped and pulled one off the other, freeing the rifle. The German-made HK something-something or other. He could never remember the exact name of the thing. If it wasn't for pissing off Collie he'd straight up call it a gun. Which it was, in his civvie brain. He picked up the weapon and cradled it like a newborn. A quick inspection informed him the magazine had a few shells remaining.

Test fire, Gus thought.

He looked around, searching for a suitable target. There were three modes: single, semiauto, and full shit-shaking automatic. The numbnuts Leather had it set on full auto, and had sprayed down the walls and marble columns before being tackled, or so Gus deduced.

Taking a shooter's stance, he placed the weapon's butt firmly against his shoulder and stared down the scope. As an afterthought, he switched the firing mode to semi-auto.

Releasing his breath, he squeezed the trigger.

Bak!

There was a fine puff of powder and a black hole appeared in the wall of the outer hallway. Gus remained in his stance, judged the soft kick of the rifle and deemed it just fine.

Bak! . . . Bak! Bak! Bak!

Four more shots. Four more holes, right around where he aimed. The scope was good. Satisfied, Gus held the weapon at arm's length and smiled at the gun. Feeling much better, he started looking for more stuff.

And quickly located the Leather fuckhead who had claimed his body armor. It took a little work, as dead people don't cooperate much while being stripped, but Gus got it off him. Dried blood spattered the armor, so he lugged it over to the bar, opened a bottle of Scotch, and emptied it over the vest. A few washcloths and some earnest scrubbing later, he deemed the vest acceptable for usage and smelling positively ornery.

It seemed tighter for some reason, until Gus realized the bastard had adjusted the straps for his lesser frame. He corrected that, got his fit, and snapped everything into place. Once finished, he inspected himself with approval and wondered what else the murderous little dicks had on them. So he got to rooting around the Leather corpses. Knives. Axes. Clubs. None of that really interested him. One of them wore a set of leather sheaths, one strapped to each forearm—which Gus thought was cool. One knife was missing but the other one was there. Figuring *what the hell*, he unstrapped the sheathed weapon, judged it exceptional, and proceeded to clean it (but with less Scotch, because he wasn't stupid). Once done, he fixed the whole thing to his left arm and sized it up.

Oh yeah, he thought.

Guns. Knives. Axe. Body armor.

Goddamn.

Outfitted again, he was feeling impressive. Damn impressive. Although that might have been the Scotch talking. Probably.

The holster for the Glock was nowhere in sight, so Gus would have to stuff the thing in his coat pocket. He just hoped he didn't shoot his dick off if he had to fast draw the gun. On impulse, he checked the load and aimed at the Dog Tongue.

And fired.

The body flinched upon impact. Gus didn't mind.

So he continued firing.

It was petty. Unnecessary. A waste of ammo, even.

Still, his scowl deepened with every shot as he emptied the magazine into the Dog Tongue's dead ass. Not feeling the relief he wanted, Gus dropped his gun arm and went to the bar. Got a mouthful of resolve into him and took the burn. Another swig and he growled, thumping a fist off the countertop. Then a smoky third because once you started, well, it was kinda hard to stop.

He needed the buzz. Just a little. Enough to take the edge off, but not to get stupefied. He needed all his marbles rolling. Inhaling deeply through his nose, he found himself staring at the winter screen obscuring downtown Regina.

That lasted for seconds, then, quiet moment over, he considered his next move.

Based on the zombie presence in the penthouse, he believed it wise to search the whole hotel for any leftovers. Any stragglers that might've gone astray. Just so there would be no surprises. The restaurants were in his head, specifically the kitchens. Every army needed food and water. With his luck, the places would be crawling with zombies. Might even find one with its ass sticking out of a bread box.

His eyes drifted over the penthouse. It was still early. Might as well finish searching the place.

A minute later he was in the kitchen.

Bottled jams and preserves, frozen bread, and strips of cured meat. Even a frozen roast which surprised Gus. There were basic condiments—nothing too fancy—and a few utensils. Everything got whisked into the duffel bag. No sign of any of the edible treats from Whitecap so Gus deemed them long gone. Eaten by the savages. There was a water jug and a big can of Oh My! grape-flavored drink crystals.

"Oh my," Gus said, grabbing the mix and studying the label. "Sugar."

He went to the nearby sink.

A strong flow of water spat from the faucet and Gus cupped a mouthful, deemed it good, and let the water continue running. When it was cold enough, he checked the nearby cupboards, found a mug, and rinsed it. He then mixed the sugary goodness in with the water and gulped it down.

"Gah," he choked, draining half before coming up for breath. Rivulets seeped into his beard and reached his neckline. He didn't care, choosing to finish the drink off.

"God, that's good," he gasped, lowering the mug and studying it. "So, so good."

The dark and empty bottom of the mug held his attention for seconds until he fastball pitched the thing into the sink. Porcelain exploded, sending shards everywhere, the clack and clatter echoing briefly in the kitchen. Chalky residue marked the point of impact, while the sink caught most of the fragments. Then he kicked in the door of a nearby cupboard, then a second one, before sweeping a collection of containers onto the floor.

In the ensuing silence, Gus stood there fuming, the anger hot and flowing. It took him a few moments to realize he'd done all that and he didn't understand why. It just happened. The impulse just . . . took him.

Calmer, but once again feeling shitty, Gus returned to the bar, duffel bag swinging from his side. With almost more than he could carry, he figured he'd come back and finish exploring the penthouse. The bag had a shoulder strap, so he hooked it over himself and let the chunky weight rest against his ass cheeks while he carried the rifle. It was a little awkward, but he would manage.

A plan formed in his head. He'd search the hotel. Double-check it was clear. Along the way, he'd find the restaurants.

Feeling the load hanging off his shoulder, Gus returned to the elevator. When the doors opened with a soft ding, he swung himself aboard and thumbed the button for the fifth floor.

All the while, the memory of smashing the mug stayed with him.

6

It took roughly twenty minutes to unload everything back in his room. When he did, he dropped the rifle and took up the Ramfist, very much enjoying every click and clack of the reloading process. Armed and ready and with a clear goal in mind, he headed back to the penthouse. There, he recovered all the Scotch and the bottle of gin, wrapped everything in bathroom towels, and returned to what was now home. He unloaded everything again, examining the occasional bottle while lining them up on a dresser and fireplace. When there was no room left on the dresser, he placed the remaining bottles on the table. After sorting things away, he looked for the clock and saw it was 12:46 in the afternoon.

Still early, so he mixed up another mug of grape drink, made himself a crude sandwich, and took everything over to a window. He sat, pulled back a curtain just a little, and chewed while staring out into the winter storm. All that stormy whiteness hypnotized him and he finished his lunch without realizing it. Draining his drink, he considered the supply of Scotch on the dresser. The earlier sips were in him, working their not-so-smooth magic, but it wasn't debilitating, which was good. There was still a lot to do.

The pile of ammunition he'd dumped on the side of the bed caught his eye. He replaced the Glock's empty magazine, then eased the gun into his coat pocket, slightly concerned for his dick. The duffel bag got slung across his back. Then he picked up the Ramfist, readied it, and faced the door.

He froze at the door. Froze for long seconds, where he stood and stared. Stared hard. And after perhaps a minute, where he was so dearly tempted to call it a day and not go anywhere else, where getting shit-faced in his palatial man-nest seemed like a much better idea, he opened the door and stepped out into the hallway.

Empty. That same long and deserted corridor. Without a sound, not even that of winter attempting to blow the building over. Soft carpet cushioned his bootsteps as he marched to the elevator and selected a button. The doors opened. He stepped aboard and a few short seconds later, exited onto the battlefield that was the main lobby. Collie's coffin was there, dimmed by the storm beyond the glass. His eyes lingered on her final resting place for several heartbeats before he went to a second elevator. A white marble plaque read:

OLIVER GREEN'S FINE DINING. 10TH FLOOR.

And right below that:

MURPH'S SPORTS BAR. 8TH FLOOR.

And finally:

PLUCKY DEE'S FAMILY GRILL (FILL YOUR PIE HOLE!). 8TH FLOOR.

Gus smirked. He was all about filling his pie hole. Damn right he was.

Selecting the floor, he got aboard the elevator. He ascended, aware of his distorted reflection in the brass surfaces. Stretched. Warped. Sick-looking and mentally rubbed raw to the bone. He glanced away, not needing to see any more.

When the doors opened, he aimed the Ramfist, prevented the elevator from closing with a toe, and waited for a reception.

None came, so he got off and let the doors close behind him.

To his left was a large waiting area with fake palm trees sprouting from huge wicker pots tucked away in the corners. Cheerful murals of tropical beaches plastered the walls. A wishing pool with breaching ceramic fish occupied the center of the dining hall. Elegant summer benches with worn varnish stood outside the entrance to each restaurant. PLUCKY DEE's name was at the top of a golden archway, which framed a rounded doorway resembling a portal onto a starship. A high bamboo partition separated the two restaurants. Where Gus stood, however, leprechaun-green lettering read MURPH's and a deep, chestnut-brown layer of imitation cobblestone led into that hidden cavern.

Crushed paper cups and tatters of used napkins littered the waiting area's floor, right up to a pair of stopped escalators at the far end. Chrome railings shone in the sparse light, and anyone going up to the next floor would have to climb over what looked like a garbage truck of trash dumped on the steps. In fact, the whole space looked as if someone had thrown a hard party and refused to clean that shit up.

Ears buzzing, Gus waited, detecting nothing. On impulse, he drifted toward the escalators. A sign there read OLIVER GREEN'S FINE DINING along with an arrow pointing to the next level. Holding his breath, Gus leaned out and peeked behind the escalators. He spotted an emergency stairwell, the door opened a crack below an unlit EXIT sign. A cold pallor illuminated a pair of long white corridors beyond the stairwell, which he realized were the skyways to the other hotels.

He returned to the restaurants.

The family eatery was first, and he walked through the bright arched entrance resembling a starship's portal. The speedy, futuristic theme continued inside, where about three dozen tables were spread across a red-and-white checkered floor. Serving trays lay in disarray across some tables. A pair of garbage bins stood just inside the entrance with trays stacked on top. A lattice of dusty chrome divided the dining hall from a buffet-style layout.

Plucky Dee's was empty, but there were signs of the place being used as a mess hall for the Leather. Pails of cutlery waited to be snapped up and dumped on trays, as well as stacks of plates and little wooden mugs. A cartoonish, space-age badger wearing a futuristic helmet branded almost every surface, with PLUCKY DEE's stamped over the character's head.

All in all, it wasn't a bad-looking place.

"Fruity Bologna," Gus whispered, remembering a not-so-long-ago conversation and smiling. Briefly. Before it melted from his face.

As he moved through the buffet, the duffel bag got hooked up in a pair of swinging doors and he had to back up to free himself.

The kitchen beckoned.

Upon entering, dashed lines of fluorescent lights lit up the ceiling. Racks and tables filled the space designed to serve hundreds in the run of a day. All manner of utensils hung over prepping tables or were stacked nearby, including a few of those meat hammers to flatten the freshest cuts. Ovens, deep fryers, and grills abounded, some crusty, some clean. Above it all, Plucky Dee the Space Badger smiled and winked, pranced and posed, clearly excited by what the staff were whipping up to serve their customers.

Gus edged around a block-sized island with a vast array of cooking appliances and proceeded past a prep station of sorts. Not a corpse in sight, though he was still getting whiffs of pissy ball sack coming off his coat. It kind of irritated him. The mindless would pick up on that shit right away and come hunting for him.

If they were around.

Near the rear of the kitchen were four stainless-steel doors belonging to walk-in freezers. As he approached them, a light flickered on, revealing what looked to be an open closet.

Holy shit.

The closet turned out to be a deep pantry, some thirty feet in length, lined with shelves five high on each side. He wandered inside, gawking at the discovery. Bottled goods filled the shelves. Plastic bins contained dark apples. Other bins displayed labels with FLOUR scrawled across the tops.

The flour stopped him.

"The fuck you get that?" Gus bluntly asked, amazed at the amount of food stored away. The handwriting on the labels was written by the same shaky hand. Bottled peaches, pears, and plums. Bottled salsa, tomatoes, and even crude-looking ketchup.

The pantry contained enough provisions to last . . . well . . . a winter. A winter and a half, even. For many, many people.

Then there were the freezers.

He turned to the first stainless-steel door and cracked it open. Like the pantry, it held a considerable amount of frozen food. Huge haunches of beef and pork. Cut-up steaks, pork chops, and enticing roasts. Frozen lake trout in metallic bowls. Whole chickens and chicken parts laid out on trays and wrapped in plastic. There were even ducks and rabbits, plucked and skinned and ready for cooking.

"Jesus," Gus said softly.

Did he just think the Leather had enough food for a winter and a half? Scratch that shit. *Two* at least, and that was living well given the volume of goodies tucked away in the freezer. And that was only the first one. The food had obviously been intended for a much larger group staying at the hotel, but now it was only him. He wouldn't go hungry, but he couldn't eat it all.

The second freezer had a similar assortment of meats, either whole or chopped up into smaller portions. The third freezer had several individual packages of blueberries and raspberries cleaned and frozen, as well as stacks of what looked to be homemade butter. The last freezer wasn't nearly as cold as the others, which left him wondering if the thing was actually turned on. A wave of garlic and onions hit him when he opened the door, and he spotted the open trays of uncut cloves on the upper shelves. Several buckets of potatoes were stored away on the lower shelves. Plastic containers with cleaned carrots filled the rear. Bags of onions. More containers filled with greens stacked atop each other. The sight and level of organization amazed him, but then his spirits sank. The freezers were a step up from root cellars, but none of the fruit or produce would keep for long. A few months, tops, and then whatever wasn't consumed would spoil.

A downcast Gus closed the freezer and left the kitchen, grabbing a bagful of blueberry muffins on the way out. There were utensils aplenty, so he took one of each. A nearby fridge had an open tub of some of that homemade butter, so he snatched it, immediately spotting a casserole dish filled with what looked to be . . .

Shepherd's pie.

Gus leaned over the dish, grimly intrigued. He moved it to a nearby table and plucked out a big soup spoon.

Looked like shepherd's pie.

An exploratory sniff suggested it smelled like shepherd's pie.

Gus dug out a spoonful and tried it.

"Holy *fuck*," he whispered, absolutely gobsmacked by the existence of such a culinary delight. And *delicious*! How the hell did a pack of heathen nutbars like the Leather have a person who could actually cook? And cook *well!* It bewildered him. It was easier to think of them as ruthless, scavenging killers rather than people who once possessed real-world skills.

The pie was cold but he didn't mind. He found a plastic container, heaped in a couple of meals, and secured the lid. The food went into the bag with everything else.

"Suppers," he said, and immediately had a flashback to another time, one where a crazy nurse tried to serve him up to her undead brood.

Then he noticed the stairs.

At the far end of the grills was a set of wide stairs curling upward. With a final look at the kitchen, Gus climbed to a second, smaller kitchen, where the prep area contained only a fraction of what was one level below. There were cases of beer, however. On the floor and stacked chest-high against one wall.

A puzzled Gus skirted the aisles, aiming his shotgun down each one, and deemed them all clear. Then he checked on the beer, and frowned at them being empties. Each and every one. The Leather had stacked the bottles along the entire length of one wall, right up to a door. Gus pulled it open.

More beer.

Tucked away in a massive cooler.

"You alcoholic dicks, you," Gus marveled, and entered. Huge. Packed with enough beverages to satisfy the Leather for the entire winter. It seemed weird, however, as he couldn't quite see the Dog Tongue allowing his troops this amount of booze. The pink-faced moosechop with the Scotch addiction, maybe. But not Dog Dick. Then again, what did he know?

He took a pair of bottles, inspected them, and tucked both away. His duffel bag had grown heavy, so he returned to the kitchen and found another freezer with food. That one he left untouched. He proceeded to a far set of doors fixed with circular windows. There he stopped and peeked outside.

Well.

He believed he'd just walked into Murph's. The second level, anyway.

The majority of lights were off, but if the hockey playoffs were on, he imagined the place would be a hopping. A few shaded windows looked out over the city, but it was otherwise dark in there. Lights flared to life when he nudged the doors open. High wooden tables shone from a nice polish, complete with stools and copper cup holders built into the surface. Long light fixtures the size of coffins and studded with black lenses hung from the ceiling, suggesting Murph's could fire up one wicked, space-age light show whenever it wanted. The whole area generated a hybrid ambience of a saloon situated within an intergalactic starship, and it worked for Gus. Especially the bar. It was huge, with a generous inventory of spirits on display behind the counter. Television screens hung all over the place, allowing patrons easy viewing from anywhere in the bar.

"Jesus," he said, bewildered by it all and imagining a young crowd filling the place. The age-old courtship ritual of seeking out a potential mate, if only for a night. The music pulsing through a person's chest. The bartenders serving up beer and mixed drinks with a side dish of whatever might be that night's special. The ghost stink of spilled booze lingering on the air in between private clouds of much too strong cologne and perfumes. The age of the drunken booty call, the one-night stands, and the muddled confusion after last call.

Gus didn't miss that age at all, so he crept through the place until he completed a loop and arrived back at the main entrance to Murph's Sports Bar. There, he eyed the escalators going up to Oliver Green's Fine Dining. *What might constitute fine dining?* his mind asked. Visions of elk shanks and other wild beastuses filled his head. The escalator wasn't working, so he hoofed it, not bothering to be quiet. The duffel bag nudged his ass with every step, urging him to mush.

As he rounded the landing and took the next set of stairs, his calves started to ache. Then they started to bitch. His troublesome heel chimed in as well, playing the same old accordion tune and just letting him know it was still there.

Oh I know you're still there, buddy, he thought. *I know.*

A faint thumping stopped him. He listened, frowned, checked his boots, and then glanced behind before looking to the top of the escalator stairs.

Boom. Boomboom. Boom.

The fuck is that? Gus thought, craning his neck to see topside. The duffel bag continued nudging his ass like his own personal boot, urging him along.

Boomboom. Boom.

Faint, but distinct. Gus squished a paper cup underfoot and, with a boot scuff, sent it flying behind him. *Gimps.* Only a gimp would make that noise, heedless of the consequences. He wondered how many.

At the top of the escalator was a wide hall decorated with thick, white, sinuous tree roots and several black-and-white photos of people enjoying an evening out. The white roots ended in a wall of stained glass, along with a few benches that should have decorated a lawn somewhere. Artificial oak trees reached the ceiling and offered shade over the benches of the waiting area. A single, wood-stained podium marked the entrance, and Gus aimed at that open archway, expecting the worst. A full-scale model of what appeared to be an eighteenth-century nobleman smiling broadly and tipping his hat stood to the right of the podium. At his elbow was a fancy sign proclaiming OLIVER GREEN'S FINE DINING.

Gus nodded at who he assumed was Oliver Green.

Boom. Boom.

That came from behind old Oliver himself, somewhere within his fine dining establishment. The nobleman kept right on smiling broadly, in complete denial of the shit happening right behind his back. Gus did a quick scan and located the elevators a few strides behind him, the doors closed and unmoving.

"You okay there, Oliver?" Gus asked the figure.

Oliver smiled back and didn't say a word.

"You being a smart-ass?"

BOOM.

Gus looked from the figure to the open doorway and back again. "You stay here," he advised.

And entered the restaurant.

A fine dining interior with even more artsy flourishes around the edges. More stained glass windows, more plastic oaks towering over white tables, and large ceramic pots filled with tall sunflowers. But all that was a little further back. Just inside the entrance, however, where Gus currently stood, it looked like someone had popped a million and one blood blisters and painted the entire floor and walls. Two tables had been overturned, their dishes trashed and spread far and wide. A thick cluster of hotel flyers was dumped in one spot. Handprints and fingerprints plastered the hallways to the men's and ladies' washrooms. A potted plant rested at the base of the wall dividing those hallways, and shards of ceramics poked out from a head-sized knob of dirt. Some six feet above that was a black soil print, dotting the point of impact the flowerpot had hit.

Boomboomboom!

Nothing moved within the restaurant. The thing playing bongos on the washroom doors was straight ahead, down the hallway below the featureless profile of a man wearing a top hat.

Gus raised the Ramfist.

As he crept closer, four LED light strips switched on, running the length of the baseboards and ceiling. Glowing white and green strips led the way to the washroom door trembling from each heavy blow.

Gus edged down the hall, more from habit than from fear of being heard. Whatever was behind the shitter door didn't need to see or hear him. It *smelled* him, plain and simple. Smelled the coat he wore. And, seeing how the door opened inwards, it was easy to see the mindless piece of shit had pushed his way *inside* but didn't have the brains to back out.

Gus stopped at the edge of the doorframe.

The drummer started swinging from the shoulders, and the door shivered from the onslaught.

"Yeah," Gus muttered, figuring it must piss off the undead shitbag knowing a fresh meal was so close and yet unreachable.

There was no handle, just a panel to push your way in, so Gus put his shoulder to the door and heaved.

The thing inside slammed back, startling him.

"You're a fresh one," Gus observed warily.

Perhaps hearing him, the zombie started hammering the door with *both* arms. A heavy-handed drum solo that threatened to split the barrier down the middle. Gus retreated and studied the opposite wall. He placed his back to it, mindful of not squishing the blueberry muffins in his duffel bag. He braced himself for impact while the zombie trapped inside continued hammering away.

Gus waited. And waited. Fully expecting the thing to smash its way through, whereupon he would blast it back.

Except . . . it became obvious Oliver Green had built his restaurant with the finest materials, because the door wasn't breaking. The door, with its surface as flowery as the rest of the décor, held its ground. It rattled in its frame, vibrated even, but refused to give.

Worse, the constant pounding was getting on Gus's nerves.

"Just . . . pull on the door handle," he growled and got a doubling of effort from the one occupant. At least Gus figured it was only one. Might be two, but he wouldn't really know until he got inside. He couldn't leave the dead bastard on the chance that it might open the door on a fluke and somehow get the jump on him when he was least expecting it. Gus had to admit the chances of that happening were almost nonexistent, but his luck went both ways at times.

The hammering continued, threatening him with a headache.

"Maybe you aren't so fresh," Gus said. "Maybe I'll come back in a day or two."

But he wouldn't sleep that night knowing a dick-chomping zombie was up here.

So he went to the door, placed a hand on it, and again tried to push it open.

The thing crashed into the barrier from the other side.

"*Goddammit.*" Gus pulled back while jerking up the shotgun. "You little bastard. Come outta there so I can blow your head off."

A lengthy rattling answered that, the noise truly pissing Gus off. Grimacing, head shaking, he sized up the door, wondering if he could put a shell through it. The wood seemed fairly thick, considering the beating it was taking.

"All right, you piece of shit," Gus said. "I'm comin' in for ya. Back the fuck away."

He pressed his shoulder into the door, forced it open half a finger, where a bloody face jammed itself into the gap in a flash of snapping white teeth. A single black eye glared, a split-second before the zombie slammed the door shut—on its own nose. There was a dollop of ink, and a rotten nub fell to the floor with a splat.

Not that he heard the splat, because the zombie resumed smashing the door.

So Gus once again placed his back to the wall, grossed out by the deadhead's nipping off its own nose. He shouldn't have expected anything less.

Across from him, the drum solo continued.

Disgusted, Gus sighed and fired the shotgun from the hip.

Boom.

The door buckled and a shredded, fibrous hole appeared in its center, complete with a puff of smoke. The hammering ceased and after the shock and awe of the Ramfist's vitality in such a confined space, Gus straightened, checked his flank and, wary of surprises, crept ahead to peer through the hole. Through that splintered mess, the mindless, a reanimated Leather of course, was already getting to its feet. Gore covered its midsection, where the shotgun shell penetrated but failed to do much else. Except open up the thing's abdominal cavity, so everything hung to the undead's ankles.

More stuff of nightmares. Raw material for Gus's memory to stash away, waiting for him to sleep, because his memory—lapdog of his brain—was a treacherous dick. He firmed up and forced his way into the washroom just as the Leather zombie attempted to stand.

Gus fired a second time, plastering the corpse against the far wall with a splatter very much like the slap of an exploding water balloon. The mindless collapsed facedown on the tiles and, when it lifted its face, he fired again.

Destroying the head completely.

The torso fell for the final time and silence, glorious silence, ruled. For seconds, Gus waited, eyeing the dead thing and savoring the stillness before energetically ejecting the spent shell.

The casing clattered off the floor.

"Ramfist," he whispered.

7

The freezers within Oliver Green's kitchen were similarly packed with provisions. The only surprise was a supply of wine, already half-diminished, and a few bottles of Scotch. Gus took a bottle of pinot, left the rest, and, having explored enough for one day, retired to his room. Shepherd's pie still in the bag and blueberry muffins still intact.

He locked the door behind him and stood the shotgun upright in a corner. Then he stripped and showered, taking his time doing so. When he was finished, the Scotch in his system had pretty much fizzled out, so he reloaded with red wine, filling a mug to the brim and slurping the excess before spilling. Mug in hand and sipping every so often, he reheated the shepherd's pie and sat down at his table. *Shepherd's fucking pie.*

The first bite was exquisite.

"Fuck me," a weary Gus sighed between chews, sizing up how much he had left. He ate in silence after that, noting that he could no longer hear any wind. Which was good. Whatever storm had parked itself over the city had pretty much dumped several feet of snow on it. Any more and the front doors would be buried.

Then it hit him.

Winter was just beginning. There would be more snow. Much more. And it would pile up. Even if he cleared the entrance, it would pile up. Maybe he could use the old pickup with a plow in the underground garage, but that would only deplete his limited fuel supplies. Thinking more on it, the rising drifts didn't bother him at all, actually, as he had more than enough snow-clearing experience. If he couldn't get out, then no one could get in. He'd made the right choice coming back and, if winter decided he would stay until spring, well . . . fine.

If only . . .

And then it hit him again, predictable in its timing. That miserable realization that something was missing. Some*one* was missing. He'd experienced it when he lost Tammy, and he was living it all over again with Collie.

He leaned forward, elbows to table, and held his forehead. He sighed a couple of times, long and hard, the sadness crippling. His throat constricted and his sinuses flooded. His eyes welled up and streamed. He grabbed some tissues and blew his nose, great honks that rattled him and left him checking for blood. The empty chair next to him got his attention and that only broke him again.

"It's not right, Collie," he croaked. "You . . . you should be here. With me. I need you here. Jesus. I need you."

No one answered him. Not even the wind raised its voice.

That terrible, profound ache of missing someone remained with him and got worse.

With a grunt, Gus chugged his wine in an uninterrupted stream. He belched mightily, causing his throat to sting. Ignoring the last few bites of food, he took the bottle, got up, and went to the window.

He pulled back a curtain, took a swig of wine and, with red watery eyes, watched the winter sky go dark.

Morning brought no real relief. He'd slept only so-so, waking often and listening to the great and imposing dark, expecting something to scratch at his door. Nothing of the sort happened, however. The long nights would be a challenge, but he reminded himself he'd done it all before. Just a matter of getting into a routine and sticking with it, starting with his continued search of the hotel. The wine left a lingering hangover, but nothing that would stop him from exploring. After discovering the zombie in the washroom yesterday, Gus figured any others would be easy to find, because of the stink on his coat. All he had to do was come within a hundred feet or so of one, give or take a foot—and the undead would come looking for him. If they were around. He wondered how much more range he would get if he had a greater scent on him. If the smell wore away, he could always pee on his coat just to freshen it up.

Pee on my coat. That put a smirk across his face. *Never say never.*

So he dressed, pulling everything on, finishing with his armored vest. He loaded the Ramfist and the Glock. Strapping on the forearm sheath took a little longer than expected, but he felt and looked cool as shit wearing it. The duffel bag would stay behind, but he brought along an Anchor Bay notepad and pen from the room's own stationery. His memory was going to shit, so he'd write down any important room numbers, especially rooms containing anything useful, that he could later transfer back to his own little palace.

When he could think of nothing more to do, he went to the door and stopped there, eyeing the locks. The surface of the door. Very much aware of the silence.

"I miss you, Collie," he whispered with a nod, the loneliness striking once again. "Wished you were here, y'know? Be easier if it was. You know me. I'm . . . I'm a follower. Better at takin' orders than . . . you know. Good intentions but half-assed execution. All that. Yeah."

A lump rose in his throat.

"I'll be careful," he croaked and meant it. "Miss you."

Nodding and wiping at his eyes, he undid the locks and pulled the door open.

The same long and empty corridor, which was a good start. He stepped out and locked up, glancing over his shoulder as he did so.

"All right then," he whispered and snorted back snot. "Let's do this."

He would start at the top in the penthouse and work his way down, going floor to floor to see if he attracted anything undead and then deal with them. There were those other places he wanted to find as well. Anchor Bay's other amenities, in addition to the restaurants. The food he'd found was far more than expected, and he wondered if the other hotels, all accessible via the skyways, would have similar supplies. It wasn't a pressing matter, so a search of the other towers could wait for another day. The brochure for the Anchor Bay listed a gym, a pool, and an arcade from the '80s, which sounded like fun. Then there was the nightclub and the driving range. Good times waited. Very good times.

The elevator ride to the penthouse was a lonely affair, one where Gus stared at the doors, neck-deep in a depressed funk. A couple of times he looked around, hoping to see Collie right there, but she wasn't. Then he wished for a sign. A flicker of light. Even a hitch in the elevator ride. Something. Anything. Just a little sign, a message from her to him, to let him know she was all right and that he should continue on.

Nothing of the sort happened, however.

The elevator slowed to a stop and he stepped to the inner corner to avoid anything rushing inside when the doors opened. He exited without incident and tiptoed through the decomposing mess strewn about the floor to the penthouse. The idea of a master key was still on his mind, and if Dog Shit didn't have one, maybe it was nearby.

Dog Shit. That was even better than Dog Dick. He wondered why he hadn't thought of that one before.

It took the better part of an hour, but a little after nine in the morning he found a brass key, with the letter *M* stamped into its end and some sort of an embedded security chip at the center. The key was in the fridge, of all places, in the ice tray. Why they put the thing in there befuddled him, but whatever. He hefted the thing and wondered if he had the key to the city. He would find out.

Done with his search of the penthouse, at least for the time being, he decided to leave. On the way out, he stopped and gave the middle finger in the direction of the Dog Shit, who remained heaped where Gus had delivered the final chop.

Deciding to forgo the elevator in favor of exercise, Gus took the stairwell down to the next level, his footfalls echoing. The noise didn't bother him so much, probably because of yesterday's zombie encounter and the knowledge that a deadhead would smell him long before anything else. Lights clicked on and off as he passed under sensors, shining down on each landing, where he would round a cement corner and continue on.

The next landing light winked on, positioned over the big and boldfaced number 24.

"Here we go, Collie," Gus said, and pulled opened the door.

If his fifth-floor nest was stately and the penthouse was royal magnificence, then the twenty-fourth floor was somewhere in between. And that was just the hallways. Which was to say, Gus immediately felt it was way above his pay grade. Soft, sumptuous carpets. Dark but tasteful wall paneling, with gold lines that shone dreamily in every bubble of light. Elegant tables held up little jade statues of exotic fairy creatures and their houses. Paintings, large and bold, depicted sweeping scenes of the surrounding prairies at sunset or sunrise.

Not at all in a hurry, Gus wandered through, getting an eyeful of everything, shotgun lowered. Sometimes he stopped, stared, and blinked. Not since Mortimer's mansion had he witnessed such obscene wealth. An aura of implied history pressed down on him, which couldn't be right since he guessed the place was only a few years old. Ten at most. The paint job was immaculate. The lines downright perfect, which made him wonder suspiciously if they sprayed the latex on with one of them fancy robotic painters. Those mechanical bastards came online a year before the zombie outbreak and Gus remembered fearfully wondering if his job was finished. Benny assured him it was not.

Benny, Gus thought fondly.

The first door distracted him from thinking anymore about his long-lost friend. He checked both ways to ensure he was indeed alone and tried the knob. Locked. So, with all the care of a bomb expert diffusing an unexploded ordnance, Gus inserted the brass key with the embedded chip and gave it a turn.

In the stillness of the hotel, the clacking of tumblers sounded very loud indeed.

He glanced around, listened for creepers, and decided all was good. He entered the room shotgun-first, stopped just inside, and cleared his throat.

"If you want it, I'm right here." Which didn't sound very diplomatic, so he added, "If you're actually alive. Let's talk."

Unless you were a leather-clad douchebag, in which case Gus didn't feel very sociable. Matter of fact, getting right down to the matter, if one of the Leather was inside, he would probably shoot the knob dead. A motion sensor light switched on, revealing the room. Grandiose. Penthouse-level poshness but without the size, and everything on one floor. Bright bathroom with what might've been gold fittings. Marble floor tiles. Shiny bidet, which left him stunned. A separate living room with a huge TV and what looked like a gaming console. Open bar with an assortment of bottles. Kitchen area, which Gus didn't understand. Whoever could afford a place like this probably ordered room service. A lot. And a king-sized bed for a king-sized bedroom.

The surprising thing was . . . someone lived here. Or *had* lived here.

A sports bra had been draped over a chair. T-shirts filled a closet, along with denim and actual leather attire. That put Gus a little on edge. He checked under the bed and got a snootful of dust that got him sneezing. When he finished, he scrubbed at his nose, and continued searching, finding an assortment of female clothing in a closet. The place was otherwise empty, which sorta disappointed him.

More to the point, he realized he *wanted* to shoot a Leather. Plain and simple. He'd gun down one of them pricks without a second thought and would not lose sleep over it. In fact, he'd probably snore his ass off, he'd sleep so good.

Before leaving he checked the hallway and closed the door behind him.

First room done.

Around eleven o'clock and seven monster-sized rooms later, Gus dubbed the floor clear of both Leather and undead. Of those rooms, five of the places were once inhabited by the Leather, as evident by the spare masks and assortment of gear. Although the Leather dressed like freaks while on active duty, in their downtime, they dressed like anyone relaxing at home, which seemed totally odd to him. Someone even had a T-shirt and pajama bottoms waiting on a sofa for when they arrived home. It was hard to process, since Gus believed the Dog Shit's minions to be obedient, brainwashed killers.

Warning himself not to get careless, Gus went down to the next floor, to find another eight rooms of jaw-dropping extravagance.

Only a pair of them appeared to be lived in, however.

Sometime after noon, he returned to his chosen room called home. There, he ate leftover shepherd's pie, marveling at how goddamn good it still tasted, and drank more sweet grape drink. He stayed off the Scotch, very much aware of the bottles, but avoided looking at them. Looking at them might rouse the urge, and Gus didn't want to be bopping off the hotel walls half cut. After lunch and a brief respite, he resumed his search and destroy mission.

It took longer than intended, but being sober and paranoid, he searched every nook and cranny and maintained silence (or as near silent as he could get) while roaming the hotel. Each level was surprisingly well kept, and it wasn't until he reached the seventeenth floor that he encountered another zombie. One that he smelled before he saw.

And it smelled like shit.

"Jesus," Gus whispered, feeling infected just from breathing in those nose-dissolving fumes.

A flat magazine propped open the stairwell door, and the ceiling light shone on a red carpet beyond the threshold. A slug's raceway of dried filth covered the carpeting. Sloppy streaks of organic sludge and mud cakes he wanted no part of.

Then he heard it.

A rhythmic locomotion that lumbered around somewhere within, perhaps drawn to the pissy perfume of Gus's coat. That honestly surprised him, considering the debilitating stink radiating off the corpse. So strong that Gus stopped and leaned against the doorframe, head lowered as if in mortal agony. There he waited, listening to the approaching hiss and thump from beyond, getting louder, closer.

"Christ almighty," he grimaced, wishing he had some ointment or nose plugs or *something* to fend off the lethal putrescence that grew stronger with every sickening intake of air.

Screwing up his face, loathing the confrontation to come, Gus stuck his head into the hall.

There, some thirty feet away, was a mindless, on its chest and crawling along the baseboards. The thing became even more animated after Gus revealed himself and the hiss and thump increased in tempo as it dragged itself along. Shards of wintry light came from open doorways and illuminated the hall. The zombie pulled itself through the nearest door, closing the distance to the living. Blue-grey hands clutched at carpeting, lifting a smiling face caked in gore, where the empty eye cavities resembled wet cigarette ash.

But it was the smell, not the sight of the thing, that made Gus weak in the knees.

He winced, covering his nose and mouth with a hand, his eyes beginning to water. He tried lifting the Ramfist, but the smell, cancerous and rotten, like something pulling itself out of a slaughterhouse shitter, repelled him back into the stairwell. Even that failed to offer any sort of escape. All the while, the rise and fall of the nearing corpse became louder, even a touch more urgent, as if doubling its efforts to reach the living. The noise failed to match the elevated beating in Gus's chest or the sudden dry heave that bent him over at the knees.

"Oh *fuck*," he whispered, his gullet aching from its induced reflex.

Exhaling, cheeks puffed, Gus stood. He sucked in a chestful of that putrid, diseased air and whirled into the hallway.

There, Mister Moe worked hard, charging the open portal, no more than ten feet away, its horrid features unchanging.

Gus aimed and fired, cringing at the thunderous acoustics, exploding Mister Moe's skull like the rotten melon it had become, spraying the walls in a jagged streak of dewy chunks. Mister Moe dropped without so much as a twitch but the smell remained. Thankfully, the doorway acted as partial cover, so Gus avoided the spatter of head cheese.

The shot failed to attract any other crawlers, for which he was grateful, as his stomach was going to turn again. Gus leaned against a wall before reaching for his knees, bending over for another retch that failed to produce anything. When the urge passed, he composed himself, then stepped out into the open, He avoided the unmoving mess he'd just created and entered the nearest room.

There he wet a towel and tied it around his face. It helped but didn't entirely remove the stink. Closing the door to the corridor helped, so he did that and continued with his search.

He did the same with the remaining rooms until he completed exploring the entire floor. The few lights that flickered on and off when he passed by made the space seem all the more empty, and a little sadder. When the sadness hit, he let it flow, taking the grief, sniffling, swallowing, and wiping his eyes and nose on his sleeves. Finding nothing else beside the deadhead in the hall, and with daylight waning, he called it a day. He crept back to his room, discarding the towel when the air became cleaner and appreciated every breath.

After locking the door, he leaned against the nearest wall and broke down, thoughts of Collie overpowering him without warning. When he'd had enough, he entered the bathroom and grabbed a fresh towel and buried his face in its softness. The tears came harder then and his shoulders shook with the release.

Some time later, Gus had a better hold of himself, but he still felt miserable. Way too miserable, in fact. And because he felt so very miserable, he filled the tub. While he waited, he placed his shotgun on a chair and inspected the Glock, which he placed on the nearby toilet lid. Everything he wore came off and was dropped onto the floor. Naked and hairy, Gus stepped into the tub. It was hotter than he was used to, but he didn't care, not even when the heat gave him pause. When he was ready, he lowered himself into the water and leaned back.

The Glock was well within reach.

Thoughts of Collie returned, bringing the pain, and Gus wept like a child separated from his parents. And when the pain became too great, he reached over and took the Glock in hand. Red-eyed, he readied the gun and studied it for long seconds before finally placing the barrel to his forehead.

Sobbing, baring teeth and snorting back snot, Gus squeezed his eyes shut and got his thumb on the trigger.

"Guh," he let out, agonizing. He pressed the barrel deeper, gouging his skin. A peal of sorrow left him, long and piercing, but he didn't drop the weapon from his head. He squealed. Sobbed. And trembled.

"I'm done," he croaked. "I'm done, Collie. I can't do it anymore. Not anymore. Not ever again. I'm done. Let me go. Just . . . let me do this."

And he meant to, with every fiber of his being, he meant to end it there, in a swanky bathtub where he was slowly cooking himself in much too hot water. No word of a lie, he couldn't go on. Couldn't do any more. Couldn't *suffer* any more, physically or emotionally. All he wanted was the bang, which he expected to hear, and the cold headfirst dive into whatever came next.

As much as he wanted to, however, he didn't squeeze the trigger. Not even when he bared his remaining teeth and swore he was going to do it. Swore this was *it* and no more fucking around. His sick hitching eased off, his arm got tired, and he eventually lowered the gun only to jam it back into place.

Finger tensed, and still, some part of him had a lock on muscle command, preventing him from budging any further.

Frustrated, Gus whipped the gun around and fired three shots into the wall. Holes appeared with puffs of powder, and fragments crumbled to the floor. He dropped the gun onto the bath mat and sank back in the tub. There, he held his head, while the water lapped at the sides.

"Moron," he whispered. "You just shot the wall."

Silence answered him.

"It was easier when I was drunk," he muttered after a while.

But, as his memory recalled, he didn't kill himself before, either, when he was back in Annapolis. Oh, he *tried*, but he didn't die. He reluctantly admitted he probably wasn't going to kill himself now. Not really. And that little bit of honest self-reflection caused him to rub his forehead and suffer. In time, the water cooled and his fingertips paled and shriveled. The urge to pee took him, so he got out of the tub to do just that. When he finished, he wrapped himself in a bathrobe and relocated to the edge of his bed. The nearby lamp provided the only light and, not caring in the least, he went to the windows and yanked back the curtains.

Gus returned to his bed and splashed down with a heavy bounce. He propped pillows behind his head and stared at the building across the street—the darkening panels which were its windows.

Scotch lay about the room. On the fireplace mantel and on the table. In fact, there was a Scotch bottle damn near everywhere he looked.

"Fine," he muttered, taking the hint. Embracing it.

8

With practiced ease, he cracked open the first bottle and started sipping, shivering as it went down. When matters calmed down, he reflected on things, then took a bigger mouthful and sent that on its way, getting into a drinker's rhythm.

By the time the sky had darkened, the first bottle was half-gone and he was feeling much better.

At some point he glanced over at the clock, purely accidental on his part, and saw it was seven twenty-one in the evening. His eyes had dried up completely and his Scotch goggles were simultaneously warping reality while also numbing it.

There was no pain. None at all.

Somewhere in there, he managed to eat something and keep it down. He also planned ahead by drinking one mug of water. Just a mug, and then he returned to regular programming, where the main character was well on their way to getting shit-faced.

He invented a new drinking game, taking a sip every time his brain remembered Collie.

Another mouthful every time he thought of the Leather.

The Leather. It didn't take long to identify the Dog Shit and his minions as the sole source of his misery. If they hadn't pressed Milo into sniping and killing Collie at Whitecap, well . . . Gus figured she would still be alive. Really alive. Maybe, maybe things could have been different. Maybe Josh Rogan could have lucked out and come up with a treatment of some kind. Maybe a serum, like in the movies. *Some* god-damn thing.

More thoughts of the Leather, circling around him, killing the reanimated corpse of the Dog Shit. That, he had to admit, didn't feel bad at all. He could do more of that. A *lot* more. To any Leather he found. Find more Leather and shoot them. Kill them without mercy, making it hurt. Like they'd done to so many of their victims. Would *continue* to do, if it hadn't been for Collie and him.

Piss-eyed and very blackhearted, Gus drank slower now, making it last while staring off into the night. Poisonous revenge seeped into his system, working mayhem on the flickering circuitry of his mind, rotting him to his core. If he didn't take care, he'd probably stink every bit as bad as the last mindless he'd executed. That would not do. The Leather, the ones who still lived, would smell him. Know he was coming for them. And be ready.

Not that it mattered, he'd kill them all anyway. Matter of fact, that sounded like an ideal life's mission. Hunt them down and kill them.

Make it hurt.

All for Collie. And yes, for him as well.

Fuck, Gus mulled, his drunken stupor deepening. *That doesn't sound half bad at all.* Fitting punishment for the crime.

No torture. That wouldn't do. That would make him no better than the vermin he hunted. Just straight up killing. *Righteous* killing, which pleased him for even thinking it.

Make it hurt, his mind suggested again.

He pooh-poohed that away. Even so, cinematic scenes rolled through his head where he utilized nail guns and hammers upon his leather-clad victims and their lack of screaming only incensed him to even greater punishments. Blowtorches. To the cheeks. The ears.

The cameras of his mind rolled.

The next day was a late start.

The Scotch he'd drank had left a wicked hangover, so he downed grape drink until he was ready to piss purple, and returned to bed for a few more hours. When he woke a second time, the room was warm, and he'd kicked off all the bedsheets. He was still in his robe, which stank of spilled Scotch. He thought of Uncle Jack, who was still MIA. Gus figured he was gone forever, if he'd ever really existed in the first place.

The day was a write-off, so he stayed in bed until evening, whereupon he got up, downed a couple mugs of water, and deemed it too late to do anything. *Tomorrow*, he promised no one. He would get an early start tomorrow. So he stayed in, laid off the Scotch, and took it easy. Sleep eventually claimed him and gave no dreams.

The next day, he woke, splashed water across his face, got ready, and, as promised, went through the last few upper floors.

The mindless were gone, as were the living. No one inhabited those rooms, which Gus found weird, since that meant most of the Leather who had lived here must have lived on the floors below the restaurants. The regular Leather, he supposed, and not the pack leaders. The more he wandered, the greater his sense of just how big the Anchor Bay was. Huge, really. As such he took breaks when needed, closing the door of the room he had just searched and collapsing in a chair facing a window. There he would stay, gazing over the snow-buried city, until he snapped out of his trance and got moving again.

When he reached the fourteenth floor, the signage informed him of the swimming pools inside. He remembered Mortimer's mansion of horrors, and the indoor pool filled with trapped zombies. That memory bothered him enough to have a good hard think about what he was about to do next. He had the Ramfist and his sidearm, but he didn't carry enough ammunition to take out a pool potentially filled with undead.

Then he realized he was wearing his pissy smelling coat and that there was no commotion beyond the door.

Cautiously, Gus opened the door just a crack, enough to peek inside.

And got a whiff, of all things, of dirt.

Nothing crawled into view or attempted to tackle him, so he slipped inside, into a big temperature-controlled room. Gus corrected himself, the place was not just a room. It was an *enormous* open space devoted to three swimming pools of various sizes. Reclining chairs and a few small tables lined the edges of those pools, and a number of fake palm trees and flower beds throughout created something of a tropical ambiance. An indoor track wide enough for two runners encircled the whole scene, with strips of artificial grass along the side. A second track ran above the first, one level up, encircling the whole area, as if one crazy loop wasn't enough for the health nuts.

Gus wandered in a little further, eyeing the largest of the swimming pools, which resembled the watering hole of some desert oasis. He stopped at the edge and leaned over, gauging the depth. The other pools were nearby, sharing that tropical beach vibe but without the sand. Those pools were smaller and not nearly as deep. There was even a pair of what looked to be hot tubs, placed within little green groves to provide a little bit of privacy. Daylight shone through a series of tall windows on the second level, coming down upon an open area hemmed in by planks and filled with dirt, resembling a large sandbox. A row of wooden shelves stood to the left of that, while on the right was a low wall of what appeared to be stacked sandbags.

Squinting in puzzlement, Gus realized how damn quiet it was. He scanned the rest of that open space, sighting a single building at the halfway point. A door was ajar, with a sign beside the entrance warning SLIPPERY WHEN WET.

"So's my dick," he muttered, and walked across beige pool tiles, heading for the place.

He entered a single hallway with a series of changing rooms and showers, as well as two saunas, which pleasantly surprised him. He'd never been in a sauna before. That got him wondering if it took only a flick of a switch to get the things going. He supposed he'd try that another day, and continued through the main hallway to an open door on the other side. He passed a drinking fountain that worked, a fire extinguisher positioned next to the exit, and a set of emergency flashlights.

Gus stepped back into the pool area, still spotting the elevators, always mindful of unwanted company. Nothing stirred. Nothing crawled into the light.

He took a moment to think. There were rooms above and bars and restaurants below. Pools in between. What a setup. He supposed any guests would need a buffer of sorts, to separate them from the entertainment floors. Sensing the place was safe, Gus returned to the big pool, and wondered how much water was in it. Then he wondered if the Dog Shit actually allowed his minions time off to simply lie back and relax here. Seemed unlikely. Maybe it was an indoor reservoir, a back-up just in case the pumping systems failed, or the power went out, or whatever. But wouldn't they need chlorine or something?

The oversized sandbox caught his eye, then. Closer inspection showed there were actually two, each perhaps thirty feet long and ten feet wide, separated by a five-foot walking space. Both sandboxes held the dirt Gus had been smelling. Dirt filled several green and brown plastic pots that lined the nearby shelving units. A cluster of tall heating lamps stood behind the shelves, waiting to be used. The row of sandbags Gus noticed earlier turned out to be bags of weed-free, high-grade topsoil (or so the label promised). Three plastic buckets were behind that, with bricks on the lids.

"The fuck you guys doing here?" Gus wondered aloud, drawn to a box stuffed with seed packages. "You gonna grow veggies up here or something?"

Apparently so.

Potato bulbs. Carrots. Onions and green peppers. There were even seeds for tomato plants and sunflowers.

"You self-sufficient fucks, you," Gus whispered, impressed. Obviously the Dog Shit wasn't just a warped, ex-wrestler warlord. He was planning ahead. That thought lingered until Gus realized the air wasn't so dry on this level. A touch on the dewy side, even, if that might be a factor in growing indoor crops. He didn't know. Still, the Leather looked like they were going to try exactly that. Maybe they already were and Gus had missed the harvest by a couple of days.

"Science," he muttered and made a silly face. He had never been stranded on Mars, but he had his fair share of chores around Adam's farm back in the day. He supposed he could plant some vegetables if he had to. Not that he would. The hotel had plenty to eat. And come the spring, well . . . chances were he'd be long gone.

On impulse he noticed there was a plastic lining underneath the bucket lids. He removed one of the bricks and lifted a lid, getting a raw snootful of human manure despite the plastic seal. Wincing, Gus replaced the lid and brick, and had the very strong urge of needing to wash his hands.

"You gotta be . . ." he groaned, made a disgusted face, and nudged the other buckets with a boot toe. All filled.

Crazy fuckers, the Leather. Shitting in buckets and using it as fertilizer. Why not. Nothing surprised him at that point.

He returned to the stairwell, descending to the gym level, according to the sign posted outside the doorway. The gym was also empty and rivaled the greenhouse pool area in available floorspace. Rows of treadmills faced a wall of windows on one end, offering a view of the snowbound city. All manner of exercise equipment occupied the main floor. Blue and yellow mats padded a section of floorspace for aerobics or yoga. A maze of ductwork, speakers, and unlit lights hung from the ceiling. There were changing rooms, lockers, very nice bathrooms, showers, and even more saunas.

The whole setup made Gus hiss like a vampire exposed to sunlight. Still, he had to admit, it was an impressive gym. Maybe he could get a membership.

Feeling hungry, he returned to his room for a late lunch. After eating, he laid back on the bed, lying on his side and facing the windows, watching the grey sky. It got comfortable real fast, and he decided he'd had enough housecleaning. A bottle of Scotch got cracked open, and he settled in for the evening. The nightclub, arcade, and golf range were the last few floors he wanted to check, out, nothing that couldn't wait until tomorrow, as he was ninety-nine percent sure he was the last dickhead alive at the Anchor Bay. Whether or not he'd brave the skyways to check out the other hotels was a matter for another day. In fact, there was no need, really. There was plenty of food in the kitchens upstairs. He doubted there were any Leather in the other hotels. He'd have seen signs of them by now. If he was truly feeling proactive, maybe he could barricade the skyways, preventing any leftover zombies from crossing over that way.

Not a bad idea, he reckoned, and added it to his mental list of things to do.

That checklist morphed into images of Collie.

Whereupon he started drinking.

9

If the gym was impressive, then the arcade was awesome.

Perched over a gaping mouth of an entrance, the sign read TechDome, its block letters heavy and cracked and drawn with love. Four different machines flanked the open cave mouth of the arcade, all of them claw machines still filled with stuffed toys. Just inside the entrance were two game cabinets turned on their side, with intergalactic pirates posing on one and battling starships on the other. Plenty of other video games waited farther in, their own profiles just barely visible in that pulse-racing pit of pixelated fun.

Across from all that stand-up glory was the golf range. Called Anchor Bay's Driving Range, it had as much appeal to Gus as the sick accordion in his fucked-up foot. Or the buckets of collected crap on the pool level. The dark interior of the arcade enticed him more, as he was slightly hungover from the previous night's drinking. So he marched right in.

Dim strips of LED lights spread out along the ceiling and floor. More red carpet, which made Gus wonder if he'd ever been in a place with so much quality fluff underfoot. It was space-agey. Neo-techy. Quietly bedazzling, even. None of the games were on, but there were probably switches for that. Even so, the darkness only partially muted the flashy artwork on the sides of the individual games. Nostalgia welled up within Gus, enough that he stopped and marveled at those arcade delights.

Centipede. Pac-Man. Space Invaders. And a plethora of others. Including pinball machines that would positively dazzle if the power was on.

Best of all . . . no zombies.

Not one undead ass muncher in sight. And he'd been inside the place for minutes, plenty of time for one to drag itself into the open and take a swipe at him. Despite the lack of mindless, he still did a slow march throughout, checking between and behind the game cabinets. Playing each one cost a token, which could be bought at a counter that resembled the podium of a postapocalyptic judge—its base consisted of stacks of cartoonish grinning skulls with electric flames flickering from their sockets.

But that's not what raised Gus's eyebrows. A sign on the counter read tokens cost two bucks.

Apiece.

Obviously the Anchor Bay wasn't above making a little side money.

"Bet you'd like this place, Collie," he said, smiling wistfully at a series of pinball machines. "Bet you would."

Feeling like he had all the time in the world, Gus strolled on through the arcade, Ramfist held at his waist. After finishing his leisurely recon, he returned to the golf range and checked that place out. A lot of green walls, but without the fake plants. Also a lot of nets and alleys, where a grey canvas waited at the very back to catch any incoming balls. Compared to all the dead glitz of the arcade, this place was much more subdued in décor. It, too, was empty of deadheads.

Gus went down to the eleventh floor, where the nightclub and lounge were located.

Another huge feature of the hotel, and every bit as dead as the previous ones. No lights were on, so he stopped at the red carpeted archway of the entrance. He stuck his head in and glanced around, spotting a few tables and chairs. A cozy-looking booth was just to his right, with a menu on the table's surface. The whole place might've had booths along the walls. No doubt a bar as well. Oddly enough, a stack of what looked to be cut and treated lumber—two-by-fours, to be exact—of some unknown length. Plastic bins filled with nails rested on top of the wood. Someone had piled the building materials off to the side, suggesting some in-hotel renovations or even repairs being completed.

"Anyone in here?" Gus called out, the echo eerie in that massive space. He waited, tingling with expectation, feeling a chill strop his spine.

No one answered.

"Figured," he grumped and turned to leave.

The smell stopped him. Faint, but just a little stronger than what was sprucing up his coat. He pulled out his flashlight, juggling that and the shotgun, which was a balancing act he wasn't used to doing. He clutched the flashlight in his left hand, Ramfist in the right, and hoped to hell he didn't have to shoot anything.

He flicked on the flashlight and moved the beam around. Booths, like he figured. Nice ones, too. Wide with curved backrests and lush leather upholstery. Only the best for the Anchor Bay. Curiously, two of the booths had what looked like open toolboxes and partially concealed power tools, which wasn't surprising, given how the green thumbs were working their magic a few floors up. Gus could only guess what they had planned for such a wide-open space. Maybe they planned on raising chickens or goats here.

The beam swept over a sight that stopped him cold.

"Holy..."

He panned back, then up, illuminating what he'd found between a pair of booths, his mouth hanging open, wide enough to catch flies if they were around. His heart went from a quick beat to a full-on race. He blinked, swallowed, not believing but certainly not surprised, and realized what the smell was.

Realized what the power tools were for. And the lumber.

The Leather had nailed a person to the wall.

A man, splayed out, hung off a mighty X made of wooden planks. Head and shoulders slumped, his flesh devoid of color. The Leather had stripped him down to his underwear, wrapped strips around his wrists and feet, and nailed the ends to the wood. When the poor bastard had been secured, they then hung him up like a trophy. They didn't stop there. Nails festooned the victim's palms, wrists, and elbows, for extra support or pain, or both. Every nailhead gleamed in the flashlight beam. Long streaks of blood led to the floor. Nails spiked the poor bastard's feet as well, right up the insteps like a single set of eyelets.

Gus slowly panned right, creeping the beam along the wall, inching over a few more booths, until it revealed another dead man, stripped down and strung up like the first. Then there was a third person, a woman, treated no differently than the previous two.

A smell reached him then, of blood, long-since soaked into the floor, faint but haunting. It failed to move Gus. There wasn't much directly below the bodies, as if whoever did the nailing had placed something underneath, to catch most of the bodily fluids. Not all, as evident by the dark stains, but most.

He discovered two more grisly decorations before he reached the waist-high stage. A DJ's turntable was situated on the right side, with a mass of cables flowing from it. Right behind that, however, were a dozen more corpses. Four were nailed to chairs surrounding a round table, while the rest were adorning a white lattice that spanned the rear wall. The four around the table had their hands spiked to the surface, while some held playing cards. One wore a casino dealer's visor. Others, practically naked, wore sunglasses. Two empty chairs remained at that poker table, waiting for unwilling players, while a dead audience watched from behind. A diorama of human agony and suffering, on full display.

Not one of them moved when the light hit them. They were all dead. Mercifully so. Perhaps they were prisoners, but Gus wondered about that from what he learned from Milo. Maybe they were dissidents, unhappy with the Dog Tongue's rule. Maybe they died somehow of natural causes, or as naturally as one might in this day and age, but he saw no gunshot or knife wounds other than the ones inflicted. Whatever the case, all notions of the Leather being industrious do-it-yourselfers were wiped from Gus's mind and the label of insane killers returned. Displease the Leather, piss them off, and you would find yourself literally nailed to a wall. Or to the last poker table you'd ever sit at.

Moving the flashlight along, he backed away and nearly bumped into one of the many tables and chairs on the main floor. The nightclub wasn't for dancing it seemed. *Nightclub.* Gus scoffed. The place was a torture chamber.

"The fuck is . . . *wrong* with these people?" he whispered, horrified to the core. He retreated, whipping the light across the opposite wall, much farther away, revealing additional bodies tacked to *X*s.

"You . . . sick . . . *fucks*."

Then he was outside, flashlight aimed at the floor, attempting to process what he'd just seen. He stood there, appalled. Dazed. Accustomed to zombies but not so much to seeing what people could do to other people.

I'm done, he decided. His nerves demanded medication.

The trek back to his room was a slow one, as he thought about the nightclub. While he walked along, his attention switched without reason to the carpeting in the halls. He realized he could walk almost anywhere in this place wearing just his socks. He might very well do that once he was sure he was alone. He was ninety-nine percent certain already. The fact that his brain switched over from bodies nailed to walls to walking around in socks wasn't lost on him.

Then he started thinking about being the only person at the hotel. He could do whatever he wanted here. Fortify the place just like his old place back on the mountain. 'Course, back then, he had the wall. There was the half-assed attempt at digging a moat, which he gave up on fairly quick. Just didn't have the energy or the drive to complete it. These days, he was in much better shape. Most of the fat was gone, and he had the saggy skin to show for it, but there was another problem. His age. Not only was he getting older, but he was getting slower as well. Oh, he *felt* as if he were still in his twenties, but the reality was he moved like a guy in his fifties. And over the years he'd sustained enough bumps, bruises, and broken bones to slow him down even more.

Then all he saw were the dead people around that poker table.

With an effort, he shoved that image out of his head, but just doing that raised the question—was something like that in his future? If not by the Leather, then by another pack of crazies? There were plenty of them out there, he knew, small packs preying on whoever came within range. He'd been captured too many times over the years, managing to escape by himself or with help. Managed to buck the odds every time, in fact. But how long could his aging ass do that?

Maybe it was best just to end it all now and be done with it.

The coldness returned, one Gus was familiar with on a very intimate level. He considered the Ramfist. Powerful beyond all expectation. Even more spectacular than the Glock, which would merely leave a hole. The Ramfist would leave a crater. Gus considered the weapon for seconds before his chest and shoulders heaved in a weary sigh.

"You lucky civvie, you," he smirked and resumed his walk, clutching the shotgun a little harder.

Back in his room, he locked the door and placed a chair against it for that little extra bit of security. The boots came off, since he had been trained since birth to kick off his outer footwear when coming home. He placed the Ramfist against the wall, handy if needed. The Glock went on the bedside table. The rest of his gear and clothing came off, everything draped over a chair close the bed. When he stood in his underwear, he spotted his store of Scotch, stared hard at a bottle, and shrugged.

The bottle felt good in his hand and the first swallow gave him a welcome cringe. *Scotch*.

"Home again, home again," he said, and had another shot.

That mouthful hit the bull's-eye dead center, resulting in his best wet dog shiver and shake. He sought out his bathrobe, slipped into it, and fluffed up the pillows on the bed, so that they were against the headboards. He regarded the painting over the bed, the one of the elven forest with a winding path. Boy he wished he could teleport there, skip along that trail on his way to whatever waited around the next bend. When he finished fluffing up his nest, he climbed in and lay there, bottle in hand. The curtains were pulled back. It had stopped snowing, but clouds brought on the shadows. Didn't matter. He intended to watch the sky grow dark over the city. The evening's entertainment, which suited him just fine. Quiet times were needed. To dispel the memories of the day before they could haunt him in his sleep.

The television got his attention, but obviously there was nothing on it. And no handy storage device packed with near endless hours of entertainment.

"Shitty cable service," he grumped, and followed that up with another drink. A backhand wipe across the mouth and beard so there was no sloppiness. Seconds passed. Gus stared at the television, then his bottle, only a few swallows gone. It was the weekend—or so he thought—and here he was, Mister Saturday Night, shacked up in a grand hotel. A hotel once occupied by killers, who liked using reanimated dead people as shock troops and who also decorated their walls with corpses.

Gus drank, not needing to remember, and hoping once again he got the opportunity for some payback on the Leather.

Some big time payback.

The fine print on the Scotch bottle label caught his eye, but it was too small to read. Then, for whatever reason, he remembered the lost and found box on the ground floor, behind the front desk.

"Forgot to bring that up here," Gus grumbled, recalling a coloring book in there. A coloring book. Let the good times roll. Not today, however, as his interest in the lost and found box wasn't enough to get outfitted again and head down to the lobby. Fuck that noise.

So he made do with the bottle.

The room continued to darken, and Gus kept right on drinking. He wondered what else he might find in the hotel. What might be waiting for him in the other hotels, if he dared to venture across the skyways. Wondered about Collie and remembered their conversations.

Not quite an hour later, the shadows thickened into near darkness. Gus had trouble finding his bottle. Fearful of knocking it over the nightstand, he switched on a lamp.

"*Jesus Christ!*" he blurted, startled by Uncle Jack sitting on the nearby couch, preening his beard with long fingers. If the old gentleman noticed the jump he gave Gus, he didn't show it. Nor did he choose to say anything at the rather rude outburst.

Gus's expression changed to a frown, and he settled back into his pillows. "Finally decided to make an appearance, eh?" he asked after a few seconds.

Uncle Jack nodded and continued to rake his beard.

"Yeah, well, next time announce yourself."

"My apologies, Gus Berry. You're quite correct in that . . . social decorum should be observed. And practiced. And yet, these old eyes of mine saw in advance that you were in a troubled state of mind and body, thus I decided to let you be. And there was a peace I chose not to disturb, if you gather my meaning. A nice, reflective evening to watch the sun go down, in a sense."

"One where I nearly shit the bed because of you," Gus grumped.

Uncle Jack said nothing to that.

Gus studied the older gentleman, sitting just beyond the lamplight. Uncle Jack's choice of wardrobe looked ancient, perhaps Edwardian. An old, but not untidy, three-piece suit in a distinguished black, marked by a high white collar that disappeared underneath the man's massive beard. There might have been a necktie underneath as well. His hair was slicked back and shone in the lamp's glow, and with God as his witness, Gus could smell a faint, but fine, clean powder.

Aware he was being watched, Uncle Jack tweaked one tip of his moustache and then the other with a practiced fluidity.

"Where'd you go, anyway?" Gus asked.

"Oh, here and there," Uncle Jack replied, and then made it clear he wasn't going to say any more. "My own matters to attend to, but never that far, I can assure you."

Whatever, Gus thought, and studied his bottle.

"You had a bit of a hard day," Uncle Jack said finally.

Gus scoffed at the understatement and took a good swig.

"Still fond of the drink, I see."

"This? This is medicine. Break in case of emergency sorta deal."

The other man held up a hand, indicating no explanation was needed.

Gus settled back and resumed gazing out the window. "You missed all the fun."

"You mean the undead still lurking about these parts?"

"Yup."

"And the corpses nailed to the wall?"

"Mm-hm."

"I . . . wouldn't call that fun. If you do, then I'm afraid you've gone further than I thought. And, for your sake, dare I say, sanity . . . I pray you go no further."

Gus wasn't sure what to say to that.

"And so . . ." Uncle Jack nodded. "To cope with all the horrors you've seen . . ."

"I'm getting shit-faced, yeah. Want some?"

"No, thank you. I'm quite fine. If not a little distressed by your own troubled state of mind."

Gus drew in a deep breath. "Not distressed. Freaked out is more like it. I mean, yeah. You saw what I saw."

Uncle Jack didn't comment.

"So you know," Gus went on. "People are . . . fucked-up. These days. I mean . . . I know they're out there. Crazy fucks who'll cut you up without blinkin'. I've come across plenty of them. But, I mean . . . how can people do such awful shit to other people? It's fucked-up. So very fucked-up. You hear what I'm sayin'?"

"I believe so."

"Good. Because . . . aw, man, I don't know. Dead people walkin' around is one thing, but livin' people doing that to their own kind? And for *what*? What did they do to deserve being . . ." he waved a hand. "You know. I don't get it."

"All manner of insanity's afoot," Uncle Jack offered. "All manner of depravity. And evil. No question."

Gus had a drink in agreement.

Uncle Jack watched him. "Are you . . . enjoying that?"

"Oh yeah."

Silence then, but it didn't last long.

"Don't take what I'm about to say the wrong way," Gus said. "I'm glad you're here. Real glad. God knows I need someone to talk to. But . . . it's just that . . ."

"You miss her."

A hot lump filled Gus's throat then and he nodded in reply, for fear of his voice breaking.

"No surprise," Uncle Jack continued, wisely giving him time to recover. "Clearly, she was an exceptional woman. Anyone could see that. A true loss. I don't believe I extended my condolences at the time, but allow me to do so now. I'm truly sorry for your loss."

That hit a tender place. Gus squeezed his eyes shut as his sinuses filled up, forcing him to breathe through his mouth until he had to sniff all that viscous slop back down. He smiled a little, one far from happy, then he nodded again and took another sip.

"These are hard days, Gus Berry. Hard, hard days. She knew that. As well as you do now. The only thing you can do is . . . honor her memory. And carry out her wishes. Which you willingly took on, I might add."

Gus nodded, still unable to speak, sniffing back the cement filling his sinus cavities. He wiped his eyes. A little whimper escaped him, but he caught it before it erupted into a full-blown blubber.

"Though I imagine you are filled with feelings of despair, emptiness, and doubt, you must remind yourself . . . She didn't leave you without first imparting some knowledge. Of what to do. And how to do it."

A wet-eyed Gus croaked, still unable to speak, and left it at that.

Uncle Jack glanced away. "I'm sorry, Gus Berry. Again, my sincere apologies. I've upset you. Just my nature to ramble on without regards for how it affects another person. A habit I will strive to remedy, I can assure you. Do you need a moment to better compose yourself?"

Gus shook his head.

"Are you sure?"

Gus nodded even harder.

"I may have a handkerchief about me somewhere, if you give me a moment."

That earned Uncle Jack a hard glare and the older gentleman backed off with a raised hand asking for pardon.

It took some time, but Gus recovered, using his sleeves until he realized at the rate he was going, he would be up to his elbows in snot. So he got up and went into the bathroom, pulled off a generous wad of toilet paper, and unloaded his nose. A couple of blasts later, Gus gripped the edges of the counter and hung his head. He eventually washed his face, scrubbing it red, and stared into the mirror, his beard dripping.

"Yeah," he whispered.

Uncle Jack waited for him, no longer concerned with combing out his own whiskers. The stately gentleman watched Gus climb back onto the bed.

"You see the . . . garden shit they had going on, upstairs?" Gus finally asked, wanting a change of subject.

"The tilled plots of earth?"

"Yeah, that."

"I did."

"What do you make of it all?"

"Industrious."

"Yeah, that's what I said." Gus finished and adjusted his pocket pearls. "And all the food in the freezers."

"You've more than enough to survive the winter."

"Yeah," Gus agreed. "More than enough."

"What are your intentions tomorrow?" Uncle Jack asked.

Gus took a breath and thought about it. "Go through the rest of the hotel. Finish that off. Make sure I'm . . . I'm the only guy here. Sorry. No offence."

Uncle Jack shooed the slip away.

"Make sure *we're* the only ones here," Gus corrected with an expression of *see what I did there?* "I'll sleep better when that's done. Then, I'll go back through the rooms where those lunatics shacked up. Might find something useful. I dunno. But the way the snow's buried the streets below? No one's gettin' through downtown."

No comment on that, so Gus continued. "So, yeah. I'll make sure the hotel is clear. But I tell you . . . if I find any Leather . . . look out. I'm . . . not feeling merciful. Hear what I'm sayin'? I'll nail *them* to a wall. See how they like it. I dunno. Maybe I'll just kill 'em quick."

Gus let that thought marinate for a moment. "Just kiddin'. I'll make it slow."

Old Uncle Jack didn't look impressed. In fact, the old codger looked downright *un*impressed, which befuddled him a bit.

"Something the matter?" Gus asked.

Uncle Jack didn't answer.

"Fine," he said, mildly pissed. "Don't answer me. I get along fuckin' fine on my own, if you haven't already noticed. Next time maybe show up when I'm about to put down a Moe. Or a Leather. You'll want to be around for that, I guarantee it."

Uncle Jack lowered his head. "You're hurting."

For that, Gus frowned, shook his head at what he thought was obvious, and sized up the bottle.

"I'm not one for hiding my meaning," Uncle Jack said. "So I'll just say what I have to say, and move on."

That sank through the Scotch fog. "Move on?" Gus asked.

"I'm leaving."

"Wha? Jesus, Jack. We're just talkin' here. No harm no foul. No need to get pissy. I mean, okay, I was pissy a second ago, but Jesus, I'm *sorry*. You don't have to *leave*."

"I do," Uncle Jack said with an apologetic frown. "I sense you're going to dark places, Gus Berry. Very dark places. You're angry. Hurt. Becoming increasingly eager to inflict pain. To instigate violence. Becoming no better than the ones who did this to you."

Gus held up a hand. "We talkin' about the Leather here?"

"In part, yes."

"You think I'm becoming like the Leather? The ones that enslave people? If they don't make you into one of the mindless? That same Leather?"

"You just said you would kill them slow."

"Yes, I did."

"Then—"

"Because the *crime* justifies the *punishment*, in my book," Gus interrupted, glaring at his companion.

Uncle Jack glared back. "You're walking a fine line between retribution and corruption."

"And you can fuck off."

That silenced Uncle Jack, and for seconds, the tension in the room became as tight as piano wire drawn across a throat.

"Men have become monsters while hunting for vengeance."

"Even sick fucks like the Leather?" Gus asked. "After everything they've done? Collie? Milo? Them kids? You forget the *kids*? Am *I* supposed to forget the kids? What they went through? What'll they *go* through as they grow up? All because of some insane Dog Shit's *minions*?"

Uncle Jack shook his head. "You're already committed, I see."

"And you're fucked in the head to think otherwise. I'm going to some dark places? I parked my truck there *weeks* ago. Make no fuckin' mistake. I'll kill each and every one of them sick bastards I find. Each and every one. For what they did."

"Well," the elderly man said and stood, dusting himself off. "I believe I've voiced my concerns. You've stated yours. This is where we part ways, then, Gus Berry."

"I goddamn guess so."

"You choose and walk your own road," Uncle Jack continued. "But I'll not accompany you to those horrible places. You understand?"

"Go ahead," Gus held his Scotch bottle by the neck and looked at the window. "You don't do shit around here, anyway. Not one soft-assed nugget. So you go. I don't need you. When did I ever? *Never*. So get the fuck out."

A chill drifted through the room as that sank in. Uncle Jack stared at him for moments, then, "Good day to you, sir."

With that the older gentleman left, walking across the room until he disappeared around a corner.

Gus watched him go. "You just remember," he yelled. "If I find them, if I find *anyone* wearin' the leather. They're dead. Each and every one. Gouge eyes, break bones, or cut throats. Or just plain shoot 'em. I'll fuck them up from here to Christmas next year. For what they did. To me. To Collie. To Milo. To *everyone*."

Uncle Jack didn't answer.

Just getting warmed up, Gus climbed off the bed and staggered after his one-time companion, looking to fire off a few parting shots. Thing was, the hallway was empty and the front door remained locked. And there was no sign of it being opened. Confused, Gus swayed for balance as he scanned the room and its many adjoining crannies, all to no avail.

Uncle Jack had made good his exit, up and gone, like a baby's fart in a thunderstorm.

"The fuck you go . . . ?" he muttered, doing a wobbly three-sixty, scowling all the way.

Shrugging, he staggered back to bed.

"Becomin' like them," Gus said under his breath. "The fuck you talkin' about. I'm nothin' like them. I never nailed anyone to a wall. I never tortured anyone. I never . . . never . . ."

The words trailed off, as a sobering thought seeped into his head.

Maybe Uncle Jack didn't mean he was acting like the Leather, as in evil. Maybe like . . . just as vicious? But wouldn't that be the same? In a way?

Maybe . . . and at this juncture, Gus really tried hard to work through it . . . maybe he meant something else, entirely.

But what that something else was, he wasn't able to identify. And with the Scotch buzzing through his head, defying space and time with every passing second . . . he realized he didn't really care.

In the morning, Uncle Jack was still gone and Gus was massively hung over.

He spent most of his time in and out of the can, groaning and upchucking. He also reminisced about the early days and wondered how the hell he'd ever lived through it all. Uncle Jack's departure didn't bother him. No sir. He figured it was the booze talking anyway. Summoning some subconscious guardian angel from the depth. Thing was, Gus didn't need any guardian angel right now. Maybe not ever, not no more. All he needed . . . was to make sure the Leather were all gone. And that nothing like that twisted road clan ever surfaced again.

The old guy might be back anyway, when Gus went on another Scotch bender. He knew what was going on there and, truthfully, didn't care. Not in the least. At least he wasn't talking to his dick.

There was enough food and drink in the room for the day, which was a sunny one. So Gus napped, ate, and drank grape drink. Around midafternoon, he started feeling a little better, just as things were turning dark outside. So he dressed, strapped on his armored vest, and prepped the Ramfist and the Glock. A few minutes later he took the elevator down to the lobby. No way was he taking the stairs. They would only make him barf again and all he needed was the stairwell smelling of puke.

Cold was his first thought when the elevator doors opened, despite his clothing. A harsh wind blew through the building, threatening to do a job on his boys. Barefoot in his boots—a detail he should have rethunk—a squinty-eyed Gus stepped into the lobby and surveyed his surroundings.

Empty. Snow everywhere. A vast drift had blown into the lobby, the crest tall and graceful and covering up more than a few bodies while trying its best to reach the front desk. Bigger drifts loomed outside the place, like the bleached backs of whales surfacing and frozen in a flash. Snow reached up to the halfway point of some windows, even, which meant a good six or seven feet at least.

Collie's flower bed grave remained untouched by the elements, as it was away from the main entrance. For that, he was grateful.

Gus avoided the drifts but not the multitude of bodies. The lost and found box was where he'd left it, on the countertop of the front desk. Careful of where he put his foot down, Gus stopped and looked inside the box. Despite how shitty he felt, half a smile hitched up his face.

Treasure galore.

Coloring book. Crayons. Sketch pad, notebooks, and pens. A child's winter hat. About a dozen or so paperback novels. A stuffed toy lamb. A leather belt with the brass belt buckle fashioned in the shape of a lightning bolt. An assortment of keys and the last item, a handheld game console, without batteries.

The keys he left behind, seeing no need for them. He also discarded the winter hat—much too small for him—and the stuffed toy lamb. The game console had no batteries, but maybe he'd find some later.

The little lamb with floppy arms, legs, and a sad smile got his attention again. Gus smirked at the toy. He placed it on the counter and aimed a finger.

"You're the guard," he said. "Anyone comes in here, you let me know. Capisce?"

Capisce, the lamb smiled back, seemingly brighter with the assignment.

Gus picked up the box and headed for the elevators.

Halfway back, he slowed to a stop.

"Goddammit," he said under his breath and reluctantly looked back at the stuffed toy.

There it was, already fallen over. Sad smile still on its face.

And it was looking right at him.

Gus wavered and turned for the elevator, but only got two steps when he halted again.

"God*dammit*."

He faced the stuffed toy.

"You just ain't gonna drop it, are you?" he aimed. "Are you? No, 'course not. You little . . ."

The words failed him, and he simmered there with indecision. With a huff, Gus marched back to the counter, grabbed the little plush shit, and stared at it hard enough to induce tears of fear—if the thing could cry.

Instead, it only smiled that melancholy smile.

Gus ran a hand over its little white head, as pure as the snow piled up around the hotel. Scratching at his eye, he put the thing back into the box, and checked to see if he was being watched. All clear, so he walked back to the elevator.

"Not a word," he warned the lamb, who gazed up at him. "Not one fuckin' word. All I need is for you to start talkin' to me. Seriously. I'm not that far gone yet. So shut the fuck up and wipe that smile off your face. Okay?"

The lamb did not answer him.

Which was fine. Ideal, really. And Gus didn't know what was so weird about taking the toy, anyway. It was a *toy*, for Christ's sake. As soft and boneless as they came. A child's keepsake and dare he say it, a security thing, meant to get one through the darkest nights. A comforting reassurance that all will be right and good in the morning. Not like the thing was going to eat or drink him out of house and home. So what was the big deal? Nothing. Nothing at all.

Still, he couldn't stop glancing at the sorry-assed little thing, even when the elevator doors were closing.

10

The sweep and search resumed the next day.

Gus picked up where he'd left off, combing through the last floors, where the lower ranks of the Leather seemed to stay. He checked rooms for bodies, living or dead, hiding or in plain sight, and left alone the dressers, cabinets, and such. Most of the rooms were neat, but a few had their surprises. One had a man's discarded pair of shitty drawers, tossed into the bathtub and left to stink. The moment Gus unlocked the door he got a whiff of the soiled undergarments and brought up the Ramfist, expecting the worst. He relaxed a little after discovering the underwear, but quickly grew disgusted at the state of them and wished he had a lighter to burn the clothing. Not a good idea, he supposed, unsure if the sprinkler system still functioned.

There were no Leather minions waiting to ambush him. No remnants of their zombie forces. No other real surprises.

Until he reached room 607.

The number resonated with him for some reason, until he remembered he had a key for it, which he used. A new, much more intense wave of bodily gases enveloped him the moment he cracked open the door.

"God almighty," he gasped and jerked the door shut. He stepped away, shaking his head to clear his senses of the debilitating fumes. Just a whiff, but whatever lurked inside was a breath stealer. A killer stink bomb of decomposing flesh and putrefying liquids best left inside a body. Gus recognized it immediately. He didn't have to go in there. He could lock it and walk away. Even make up a sign with the recovered paper and crayons if he really wanted to.

Instead, he readied himself to enter the room. Undoing his coat and yanking his undershirt up over his nose, he took one last breath of air and opened the door.

"Oh . . ." was all he could manage, wincing at what had to be ground zero of the olfactory tactical strike. Only by sticking his head up a dead man's ass could he have discovered something worse. That appalling stench repelled him. His stomach clenched and threatened mutiny if he didn't get some fresh air soon. There was no clean air to be had, however, only that unseen, throat-clawing vise that rotted his nasal cavity and pinched his windpipe.

Fuck it.

Gus raised the shotgun and blasted out the far window. A curtain rod dropped and a backlash of sub-zero air raged back, ripping through the interior and out the open door. He staggered against a wall, the air once again breathable. The polluted stink weakened but was far from banished.

With the curtains puddled on the floor, sunlight blazed inside, revealing a space empty of the usual upscale décor Gus had grown accustomed to seeing. Instead, an imposing assortment of medieval blades, clubs, tongs, and whips lay around a single bare mattress, where a man had been stretched out, tied down, and stripped to his undershorts. A hotel towel covered his face for some reason, but everything else was on display, and the length of his entire body resembled a mottled palette of greys, blues, and purples, with streaks of maroon. The maroon had leaked onto the mattress, saturating the foamy texture to the point where little pools had congealed. The sight of the dead man, who had obviously been beaten, pinched, whipped, and cut during a long and drawn-out session of agony, weakened Gus in the knees. Worse, the poor soul wasn't long gone, judging by the relative freshness of everything.

Matter of fact, everything looked so fresh, Gus wondered when the guy had actually died.

Then the real horror hit him, powerful enough that he stood and stared, hoping beyond hope that the guy was long dead and that he *hadn't* missed an opportunity to save him . . . if he had come straight to the room the moment after finding the key.

"Oh fuck me," Gus moaned, ice forming in his guts. He lurched to the bedside and stood there. "I'm sorry, man. I'm so sorry. I . . . didn't know you were here. I didn't know. I just didn't."

Guilt-stricken to the core, he pulled back the towel.

A young guy, swollen eyes closed to slits. Mouth partially open as if snoring, allowing a glimpse of the other tortures the poor bastard suffered through.

"*Fuck,*" Gus blurted and covered the face again. He stood there, unable to fully grasp what had taken place in this room, truly hoping the man had died days earlier.

But suspecting the worst.

"All right," Gus finally said, iron in his voice. "All right. First thing's first."

The rest of the torture chamber was empty. Gus cut the ropes, keeping the body in place, and waited for a reaction. Nothing happened. The guy died as a person, which depressed Gus all the more, but also moved him to do the right thing. So he returned to the last room unoccupied by any Leather, and propped open the door. He stopped for a quick bathroom visit, splashed water on his face, and rubbed a finger's worth of fragrant hair conditioner under his nose. Then he wrapped a towel around his face, outlaw style.

He returned to the torture chamber, gathered up the dead man, and lugged him back to the other room. There, Gus dropped the body onto the bed and covered him from head to toe in soft duvets. With as much fatherly gentleness as he could muster, he tucked the blankets in the right spots, to ensure the deceased was comfortable. An idea came to him then, and he pulled open the drawer of the nearby nightstand. The Anchor Bay might be a swanky hotel, but they still followed tradition, tucking a small Bible inside. He took that, ran a hand over the cover, and placed it on the dead man's chest.

Once finished, Gus stood back, studied the makeshift grave, and nodded at it all.

"Best I could do. Sorry again. It was either this or the tub, and I think this is cozier. I could . . . cremate you, but," he sighed, "not up here. Be too messy. Anyway. The bedroom seemed to be the better choice for . . . you know. For a lot of people. I found plenty of folks who, ah, gone to their final . . . rest. In their beds. Over the years. So . . . yeah. Hope you're in a better place. Now and forever. Amen."

Memories struck at him then, of when he'd been captured and tortured by some very twisted people. Gus gazed upon the covered body, knowing it could have been him so many times over.

"Evil fuckers," he whispered, hating the Leather just a little more, knowing they deserved everything they got. He located a notepad and pen, wrote DECEASED PERSON in block letters on it, and laid it on the body's chest, just below the Bible. Unsure of what else to do, he left the room, closed the door, and hung the DO NOT DISTURB sign off the knob. He took out his knife and scrawled DEAD PERSON INSIDE into the surface. It took a while, but he got it done.

When he did, he went back to checking rooms.

Around midafternoon, Gus declared the Anchor Bay free of Leather and mindless. It felt hollow, though, as he was still aching over the grim discovery of the Leather's last victim. That was going to be a hard one to forget. And he wasn't entirely sure if he should forget.

Gus dragged his ass home, scuffing the carpet at times, wary of corners. Before long he was facing his door. Once inside, he locked everything up and stripped down. After tucking away his weapons, he wandered into the bathroom and put hot water in the tub. A deep soak was becoming addictive and, while he had no idea about the water situation, once again he didn't really care. After the horrors of the day, a bath was needed. So he soaked in silence, listening to the slow drips of the faucet while breathing in steam. The water eventually cooled, so he got out, cleaner, yet knowing he'd never be clean again. The bathrobe fought him as he put it on, all the way over to the bed.

Where the little lamb waited, propped up against a pillow.

"How you doin', you little shit?"

No response.

"Yeah, I know," Gus said and laid down beside the stuffed toy. "Good thing you weren't with me today. Man oh man. What a shit show. The Leather . . . you know what they did? They . . ."

A side glance at the slumped posture and the sad little smile stopped him from continuing. "Yeah," Gus muttered. "You don't need to know. We'll just leave it at that. Anything on the TV? No? That's fine. Didn't feel like watching it, anyway. Never anything good on. How about a drink, then? Hm? We got Scotch. Lots of Scotch. Something to take us into the evening? Howzat sound?"

The lamb didn't answer.

The remaining bottles waited. Gus considered them all before glancing back at the toy. "You don't talk much, do you? No sweat. I like that. You don't have to say a word. Just listen. I'll do the talking, okay? Rather talk to you than my dick. Ha. That would be something. Anyway, Jack will probably pop in here sooner or later. I don't doubt it. Probably scare the livin' shit out of me again when he does. 'Til then, what do you want to do? Hm? Any idea?"

Gus waited an acceptable amount of time before carrying on. "Okay, I'll take care of entertainment. You just relax."

He rolled off the bed, gathered up the lost and found box, and pawed through the contents.

"Game thing here." He held up the device. "No batteries though. I'll have to put that on the list of things to get. Must be some batteries around here somewhere. Some new ones. Those things last years in the package." He checked the size. "Triple A.

Needs four of them. Wonder why they don't just pop a D cell in there? Probably makes it look fat. All right. Triple A. I'll keep that in mind. Hey, you got a name?"

Happy to listen but still not responding, the lamb's gaze remained on the bed before him, pleasantly content to do so.

"No name?" Gus asked. "Can't have that. Gotta have a name. I'll give you one now. How about . . . Toby?"

Not a word.

"Yeah, maybe not," Gus said and scratched his neck. "Toby wouldn't like it either. He's weird like that. If you were a next generation Mustang or some other thing he'd be all for it. But not a, you know, you."

Gus examined the contents of the box before aiming a finger at the toy. "Boxy? No? Foxy? You are a cutie, I'll give you that. No? Well, fuck, we gotta call you something. Lambchop? No, I think that's been taken. Lamb something. Lamb . . . *be*? Nah, sounds like a deer and I've seen that movie. The ending tore my guts out. Oh! Oh! Lam—*me*? Lammy? 'Eh? 'Eeeeeh?"

With an oddness that bordered on eerie, a shard of dying sunlight stabbed through the curtain slit. That sliver of brightness razored across the bed, not a few fingers away from the stuffed toy. It didn't hit, but it came close. Close enough for Gus to take it as a sign.

"*Lammy*? You like that? Huh? Well, it's *you*. Lammy. Sure, why not. Beats my next one, which was Floyd. White Floyd. Or Floyd White. Jeez, that's not bad either. Lammy Floyd White. That could be your last name. Lammy for short. All right. Done. Let's make it official."

Gus reached for the nearest bottle of Scotch and cracked it open. He toasted the little stuffed animal. "To you, Lammy. May you never grow up. May you never grow old. And may you never . . ."

A lump of emotion welled up inside him, stealing his voice. His eyes watered. He pushed through, however, needing to finish. "May I . . . never run out of toilet paper. 'Cause . . . it'll be your ass then. Haha. Kiddin'. I can use the shower head in there, so yeah, no worries."

He drank, a light sip that turned into a full swallow, and offered the bottle to Lammy. "No? Yeah, best not. Get this on you and you'll smell like Scotch forever. Smart. You stay clean and sober. I'll do the drinking."

Another shot and he placed the bottle down. Something in the box caught his eye. He reached in and pulled out the Christmas coloring book and crayons. The crayons were brand new. A box of forty-eight, even, which was one of the more expensive packs. The coloring book had all the classic characters and pictures of the season, all laid out in thick lines for the shakiest of hands. Even better, every picture was a color by number, with the legend at the upper-right corner.

"All right," Gus said in approval, flipping through the pictures. "Hm. Oh . . ."

A decorated tree situated next to a fireplace caught his eye. Only black-and-white now, but he would change that. Excited to get started, he cleared a space on the table, moved the Scotch bottle to the side, and sat down. Checking the legend, he saw that number one was green. There were a good many sections marked with number one. Gus flicked open the crayons and found a surprising number of shades.

The first extracted crayon resulted in a frown. "Green-yellow," he muttered in distaste. "Sounds like snot. Flu snot. You know what I'm sayin'? Dark and all chunky, like. Another one here. This one's darker. Hm. Yellow-*green*. Christ, *that* looks like snot too. But it's lighter. See? Like sinus infection snot. What's with all the snotty colors, anyway? Shit's fucked-up. Whatever. All right. Here we go." He paused for a quick rub of his nose and pulled out a third.

"Green," he announced after inspection. "The traditional color of a Christmas tree. You other greens can fuck off back in the box. Back, I say. I command you. There. Okay, let's roll this bird."

He started in, got a good swath of green going, and snapped off the crayon. Frowning, Gus held it up, shrugged, and looked for another green green. Of which there were none. Realizing he'd have to make do, he peeled back the paper from the broken tip and started in again—with less pressure.

In time, he shaded in all the greens and saw that yellow was number two.

"In my day," Gus said to Lammy, "a yellow number two means a trip to the doctor."

He smiled at his joke and saw Lammy smiling too—and damn if it wasn't a little less sad. Gus sat back, had some Scotch, and regarded his companion. Uncle Jack still hadn't appeared, and Gus was beginning to think the old timer really had left him. Fine. Whatever. He had plenty of company right here.

He leaned back and sighted Lammy. "What're you doin' over there, anyway? I mean, you can't see what I'm doing here. Stop bein' antisocial. Here . . ."

He stood, scooped Lammy up with one hand, and brought the toy back to the table, where he sat him down with his back against the Scotch bottle. The toy flopped over twice, but Gus steadied him, charging him with a glare and a finger not to fall over again.

"There you go. Okay? Now you can see what I'm doin'. You can supervise. See this? This shit's fun. Oh my Lord is it ever . . ."

He glanced up every so often, to see if his new little friend was watching him.

And much to his delight, a happy looking Lammy watched him the whole time. The toy kept his back against the Scotch bottle, just fine with where he was. Gus finished coloring the Christmas tree and all its trimmings in a little under thirty minutes and presented it to his new friend.

"Eh? Howzat? Nice, right? Goddamn right it's nice. That's art right there. Sure, it has numbers, but I like it like that. No thinking required, just . . ." He chopped a hand. "Get in there and color. Straight to the fun. Damn, I'm buzzed. Let's do another."

The room was getting darker, so he flicked on a light, settled back down, and selected another picture. One of a little girl going headfirst down a winter hill on an old-fashioned sled. Feeling no need to rush, Gus took his time, careful of staying within the lines and, of course, talking to Lammy all the while.

"They want blue for number five, man. Blue. But there's like, four different shades of fuckin' blue in here. This must be an 'advanced artist' box of crayons or something. I mean, I can see turquoise, okay? Even *cyan*. I think that's how you say it. But, seriously, what's the difference between this and *this*?" He presented two crayons to Lammy. "This is fuckin *midnight* blue. And this little greasy stick of shit is *navy* blue. Can you see a difference? 'Cause I can't see a difference. Ergo, there's *no* goddamn difference, but they *named* them different. Okay. Maybe one's a *little* darker. Just enough to start a fight. But really? Really?"

No argument from Lammy.

Gus appreciated that.

Supper was a standard sandwich, but the bread was starting to spoil. Gus pinched off the moldy bits and flicked them into the nearby trash. He could still taste a little residual grossness mold here and there. Next time, he'd toast the bread. He'd have to head back to the kitchens soon. Not today, though.

When he tired of coloring, he picked up Lammy, selected a science fiction paperback from among the books in the box, and retired for the night. Gus got into bed first and situated Lammy on the next pillow over, turning him so that the stuffed animal was looking right at him. That got a little weird, however, so Gus adjusted him until the little guy was looking at the book. When they were both settled in, Gus dimmed the bedside lamp just a touch and started reading. He squinted at times, which made him wonder if he needed glasses. *Good luck with that*, his brain said. So, he got his arms above the blankets and straightened them out until he could comfortably see the words.

When he reached the end of the second paragraph, he did a curious thing. He glanced over at Lammy.

"You, ah . . . want me to read this? Like, ah, out loud? To you?"

It was a trick of the light. Had to be. But, Gus thought, nay, could *swear*, that the little stuffed animal's head actually dipped forward. Just a smidgen. That was impossible, of course. Gus might have unconsciously shifted in bed, perhaps, causing the toy to move, but he wasn't sure.

Regardless, he took it as a yes.

"Well, okay. Look, next time, let me know, all right? I'm not a mind reader here. I don't mind reading out loud. And I'll keep my voice low, too. I sound better that way, anyway. My voice gets all smoky n' shit. Downright sexy, if'n you ask me."

Which was what Tammy used to say. Maybe Collie might have said it, too.

"You ready? Okay then. Here we go . . ."

And so Gus read to little Lammy, right up until they both fell asleep.

11

The next day, Gus rose and went through his morning routine. He ate leftovers from the fridge. Then he brushed without toothpaste, flossed, and rinsed. When he was ready, he dressed and slapped on his vest. As he readied the shotgun and sidearm, he glanced over at the bed.

"I'll be back for lunch," he told Lammy, who sat with his back to the pillows. "If I'm not back, well . . . I'm probably dead. Then you're on your own."

Gus thought that was leaving on a bit of a down note, so he added, "Just kiddin'. Sorta. Be back in a few hours. Guaranteed."

Lammy's smile seemed reassured.

Gus needed to leave the toy in a good mood. When he closed the door, he paused and sized up the hallway. Not a piece of meat in sight. Ramfist ready, he squared his shoulders and headed for the stairwell.

A short time later, he was back in the lobby, sizing up the Sahara-sized snowdrifts settled around the Anchor Bay. Not much had come inside since the last time he'd been there, mostly because of the awesome amount of snow already blocking the entrance. Gus trudged over the mess of bodies, hating every step, and stopped when he was close enough to the front doors.

No tracks to be seen in those pristine curves and peaks. In fact, anyone coming into the place would need a plow to clear the way. Or a monster snowblower. Else they risked getting bogged down at the waist. And if any of that happened, well, he would know about it.

All right, he thought, feeling better about the front door. Being snowbound wasn't a bad thing, not in his opinion. The parking garage popped into his head, so he'd have to check that as well.

But first . . .

He stopped before Collie's grave, partially cloaked in shadow due to a high drift rising up the window. Gus studied the flower bed from one end to the other, nodding until the sobbing started. He let it, figuring it was a good thing, and that made him even more miserable. He tried to let Collie know he was okay, was doing fine, but that he missed her terribly. His voice failed him every time, pissing him off.

When he got himself under control, he wiped his nose and firmed up, determined to say a few words.

"All right. I'm good." He squeaked and rolled his eyes. "God . . . *damn*. Place is clear, Collie. Snow's so high. No one's getting in here. Not until spring. It's clear. So . . . goddamn empty. Miss you. Wish . . . I wish . . ."

That was it. His throat clamped down the rest. So he waved, mouthed, *I'll be back*, and walked back to the stairwell.

"Christ Almighty," he gasped at the end of the hitches. Tammy's death hadn't affected him so badly. Or had it? He couldn't remember. Probably because it had been the start of everything zombie, and he'd been in shock. And constantly shit-faced.

"Walk it off," he told himself. And immediately slumped against a cinderblock wall as another wave of sadness overwhelmed him.

Minutes later, emotionally exhausted, he entered the underground garage. The main floor was untouched by snow, but like the lobby, the last couple storms had dumped an avalanche's worth of sugar onto the entrance. The unblemished powder had poured all the way down the ramp, creating an indoor ski slope. The winds had also blown great white ribs up either side so that it resembled the ancient opening of some gigantic, arctic trapdoor spider.

Once again, there was no way anyone could enter without leaving a trail. Security cameras were all over the place as well, but Gus wasn't sure if they were working or where the workstation controlling them all was located.

That made him curious.

He returned to the lobby and in short time found an unlocked door down a hallway, labeled SECURITY/LOSS PREVENTION.

Gus entered shotgun first.

The lights did not come on, so he had to feel for the switches. He found one and lit up a room filled with computers, workstations, and dozens of monitors. One wall had a series of screens, sixteen at least, stacked four across and every one dead to the world. The sight of all that tech lifted Gus's spirits for all of two seconds, when he feared it was all beyond him. He stopped at one computer station that looked important and powered it up. To his surprise, the screen came alive as it ran through its start-up routine.

Then it asked for a password.

Gus sighed. He poked at the keyboard, spelling out FUCK YOU, and tapped ENTER. ACCESS DENIED. But the computer didn't lock him out and offered him another try.

SUCK MY CACK, he typed and tapped ENTER.

ACCESS DENIED, the computer responded and offered yet another shot.

Three tries for a dollar, Gus thought, and gave the machine the finger before switching it off. Didn't need the surveillance system. Not really. He'd just do a walkabout, which he'd been prepared to do anyway.

There were no weapons in the room. An adjacent locker room had no weapons. No armor. No nothing, except some sharp grey suits which mildly surprised him. He left them in their lockers.

No reason to stay, Gus departed for the elevator, intending to start from the penthouse level and work his way down.

To start what would become a daily routine . . . until spring.

And for the next couple of days he remained vigilant, conducting daily patrols of the building. Each morning he would deck himself out, armor and weapons, and head down to the underground garage. At the ramp he would check for tracks, then his truck, before moving on to the other vehicles, just to ensure all was fine. After that, he'd travel to the lobby and scout for footprints. Collie's final resting place would be a stop on his tour, where he would stand, clearing his throat and wiping his eyes until he got it out of his system. It was best to let it out whenever it came on. Just take the pain and let everything gush. Until it stopped. After the first visitation, and to spare his sleeves, Gus located and left a box of tissues on a table near the flower bed. He dragged a trash bin over and placed it a few feet away from the gravesite, for convenience's sake.

After that morning routine, he would ride the elevator to the penthouse floor. From there he would commence his patrol of Anchor Bay, a guarded walk through all the floors, until he reached his room. He made a point of leaving all the doors open, so that there would be no surprises. And to allow some much-needed daylight into the corridors.

The two skyways on the tenth floor became a rest point on his patrol, and he would stop and gaze across those square tunnels of glass and steel, to the not-so-distant entrances of the other hotels.

The skyways were something else.

Red carpet went all the way across the potentially nerve-racking, aboveground tunnels of reinforced glass and steel crossbeams. Plush chairs lined the sides, arranged around little circular tables every fifteen feet or so, for those brave souls who wanted to stop, sit, and gaze down upon the city. Maybe patrons wandered over from the nearby Oliver Green's Fine Dining, found a seat, and watched the sun set while enjoying their cappuccinos.

When he stood upon the threshold of the skyway for the first time, so many floors above the ground, Gus realized he didn't want anything to do with the other hotels. They seemed incredibly dark, as if the Leather had switched everything off to conserve or channel all existing power to the Anchor Bay. The stark openness of the tunnels unnerved him as well, and even as he watched, a blast of wind pounded the glass hard enough to make the panes shiver. There were no signs of passage. No messy spatters from walking corpses. No telltale upturning of the furniture, and best of all, no lingering dead ass stink.

On his first day patrolling, he took a couple of hours to pull all the furniture back and heap it across the opening of both skyways on the Anchor Bay side. It was a meagre defense at best, but at least a tripwire, if something attempted to creep up on him from those quarters. Every day after that, he would check on the barricades to see if they had been bashed aside, or altered in some suspicious way, before continuing to the lobby. There, he would inspect the entrance for tracks, and then complete the loop by returning to his room. Inside, he would greet Lammy with a nod and a wink, and down a drink or two of Scotch to mark the end of another daily prowl. Those would be the only drinks he would take, as he did not want to be hungover the next day, wasting a day on recovery.

In the evenings, he would read or do a little coloring with Lammy nearby. More often than not, he would talk to the toy. Lammy would not talk back and that was fine. He was there, though, with that constant smile Gus was beginning to find very comforting . . . and much needed.

Uncle Jack did not return.

And Gus didn't miss him. If the old codger was only going to lecture him on how dark he was becoming, especially on matters of the Leather, well, Gus didn't need him. At all.

That was the first week.

At the start of the second week, Gus stopped on the gym level, and decided to do a more thorough walkthrough. Solid rubber mats covered half the floor space. Treadmills and funky hiking machines lined the place in rows, with helpful illustrations to show what muscle or groups of muscles they worked. Long racks of free weights and benches stretched out along the walls. Medicine balls rested on stretch mats.

Freestanding punching and kicking bags. No ghost stink of sweat or ass lingered on the air. The place was clean, as if freshly taken out of a box. Much cleaner than expected, and not a piece looked out of place.

Gus stopped beside a series of hexagon-shaped dumbbells, each pair heavier than the last, resting on a lower rack.

"No way," he said in disbelief, spotting the numbers on one set of dumbbells. He got in close to make sure there was no mistake.

A hundred pounds.

A single dumbbell weighed a hundred pounds.

"Get the fuck outta here," Gus muttered, bending over the thing. Curious, he put the Ramfist aside and took a hold of the nearest dumbbell.

One tug and he gripped it with both hands.

And lifted.

"*Christ almighty*," he blurted.

He cleared one end off the rack, but realized it was going no further without internal rupturing, so he dropped it. That sent a little boom echoing throughout the gym, which caused Gus to look around.

"You're fuckin with me." He aimed at the weight. "Someone actually lifted you? In one hand? Fuck off."

What left him in total dismay was the *second* set of hundred pounders. As if there were two meat gorillas curling those things at the same time.

"Yeah, right," Gus scoffed, not believing it for a second. He took his shotgun and wandered along the rack, going down in weights. He stopped at the fifties, managed to lift one with both hands, and dropped that with a grunt. Rubbing his palms, he decided to move down the line a little further.

Thirties. Nope.

Twenties. Closer, but it took some effort.

Tens. Not bad. Doable. Comfortable even. At least he wouldn't blow out his ass ring trying to lift it. Gus faced the wall mirror, which provided a view of almost the whole gym. He test-curled one dumbbell, up and down, elbow jutting outwards with the movement. Inhaled when he lifted, exhaled when he lowered. His screwed-up foot squeezed out a few painful notes but didn't get any worse.

After doing three reps he placed the weight next to its companion and nodded. *Not too shabby*, he thought, pleased with his performance, considering he wasn't one for exercise. Work had been his exercise. While he didn't puff out his chest when standing next to obvious gym rats, Gus secretly suspected they all took supplements of some kind. Including illegal ones. He was more into cardio, thinking back on how he shoveled snow back in the day.

He remembered how he always told himself he could get into shape *if* he had the time and money.

Well . . . he presently had the time. No money, but all the necessary equipment was right before him.

Shrugging, he gripped two dumbbells, squared himself up in the mirror and straightened his back. Curled. Up and down. Breathing in on the upswing and out on the down. By the fifth repetition, his face was bloodred and on the verge of blowing all its gaskets and grommets. His arms burned and his heart hammered away, wondering what tomfuckery the brain was up to, and yammering for an immediate cease and desist.

"Fuck me," Gus panted and lowered the weights onto the floor. Even that was a feat, as he couldn't rightly bend over all the way, and his back cracked in ways that widened his eyes.

"What the fuck?" he blustered as he straightened. "I mean, I'm not *that* old."

But he wasn't in that good of shape, either. He had some endurance, sure but the muscle strength could use some work.

His reflection stopped him. Battered. Scarred, with parts missing. Tired eyes. And a lot hairier around the beard. Depressed by the sight, he wandered over onto the mats where the punching bags waited.

Placing his weapons on a nearby bench, he selected a bag. Regular-sized, with a few bruises of its own, but in good condition overall. The placement of the bags puzzled him, and he wondered who the hell would start swinging at the thing while everyone else was pumping weights. Someone did, he supposed, or else the bags would not be here.

He assumed a fighting stance, which Collie had drilled into him over the last few months. His hand with the missing fingers had bothered him at first, but she insisted that when he landed a punch, those first two knuckles were all he needed. And that if it still bothered him, he had other weapons available.

Gus squared up the punching bag and jabbed.

Pop.

Pop-pop.

"*Stop punching like a five-year-old, and punch like a killer,*" Collie said from behind the bag.

Gus remembered the training sessions.

Bang!

Hard, but not hard enough to damage his hands.

"Breathe out when you let it go," Collie spoke.

Gus remembered that tip, and how it also applied with the weights. Breathe out when he lifted. *Forgot that*, he realized. He drew back an arm and let it go.

Bang!

Then he was back, back in the dojo inside that motel. With Bruno and Cory Shale, practicing their own striking in another part of the modest workout area.

"Use that power," Collie instructed. *"Extend the whole arm. Snap it out there, land, and pull it back as fast as you can, because if the guy you're fighting knows anything, he could be waiting for the counter."*

Bang-bang.

Gus dropped back a step, once again at the Anchor Bay, grimacing at the pressure in his foot. *Joseph and Mary*, he was a mess. A rusty derelict that had somehow been refurbished. He stopped, took off his coat because he was serious, and went back to the bag.

Laid another fist into the leather. Then a follow-up.

"My luck, the guy I square off against will be an ex-heavyweight," Gus said.

"Don't be so sure, my young apprentice," Collie informed him. *"Training didn't grant immunity against infection. The virus took anyone. I'm here to tell you, most walking dicks are winging it. Going by whatever they saw in the movies. Sure, some learn by hard knocks, but actual training? Of whoever's left running around out there? No more than five percent. And that's being generous. That's it. You hearin' this?"*

BANG, and that one stung the knuckles.

"What about that guy you fought in the trailer that time?" Gus asked her. *"When I was stoned out of my gourd."*

Collie smiled, the flash brilliant. *"He was the real deal. In the flesh. Wondered about him, sometimes. Someone like him . . . in this day and age? Yeah. He was a special kind of dangerous. A nightmare, really, to untrained civvies. Just his luck he ran into me."*

Back in the now, Gus smiled and hit the bag twice more.

"Good," Collie said during another training session. *"You're improving. Getting off the jab. Try bouncing back more."*

"This is as good as it gets, Collie."

"What? Your feet are flatter than my baby sister. Ha. That's a joke. Goddammit Bruno, the fuck you stopping for? This look like a talent show to you, chuggernuts? Keep swinging or I swear to sunny Jesus I'll come over there and twist your nuts off."

Back in the now, Gus smiled again, one that quickly faltered. He did a two-strike combo on the bag, his knuckles starting to really ache.

"That's it," Collie said, watching him in another time, appraising him, then frowning with good humor. "Stop looking at me and concentrate on what you're doing."

"Sorry, Collie." Gus panted, his voice echoing in the Anchor Bay gym.

"Keep up the good stuff," she said. "You'll be someone's nightmare one-on-one. Hand-to-hand. I guarantee it. Hell, if I'm around, I'll fucking stop to watch."

"If I'm around," Gus repeated, interest disappearing, his punches losing power. He stopped, knuckles throbbing, the bag swaying.

"Why the fuck did you *leave*, Collie?" he barked at the gym. "*Why?*"

She didn't answer him, and his memories left him cold.

No longer feeling like boxing or anything else, Gus hauled on his coat, gathered up his gear, and walked out of the gym.

Two more winter storms lashed the city that week, piling on even more snow which, at the rate it was falling, totaled five feet at its lowest depths, and eight feet at its highest peaks. Changes in the wind whipped the white stuff all around the hotel, to the point where, in the morning, the sun was a bright ball wrapped in gauze. Snow pressed up against the windows, offering dramatic cross sections of the deepening drifts. Collie's flower bed grave lay well within the shadows, as did most of the lobby. The entrance to the garage also got its share of snow. What once was a beginner ski slope had become a cliff, waiting for the unsuspecting to fall through.

Snow. Gus stared at it through his room's window.

And it was only November. Perhaps edging into December.

The rate things were going, the lobby would be submerged in darkness by January or February. He remembered seeing old black-and-white pictures of kids sliding down snowdrifts rooted against two-story rooftops. If he had to, he supposed he could blow out a window on the second floor and do just that. Otherwise, he was indeed stuck in the hotel for the winter.

When he turned from the window, Lammy was watching him.

"You don't believe me?" Gus asked the toy, who didn't seem impressed at all.

"You don't believe me. Well then, that's it. We're going for a walk here, buddy. Just you and me. It'll wipe that smile off your face that's for sure. Be good to get you out of here, too. You're spendin' too much time by yourself."

The next morning, they stood in the hotel lobby. Gus pulled Lammy out of his inner coat pocket and held up the toy, to better behold winter's might at ground level. Lammy's smile remained unchanged, however. Gus even checked to make sure.

"See what I'm sayin'?" he asked his companion. "Yeah? Well, now you know."

He stuffed Lammy back inside the coat. "Get in there. The lobby's freezin'. Freeze your squishy ass off. Now, the big surprise. Since you're here... and I'm too damn lazy to bring you back to the room, you wanna come on patrol with me? Hm? Howzat sound?"

No answer, which Gus took as a yes.

"All right. Here we go."

One long elevator ride later, one where he wrapped a towel over his mouth and nose, they got off on the penthouse floor and went for the stairwell right away.

"Place stinks, I know," Gus strained as he hurried down the steps. "But it's clear. Nothing living or dead could take that shit. I know I should open a window, but getting to one? No way. Not this monkey."

He halted on the stairs. "Listen. Hear that? That's just you and me, buddy. You and me. Coat? This coat? Uh, yeah, the Leather pissed on it. Yeah, I know, gross, but hey, it attracts the mindless. Yeah, I *know*, but it's better *hearing* them come at you rather than them *jumping* out at you. Understand me? Can't tell you how many times I almost lost my shit when some undead asshat just flopped out right in front of me. This way, at least, I can hear them."

Gus stopped and opened up his jacket. "You can't see anything in there, can you? Hold on."

One quick adjustment later, Lammy's head was wedged into the open neckline of Gus's coat, smiling out at the world.

"Better?" Gus asked. "Better for me. Frees up both hands. You just hold on and watch the world go by. Check the place out. I know right? The cat's ass. And the rooms? Fuck me. Bet it costs an ordinary schmuck a year's salary to stay here. But I like where we are now. Out of the way, sorta. And yeah, I left the doors open. In case something wanders in there. I mean, I'm pretty sure the place is empty, but..."

Gus gripped the shotgun a little harder.

"You can never be too sure."

For the rest of the morning, Gus showed Lammy around, introducing each floor and its amenities as they entered through the stairwell door. He showed his companion the swimming pools and the budding greenhouse. Then the arcade and the golf range. At noon, Gus went back to his room and ate a quick lunch. Lammy sat on the bed and watched. Gus felt him watching, so he brought him over to the table, sat him down with his back to a bottle of preserved beets, and proceeded to cut off a triangle section of his sandwich for the toy.

When Lammy didn't eat it, Gus ate it himself, glowering at the stuffed animal and sending a message, *Don't ask for it if you're not gonna eat it.*

When he finished, he wiped his mouth, packed up Lammy, and went back to the upper floors. When they got to the gym, he stopped at the bench press.

"See this?" he said to Lammy. "This whole place? Something, 'eh? Figured I might as well make use of it. Never was one for lifting weights but what the hell, right? Ah, you mind watching while I squeeze out a few reps? Huh? Won't take long."

Lammy didn't mind at all.

The bar was heavy, and Gus didn't know the exact weight. The plates were labeled as tens, and he placed one on each side. He'd done fifteen reps the day before, which had given him a comfortable burn. He was still somewhat sore, but thought he could manage an extra set.

Which he did, getting the blood moving. He exhaled when pressing, inhaled when lowering. The bar rattled when he set it back at rest position, finishing the set. Lammy watched all the while, offering silent encouragement.

"Not bad, 'eh?" Gus panted and got no reply, which he took as agreement.

"I figure, you know, get in a few reps every day. Yeah. With all that protein upstairs? By the end of the winter I should be fuckin' cut. Huge. Or fuckin' crippled with gout. Ha. Oh don't worry, I'll eat the veggies, too. That'll help. And should make the morning crap go easier. Don't want to be squeezin' out shit bricks in the morning. C'mere..."

He transferred Lammy to a bench before the dumbbells. There, he stripped off his coat and grabbed a pair of weights. Facing the wall-length mirror, he straightened his back and started curling, alternating one arm and then the next, breathing properly this time. Ten of each and he dropped the weights back into their resting place.

"*Wooo*," Gus let out. "Light-headed. And red! Look at my face. Christ, you think I had a moose cock shoved up my ass. Man o' man."

He did a quick flex—right arm, then the left. "'Eh? Grrr. *Grrrrr*, I say. A winter's worth of this and I'll be a monster. A *monster*, I say. You just wait."

Lammy kept right on watching.

"Come over here," Gus said and brought the toy over to the punching bag. "Watch this."

He rolled his shoulders, loosening them up. Then he took a breath and started punching. A series of left jabs, first. Then right jabs. Then body shots from the right and left. Gus did twenty for each, feeling the pump all the way to his shoulder.

When he was done, he was breathing hard and wiped sweat from his face.

He plopped down across from Lammy.

"Not bad, right? Not too bad at all. Just the single punches first, y'know, to get started, but Collie... she wanted me to work on combinations as well. Twos and threes to start, then as many as I felt good about. To get used to it. I was only shadowboxing before, because there was no workout bag. But here? I can throw it."

He inspected one set of knuckles and then the other.

"I'm no boxer, you understand. But . . . she was training me. Got the basics in, and a few self-defence techniques. Just a few. She said . . . it's better to be able to do a few of them *well*, than all of them shitty. That's how she said it, too."

Lammy took it all in.

Gus waved a finger at him. "I like you. Nothin' gets you down. Sorta reminds me of another person I knew. Good guy. Great guy. Except he would . . . well, you know. He would talk back. Just puttin' it out there. Somethin' on your mind . . . you let me know. I mean. I thought Jack would be around a little more often but nope. Don't know where he is. All that me getting dark and shit is just that. Shit. He's probably just pissed I'm drinking Scotch or something or other. Though, between you and me? I should probably cut back. Stop it entirely. Had a problem back in the day. With booze. Brought on by all the zombie shit goin' on. I got through it with some help from friends, but . . . recently . . . with Collie . . ."

His voice cracked and he looked away, anywhere but at Lammy.

Gus forcefully cleared his throat and composed himself. "You can fall off the wagon at least once. But to be clear, I'm not falling off the wagon. Okay? Just need to get through this. That's all. Promise. Just a little nip here and there to take the edge off. S'all I need."

The mirror showed his reflection, red-faced and hunched over, elbows to knees, talking to the plush toy sitting on a bench across from him. He sighed at the picture and stood up.

"All right. I'm good. Come on. We got the rest of the place to go through. I'll take you down to the skyway. Those things are scary. Seriously. You ever see those hotels with the little glass rooms with the see-through floors? So you can shit yourself twenty floors up? It's kinda like that except it's only ten floors or so. And you can't see through the floor. Like *that* helps."

Gus pulled on his coat, zipped it up, and stuck Lammy back in so that he peeked out from the parted V at his chest.

"Right below that are the bars and nightclubs. I'll show them to you. I should stop in one of the freezers anyway and get something out for supper. The fridge back in the room's gettin' a little low. Can't believe an outfit, a . . . *cult*, like the Leather, stocked up on everything here. They gotta be gettin' it from somewhere. I mean, they gotta . . ."

On his way back to the stairwell, Gus wandered by the elevators and noticed the light display over the doors was showing the twenty-third floor.

Which was weird.

Because when he'd taken the elevator, all the other elevators were in the lobby.

And as he puzzled this out, with Lammy's smiling chops sticking out from his open coat, another strange thing happened.

The elevator light winked, signaling the lift was in transit. Until it reached the twenty-second floor, where it stopped.

Realization crunched his brow and his mouth slowly hitched into a scowl.

He had visitors.

12

Gus raced for the stairwell.

A back draft of stale air as he pushed through the door. He stood there, shotgun raised, listening for any voices above him. Nothing, so he pounded up the steps, cringing at the first landing. He stopped and pulled off one boot, then the other.

In socks, he hurried up the steps.

Lammy's little head bounced and flopped with every step.

Using the elevator might alert the visitors that he was on his way. As he rounded the landing for the fourteenth floor, he slowed down to an energetic hike. He wouldn't make it at the pace he was going and anyone in the stairwell would hear him puffing well before they saw him.

So he paced himself, taking the burns of exertion.

Thank God I'm not a smoker, Gus thought as he rounded the corner for the seventeenth floor.

His breathing got deeper, however. Real deep by the time he got to the twentieth floor, so he stopped, put his back to a wall, and tried to catch his breath.

They're gone now, came the frantic thought. *Gone. Maybe even back downstairs. Holy shit. The front door was wide open and there was no one in the lobby. That's why there's a shit ton of snow down there, remember? Don't matter. Not going to stop anyone, only let you know when someone came* into *the place.*

Gus rubbed his face, feeling sweat. When his breathing got better, he soldiered on, hoping Collie would approve.

Big block numbers painted black said 22.

Hoping his heart wouldn't explode, Gus reached the landing and put his shoulder to the cinder blocks, aiming at the door.

He waited. And waited.

And listened.

Had to admit, the fire escape door silenced things pretty good. He couldn't hear shit from the other side.

Now what? Gus asked himself, glancing down at Lammy's bare white head. If it were zombies, he could just make a racket to draw them out and be done with them. Zombies, however, did not operate elevators. His heart hammered, urging him to do something. Anything. Then the stairwell door opened right before him and the Leather—as there was no doubt from the bulky coat and old ninja mask—stepped in as if nothing was wrong. He glanced at Gus and froze, petrified by the sight of the armed stranger, and Gus was close enough to see the Leather's eyes widen as he fired the Ramfist.

The acoustics in the stairwell weren't as good as the ones in his old apartment building, but the testicle-hefting boom and reverb of the mighty shotgun shook Gus right down to his boys, who immediately hoisted themselves to higher ground.

The blast bounced the Leather through the open portal, slapping both man and door off the cinderblock wall, leaving a gruesome splash at the point of impact. The door rebounded, smacking the dead man, whose bulk prevented the door from closing. The shot shredded the back of the bulky coat, leaving a nasty wet crater of meat and bone.

The sound and fury of the blast faded, and Gus's shock dissipated with it.

Ramfist.

He immediately peeked into the hallway.

Empty.

The stairs behind him were also clear.

Stepping over the corpse, Gus entered the hall shotgun-first. He streaked past an elegant table holding up a little statue of some exotic fairy creature, past a grand painting of a red sunset over a prairie, and darted into the first open doorway. Once in the room, a thunderbolt of uncertainty struck him.

How many are there?

He had no way of knowing . . . until he hunted them down.

He spared a look at the stairwell. Blood was everywhere. An explosion of red from the fallen minion. Blood and other matter splashed the walls and soaked the carpet, where the luxuriant edges absorbed the flow.

Gus once again peeked ahead. He checked right and left, then looked back to glimpse a black shape darting into another room halfway down that suddenly ominous hall, where thin lines of gold gleamed. Just a glimpse, but there was no mistaking the figure dressed in leather.

Christ Almighty. He just *had* to leave the doors open. Thought he was being so goddamn smart. Gus took a breath, pressed the shotgun hard against his shoulder, and locked onto the next room some ten paces away on the opposite wall.

The Leather remained out of sight.

Gus became very aware... of just how damn quiet everything had become. It wasn't a zombie out there trying to kill him. It was a sadist. Outfitted with medieval weapons. *If* he was lucky.

He took a shaky breath and realized he was trembling.

Then he realized that the Leather were responsible for Collie's death. Her first death, anyway, when they forced Milo to shoot her from the back of the buggy a lifetime ago. He remembered the Leather had either killed, converted, or enslaved whoever was left and decent in a world gone insane. That they had used the undead as shock troops in their assaults. And that now, after Collie was gone, he had a hotel potentially full of them.

Then a weird thing happened.

Gus wasn't scared anymore, because he'd already been through and survived a ton of terrifying shit. Shit much more terrifying than a handful of primitive dickhats running around, wearing Halloween costumes from some abandoned warehouse, attempting to take over everything.

And he had the Ramfist, which spiked his growing confidence.

Matter of fact, standing there with his shoulder against the doorframe, the more he thought about it all, the more pissed off he became.

"Little—" *shits* he was going to say, when a battle axe came whistling around the corner, aimed at his head.

He ducked, the wind from the blade brushing his scalp, the great axe sinking into the door frame with a *whuk!* Fragments showered him as he aimed at a Leather minion wearing—of all things—the grey-black face of a mythological satyr.

Fucking *Pan* himself.

And Pan was fast.

Releasing the axe, a gloved hand grabbed the shotgun barrel and shoved it away. Pan tackled Gus, pushing him back while Gus was still attempting to stick the thunderrod up under the minion's chin. But his left arm shot out instead, clutching Pan's wrist, to clutch a descending curved knife that might've once been used to sacrifice virgins.

They rolled. Across the wall, into the room, until they stumbled and fell. Their heads clacked off table legs. An urn, of all things, fell and clopped Gus across the nose, bringing tears to his eyes. Pan wrenched his knife away and a bolt of panic surged through Gus. He swung his arm blindly, not knowing where the knife was, only that it was on that side. He blocked Pan's stab, his forearm stopping the minion's thrust, but then felt the slow sink of pointed steel into his ribs, sliding for the gap in his vest.

Which sent a burst of panicked strength through him.

A surging Gus twisted out from underneath and shoved the Leather onto his side, pinning the knife arm. Gus scrambled, latching onto a throat and driving a knee into Pan's forearm, while that goddamn satyr wannabe punched him in the kidneys. The blow buckled Gus and lessened his own punch—launched a microsecond later—torquing Pan's head to the left. The gleeful face snapped back. Gus pawed a hand across the man's mouth, crimpling latex against flesh and bone. And executed dirty fighting 101.

Elbow to the face. With all his upper body weight behind it.

It was a nasty little move Collie had taught him.

That first anvil of bone brutally pounded the Leather's chin, bouncing the head off the floor. Gus landed a second elbow, suddenly furious and needing to inflict more than just pain. He needed to dispense *punishment*. Pan's entire head rattled upon impact and Gus didn't stop there. Couldn't stop there. Because in a life and death struggle where the winner walks away, Collie had taught him to strike hard and fast, with killer intentions.

So Gus landed a third elbow, resetting as fast as he could, and then dropped about a half-dozen more.

Pan stopped moving.

Stopped moving after the third, really.

But Gus wanted to make sure. Needed to make sure.

Gus dragged himself off the motionless man, drained from the short but intense fight. He staggered back until he banged into an open closet. That whirled him around and he slapped the row of hangers there, whipping them along the metal bar. Lammy was on the floor, having fallen free during the brawl.

Breathing hard, Gus gathered up the shotgun, then Lammy, stuffing the toy into an inside pocket. Then he stood over the fallen Pan and aimed at his face.

"How many are here?" he gasped.

The Leather didn't answer.

Gus kicked him in the balls, which was dirty fighting 102.

The fallen man didn't react to the blow. Blood trickled from underneath the mask, soaking into the carpet.

"Fuck," Gus huffed.

He didn't even have a roll of duct tape.

The idea of taking a prisoner entered his mind, but only if he could find something to tie up the Leather.

"Oh, you bastard," Gus panted and checked the hallway outside the room. Empty.

There was a moment's flutter, then recognition as he sighted the curtains over the windows. Seconds later, he had cut off two long sections of string and used both to bind the Leather's wrists. A pair of bathrobes hung in the closet, and he stripped the belts off them. In less than a minute, he had Pan's hands tied behind his back and his ankles bound.

The bindings looked flimsy, especially around the ankles.

"Your unlucky day," Gus growled and stomped on the Leather's ankles, breaking both of them.

Pan shook but he did not wake, which was weird. You'd think someone being so viciously incapacitated would come around. Pan did not.

Gus kept the curved knife. A quick pat down revealed no other weapons. He took the axe.

And kicked Pan in his face.

Gus left the room, closing the door behind him.

No other Leather challenged him. The minion he'd shot and killed by the stairwell remained there.

The lit numbers of the elevator panel indicated that it had returned to the lobby.

How many left in the hotel? No way of knowing.

He summoned an elevator and waited for what might have been the longest minute of his life. When the lift arrived, Gus set the axe down, slid to one side, and readied the shotgun.

On impulse, he brought up the wooden end and steadied himself.

The doors opened with the softest ding . . . and a Leather stepped out.

Gus punched the Ramfist's solid walnut butt into the figure's face. The blow stopped the Leather cold and left him wonky from the ankles up. He staggered back into the elevator, falling against the wall. Gus smashed the Leather's head a second time, flopping his victim flat.

Just the one.

Seeing no need for two prisoners, Gus unsheathed his forearm knife and sank it deep in the Leather's jugular. There was no thought to the killing. Just pull the blade, stab it hard, and yank it out. A quick wipe and he returned the weapon to its sheath. Senses thrumming now, he retrieved the axe and threw it into the elevator. Then he got aboard and jammed his thumb against number three.

The doors closed. The leather-clad individual on the floor continued to bleed. A grim-faced Gus ignored him.

The ride down didn't take nearly as long.

The other elevator was in the lobby, which meant there were Leather down there. Gus just didn't know how many. When the lift stopped on the third floor, he got out and went for the stairwell. Still in his socks, he descended to the second floor. From there, he snuck to the mezzanine overlooking the lobby and crouched behind a set of sofa chairs. The crackle of both knees paralyzed him, but he didn't budge.

No sound from below. Gus exhaled and waited a short time before shuffling closer to the railings.

The entrance had tracks. A mess of them, telling of a struggle to get through all that snow. Beyond the tracks, parked next to the ruined opening, were two snowmachines.

Gus stood, searching for any Leather moving about below him. Spotting no one, he retraced his steps to the stairwell and descended to the lobby.

Boot tracks, several sets, coming in from the cold. They trekked across the floor of bodies and proceeded to the elevators, the snow diminishing with every stride. Four sets, with an extra set heading back out into the cold, ending at the. A track that turned around and went away from the hotel, back out into that glaring white maze of the city.

Gus squinted, understanding full well what it meant. The other machines were switched off, waiting for their owners to return. He shielded his eyes with a hand, searching the streets for movement. A wind blew along the avenues, haunting the cityscape, but the Leather was long gone.

The two other snowmachines, however, were parked and sunk deep in the drifts.

Then he remembered a conversation from not so long ago.

"And no idea how they do their communications?" Collie asked.

"None," Milo answered. "We figure straight-up messenger."

Straight-up messenger.

How long since Collie had killed the Dog Shit and Gus had taken up residence in the hotel? Two weeks? At least. Going on three. Before the Dog Shit, there was that pink-faced bastard called Joe. Was this a regular visit? Or had the Leather crew living at the Anchor Bay been quiet for too long? Did they usually come in on snowmachines? Gus couldn't remember how much mileage one of those rigs could get.

Then the cold reality hit him.

Four messengers. And he just killed two of them.

They came to the Anchor Bay, saw the smashed front doors, the corpses, and their first impulse would be . . . to seek out the Dog Shit. Or whoever was in charge.

The penthouse.

They would have gone to the penthouse first, discovered that the Dog Shit was dead, and immediately decided to leave. At least one of them did, while the others searched the hotel, floor by floor. The one who had left would report that the Dog Shit was no more . . . to a superior.

Wonderful.

Whoever was left had far too much of a head start, so Gus didn't think about pursuing. Besides, he had a prisoner to attend to.

He spotted a golden luggage cart nearby.

13

The Leather woke when the wind hit him. He groaned, head rolling, and realized with a dazed jolt that he was tied up and lying on his side. He looked around and eventually spotted Gus pushing the luggage cart. The same cart the Leather was presently heaped onto.

The elevator doors tried to close, but instead they pinched the cart's sides and slid back open.

Gus shoved the cart along the rooftop terrace and stopped in a snowbank, thankful he took the time to retrieve his boots. He snarled at the biting cold, and regarded his prisoner.

Pan watched him in turn, remarkably quiet considering the beating he'd taken.

The elevator doors closed behind him, but Gus didn't take his eyes off the Leather. Gus wandered two steps out into heaps of snow and knew he had a problem—he had failed to anticipate how much of the white shit had fallen on the roof. He couldn't push the cart through all those drifts. Couldn't pull it either. Even the stacked building materials were buried and nearly unrecognizable. A snowy thicket of garden chairs was heaped against a wall. There was a smaller hand trolley, coated white, and propped up against a pile of unused cinderblocks, all but hidden in powder. The cinderblocks had sheltered the trolley from the worst of the storms.

Gus trudged over, scooping snow from his path as he went, until he reached the trolley. He dusted the thing off, pulled it out, and hauled it back, using it for balance as he hiked through the thick snowfall.

"Right," he announced as he drew up alongside his captive. "Time for that dick move sucker punch."

Pan's eyes narrowed, a split second before Gus cracked the guy. Hard. Straight across the jaw. Hard enough that the head rattled like an off-kilter speed bag.

The Leather remained conscious, however, and didn't say a word.

Gus shook his head. "You got the shittiest luck," he muttered, and unloaded a salvo of heavy blows upon the prisoner until the minion was knocked out cold and bleeding.

Not that Gus gave a shit.

Securing the Leather to the trolly, Gus tipped the load back and hauled his prisoner through the snow. Sometimes he had to use his hands to shovel his way through some of the bigger drifts, inching his way forward. Toward the very place that killed him inside and yet drew him close.

The glass partition where Collie had dived.

It was a slow and agonizing process, taking perhaps an hour, sapping his strength while the elements sought to freeze him. A brutal wind buffeted his frame but he didn't stop, not until he reached that waist-high barrier, where the city spires rose up around them. There was a flurry on, and the streets below resembled snowy runways.

Gus didn't gaze into that chasm long. He turned to his prisoner, sized matters up, and cleared the powder piled up against the base of the frosted partition. After dredging enough clear, he pushed the trolley and its baggage as close to the rail as he could get.

Then he stepped in front of the Leather, between his spread legs.

And rudely pulled the Pan mask off the prisoner's head.

The man was battered. Severely bruised and bloody from half a dozen places where his swollen skin had split apart. Dark hair shorn to the skull allowed an excellent view of the damage Pan had sustained. Both cheeks bled from blue-red welts resembling oversized robin's eggs. A purple eye wept blood while a bloated lip drooled spawny froth to his neckline. A scream of wind lashed flakes across the prisoner's head. The minion glared, cranked his head as if attempting to wind himself up, and snarled in either pain or anger, showing broken and missing teeth.

He stared hot hatred at his captor.

An unflinching Gus scowled back.

They stayed that way for long seconds, neither man said anything.

"How many of you little shits came here?" Gus finally put to his prisoner.

Pan blinked, starting a fresh trickle of blood from his eye. He winced and lowered his head, ignoring the question.

"There were three snowmachines parked out front. One's gone. Where did it go?"

Pan sniffed. Sniffed hard. Drawing back great disgusting gobs until he choked, coughed, and spat. A chunky red gob spattered the minion's knee. Then he sent another meteor into the snow and met Gus's gaze.

Gus waited, taking the wicked cold. A person could get frostbite in such temperatures. He wondered how long before it would happen, then he realized he didn't really have to wait at all.

"Not going to talk?" he asked Pan.

The Leather smirked, as if knowing Gus wasn't going to do shit.

Gus didn't have time for this silent posturing. Thing was, however, for all his tough talk, he had discovered he wasn't one for torture, either. At least he didn't think he was, dismissing the beating he delivered to his prisoner. The more he looked at the unmasked knob before him, however, the stronger the urge to just smash the defiance from the prisoner's face. Gus's anger began to build. The Leather were slavers. Killers. Terrorizers and deceivers. They preyed upon the weak. Weaponized the dead. And, in the end, he held them accountable for Collie's death. They forced Milo to pull the trigger, which started, or at least accelerated, the same process that had claimed Wallace. If Collie was still alive, who knew what Josh Rogan might have been able to do with her. There was no knowing now, no *what ifs*, no *if onlys*.

And that ate huge holes in Gus's heart and mind.

"Where did you come from?" Gus tried once more. "Hm?"

Pan eyed him, sly and bleeding. He slowly prodded his swollen lips with a bloody tongue.

He did not answer.

Gus's cheek twitched.

Without warning, he grabbed the trolley by the lower bits, his wrists pressing against Pan's buttocks. Then he groaned, lifting with his legs, and hoisted the Leather and the trolley up to the rail. It was hard. Pan was heavy, thrashing even, but stopped when Gus got him up on the edge and heaved . . . pushing Pan out near the halfway point.

Where he hung over the drop.

His smile gone, Pan's breathing quickened. He glanced from side to side, realizing his predicament.

"Last chance," Gus strained from between the Leather's knees.

And Pan did the last thing Gus expected.

He laughed.

It started off as the nervous sputter of a flooded outboard engine. An organic snort of glee and rage, and then bloomed into a full powered bray, as if he'd just heard the best joke ever. He eventually whooped, like a cowboy strapped to a falling nuclear warhead. All the while, he regarded his captor with that wrecked and bloody grin.

A little red light went off in Gus's head.

He pushed the trolley over the railing. Two hard shoves before gravity sucked the offering down—but when it got a whiff, Gus simply stepped back and let it go.

Pan flipped over and dropped from sight.

He screamed laughter all the way down.

When it was over, Gus walked back to the elevator, not bothered that he had just executed a man.

Not one shit.

Only two things occupied his mind.

First, he returned to the twenty-second floor and immediately searched the Leather he had killed.

Key fob.

Two of them in fact. He extracted the devices from the ass pocket. Pressed a green button. Then the red.

All right, that's one, Gus thought. He searched the other one shortly after, retrieving more key fobs. Then it hit him—he didn't search the last little bastard, which meant . . .

"Fuck . . ." he groaned. How had he lived this long? It amazed him at times.

Pan had landed in the same area where Collie did. Gus stood in the lobby and gazed out through the window. He could see a body-strapped-to-a-trolley-shaped-outline of a hole, but that was it. No sight of the Leather strapped to it, so deep was the snow. If he wanted to search the body, he'd have to shovel through some mighty high drifts.

Fuck that noise.

He could wait until spring.

Then he had another idea. He held up the key fobs. Clicked the start button of the first. Then the second.

One snowmachine flared to life.

Nodding approval, Gus checked the fob and pressed the red button for three seconds. The machine switched off. Then he considered the other fobs, shrugged, and pressed the remote start buttons.

Nothing.

The third fob started up the remaining snowmachine.

Gus scratched at his temple, thinking things through. He had the fobs for two machines, so what were the other ones for? Obviously they were used for individual rides, so where were they? And what kind of machines were they? There was no brand logo on the thing.

And should he leave the other snowmachine functional?

"Sorry amigo," Gus said, and took aim.

He fired from the hip.

There was a *pang!* And the snowmachine bucked, spinning to one side and creating a spiral in the snow. A huge, crimped hole appeared in the fiberglass shell covering the engine.

Gus studied the damage. He hoped he'd done the smart thing. He took a moment to think about where to leave the untouched snowmachine, and decided it was fine right where it was. At the very least he could park it in the garage, but he remembered the snow cliff filling the entrance. If he tried driving the machine over that, it would fall, and he would risk damaging it.

The growing cold forced Gus back to the elevator, but he wasn't going back to his room just yet. Not with the possibility of more Leather running around his house.

That was one thought Gus didn't want to dwell on, so he occupied his time by, once again, taking off his boots.

When the elevator doors opened, he peeked around the corner. Only mindless corpses between him and the front doors of the penthouse. Nor did anyone hide in the stairwell. Shotgun aimed, Gus stepped out and let the elevator doors close behind him. He snuck toward the penthouse entrance, tiptoeing over the droves of rotting dead, and wished he'd worn a mask.

A quiet dread permeated the penthouse, thick and chilling to the bone. He stopped and peered inside, waiting for a shout of alarm. Gus leaned past the threshold a little farther, aiming the shotgun at the area beyond. Nothing moved.

Knowing the stink was going to make him sick, he went inside.

The usual corpses heaped upon the floor, only more decomposed than before. One or two may have been moved and searched, but he couldn't be sure. The penthouse was huge, so he'd have to go through the whole thing, making like a ninja.

Which was right about when he caught sight of the Dog Tongue's body splayed out on the tiles where Gus had left him.

He stopped and stared, unable to understand what he was looking at.

The dead man's head was missing.

14

Three weeks earlier.

Hard northerly winds rattled the steel mesh fence surrounding the refinery. A six-vehicle convoy leaving the facility rolled to a stop before he gates. The Mallet shifted in the passenger seat and stared at the entrance to the site, longing to be back in his room. It had been a long grind these last few months. He had had enough of overseeing day-to-day operations and looked forward to a long and peaceful winter. Next to him, his driver drummed his fingers softly on the steering wheel. Neither man said a word.

A thick-necked minion wearing a heavy coat lumbered past the tankers and continued to the gate. There, he twiddled with the lock, fumbling with it for long seconds. Finally, he shoved half the gate aside and then the other. Once done, he stood aside as a few snowflakes hit the windshield of the lead tanker.

"Starting early," the driver said, the words carrying in the silence of the cab.

The Mallet turned his masked head until he spied the profile of the driver—who became quiet and did not speak again. Message delivered, the Mallet pushed his sunglasses up on his face and regarded the gate. The driver drove on, passing the minion standing aside.

For the last six months, this group of Leather had been preparing for winter, like a small detachment of army ants. As of today, the refinery entered a stage of shutdown before the snow came. The Chemist, returned from Vampire Joe only two days earlier, had arranged it so that the automated system would not need any human operators during that time. The facility would monitor itself for months with minimal supervision until the spring, when the Leather would return to the site, fire up the great machines, and start refining the much-needed fuel of the day.

Affectionately called Dog Piss. Premium.

The driver didn't offer any more comments as he drove, which was good. The Mallet didn't speak to him in the first place. He didn't want to discipline his driver. He was a good driver. Just needed to keep his mouth shut was all.

Flat. An exceptionally flat part of the world. A prairie of wilting wheat split down the middle by a single two-lane strip of pavement. Some hills fringed the absolute edges of the scene, far and forlorn looking. There might have been deer or caribou out there at one time, but these days, not even a prairie dog. It was drab. Hugely empty, where the horizon divided the yellows from the greys.

The engine grumbled with each shift in gear before smoothing out, a sound the Mallet enjoyed as it put him to sleep. A season of sleep lay before him. As much of it as he wanted.

The side mirror offered a shrinking image of the refinery left behind. The Mallet only gave it a fleeting glance before he leaned back in his seat, turning somewhat away from the driver. The weapon which gave him his name of choice rested against the door, and he had to adjust it a little to keep it from falling.

He then closed his eyes.

When he opened them, he was back at the Grand Robertson Hotel, the tanker chirping shrill warnings as the driver reversed and parked. The Mallet tugged on his leather mask spiked with chrome and sighed heavily.

"Home again," he said and swung himself out of the rig. Sub-zero air woke him, prompting him to grab his mallet. Gripping it just behind the head, he walked toward the main doors and stopped for a moment to study the sheer size of the parking lot.

It was an immense space, encircled by two dozen parked transport trailers and sandbags that in some places created ramps right up to the top of the trailers. Guard posts made of more sandbags ringed the roofs, facing the roads, providing a clear view of visitors coming down the streets of North Battleford. Within the makeshift fortifications, the remaining vehicles of the convoy rolled to a stop. The Chemist jumped out of one of the pickups, while the inflictor called the Dragon dropped to the ground on the other side. The Chemist adjusted a set of motorcycle goggles and walked on. The Dragon followed. The inflictor wasn't as tall as some of the others in that fearsome brotherhood, but he was bulky, with broad shoulders. Beefy and formidable in his black insulated clothing. A plain leather mask covered his whole head, and on that mask, stenciled in red ink on the right profile, was a dragon. The beast stood on its haunches, claws extended and ready to fight.

Another inflictor, the Hook, appeared behind the Dragon after parking another truck. Both inflictors guarded the Chemist, who controlled and directed all facets of the production and storage of Dog Piss Premium.

The Hook was tall—six-foot-three or -four. Maybe six-five with motorcycle boots. A physique as thick as a rum barrel. A heavy hide of a leather trench coat kept the man warm, while his mask was a simple muzzle that covered everything below his sunglasses. A black winter cap was pulled down over his ears. Side by side, the Hook was a few inches taller than the Dragon. The Dragon, a few inches wider. Both men were, to put it bluntly, scary as all fuck.

The Hook slowed to a stop and faced the Mallet as the men approached the hotel entrance, some fifty feet away, and waited for the leader to make his move like a gunslinger of old. As his namesake implied, the Hook possessed a huge set of meat hooks that he used on prisoners whenever given the chance. Only on those special occasions, however. Most of the time, the man used a pair of thick gladiator swords plucked from some dealer's shop in downtown Vancouver.

The Mallet ignored the posturing and headed for the revolving door, swinging his namesake with every step. The cold followed him into the lobby like an unwanted dog. He stopped before the only working elevator in the place. The others had been ripped apart by a sizeable blast. Perhaps a last-stand scenario involving survivors with explosives of some kind. Or so the Mallet figured, considering the number of undead that had once spattered the place and had to be cleared.

Not that it mattered. Some days it seemed like the Leather had been harvesting and clearing places of the undead for years. Not the Mallet, however. Mopping up that chunky mixture of spilled people paint was a nasty job given to the lessers.

"Yo' Mallet," a voice called out from the nearby coffee shop.

That stopped the leader cold, as if he'd just taken a stake through the heart.

"How you doin', son? All good? Got all your winter preppin' done? Cupboards filled to the brim and all that?"

A figure emerged from the coffee shop, dressed for winter, his bright coat open to the waist, revealing an expensive sweater underneath. Nice boots, as well, as the man obviously looted from the very best. As he walked over, he slapped a pair of gloves off the back of a nearby chair. He had sunglasses propped up high on his hairy, gel-slicked head, and smiled, showing a mouth full of original teeth.

The Mallet considered smashing that mouth.

"Been waiting for you to get back," the man—named Trunk—said. "Your boys here didn't know when, so they gave me a room on the second floor, along with some grub. They treated me good. Can't complain, not one bit. Figured I tell you who's been naughty or nice, you know, in time for Christmas."

Christmas? the Mallet thought, slightly cocking his leather-wrapped head.

"Got some information for you," Trunk said, stopping a short distance away. "For the usual price."

Business, was it? the Mallet thought. Then, "Wait for me in my office."

Trunk waved that away. "Can't wait for that. Gotta gear up and get out. Besides, you'll want to hear it now."

The Mallet stared for a moment, letting the silence swell. "All right."

"The usual price."

Another stare. Followed by a barely noticeable nod of the Mallet's head.

"Shake on it?" Trunk extended a hand. His other hand hooked the flap of his coat and pushed it back, where it revealed a holstered sidearm.

The Mallet regarded the weapon for only a moment.

A shot of freezing air heralded the entrance of the Chemist and the pair of inflictor bodyguards. The Chemist was a bundle of insulated material, complete with a brown mask of leather, studded with chrome rimmed holes for breathing. Steam flared from those holes.

When the Chemist stopped, the inflictors stopped as well.

The Mallet gripped Trunk's hand and pumped it exactly once before releasing. "Out with it."

"Sorry," Trunk smiled false sympathy, "I misspoke. Usual deal means for each place. I found *two* this time around."

"Two?"

"Two. Ah-*haaa*. See what a good boy I am? The *best*, I tell you. The *best*. I can sniff them out anywhere. Prime meat, too, you'll be happy to know."

"Where?" the Mallet asked, light flickering over his sunglasses.

"Ah-aaa, hold on a second. Two places. That's twice the goodies. Okay? Understood?"

"Twice?" the Mallet repeated.

Trunk nodded, smile still in place, bordering on a little too much bravery. "*Twice*. You guys been producing day and night right up 'til now. Don't bother denying it. I know. I see the tankers. I *know* you got the goods. The secret sauce. I like that name better than Dog Piss. That's harsh, you know. Who the fuck wants to fill up with something called that?"

The Mallet didn't comment, his sunglasses tracking Trunk as he prattled. The Chemist stopped a few paces from the Mallet, while the inflictors were right on her heels, casting ominous shadows across the floor tiles.

Without missing a beat, Trunk nodded at them all, seemingly oblivious to the sunglasses trained on him. Or perhaps he didn't care. His right hand still held his coat back, showing off the gun.

"So we good? Twice the info for twice the payment?"

The Mallet considered it. "We're good."

"Excellent. You're a gentleman. And a scholar. Always a pleasure doing business. Oh, and an upgraded room for the night."

"Upgraded?"

"One of them suites."

The Mallet didn't move. "What about what you said about gearing up and getting out?"

Trunk's smile softened. "Only for the night. It's cold and dark out there. I'll be on the road first thing in the morning. Maybe I'll head south this time. Head stateside. See what's happening down that way."

The Mallet took time absorbing all that. "A suite, then," he finally said. "What have you found?"

"Fully furnished?"

The Mallet stared. "They're all furnished."

"Not trashed, I mean. Sometimes I think you folks get into some weird shit, dressed like you are. Anyone coming around here would think they stepped into some kinky ass shit. I mean hip-deep. No offense."

The Mallet didn't flinch. "Not trashed."

"And with running water. Hot, too, please."

The Mallet twirled a finger, indicating Trunk to get on with it.

"All right, then," the other man said. "We're in business. Not that I expected anything less, you understand. Your outfit has always treated me good. And with respect. That's hard to find these days."

The Leather gathered around the parley and did not move.

"Yeah," Trunk said a tad warily as he eyed them all. "So, two places. One's bigger than the other. The big one's to the northwest. Place outside of a town called Smoky Lake. TCH 16, to—"

"I know the town," the Mallet interrupted in a quiet voice. "No one's there."

Trunk's wet smile widened, as if expecting it. "That's why you got me, right? Call me the bloodhound. I can sniff these places out. And you're right. No one's in the town. You head north of Smoky Lake. Some hundred klicks or so on the 855. It's tricky to find because they knocked down the signs. But it's there. Old road among a few. Straight stretch really. Campgrounds called Flat Hill. About a kilometer square and surrounded by nothing but wild country. A little village of cabins all around a small lake. About fifty or so people, young and old. No kids, from what I saw. Anyway, not a bad little number. Be tricky to get them but, hey, that's not my problem, right? I only show you the way."

The Mallet kept right on watching him. "And the other place?"

"That one I found on the way back here. I took the high country. That's where the people are. That's where they're *all* hiding. Well, not hiding, but away from all the shit. You know what I'm saying. Anyway, I stopped to take a leak on the side of the road and saw smoke. You know what they say, about where there's smoke and all that, right? Ended up at another small place, built up along Midnight Lake. Know that one?"

The Mallet shook his head ever so slightly. He did not know that one.

"No? Really? You got to get out more. Spend less time at the cabin. Get some of your boys to scout shit out. Plan ahead. Just kiddin'. Don't kill me. Please. Ha! Nah, seriously, it's just up the road from here. I mean as the crow flies and all that. Wait. You don't have anyone in your outfit called the Crow do you? No? Maybe I'll take that one. Unofficially. All right, take the 4 straight up north. There're even signs. Guess they never had trouble with anyone, and zombies can't read, right? And in a way they're right. Way out in the middle of butt-fuckin' nowhere. Like an itty-bitty mole on a hairy taint. East to miss. Seriously. Gross imagery aside, that's where they are. Not as many, though. Only a dozen. Small group but every head counts, right? More mayhem for your zoo, right?"

The Mallet nodded. "That's right."

Trunk visibly relaxed a bit and even let his coat flap go, covering up the gun. He rubbed his hands together. "That's all I got. Until next time. So, ah, mind if I take a look at what's behind the front desk there? And where are the suites in this place? Only five floors so . . . what? Top floor? On the wings or something? Geez, do you have anything with a Jacuzzi? That would be sick. I mean, *fuck*."

"That's all?" the Mallet pressed. "Those two places? Nothing more?"

The Trunk chuckled. "That's all? 'Course that's all. For now. I'll head south tomorrow. After I rest and gas up. My rig's parked out front there. The big SUV. Fuck pickups."

"Fuck pickups," the Mallet repeated, letting the sound slide off into nothing. Then he did a curious thing. He lifted his hand and fluttered a finger at the mercenary man before him.

Trunk was still smiling when a crossbow bolt sank into the shoulder blade of his gun arm. He grunted, his smile gone, and fell to his knees. A groan then, as if lifting something incredibly heavy, and he looked up in time to see the Hook, who had already unsheathed his namesakes, sink four inches of stainless steel into Trunk's *other* shoulder.

The Hook yanked him forward.

Trunk landed on the floor in a bloody sprawl. He rolled over, bleeding all the way, and groped for his sidearm with his still functioning right arm.

The Hook closed in.

"Don't kill me!" Trunk screamed, lifting his empty hand halfway.

The Hook impaled it, straight through the meat of the palm, the metal bright and bloody.

Trunk's screaming took on a new pitch.

The Hook kicked the man's face, flattening him out and ending the noise. The inflictor didn't stop there. He stretched out the hooked arm and looked for his partner, the brute called the Dragon.

The Leather was already approaching, holding exotic twin blades in each hand, what he called his claws. The curved knives could easily fillet a fish . . . or something much bigger.

"Stop," the Mallet ordered quietly, halting both inflictors as they regarded their leader.

Using the mallet as a cane, the Leather commander walked over to Trunk. The mercenary was half-conscious and cringing. Blood gushed from a nose squished to the right. Half of his face had swelled, causing an eye to narrow to a slit. Stains marred the man's expensive sweater from what dripped off his chin.

"Last time you were here," the Mallet recalled, "You . . . showed no respect for the Leather. What we've done. What we *are*. Even today, you are a little *too* comfortable around us. Bothered me then. Bothers me now. I don't think you fear us like you should. So, shortly after our last encounter, I talked matters over with the Chemist, who agreed. So I *planned ahead*. For the next time you graced us with your presence."

Trunk shuddered and opened his mouth. Blood lined his teeth.

The Hook shook the mercenary's impaled arm, producing a wail of pain.

The Mallet gestured at the two inflictors, and they stretched out their victim. Trunk had the presence of mind to beg, to blubber, really, but the Leather weren't moved. The Mallet stooped and extracted the gun from Trunk's waist. A quick pat down produced two spare magazines from the coat pockets. The leader handed everything over to the waiting Chemist, who inspected the weapon and nodded.

"Thank you for your service," the Mallet said to Trunk.

"Don't kill me!" Trunk wailed. *"Please don't kill me!"*

"Sadly, I have to," the Leather informed him. "We're in need of fresh meat."

He addressed the inflictors. "Take him to the trailer. But don't break his legs. They'll crush him to a pulp if that happens. Come see me in the office when you're done."

The Mallet turned his back on the mercenary, who shrieked as the inflictors dragged him out the revolving door and into the cold November evening.

Wasting no time, the inflictors hauled Trunk over to a parked transport trailer, one with a set of metal stairs that was almost level with the top. There, they hooked his arms and carried him up, screaming, wailing all the way. On the roof, a minion waited beside a wide opening, holding its lid, crudely modified for the trailer.

"NO!" Trunk squealed upon spotting that gaping maw and the darkness below. *"No! I'll be good! I'll do anything you want! Anything you want! I'll be a Leather! I'll be a Leather!"*

The Dragon punched him, a crushing shot to the guts, one that might've made contact with his backbone. Trunk doubled over, gasping for air. He clawed weakly at the edges of the hole even as the inflictors lowered him into the trailer.

There, things grabbed at his ankles, his shins, then his knees.

A terrified Trunk croaked at the writhing contact, and continued to hitch, trying to force sound past his mouth—until grey hands grabbed his upper body and covered his face. Fingers hooked into his eyes and mouth, pulling him down into that vat of darkness.

The minion let the lid drop, and it slammed with a resounding clatter.

Within the trailer, Trunk regained his ability to scream.

Until it petered out to a submerged gurgle . . . and stopped.

A knock at the door and the inflictors lumbered in, stopping just inside of what had been the manager's office of the Grand Robertson Hotel. Now, however, the Mallet had claimed it as his own, and he sat, stretched out behind a large desk. His namesake rested by his side, its head to the floor, and he kept one hand on the end as if piloting a ship.

The Chemist sat opposite him and both looked up as the bodyguards entered the room.

"All done?" the Mallet asked.

Both men nodded. The Dragon glanced at the Chemist.

"Should've done that long ago," the Chemist said in the scratchy voice of a lady who might have smoked far too much back in the day. She clasped her hands over her midsection.

"He was valuable." the Mallet reminded her. "As it is, now we'll have to find someone else to do Trunk's job. Not an easy thing to do. You have to be totally ruthless. Without a conscience, really. All while being outwardly charming."

"He was a prick."

The Mallet conceded that. "He was. All that. And now he's dead."

"Undead," the Chemist corrected, glancing away. "Or at least soon to be."

"Yes. Did you lower him in?" the Mallet asked the inflictors.

The Hook nodded.

"And you didn't break his legs?"

Both inflictors shook their heads.

"Excellent. Don't need any crawlers in the collection. Too much of a mess. They get walked on by everything else in there. Starts to look like shit from a flattened tube of toothpaste. Then there's the smell. Been there, done that."

"As if they don't smell bad already," the Chemist added.

"As if, indeed," the Mallet concurred. "All right, then. Next item. Winter is coming. Just around the corner, in fact. We're all stocked up for guests who might happen to drop by—"

"Who's dropping by?" the Chemist asked.

"No one. I'm just saying if they did. And could be anyone. Maybe one of Vampire Joe's people."

That quieted the Chemist.

"Not too keen on him?"

"I can work with him," she answered, careful with her words.

"You're done with your deliveries?" the Mallet asked, steering around the previous question.

"Yes. Unless I get called down to troubleshoot something, but I can't see that happening."

"Then you're done. Relax. Enjoy everything the Robertson has to offer."

The Chemist didn't reply, not that it bothered the Mallet. She was like that at times. And truthfully, he didn't like Vampire Joe either. The man was a murderous dick. But the Mallet kept that opinion to himself.

"In any case," he continued. "Before the infamous Trunk got dunked . . . he gave us the name and locations of two new grab bags. Full of people. Now, let me be clear. We don't need any more mouths to feed. Not going into winter with that. Spring . . . that's different. We could put them to work. But that's *spring*. This is *not* spring . . . and we *are* running low on cannon fodder."

The other three listened.

The Mallet watched them all in turn before stopping at the Hook. "What's the head count in the trailer?"

The Hook regarded the Dragon.

"Two dozen," the bulky inflictor replied. "At most. Give or take a head or two."

"Let's just wait until spring," the Chemist said. "The snow could come down any time."

"That it could," the Mallet agreed, smiling behind his mask. "That it could. I was thinking the same thing."

"And we could lose a crew."

The Mallet nodded. They could, indeed.

"I can go get them," offered the Dragon.

Three heads turned his way.

"You know where these places are?" the Mallet asked.

"I'll find them."

No one said anything to that, and again, the Dragon ever so subtly eyed the Chemist, who met his neutral gaze for seconds before turning her attention back to the Mallet.

"What do you think?" the leader asked her.

"Your call," she said.

"I value your opinion."

"If we send one, might as well send both."

"And leave the Dog Tongue's most precious asset unprotected?" the Mallet asked her back. "I like having my head right where it is."

"I'm not the Dog Tongue's most precious asset. That installation we just locked up for the season is."

"You can debate Lord Dog Tongue over that."

She looked away without another word.

"You think you can do it by yourself?" the Mallet put to the Dragon.

"Yes."

The Mallet considered it. He wasn't about collecting live slaves. Didn't need any extra meat puppets. But he *was* about keeping the fuel flowing, which was why the Chemist was here, and the reason she was so heavily guarded. Still, of all the inflictors, the Dragon was the Dog Tongue's most . . . reliable, when it came to extracurricular duties like the one being proposed. The Dragon had performed such operations before, until he was promoted to bodyguard duty and taken out of the field. Taking in a trailer full of mindless was fine enough. The mindless would stay in the trailer until needed and would keep over the winter months. Unlike any new meat needing to be converted. Having been converted himself, the Mallet wasn't up for converting someone else. It took time and energy. An incredible amount of cruelty. He'd just as soon kick back and enjoy a quiet winter. Get back to conquering when the snow was finally all gone.

"And you're good with this?" the Mallet asked the Chemist.

She raised both hands in tired exasperation. "No one listens to me, anyway."

The Mallet ignored that. "Hook?"

"Fine with me," the inflictor rumbled. "I'd send him if I were you. I'll keep watch over the Chemist. Until he gets back."

Silence then, with the Dragon once again, and ever so slyly, making eyes at the Chemist.

The Mallet sat up, placed his elbows on the desk, and pointed.

"Gather your troops, but no more, as we'll be at half strength until you get back. Bring back a trailer full and, well, I'm sure the Dog Tongue will be pleased. Very pleased. I'll write down the directions before you leave. Just in case you get lost."

"Should we notify Vampire Joe?" the Chemist asked.

"What for?"

She waved a hand. "He is head boss around these parts."

"Point taken. Maybe in a few days. Unless he sends word first. He's stretched thin like the rest of us. And the Dog Tongue's coming this way. Yes, I know I didn't tell you. And yes, it's late in the season, but it's happening. Everyone between here and there will be coming with him."

"The Dog Tongue," the Chemist repeated. "Coming here."

"Yes."

"Why is he coming this way?"

The Mallet shrugged. "War. Conquest. Boredom. Maybe he's never been this far east. Who knows? Ask him when he gets here. If he stops by to visit. He might or he might not, preferring to stick with Regina and nowhere else. Like you, nobody tells me anything. We just make the Dog Piss."

"I make the Dog Piss," the Chemist countered. "And deliver it, come to think of it. And perform maintenance checks on the facility. What is it you do again? Oh yes. You watch me work."

"That we do," the Mallet agreed, a hint of playfulness in his voice. "And we take our job very, very seriously. All right then. Muster your troops, Dragon. Fire up your machines of war. Go forth and claim whatever meat is out there. In the name of the Dog Tongue. Seventy heads or so, was it?"

"Fifty or so at the campgrounds called Flat Hill," the Chemist supplied. "And a dozen at the other place. Seventy is a reasonable estimate."

"Just in time for Christmas," the Mallet said, rocking his cherished weapon as if changing gears. "Good hunting."

The Dragon nodded at his commander, then fist-bumped the Hook. He looked at the Chemist. With a gentleman's grace, he dipped his head in her direction, as if they were in some noble's court and not the office of a backcountry hotel.

The Chemist didn't dip her head in return.

15

The gruesome discovery shocked Gus down to his frizzies and left him in a state of confusion, all the way back to the lobby. There, he dragged out a chair and sat down heavily in one of the areas less polluted by the dead. Despite the chilled stink on the air, he leaned back and placed his shotgun across his lap. He made a face and focused on the tracks in the snow as daylight retreated across the streets.

Eventually, he pulled out the remaining mysterious key fobs and held them.

He wondered where the Leather came from. He wondered how many klicks they could travel on one of those machines, in the freezing cold and the wind. They had to be close . . . or . . . what? What was he missing? A smaller group of them in another part of the city, maybe snowed in like he was? He held up the fobs and wondered what they switched on. Other snowmachines? Maybe broken down? Or was it for something else? Maybe a truck or two? Personal rides? Or big machines hauling trailers? A truck would give them greater range, but then it came back to where they left the truck, and if there *were* trucks, why didn't the driver of the missing snowmachine have at least one of the fobs?

Mysteries.

The worst being the one who got away. Was he back there yet, to that place from whence they had all come?

And did they know about him?

That stuck in his mind.

As far as he could tell, only a handful of Leather came to the Anchor Bay. Perhaps delivering a message, like Milo had said. One of them had left, presumably with the Dog Tongue's head. The others searched the floors. Perhaps for him? Or other survivors? The frozen mess of dead bodies in the lobby would have stopped the Leather in their tracks. The discovery of the dead Dog Tongue would have been another sizeable shock. A messenger would think the Leather at the Anchor Bay had killed off the last freak, then left a handful of goons, before running to report in.

Why else would they take the Dog Shit's head?

Gus mulled that last part over, morbidly stunned that they . . . actually *took* . . . the Dog Shit's *head*.

There was a chance they didn't know he was at the hotel.

"All right, so what?" he asked and sighed through his nose. *So what* was he had a choice. He could wait for them to return, however many that might be, and greet them at the door, guns blazing. He could also retreat deeper into the hotel, in *any* of the hotels, and make their lives miserable. Waging guerrilla warfare on their sorry asses, until either they won or he killed them off.

His eyes fell upon the last snowmachine.

Or he could get on that ride and follow the single track all the way back to wherever. Go on the offensive and deliver a little more payback for Collie. For Milo and the kids. For the people of Camp Red Wolf. For *anyone* the Leather might have killed, maimed, or flat-out enslaved for fell purposes.

That was the choice.

Back in the early days of the zombie apocalypse, when all was said and done, and he was facing isolation and a perpetual shitty ass, he used booze to cope with the day-to-day madness. He leaned especially hard on the drinking to get him through those days when he had to venture into Annapolis to scavenge for supplies. There was plenty of alcohol around if he needed it. If he wanted it, for what he was thinking about doing. And what he was thinking about was revenge, on a level equaling mayhem.

Thinking hard on it, in fact. Hard enough that his blood pressure was rising, as if the black iron kiln that was his heart was cooking up a full head of destructive steam.

Another heavy sigh, released through the nose, as he studied the snowmachine.

It was going to be dark soon. He'd be traveling in the night. Hated traveling at night. But whoever had left would be doing so as well.

Then another thought came to him. As awesome and terrifying as the Leather was, as the Dog Tongue purportedly was, and after all the death and destruction at the Anchor Bay, he wondered . . .

If whoever was driving that snowmachine was afraid.

Afraid of who had killed the all-powerful Dog Tongue.

That was the truth, Gus could sense it. That sealed the deal.

He rose, Ramfist at his side. Within minutes, he was back in his room packing the duffel bag full of whatever it would hold. Especially the ammunition. The HK rifle prized by Collie went in there as well, but barely fit. Her Sig went down the small of his back, tucked into his waistband. When he finished packing, he stopped and stared at the remaining bottles of McDonovan's So Very Fine Scotch. Then there was all the alcohol in the restaurants as well.

He didn't need the booze anymore.

Not for what he was going to do. The fear had been replaced by something far deadlier.

And as such, he didn't touch one bottle. Not even a parting sip.

He patted down his coat. He would have to stop at a clothing store and rummage around for something warmer and a little less pissy. He'd also need extra layers as it would be cold on the machine, but until then, he stuffed the Glock into a pocket.

And discovered Lammy was already in there.

"The hell you doin' in there?" he asked and held the toy up. "Did I put you in there? Must've. Well... Look. I gotta go. I gotta go look for the rest of the dickheads that came here. See what's up. And... and make sure they don't start anything like this again. You understand?"

Lammy smiled back. He got it.

"It's gonna be dangerous," Gus explained. "Might be best for you to, you know, stay here."

Lammy got that, too.

Gus wavered and jammed the little toy into his other coat pocket. He didn't have many friends, and after the last few weeks, he found he wasn't keen on leaving one behind. Without another thought, he hung the duffel bag off his shoulder and lifted the shotgun.

One more thing to take from the hotel. From the Leather.

He rode the elevator to the twenty-second floor and located the first Leather shit-pouch he'd shot. The mask was intact. There was nothing special about it, just a regular facemask, a balaclava with a leather skull cap.

Gus pulled it off the dead man. Stuffed it in his pocket with the Glock. Left the rest.

On the way back down, he wavered again and made a detour back to his room.

There he emptied the lost and found box on the bed. *Lost* and *found*. The words struck him hard. Considering everything he'd been through, he most certainly could relate. He took a pillow from the bed and lined the box with it. Then Gus pulled Lammy from his pocket, placed him inside, and made him as comfortable as a stuffed toy might be in such a place. Looking down upon his little companion, Gus might've intended to say something, assuring him that he would be back, that everything would work out, or some such parting thought. Something reassuring, not only for Lammy, but for himself.

But Lammy was just a toy.

And a toy would not want to go where Gus was going.

A short time later he returned to the lobby and the front desk. There, he placed the box behind the counter, easily found if someone looked. Gus smiled a little smile, matching the one on the stuffed animal's face looking up at him. His smile faded into a scowl, then one of regret. Then he nodded with purpose.

"Someone will find you," Gus said. "Someone will."

Still, it was hard to leave the little guy. Gus did it, however. He left Lammy and walked back to the snowmachine. The storage compartment was empty, so he jammed what he could in that, making room in the bag for his shotgun. The rest would hang off his back. Mounting the machine, he started the engine, and wished he had a pair of goggles.

On impulse, he glanced over his shoulder, back at the smashed entrance to the Anchor Bay. And at the lost and found box, half expecting to see the little stuffed bastard peeking up over the rim. It didn't happen.

He focused on the tracks ahead.

"Here we go," he said, and squeezed the throttle.

The snowmachine sank a little as Gus turned it around, at one point teetering on tipping. He lined himself up with the other tracks and drove off in the same direction, with the sun starting to set between the buildings. The wind blasted him full on, attempting to blow him off the seat, but he powered through, rising and falling among the accumulated drifts. The scale of those mighty swells surprised him. Whole avenues were buried, but he followed the track left by the departing messenger, keeping his machine on the packed snow. The sound of his pursuit rebounded off downtown Regina as he weaved through lumps of stranded traffic. An intersection lay ahead, with the blind eyes of a white-capped traffic light not six feet overhead, such was the height of the snow. The straight strip beyond encouraged him to squeeze the throttle a little more. The snowmachine ripped through the intersection, spraying powder in his wake. Shop fronts whizzed by. Some caught his eye, some even having new coats, but he didn't stop for fear of being bogged down off the packed track. Thus far, his coat was protecting him from the cold.

The fuel gauge showed a tank nearly half-empty. A troubling sight. Gus hoped this venture into the suburban wild wasn't a mistake. He was driving blind, with no idea where he was as the Leather had removed most road signs. Metal posts with beaten or twisted tops were missing their signage. Instead of tidbits of much-needed city information, human skulls topped the roadside posts. Each and every one. Some grinned at him with spotty smiles, while others had their jaws missing entirely. Worse still, some kept their skin, while others had streamers of hair waving in the wind.

The only thing he had were the snowmachine tracks he currently followed, which sometimes folded into one before widening into two or three.

The evening deepened. The buildings shortened and disappeared. Rooftops of houses appeared over tall fences, eventually replaced by deserted commercial lots. Even those became fewer, spaced out over larger open swaths of territory, until only a blank slate of white remained on either. Clumps of snowcapped trees appeared, growing into lines, but by then the darkness became absolute. Gus switched on his headlights. The tracks continued west, leaving the city far behind. The night cleared, and starlight dappled the land. At times he looked up, distracted by the heavens and their bands of cosmic dust.

The tracks eventually turned north, or what he thought was north, but in truth, he had no idea. The Dog Tongue's gruesome lines of skulls continued on both sides of the road. After a short time, two shapes loomed up on that near featureless prairie, and the headlights revealed a pair of pickups with attached snowplows, sitting behind a piled-up crest of snow.

The tracks looped around the vehicles.

Gus did the same, seeing a wake of piled up snow.

Not realizing how high it might be, the unexpected drop at high speed surprised him as he and the machine dropped onto pavement. His chin clacked off his upper chest as he instinctively braked to a stop. Rattled, he glanced back at the abrupt drop-off he misread—a clear cut of snow shoved up perhaps three feet high.

"Jesus," Gus swore and pulled up beside one of the trucks. There he killed the engine, shrugged off the duffel bag (which was both strangling and exhausting him), and dismounted.

He readied the Ramfist, slapped its butt against his shoulder, and aimed wherever he looked.

Snow-drizzled black ice glazed a strip of plowed highway. The uncertain footing forced him into an impatient shuffling, which no doubt resembled a guy in desperate need of taking a dump. The shotgun felt heavy and his hands trembled from the time spent controlling the snowmachine. Gus glanced around, very much aware that he was alone, in the middle of goddamn nowhere, at night. Still, if anyone was guarding the machines, they would have made themselves known by now. And he would have already been dead.

A cleared lane stretched out into the dark behind the parked vehicles. The first truck was empty. As was the other one. One truck hauled a flatbed trailer, unhooked and tipped to the pavement. Ramps hung from empty box beds. Snowmachine tracks left the trucks and trailer alike. Four red gas cans lay in the rear of one pickup, while the other had two. Squinting and hearing only wind, Gus continued his recon, stopping on the far right to examine the highway. Two lanes, plowed just shy of its actual width.

And a set of tire tracks, reversing in a three-point turn, where the driver had slammed the tailgate of his rig into the plowed ridge of snow, stamping it with a clearly defined outline.

Gus faced the road. Fresh powder snaked across the blacktop. Heads lined the sides, disappearing into the night. He turned to his left, thinking matters through. The Leather had come from that way, with their plows flush to the asphalt. When the snow got too much, as evidenced by the white wall directly ahead of the remaining vehicles, the Leather stopped, unloaded their snowmachines, and continued to Regina.

As an afterthought, Gus fumbled for the key fobs he carried. He chose one and thumbed the remote start.

The red pickup to his right flared to life.

Oho, he thought, and thumbed the other.

The other pickup roared with ignition.

Mystery solved.

Gus checked on his ride and saw that he'd stopped out of the way of the pickup, and that he had enough room to back up. For the next minute, he transferred his gear from the snowmachine to the red pickup. Then he shook the gas cans, discovered them all full, and transferred them over. The snowmachine, he left, as he didn't think he'd need it. He left the key fob for the spare truck on its driver's seat, and stuck the fob for the snowmobile in the little storage compartment. When he'd done that, he gave the seat a fond pat on the rump. Shivering, he clambered aboard the truck and placed the Ramfist on the passenger side.

A joystick control box situated by his right knee momentarily befuddled him. He reached out, gripped it with his fingers, and gently applied pressure, pulling it back. The edged blade fixed to the front rose in a ghost whisper of hydraulics.

"I'm a fuckin' genius," Gus said and thumbed the joystick forward.

The blade lowered.

"All right, you fuckers," he said, grimly, raising the blade once again. "All right."

The truck's lights lit up the road as he reversed and turned the machine around. The headlights illuminated the road in a broad swath, and the rows of spiked skulls along the way. Every thirty feet at least.

The easiest thing in the land to follow, really, if it wasn't so goddamn evil.

He hit the gas and drove onwards.

Light snow had fallen on the road and the fleeing pickup had left clear, broad tracks. Gus kept to the middle of the highway, his mind drifting from thought to thought, tethered by a molten metal desire to kill off the Leather. Each and every one, for . . . essentially what he figured were crimes against humanity. At least that's what Channel Seven's *Maritime News* would call it. Fuckin' crimes against humanity. They'd even have footage of all the skulls, with a viewer discretion warning just before showing a parade of all those noggins, some bare and some not so bare, staked alongside the highway.

So many skulls. So many, many skulls.

He had no clue where he was going, except he was headed northwest, as indicated by his dashboard compass. Didn't really need the headlights on as the moon was out and glowing, making it easy to distinguish the blacktop from the snow-covered prairie. He wasn't tired, despite the nonstop nature of the day, and he stayed alert, scrying the dark ahead. Above all, he tried not to look at the constant stream of spiked heads.

Power poles ran parallel to the highway. Several dark and ominous towns drifted by, radiating menace, the houses and commercial buildings lightless and snowed in. He passed them all without incident, following the plowed road straight on through. Whoever the driver was, he didn't stop anywhere along that road of skulls. Matter of fact, he didn't see any abandoned cars on that strip, which was weird. Shallow, sunken depressions passed by. Distant, blackened shapes resembling grain silos. Snowed-in farms and homesteads. Even gloomy husks looking a lot like tractors. All between long stretches of emptiness and brief clumps of forest, seemingly strung together by power poles.

And the ever-present skulls.

It was disconcerting. Hypnotizing.

"Christ Almighty," Gus muttered around 8:46 p.m., glancing at the dashboard clock and then the passing landscape. "John Denver would've fuckin' *hated* this place."

He'd never been this far west before. Word was it was flat. The roads straight. But until you drove it—at night, no less—you had no idea just how spectacularly *vast* it all was. Probably was even more awesome in the daytime. There was an urge to floor the accelerator, but he suppressed it, for fear of hitting a patch of black ice and ending this entire episode.

So he continued on, watchful, driving down a frosted, seemingly *endless*, runway.

The highway went right through the city of Saskatoon, perhaps even splitting it right down the middle. Someone had cleared the traffic, rudely shoving vehicles aside to create a single lane. As usual, skulls marked the sidewalks, but much fewer than before. Gus did not deviate from the road, but if he was on heightened alert before, he was doubly so while driving through the city. Thirty minutes later, Saskatoon was behind him. The prairie returned and the road kept rolling northwest.

Around midnight, the harsh glare of the headlights revealed a particularly noticeable skull spiked on a post, in a pothole, right in the center of the highway. A skull that made Gus sit up in his seat and take grim notice.

The big horns and head of a buffalo. Or a bison. Or maybe they were the same thing? Oh what a time to miss Google.

Minutes after that, however, he saw the reason for the buffalo skull. For the first time since he started driving, the plowed road offered him a choice. Continue straight . . . or turn right.

Gus braked, leaned over the wheel, and saw what might have been flickers of candlelight in the distance.

He turned right.

The headlights slowly unveiled a piecemeal wall consisting of parked tractor trailers, wooden pallets, and sandbags. Atop that chaotic fortification were sandbagged guard posts. The road ended in the broadside of a city bus, and beyond it all, mostly hidden by darkness, was a four- or five-story hotel.

In Gus's mind, it wasn't a fortress. It was a nest.

He rolled to a stop, switched off his headlights, and reached into the passenger seat. Not for the Ramfist, but for the leather mask he'd taken from a corpse. He pulled it on and adjusted it. The damp contact nearly turned his guts, as he realized he hadn't wiped off the inside.

"Shit," he muttered, and was about to take the mask off when a figure appeared in the guard post atop the wall.

Forgetting the sweat-slicked insides of his mask, Gus lowered his window. The next part would be a roll of the dice. A shot in the dark. A one-legged man's kick at a set of nuts. He stuck his head and arm out, making sure the minion on the wall saw him. More specifically, saw the mask. Gus remembered Milo's information on the

Leather. Remembered how the soldier had said they got their news by relaying messengers between their groups. The mask he currently wore was taken from the one Leather left behind at the Anchor Bay. If this was a small outfit, the guard might recognize the mask . . . and he might also recognize that the mask didn't belong to the original owner.

The Leather didn't talk much. Gus hoped the guard above was the same way.

The minion didn't move right away, and when Gus's ball sack started tightening, the guard turned and walked out of sight. Gus kept one hand on the gearstick and, with his foot firmly on the brake, shifted into reverse.

When the bus started up, it startled him. Seconds later, the machine rolled ahead, granting access to an inner parking lot.

Gus shifted into drive and drove through, into a small area filled with vehicles, including a pair of fuel tankers. He turned for the main entrance, where the lobby had lights on, and stopped with the driver's side angled for the doors.

In his side mirror, the bus was already rolling back into place.

Gus checked himself before staring ahead. He could try bluffing his way inside. Perhaps even try dispatching the sentry before entering the place. Then he could go into full stealth mode and infiltrate the building, picking off the Leather one by one.

He gathered up the shotgun. Got out of the truck. He fished for the key fob in his pocket and locked the rig. Because you just never know.

A guard was walking toward him, maybe already noticing Gus wasn't wearing leather from the neck down.

Gus turned to face him while casually bringing up Ramfist.

The sight of the weapon froze the Leather in his tracks.

Boom.

One shell, but it propelled the Leather bastard back as if struck by an oversized wrecking ball. The minion splatted the side of the distant bus and did not rise.

Gus had already turned and was hurrying to the doors of the hotel.

A Leather appeared in the lobby, crouched and ready for action, carrying—of all things—a bat.

Gus stopped and aimed.

The Leather turned and ran.

Not fast enough, however. Gus pumped off two shots in his direction, the glass door imploding as the ejector spat shell casings. Jagged slivers sprayed the entryway as the Leather—a stride away from a full sprint—got launched sideways over a small set of living room furniture, whipping around a sofa chair.

Gus swung the Ramfist left to right and back again, searching for targets. No one stuck their head up. No one came at him from the parking lot. He faced the door and aimed from the hip. The front doors flew apart.

Narrow-eyed and focused, Gus marched inside.

If the fuckers weren't awake before, they were now. He intended to put every last one back to sleep.

The lobby was a small one, dimly lit as if conserving power. Gus aimed wherever he looked, searching for targets. A hurried walk, and he was in an empty cafeteria draped in shadows, much smaller than the restaurants of Anchor Bay. An elevator to the upper floors was across from that. Gus jogged back to the lobby, glanced down a hallway displaying signs for the indoor pool and gym. A distant stairwell was at the end of the corridor.

That was one.

Back in the lobby was the elevator, as well as a second stairwell.

He crossed the floor, avoiding the widening blood pool from the Leather he'd just gunned down. The man's entire side was flayed open and steaming, but Gus only spared a quick look.

The elevator wasn't moving.

He squinted at the readout above the doors, waiting for the thing to start descending. The mask bothered him. With every passing second his need to get moving grew increasingly stronger. After what felt like the longest minute of his life, he aborted, and huffed it over to the stairwell. There he placed a shoulder to the wall and waited. The pickup was visible from where he stood, and no one sought to flank him. That was fine. Excellent even, as he'd left the German HK rifle in the locked-up pickup. Along with the rest of his supplies in the duffel bag.

He waited a few seconds more then cracked open the stairwell door. Spotty lighting shone over beige cinderblocks and bright red railing. Holding his breath, he waited, and heard the barest thump from above. One that might've been a door closing.

He slipped over the threshold, keeping a boot heel there to prevent the door from closing.

A shuffle-slap as someone hurried down the stairs, getting louder. A shadow then, just up the flight of steps, becoming increasingly dark on the landing wall.

A Leather head poked around the corner.

Gus fired, the shot deafening in those close quarters. The head disappeared as if it never existed, spattering the wall with a wet slap that the concrete confines amplified to even greater effect. The body dropped into the open, every bit as dewy as the gruesome matter streaking down the cinderblocks.

The urge to check the elevator overcame him then, so Gus pulled back and did just that.

No movement.

He jammed a finger onto the button marked "L" and summoned the elevator. The thing clunked into movement, sinking from the fifth floor. Without hesitation, Gus rushed back to the stairwell and started climbing bloody stairs. The worst of it was on the landing, where he trod through the bloody mess he'd just made, ignoring the tangle of fabric and mangled head pulp. The second-floor door loomed, Gus hauled it out and entered.

Long hall, barely lit by ceiling lights. The air cold, surprisingly so, as if someone left a window open. Blue or black carpet on the floor, and most importantly, not a Leather in sight. The rooms' doors were closed. Gus tried the nearest knob. Locked. He moved down the hall, breaking into a jog. He reached the next stairwell, glanced back, and saw no one in pursuit. Gus pushed through the door, checked up and down, and huffed it to the next landing. There he spun around the corner, aiming as he went, and discovered all was clear. Then he was on the third floor, chest heaving, his calves barking, and sweat slicking his face.

Without pause he hauled open the door and charged.

Empty hall. Practically a mirror image of the second floor, with every door in sight closed. Gus speed-walked along, ready for someone to pop out ahead of him. At times, he tried the doors to the rooms, but each one was closed. He passed the elevator, the display showing the car had reached the lobby. He passed an alcove with a row of vending machines, and what looked to be an open freezer for ice.

A thread of light lay across the carpet up ahead, two doors away.

That stopped him. He retreated to the alcove, taking cover and placing his shoulder to the corner. There he waited, licked his lips, and peeked out.

That thin filament of light was still there, across the floor.

Gus sized up the hall and slipped around the corner, knowing someone was waiting behind that door opened just a sliver. Heart hammering, his fucked-up heel pulsing pain, he crept toward the door with barely a sound.

Ten feet to the door. The wire of light didn't move. Five feet.

He stopped, back to the wall just outside the door, Ramfist aimed at the floor. His chest demanded more air, being on the verge of exploding.

The light wavered, whoever behind the door listening, and then widened.

And as the light fattened, so did Gus's eyes, until the tip of a man's head slowly edged around the corner.

Gus slipped his right hand underneath the Ramfist, with barely a whisper of fabric, hiking the weapon high enough to clear the magazine . . . and reached the knife sheath strapped to his left forearm.

The head came around the corner, looking to take a peek of the hall.

Gus whipped that nasty blade from its sheath in one surprisingly fluid motion, to sink the whole weapon under the man's chin, where a jawbone stopped the steely crossbar in a grisly spurt of scarlet.

The man dropped with a thud, pulling the knife from Gus's grasp.

Whereupon he barged into the room, shotgun raised.

No one. Just the single room, inhabited by the lone minion, whose right leg twitched twice before going still.

Gus moved back to the doorway and checked on the hallway.

Clear.

He stooped and twisted the head around until he could retrieve the knife. A quick wipe on the dead man's spine, and he sheathed the blade, taking a second to marvel at the killer feat. He'd probably never be so fast, so accurate again with the weapon. Another glance around and he left the room and didn't stop until he was at the next stairwell door. He paused, listened, and pushed through.

Up the stairs and around the corner.

Fourth floor.

A quick peek and Gus barged through the door, where he whirled left then right and spotted a Leather with a crossbow at the end of the hall—just as the Leather released the bolt.

Gus's first impulse was to duck, but since he was already moving, the missile hissed by his head, close enough to feel its flight. He slammed into the wall, dropped to a knee, and fired back. The Leather's leg exploded in a burst of gore, the impact pitching the figure forward, spent crossbow clattering to the floor.

Then she started screaming.

Gus clambered to his feet, his heel playing those familiar fiery accordion notes with every step.

She was still writhing on the carpet when he reached her.

He placed the barrel of the shotgun to her head. "How many more?" he demanded.

"Fuck you!" she wailed back—and swiped at his shins with a knife.

Gus dodged that, easily evading the slash, and meant to finish her off.

When something urged him to turn around.

He did, in time to meet the full-on rush of the next attacker, swinging a machete at his head. With a speed born of adrenaline-fueled fright, he blocked the blade with the Ramfist and kicked out one knee of the Leather. The man went down and Gus slapped away a hand clawing for his chest. The Leather hit the carpet while grabbing for an ankle. Gus backed up and nearly tripped over the screaming one-legged minion behind him. He steadied himself and shot the machete owner through the chest. The blast flattened the Leather against the baseboards, opening a massive crater of meat and bone and flesh spraying the wall in a horrific sunset. Gus pivoted and shot the one-legged minion at his feet. That Leather bucked and skidded some five feet away, leaving an oil slick in the carpet.

Breathing hard, Gus placed his back against the wall and looked both ways. Empty hallway once again. He adjusted the mask, hated the feel, and ripped it from his head. Tossing the loathsome thing aside, he exhaled with a sputter and glanced around before finally settling on the ceiling. Aiming the Ramfist, he walked for the stairwell door, taking a moment to roll his shoulders.

"How many's that?" Gus asked aloud, gulping down air. "Huh? Can't be . . . too many of you fuckin' knobs left. Can't be."

He pushed through the door and, upon deeming it clear, calmed his wheezing. The short but meaningful combat had fatigued him, his body asked for more time to recover. His nerves hummed along as well, all for a breather. He ignored it all, telling himself he had plenty of juice left. Just had to slow down was all. Just slow down. That thought in mind, he carefully hauled his ass up the next two sets of steps, until he got to the door of the fifth floor.

For some reason, he suspected the main event would happen on the fifth. Damn straight it would.

Deep priming breaths through his nose, Gus firmed up and pulled the door open.

Empty hall, with the same sparse lighting. Doors were all closed. He proceeded, danger sense tingling—ringing really—just inside his ears, sounding like a pair of cowbells being frantically swung, warning him of a twister coming straight at him. That might be so, he figured, since he'd been firing away without worry of waking the goddamn neighbors. He moved ahead, bent over, as if tracking some vicious brute of an animal. A few steps and he'd stop and listen. On impulse, he'd reach out and try the odd doorknob. Each one was locked.

Then he noticed it.

Just up ahead—where the hallway was darkest—was one door not entirely closed, shining a golden wire sliver upon the carpet.

Just like before.

Gus aimed the shotgun and, in addition to the ringing in his ears, felt the railway track shiver of a very nasty engine coming straight at him.

Edging forward, Gus flexed fingers on the Ramfist. That thread of light blazed white hot, making him wonder if someone had merely forgotten to close the door when leaving. Maybe he'd already shot one of the bastards on the lower floors. Maybe they rushed below after hearing him fire off a couple of rounds. The place was no Anchor Bay, so maybe sound carried a lot—

That sunny filament of light dimmed just a bit, stopping Gus in his tracks. Someone was on the other side of that door, waiting for him like before. That notion stunned him for a split second, wavering over the next thing to do, when he aimed at the door's center.

And fired.

A hubcap-sized hole appeared, shredded and smoking, and the door crashed off the inner wall as if a tornado had come a knocking. Gus charged in, knocking back that wrecked barrier and stopping just inside the room. There, splayed out before the window and twitching like a spider shriveled up by a live wire, was one less Leather. A long-shafted mallet lay inches away from shivering fingers, while the owner's legs relaxed, and the carpet struggled to absorb everything stemming from a grisly, half-moon hole in his lower rib cage. Unmoved by the sight, Gus glanced into an empty bathroom and a sitting area and deemed them clear. He moved deeper inside the room, stopping at the foot of a queen-sized bed. A surreal painting of what might be interpreted as falling raindrops hung above the bed, when the *second* Leather, pressed as deep as possible into an open closet on the bedside right, aimed a handheld crossbow at him.

And fired.

The bolt hit Gus in the chest, blunting its steel head against his body armor, but twisting him around enough to glimpse the much more deadly surprise stomping into the room. Another minion, swinging, of all things, an oversized *meat hook* at Gus's head.

That caused a cockle squeeze of heart attack proportions within Gus's chest.

He blocked the hook seeking to impale his ear with the Ramfist. The connection locked up both weapons, nearly yanking the shotgun from Gus's hands.

The Leather's follow-up *slap* to the head completed the job.

Gus didn't really feel the blow, but a part of him heard it, flattening his ear and maybe even exploding it, such was the force mustered behind that openhanded strike. He crashed into a large television and rolled along a fireplace, trying to get control of his legs while reality warped into an underwater feel. The meat hook came down, swung with murderous wrath, and sank three inches into the wooden surface where Gus only barely managed to jerk his hand away. The Leather released the weapon and grabbed Gus by the shoulder straps of his vest.

"*Yuh!*" he got out as the towering Leather ogre lifted him off his feet, spun, and heaved him across the room.

Gus crash-landed atop an end table, limbs flailing, sending a lamp flying. He tried to right himself, still struggling with a lack of gravity from being clocked upside the head. The table dumped him onto the carpet—just for a split second—as a hand grabbed him by the collar and the lower end of his armor.

Gus looked up, saw a knee, and punched it.

The ogre rammed him headfirst into the wall.

Black stars exploded before Gus's vision, a bright galaxy of motes that should not be there. He flailed, hit something, and blindly reached for the knife on his forearm.

A fist crashed into his head. Then another, and a follow-up third. Devastating blows swung by a much larger opponent standing right over him, seeking to break open his skull. The memory of being beaten up by a white ninja entered Gus's stunned mind. He thought there would be a kick soon, one that would off-balance the ninja, enough for him to regain the initiative and get some payback.

Except this was no ninja. And it wasn't the past.

Hands pulled him up, shook the living shit out of him, and launched him across the room. Gus skidded across what might've been another table, just before he and the table went tits up and spilled onto the carpet. Flat on his back, groaning, Gus was distantly aware *it* was coming for him. Multiple damage reports fuzzed his brain. Pain pulsated throughout, rushing along nerves with wildfire speed. Every sound came through an amplified bullhorn. He balled up a fist and hammered at a boot toe—and grunted loudly upon contact with the steel-tipped nose.

It was becoming that kind of fight.

The Leather easily pulled Gus up, shook free whatever unholy shit squirts were left in him, and slammed him against the wall. A hand kept him there. Another heavy slap nearly broke his jaw. A *second* slap nearly tore his head from his shoulders. Things rattled underfoot, sounding like broken glass grinding underwater. Angry eyes above a leather muzzle peered into his, blue and evil and bursting with wickedly eager intent.

"*Erk,*" was all Gus could say, and realized the bastard held him aloft by his throat. The Leather squeezed, hard enough that Gus's eyes nearly popped from his head.

Then he remembered dirty fighting 103.

The dick punch.

Gus swung a fist into the crotch of his attacker, mashing it into what had to be a steel cup.

God . . . damnit, Gus's brain exploded in agonized bewilderment.

It was *exactly* that kind of fight.

Despite the armor, however, the unexpected strike to the corn giblets seemed to slow the behemoth. Or so Gus sensed. Not that it mattered. A heavy fist slammed into the side of his face. Something ejected from his mouth. Then two more punches, hard boulders of toughened meat and bone, in slow-motion succession and damn near face-shattering. Gus's legs went to jelly, but the hand kept him upright.

Then a *second* hand clamped down on his windpipe. More specifically, the fingers, and those fingers didn't just seek to choke Gus to death, they clutched and gouged at his trachea, intending to rip out his throat.

"*Hook!*" someone screamed.

A battered and bleeding Gus—along with the one called Hook—glanced in the direction of the open door.

There stood the *other* Leather, the one from the closet, who'd once held the crossbow.

Who *currently* held the Ramfist.

The Leather fired, blasting the ogre away from Gus, punching him out the nearby hotel window in a sparkling spray of jagged glass. There was a flutter of size fourteen boots and the killer who almost claimed Gus's life fell from sight.

Gus sank to the floor, clutching his tortured throat. Cold air rushed into the room. It wasn't enough to clear his head. He landed on his ass and rolled onto his side.

The Leather with the Ramfist crouched right before him. Gus pushed away a hand and the Leather slapped him back.

"*Stop it,*" a woman's voice commanded. "Listen to me! *Listen!* Did you kill the others?"

Dazed and confused, Gus stared at her.

"How many did you kill?" she demanded, her words taking on a sickening echo.

Which was just about when a deep and terrible darkness reached up, grabbed his consciousness by the ankles, and hauled him down.

16

Hands slapped him. A vicious, stinging pitter-patter of connections that summoned him from the cauldron of unconsciousness. Gus cracked open a single eye, holding up his hands in a plea of *no more*. No more indeed. He felt as if a battle tank had rolled over him.

Brown eyes narrowed to slits examined him. A leather mask surrounded her head, designed to resemble someone suffering massive head trauma. Motorcycle goggles were perched on her forehead. The mouth however was studded with chrome-rimmed holes. She stopped the next slap, which was already poised to let rip.

"Get up," she said.

Gus didn't answer, so she slapped him again.

"Owwww," he wailed in a high protesting pitch.

"Gonna be worse if I have to put my boot up your ass," the Leather said. "And if that doesn't work, then I'll leave you here for *them*."

Gus cringed—bleeding, breathing—and studied what was talking to him. "Huh?"

The Leather glared at him, for what seemed like a long time, and then shook her partially mummified head.

"Goddammit," she swore, and leapt to her feet.

Gus spaced out, but gradually realized she was at the door to the room, peering one way and then the other. Then she padded back to him, still carrying the shotgun. She wrapped a hand around his poor aching and bewildered head.

"Last chance, okay?" she warned, peering at him from beneath a lowered brow, accentuating the seriousness of her message. "You either walk out of here with me *now* . . . or I leave you. For the dogs. Which is it?"

He felt the tightness in his face, the rivulets running into his eyes. "Walk," he managed.

The Leather nodded and hauled him to his feet. He stood, leaning hard against a wall, and swallowed blood. A *lot* of it. That metallic swill brought a grimace to his face.

"Spit it out, if you got to," she told him. "Your teeth are over by the window."

That opened both his eyes.

But she was already pulling him away from the wall. Gus didn't resist. Couldn't resist. He felt boneless, tender all over and swallowing blood, and for some reason, he wasn't seeing so good.

Then he was at the door and pushed against the frame.

The Leather took charge, still holding the Ramfist. She checked the hallway again.

"You in there?" she asked him.

Gus winced and nodded.

"You kill anyone else in here?"

Another nod, but his throat stung, and a quick check showed blood on his hands.

"How many? Can you remember?"

"Uhh, four? Five, maybe? With one outside, and one . . . in the lobby?"

"You sure?"

"Yeah. I think so."

"You got any more shells for this thing?"

Gus nodded, still functioning at a trickle of comprehension. He reached for the extra magazine and pulled out the Glock instead. The Leather froze at the sight of the sidearm and drew back a step. Gus realized he had a gun on her, realized there was a good chance the shotgun was empty.

"Remember," she said. "I could've let him kill you."

"Yeah," he said back.

"But I didn't."

Which was true. "Why didn't you?"

She held up a cautious hand. "Look, we don't have time for this. The good news is you killed them all. Everyone at the hotel is dead. Okay? We're the only ones left. The *bad* news is there's still one crew out there. And the guy leading them is a stone-cold killer, who will be tremendously *pissed* by what's gone down here tonight. That crew could show up here any second. *Any* second. Got it? They might be pulling up to the outer gate right now and wondering why there's no one letting them in. So. Let's get away from here *first* . . . and catch up on shit *later*, which doesn't really matter *now*. That sound good?"

Halfway through her little speech, a wave of wooziness swarmed Gus, and his knees wobbled enough that he dropped the Glock. His head slumped forward and he barely had the strength to stay vertical. Interestingly enough, the Leather didn't grab for the weapon, but when she finished talking, he realized, somehow, that the gun wasn't in his hand anymore.

She had it, and it bewildered the fuck out of him.

Even more interesting, however, was that she offered him the shotgun. "Take this."

Gus did so, regretting it as the weapon felt like fifty pounds.

"Here we go," she said, and pulled him along by the shoulder, until he was ahead of her.

"Go straight," she ordered, her hand pressed between his shoulder blades. Gus limped ahead, his head throbbing, mouth and throat hurting, and pretty much everything below the neckline aching. Even a not-so-mysterious buttery sensation between his ass cheeks he didn't want to think about. The good news was, with all that new and tormenting pain, his fucked-up heel didn't bother him so much.

"Stop," she said, holding onto his vest. She turned him to a wall. The wall opened, and he realized it was the elevator.

She pushed him in before he could suggest the stairs.

Gus staggered into a corner and there he stayed, bent over and taking the time to massage his jaw. Something wasn't right there, so he stuck a finger in, and discovered two missing molars in the back, upper-right side. When he pulled his finger out, blood coated it right down to its base. More dropped to the floor, in dollar coin dollops.

The Leather examined him as a mortician might, tapping the Glock against her thigh. "Still with me?"

Took a second, but Gus nodded, and felt his face.

The elevator doors opened. He didn't even feel the thing touch down. The Leather stayed back, aiming left then swinging to the right before stepping out of the lift. There she stopped and glanced back at him. "This way."

Gus came to, but not in time to respond.

"You coming or what?" she asked.

He heard her that time and nodded, his neck warning him not to do that too often. So he straightened, taking the pain, and lumbered out—banging a shoulder off the frame hard enough to nearly wipe out again. He mashed his face against the frame and stayed there, until the doors tried to close and nudged his forehead.

Gus didn't even have the juice to swear, but somehow, he got out of the elevator.

The Leather had already circled the blood pool of the corpse on the tiles. Gus trudged right on through, heedless of the mess and growing woozier with every step. The cold air revived him a little, and when they were outside she turned to him.

"You drive up in that?" she asked.

The pickup.

Gus nodded.

The Leather went to the driver's door and tried to open it. "Got the keys?"

Gus fished for them in his pockets, eventually locating them. He held them out with his hand with the missing fingers. The Leather took the fob without comment and opened the doors.

"Get in," she ordered yet again. "I'll drive if you don't mind."

Not at all, Gus thought. Not right now, anyway. He leaned heavily against the machine as he made his way around it, but when the passenger door was in sight, the world went wobbly once again. He slid down, until his knees hit the snow, and bowed until his head touched ground.

"You are a mess," a voice said.

A croak of metal, a sensation of flight, and somehow, he was magically sitting aboard the truck, the duffel bag stuffed into his lap. A seatbelt strapped him in place, yet he had no memory of doing it. A loud bang roused him, but when he looked, his door was already closed, the bus closing off the parking lot had been moved, and the Leather was behind the wheel.

She glanced over. "You smell like shit."

Gus didn't comment because the truck reversed, lurching him forward. The seatbelt held him in place, but the force was hard enough for him to bare whatever teeth he had left. Then the truck rocketed forward and he was thrown back into his seat. That was enough for the frayed circuitry of his consciousness to *snap crackle kerplop* before everything went black. When he opened his eyes again, they were on the open road, but they'd stopped. He looked over at the driver, who was bent over the steering wheel in a display of deep thought.

"Huh? Whad-I-do now?" he asked weakly.

The Leather spared him a glance. "I have to make a detour," she said. "And it might endanger us. Will certainly take a couple of hours."

Gus barely heard any of that.

"Yeah," she said. "Thought so. All right. We go. You just stay there. Get your marbles back, if that's possible. When you wake up, we'll talk. Sound like a plan?"

But he was already going under again, out before his chin dropped to his chest. He floated, but it wasn't bump free. Sometime later, he wasn't sure when, the pickup slowed to a stop, and he managed to lift his head.

"Mind if I keep this for a while?" she asked, holding up the Glock. Her voice had a painful reverb which caused havoc in Gus's skull. Nor did he have the capacity to answer her.

Then a strange thing happened, something he was powerless to stop. The Leather reached across the arm rest and placed a surprisingly warm, comforting hand against his forehead. She pushed him back, gently but forcefully. She leaned over, peering intently into his eyes, examining his face. Once finished, she withdrew and let him be.

Then she was gone in a rush of cold air and a door slam.

Fuck, Gus thought with widening eyes. He'd hitched a ride with a ghost.

In the glare of the headlights, she materialized before a padlocked gate.

Weird, he mused, and promptly passed out.

Something crashed in his personal dark, followed by the sensation of movement. That brought him back, and he realized he'd slumped forward, mashing himself against the uncomfortable lump that was the duffel bag. The Ramfist and HK rifle were both lodged against his door, which was surprising. And he believed the Leather was right. He just might've shit himself. Certainly a s*hart*—which was when a person wasn't sure if he'd shit himself or simply farted. He'd have to investigate at a later time.

A boom jolted him, rocking him in his seat.

The Leather stopped the truck and got out. She faced the rear, looking back, as bright light danced across her profile. She stood that way for moments, with one hand on the door. An even greater flash of light across her mask and night sky, followed by a series of faraway pops that might've been gunshots. Then the brightness subsided, but the explosions continued.

A confused Gus looked into his side mirror and blinked.

There was a fire back there. Many fires, in fact, flaring up like tall geysers, illuminating a burning kingdom of pipework, containers, and other structures unknown to him. All behind that high steel mesh fence.

The door slammed and the Leather—back in the driver's seat—placed the Glock in the nearby cup holder. Seconds later, they were on the move again.

"Can't tell you how satisfying it was to do that. A real rush. I had to do it, you understand. Had to blow it up. All of it. If I didn't, they still would have had the capacity to produce and refine without me. I was just the overseer, but enough of them had watched me to understand the process, the steps needed, to keep the Dog Piss flowing. It was mostly automated, anyway. This way, it's *gone*. Now and forever. And all they have left is *all* they have left. Once that's gone, that's it. Unless they can find some electric rigs. Even then . . ."

She quieted, sparing glances at her mirrors, but kept on driving.

"Three hours," she said in a much more subdued tone. "Back to the hotel. Once we drive by it, that is. Just understand, it had to be done. I just hope we don't see them and that they don't see us."

"You . . . blew something up?" Gus finally asked.

The Leather glanced over. "Hook really messed you up. You probably have a concussion. And yeah. I blew up the site. Been planning to do it for months, really. Easy when you know the system. The dos and don'ts. Part of the master escape plan. But the original plan was for *me* to be standing in the middle of it all when it all went up. That plan changed. Because of you. I mean . . . how'd you do it?"

They hit a series of potholes, which the truck cushioned, but the rattling motion got to Gus.

"Pull over," he lurched, gasping for air. "I'm gonna be sick."

"You mean puke?"

Gus was already fumbling for the door latch.

The truck decelerated rapidly, but he couldn't wait. The meagre meal in his guts wanted out. So he opened the door over moving ground, and spewed a great multicolor jet. When he was done, he stayed that way, hanging there, letting the cold air work its magic.

"You're definitely concussed," she said in a worried tone. "Feel better?"

"Muh . . . might be. Need . . . a second."

Which she granted.

How much time actually passed, he didn't know, but eventually Gus leaned back and pulled the door shut. When he did, she started driving again, and he rested his weary head against the window. And slept.

17

Two and a half weeks earlier.

Snow fell around the campsite, great fluffy chunks floating on the barest of breezes, calming and pleasing to the eyes. The Rocky Mountains filled the background, a grey and imposing ridge that fenced off the world. Low clouds obscured their peaks, but somehow that only lent a haunting, dare he say *forlorn*, majesty to the picture, which the Dragon appreciated even more. It made him want to snap a few photos. Better still, just drop everything and paint. Just paint. Landscape pictures. Like that dead guy used to do on PBS.

The Dragon tasted the cold winter air, breathed in a deep chestful of it, and studied those distant peaks with an artist's eye. Thoughts of his old life, when he would put a wet brush to canvas and attempt to re-create scenes like the grandly poetic one before him. Shrugging, he released the grip of one his claws, to adjust his ankle-length leather duster. Once done, he gripped the claw again—one of two very personal weapons consisting of a set of blades attached to a single cross grip. A forearm brace was attached for extra support and cutting power.

He stood with his legs just a touch wider before all that inspiring mountain glory, ignoring the men and women sniveling behind him. He barely heard their misery, their pleas for mercy. Didn't pay any attention to it, in fact.

When a pair of birds flew over the forest heights, he held his breath and watched until they dove for cover. The animals didn't take wing again, so he went back to gazing at the mountains.

Pretty, he thought. *So very pretty.*

The sight prompted a heavy sigh. He reluctantly turned, facing the first line of prisoners bound and gagged and kneeling before the closed lid of the tractor trailer. There were five of them on the roof, along with two Leather guards. Both had the dual scabbards of katanas strapped to their left sides. Their masks—one red, the other golden—depicted tusked Japanese demons called *Tengu*. They even wore matching pieces of samurai armor over their winter clothing—broad shoulder guards, armored sleeves, ribbed chest pieces, and matching skirts. The minions were called Red and Gold, or those were the names the Dragon gave them. Those two were history buffs—or rather, historical *war* buffs—and could name each individual piece of their samurai armor. Not that that knowledge impressed the Dragon. Frankly, he couldn't give a shit. As long as the armor worked. And kept Red and Gold in line. Happy, even, to be able to live out whatever fantasies of conquest played through their heads.

Once again, the Dragon didn't give a shit.

Red and Gold were not inflictors. They weren't commanders either. They were just two of a preferred half-dozen Leather the Dragon used on missions such as these . . . because they didn't mind doing whatever they were ordered to do. Kill, butcher, maim, disfigure, or blind. Weapons, power tools, basic tools, or just bare hands. If he called for it, they hopped to it. That was a psychopathic quality the Dragon very much appreciated. He hated to see hesitation when he gave an order.

"Please," one of the prisoners begged, and that alone surprised the Dragon, enough to attract his attention.

"Please," the man repeated, red-faced and teary-eyed. Messed up hair and blackened eyes. He rocked back and forth on his knees, hands tied behind his back with plastic cords. On the roof before him was a cloth gag, wet and ragged.

The Dragon cocked an eye behind his mask. Someone hadn't done their job. He conveyed that thought with the slightest look in the direction of his two minions.

Red stepped forward, admitting his guilt, and picked up the gag. With two fingers he stuffed that moist ball of fabric into the prisoner's face, turning the man a darker shade of red, his cheeks puffing and nostrils flaring to catch a breath. When Red was done, he slapped the prisoner's head hard enough to splay the man across the roof. Part of that was theatrics, the Dragon knew. Though Red was a powerful man, he wasn't powerful enough to knock a kneeling man flat. Not in the Dragon's mind. Then again, the whining little bastard did look in harsh shape.

Not that the Dragon gave a shit. He realized he felt that way about a lot of things.

Seconds later, and much to the dismay of the gathered Leather, that same prisoner spat the rag back out onto the roof.

That got on the Dragon's nerves. He delivered another telling look at the minions before slashing his hand across his throat and twirling it at the crowd below.

Understanding the sign, Red grabbed the offending prisoner by the armpits and hauled him to the trailer's edge. Roughly three dozen prisoners were assembled below, less than Trunk had reported, which annoyed the Dragon. Some of them were on their knees, most on their bellies, but all bound and gagged. At points stood just four Leather guards, but like Red and Gold, they were particularly fearsome. Unquestionably murderous. And possessing no qualms about breaking a person in two, if the need called for it.

One of them wore a steampunk mask, with scuba air tubes at the mouth and draped over the Leather's shoulders. That one wore a huge ankle-length duster that could very well have been bulletproof. They called him Slipknot.

Next was Slit, who was short but powerfully broad, similarly dressed in a leather duster, but his mask resembled more the standard plague variety, with huge black lenses covering his eyes. The minion held a double-bladed battle axe across his pelvis, his gloves armor-plated and spiked. Those emotionless black lenses scanned the group before him like they were caged rabbits on the verge of being butchered.

The third of the group was a tall troll of a man called Leech, with spiked shoulder pads over his own duster. A fanged lower jaw jutted from his masked face, where, like Slit, opaque lenses hid his eyes. A mace drooped from one fist as he watched for troublemakers. The mace bristled with chrome spikes. After an operation, Leech would sit quietly by himself, plucking free any organic matter stuck among the spines... before it started to stink.

The last of the Dragon's group resembled a worn and grizzled leather-wearing biker, complete with black helmet, sunglasses, and a facial muzzle decorated with a broad smile of vampire teeth. The man called Bonemaker cradled the only crossbow in the group, but like Red and Gold, a short katana hung low on his right thigh.

They stood around the prisoners. Only the four of them. Six in all, not including the Dragon. But he considered them an army, handpicked and kept very close to himself. In his mind, theirs was a very dangerous business, in a very dangerous world. People died all the time for whatever reasons, at the most unexpected times. They would *continue* dying at the most unexpected times. Even the Dog Tongue. The Dragon considered himself loyal to his liege and master, but in truth, he was not blindly devoted. Certainly not fanatical. The other inflictors were, and that was fine. Let them. No skin off the Dragon's ass. In his mind, fanaticism was short-lived, and he wanted to enjoy this new world and all its pleasures to the fullest. Now, he wasn't a traitor. Far from it. He would follow the Dog Tongue without question, but he wondered what would happen if—and when—the Dog Tongue died. Who would take the man's place? Certainly not any of the other inflictors, who were supposed to be physical incarnations of brute force, and extensions of the Dog Tongue's unbreakable will. Certainly none of the chosen commanders like the Samurai or the Vulture, all of whom could follow orders but ultimately lacked vision. None of the insane ones, like Vampire Joe and his heathen killers.

No, if he was still around, if he made it to the final level of the game, the Dragon intended to be the next leader of the Leather. The six executioners around him would be his new inflictors. When the time came, of course. And when it did, he would create a new order. In time, an empire.

After the Dog Tongue had fallen, of course. Until then, the Dragon would carry out his orders, like a good inflictor should.

Red stepped back from manhandling the prisoner to the edge of the trailer, where the sobbing man's knees left bloody streaks. Seeing where he knelt only prompted the man to sob even louder. Red placed a hand on the prisoner's head and regarded the Dragon.

Who nodded in return.

The Dragon wasn't exactly sure of Red's or Gold's background. Not that it mattered. One thing was for certain, however. Of all the Leather, they were experts with their swords. Perhaps even masters.

Red released the prisoner's head, which bobbed on shuddering shoulders. The Leather bent his knees, squared up his stance, and gripped one of his katanas.

Sensing danger, the uncooperative sniffler glanced back and his eyes widened. *"No! Wait—"*

Where it ended, because Red pulled his katana and swept the prisoner's head from his shoulders in one broad cut. The decapitated body toppled from the trailer, a thick jet of scarlet spewing from the neck. The corpse went splat at the bottom, crumpling upon frozen ground. There were a few muffled grunts. A few startled squeaks. One wailing scream of horror, quickly stifled.

In the end, there was silence.

With practiced grace one simply didn't see every day, Red held that finishing pose for seconds before straightening and running the flat of his blade across a sleeve. Once on each side as if folding it, before returning the weapon to its scabbard.

The Dragon didn't like insolence in the captured meat. He suspected that there would be trouble with more of them, and while he wasn't above making an example of one or two, it did cut into the bottom line.

"Into the pit," he commanded imperiously. "All of them."

Red and Gold got to work, and while they carried out their orders, the Dragon descended from the trailer's heights by way of a set of portable steps waiting at the side. His heavy boots clacked off the metal steps with each footfall, the sound carrying, his claws swinging.

Screams shot out from atop the trailer, alerting the others to the horrific fate awaiting them. There was squirming. Moaning. One man toppled over face-first, passed out from his own mounting terror. The woman beside him kept it together much better, shivering but not fainting away. The Dragon ignored them all as he stepped toward his own pickup, where his favorite weapon waited.

His pride and joy, really.

He unfastened his claws and dropped them on the lowered tailgate. After rubbing his wrists, he casually picked up the rifle-sized nozzle belonging to his flamethrower unit. The tanks were in the box bed and already opened, so he didn't need to fiddle with that. He cradled the nozzle, flipped the connecting tubing so that it hung just so, and aimed it at the collection of people. When he was ready, he gave the signal to Bonemaker and Slit.

They picked the nearest person, a woman, and lugged her to the top of the trailer.

The Dragon watched the rest, flamethrower at the ready, fingers flexing. What he couldn't convert, he sure as hell would cook. He sniffed, kept glancing toward the mountains, and shifted weight from one foot to the other. Seconds later, he ended his fidgeting with a soft clearing of his throat.

One of the prisoners spat out the rag jammed into his mouth. The Dragon saw it, sighed, and grimaced behind his mask. Seriously, there was simply no capacity for learning with some people. He motioned for Leech to intervene, and he hefted his dreaded mace and stalked through the crowd.

The Dragon brushed off a section of the nozzle and remembered something. Information. Some of these isolated settlements knew of the existence of others, perhaps in addition to the two places the now mindless Trunk had revealed. Places they perhaps traded and did business with, which was all fine and dandy. They would know, and would be very willing to disclose the whereabouts of any nearby settlements, especially after some torture. It would be messy, but that was the job, and the Dragon intended to gather up all the meat he could. To please the Dog Tongue. And to deflect any suspicion from the Leather's current warlord. Not that there was any at the moment. At least not in the Dragon's mind.

Just as Leech reached the chosen prisoner, the Dragon held up a hand, stopping his henchman like a well-trained dog.

Then he gave new orders.

18

The truck stopped again, and when the slamming door woke Gus, he squinted against the harsh glare of morning. The sun beamed down upon an open plain blanketed in snow, and the resulting diamond shine blinded him. Snarling, he reached up for the visor, pulled it down, and swung it over to shield his profile.

Seconds later the driver's side opened, and she pulled herself in. The following door slam was as good as a spike going through his ears.

"You have to do that?" he asked, none too pleased.

"Do what?"

"Slam the fuckin' door."

"I slammed it?"

Gus grunted *mm-hm*.

"Oh, sorry," she said. "Feeling better?"

"No."

"You're not sick though, right?"

"No."

"Got any more fuel?"

Gus regarded her, his mouth hitching in puzzlement.

"I just filled this brute," she explained. "Everything you had in the fuel cans. The Leather like the oversized tanks on their vehicles. Greater range, and cuts down on constant refueling. That's why you see a lot of trucks. There's bikes, too, but, anyway. I digress. So, the fuel in the rear—that's all that's left?"

"Yeah."

"All right." She started up the machine. "Got three-quarters of a tank. That's good for roughly thirteen hundred kilometers. It'll get us past Regina, and well into Alberta."

"Alberta?"

"If I can get us there." She checked her mirrors before getting the truck moving. "They will come after us. Especially after me. And if they find you, well..." She sliced a thumb across her throat. "If you're lucky. If you're unlucky, and you probably will be, they'll tie you to a bumper and drag you across the Trans-Canada. Until there's nothing left of you. I've seen it happen. Four times. You think folks would only need to see that once to stay in line. Nope. The Dog Tongue liked to give reminders."

Gus stared at her profile for long moments before the obvious question came to him. "Who are you?"

She didn't answer right away, then. "I'm the Chemist. I mean... well, that's what they called me. My real name's Maya. You call me that."

"Why'd they call you the Chemist?"

"I'm a petrochemical engineer."

Silence. Then, "What's that?"

"You know anything about low carbons? Low-carbon environments?"

"No."

"Global energy transfers?"

"No."

"Huh. Well, in a nutshell, I monitor active well performances and share technical observations with the on-site team to ensure yield quotas. I formulate and evaluate optimization strategies if we don't meet those quotas and plan reservoir efforts by developing forecasts and recoverable estimates. Depending on time, I'd assess reservoir performance, risk and reward, and any other uncertainties that might arise. I'd also monitor production and key performance indicators. Also, specifically, and most especially, I oversee the refinement of crude petroleum into viable, high-grade fuel sources."

Gus blinked. "Oh."

Maya checked her mirror. "Yeah, I get that a lot. In layman's terms, me make gas."

"You make gas."

"Yup."

"That's... all you had to say. You make gas."

"Dog Piss Premium."

"Excuse me?"

Maya shrugged and glanced over. "That's what we called it. I dabbled in other fields as well, picking up things as I went along. Learning from senior engineers and other people. Hell, you'd have to pick up a few things around our lunch table. With the chemical freaks and the lab rats. Even the sump pumpers."

Gus didn't know what they were, so he didn't comment.

"You're not into oil and gas?" she asked. "The industry, I mean?"

"Uh, no. I, ah, painted."

"Oh, an artist?"

"No. House painting." Gus held his pounding head. "Interior and exterior, ah, applications. Latex mostly. It was . . . cleaner."

"You a prepper or something?"

"No."

She studied him, her eyes narrowed. "How did you do it? Kill the Dog Tongue?"

"I didn't," Gus admitted. "The person I was with did it."

"You were part of a group?"

"Just the three of us."

That caused Maya to do a double take. "*Three* of you? Three of you killed the Dog Tongue? In Regina? And his army?"

This time, it was Gus's turn to shrug.

"You don't mess around," Maya exhaled and smiled. "You killed the Dog Tongue."

"I was with a couple of soldiers. One was special forces. The other was a sniper. The special forces operator, she . . . had an idea. She used the mindless against the Leather, wiped them out with their own zombies."

"She turned the Dog Tongue's mindless on him?" Maya asked in amazement, taking a few seconds to absorb the concept. "Oh wow. I would have loved to have seen that. From a distance, of course. You know the Mallet? That was our handler. He sent messengers down to the Four Towers."

"I killed them. Most of them. One got away."

Another look. "That was *you*?"

Gus didn't say anything to that.

Maya shook her head. "When our guy got back—the one who got away—well, he had the Dog Tongue's head. Can you imagine that? Dude brought back his head. To prove the Dog Tongue was, in fact, deceased. No one would have believed him otherwise. We were stunned when we saw that thing. I mean *stunned*. Jaws dropped. The Mallet was speechless. And then the report that everyone else was dead? Oh my! That was the main force. Well, all the reserves. The Dog Tongue had brought everyone, pulling every able body from his assets in BC."

Gus rubbed his head. "Why'd he do that?"

Maya shook her head. "Who knows? Only the Dog Tongue knew. And no one dared to ask him. Ask questions around him and people risked being killed. Sometimes even tossed into a trailer and transformed into a mindless. That was the worst. We—*they* always needed them. I have bad news for you, though. There are two other armies out there. Both heading east."

Prodding his face with a finger, Gus shook his head. "No . . . we got those, too."

It was a good thing the road was plowed and empty as Maya was clearly distracted by the news.

"Okay, *wait*. Wait. Let me hear that again . . . you're saying . . . you destroyed all *three* army groups?"

Gus tongued the holes of his missing teeth and nodded.

"All three. Including the trailers full of mindless?"

"All of it," he answered. "Living. Unliving. Gone. There's nothing east of Regina."

That stunned her into silence.

"Unless there are some little pockets left," Gus added.

"None," Maya said, coming out of her daze and sounding relieved. "The East was the last frontier. The plan was roll over it, absorb what we needed, replenish the ranks of mindless, and then, after the Dog Tongue consolidated everything and the time was right, we'd turn south. Invade the States. Or what was left of it."

"Isn't there a wall of radiation or something down that way?"

"Word was the Dog Tongue knew a way down there. Don't ask me. I'm glad he's dead. Beyond words, really."

"That why you saved me?" Gus asked.

Maya took a moment to process that before shaking her masked head. "I didn't. I saved myself."

"So . . . why am I still alive?"

"One good deed deserves another."

His head hurting, Gus quieted for a few seconds. "So, if there's nothing east and nothing north or west . . . why are we running?"

Maya dipped her head. "We're running because . . . before the messenger came back with the Dog Tongue's head, we'd received—well, the Mallet received and then killed the guy—information about two small settlements. The Leather usually wait and infiltrate before opening the gates from the inside. Or they identify the water supply and dump a few mindless in there, to contaminate and infect the settlement's inhabitants. Once they even launched the decapitated head of a mindless over a wall. Can you imagine? Or sometimes, they just roll up, engines revving in a show of power, and intimidate the people into surrendering. With all the Leather movement going on, and seeing we were off the beaten track so to speak, the Mallet decided to let one of the inflictors run a solo operation. With a small group of handpicked killers."

Gus's head started hurting even more.

"They left roughly three weeks back. Haven't seen them since, but that's not unusual. If it went to a siege, well, sieges take time. Contaminating a water source takes time as well. Same for releasing gas clouds, to make people too sick to fight. Whatever option they employ, after all is said and done, they might just camp out for a few days. Or they might get a lead on some other place where there's survivors, and make a move on them, depending on their strength. See where I'm going with this?"

Gus saw. "Could they be dead?"

Maya held up a finger. "Slim chance but yes, a possibility."

"Why slim?"

"Because I know the monster that offered to go get those people. He's an inflictor. You know about them?"

"Not much."

"Well, they're the Dog Tongue's personal bodyguards, who he'll deploy within certain groups just to ensure loyalty amongst the troops. Because I was here, making fuel, there were two assigned to us. We were deemed to be too off the beaten track to participate in maneuvers, but too important to leave unprotected. You understand?"

"Yeah," Gus said.

"Well, those two assigned to me were perhaps the most vicious of the whole bunch. They made sure I was good while keeping an eye on the commander. Even the Mallet wouldn't make a decision without first consulting them or the Dog Tongue, because if he made a move without permission, they would kill him. And then there was Vampire Joe in Regina. Did you kill him, too?"

"Guy with his face painted?" Gus asked. "Had an English accent?"

"Fake English accent."

"We killed him."

Maya hesitated in a moment of shock. "Well done," she said, trying to keep the awe out of her voice. "Okay then. All that's left is the group still out there. And they could return anytime, which is why I'm speeding here."

"And he's bad?"

"Bad? That's the understatement of the century. Like I just said, they're two of the most vicious individuals I'd ever encountered, and I kept my mouth shut as much as possible around them. The one who did the job on you? He was called the Hook, for reasons I think you'll remember. The other one? Gone hunting? He's called the Dragon. Both would bite your testicles off. But one would actually force you to have a bite."

That chilled Gus. "Which one did you shoot?"

"The one who would just bite your nuts off."

". . . Great."

"And that one will be after us," Maya finished.

Wonderful, Gus thought, again tonguing the holes of his missing teeth. "Called the Dragon, you say?"

"Yeah."

"Why the scary names? Why not Lenny? Hm? Or Sharla? Or, or *Ian* or something?"

"The Dog Tongue gave them their names. I don't know the thought process behind it. Maybe symbolic. Or based on what they reminded him of."

"And the Dragon reminded Dog Shit of a dragon?"

Maya chuckled and the sound, tinged with a hint of smoker's cough, caught Gus off-guard. There was an actual person under that mask.

"Good one," she said. "And so true. That guy . . . that *monster*."

"I swear to sunny Christ this is makin' my head hurt more," Gus said, holding his forehead. "All right, so this Dragon will come after us. Because you shot his buddy and blew up some property."

"Oh, yes."

"Maybe he'll just think you're dead?"

"Always a chance."

"But you don't think so . . ."

She shook her head. Then, without warning, she reached up and clawed at some of the bindings of her mask. One buckle came free with a rip. Then another.

"Take the wheel," she said. "Just for a few seconds. Can you do that?"

Gus did, reaching over and holding onto the wheel. As he steered, Maya removed the rest of her leather mask. When she was done, she tossed the thing into the back seat and regained control of the vehicle.

"Thanks," she said. "Just realized I didn't need to wear that thing anymore."

". . . Yeah." Gus didn't know what to expect to see, but he certainly didn't expect what he was staring at now. Her hair was red and shorn close to the skull like Collie's. Probably to better fit the mask. Blue eyes, puffy and needing sleep. Average nose. What really got his attention, however, was the full bloom of scars and raging acne covering her features. A dark, rough patch of wheel-like bumps reached around the base of her neck as well.

"Not polite to stare," she said.

Gus blinked and looked away. "Sorry."

"It's the mask. We wear them all the time. Only time we don't is when we're in our rooms. The amount of irritation your skin endures. The dermatitis. It's terrible. Worse in the summer when heat rash hits. I've overhead some say they got blisters, which eventually broke open and oozed. That's when things get really serious. The infections? Oh *man*."

"Bad?" Gus asked.

"Oh yeah. *Terrible*. Worse since we can't secure any prescription drugs. Hydrocortisone. Antihistamines. What expired medications we found only worked a little anyway. What I wouldn't give for a tube of aloe vera. Moisturizers work but you have to keep the mask off for it to do any good. No sick days in the Dog Shit's ranks. It's march or die. Or get chucked into a trailer."

"Holy shit. So why are you one of them?"

Maya's head swiveled about so fast Gus might've heard it crick.

"I wasn't one of them. I was never one of them. Not really. I . . . I just made the gas. I convinced the Dog Shit I was too important for all the other shit, and that worked for a while. But I never . . . I didn't . . ."

And that's when it happened.

That's when Maya's lower lip trembled. She clenched her jaw to steady it, bore down hard, screwing up her lips, and concentrated on driving. Sniffing every now and again, to drain her sinuses.

She couldn't stop the tears, however, which ran down her inflamed cheeks.

The trip became a quiet one after that, as Gus decided to keep his mouth shut. Maya continued driving, regaining control over herself and staying silent, until they rolled toward what looked like a small city.

"North Battleford," she announced and nodded. "Fastest route is through. We got the plow but I'm not plowing shit if I can help it."

"Why's that?" Gus asked, his headache pounding once again.

"The Dragon will see it. Skull Road was meant to be like the old Roman road system. Marked and heading back to Vancouver. We . . . we just need to be careful for the next few days. Get far away from all this snow. Or at least hope for *more* snow, to cover our tracks."

"I could get out and shovel."

"You think? You don't look that great over there."

To be honest, Gus didn't feel that great. Which was an understatement.

"Our only hope is . . ." Maya cocked her head. "We drive and get someplace where there's no snow, then *keep* driving without fear of leaving any tracks. I mean, if we plow another road around here? They'll know it was us. And frankly, I don't think you're in any condition to shovel any snow."

Gus supposed not.

The city scrolled by without incident. After rolling through the dwindling burbs, the hotel fortress came into view, with its makeshift wall of transport trucks and sandbags.

Maya stepped on the gas and drove past it, glancing at the open gateway and the parking lot beyond.

"You see something?' Gus asked, rubbing at a temple in an attempt to alleviate the pounding inside his skull.

"No. I just want to be gone from here as soon as possible. Well, *shit*. I didn't blow the other tanker. Goddammit. Not like I'm making this shit up on the fly. Well . . ." she fumed, clearly mad at herself while vacillating. "Nope. Not going back. No way. God-*damnit*."

"We could fight them," he suggested with a wince.

"You sure about that? You can't shovel snow but you think you're up for another fight?"

Knowing he most certainly wasn't, he sank back in his seat and stared at the road. His attention drifted to the Glock, barrel tucked down in the cup holder, then at Maya's profile. Worse, his head really started to ring. Then he studied her again, for a few seconds more, until she met his gaze.

Grimacing, he looked back to the road.

"You okay?" Maya asked.

"Headache's getting worse."

"Then you rest," she said. "I'm surprised you're still conscious to tell the truth. I'll let you know if anything happens. Otherwise, I'll wake you up when we get somewhere safe. Or at least safer."

Gus thought about that. Someplace safe. Was there a safe place left in this world? He wondered. He stole one last glance at his Leather—*ex*-Leather companion—with her terrible rash. He could barely believe it. She was a Leather. Part of the same pack of road savages that had taken everything from him. She was also a Leather trying to escape, and what convinced him was that she'd saved his ass when he was on the verge of having his neck wrung. She could have very easily shot him and be done with it, but she wanted out of the Dog Tongue's nightmare.

She'd saved his life.

Saved by one of the Leather.

Maybe his headache wasn't from getting his ass kicked after all.

He closed his eyes and tried to relax. Then he was asleep.

*

"Hey," Maya said, waking him up after what only seemed like seconds. "Does it get any better than this?" she asked while pointing.

Gus came to his senses, rubbed at his battered face and immediately regretted it. He tried to widen his eyes, to see what she was pointing at.

At a scene he remembered from the previous day.

A cleared two-lane highway. Abandoned pickup and snowmachine. They were at the road's end, facing a wide heap of plowed snow, and beyond that, a landscape that resembled an Antarctic icefield. The wind had picked up, blowing ephemeral sheets across the surface. Just looking at it gave him chills, despite the warm interior of the truck.

"No," he answered. "It's like this all the way to Regina. Then it gets worse."

"You could have mentioned this earlier. Ideally when I was talking about leaving a trail in the snow."

"Yeah . . . Sorry."

Maya sat back and sighed. "Well, shit."

"Anchor Bay is there," Gus suggested. "We could hole up. Make a stand . . ."

"And it would be a last stand," she countered. "Because they would find us and come at us hard."

"We have the guns."

"Have you looked at yourself? They'll send in the mindless first. That's what they do. They'll corner us and wait us out. I don't like our chances. Shit. Shit, shit, *shit*. This is becoming amateur hour. Let me think."

Gus waited, wondering just how bad he looked. There was a mirror set into his sun visor, but he didn't bother to check himself out. It would only demoralize him. Every time he spoke, he felt the tightness in his swollen face.

"All right," she said, looking around as if searching for an escape hatch. "We turn this around and backtrack. First road I find, we take it. Plow it. *Shit*. I hope this thins out enough so that we can lose them on an open road. We don't stop unless it's to take a leak. Sound good?"

"And if they catch up to us?"

"Then we fight, just like you want to. We use your guns. It'll probably come down to that, anyway. And for the record? I'm a terrible shot. I used that cannon of yours on the Hook, but that was close range. Lucky all I had to do was pull the trigger."

Lucky indeed. "Let me do the shooting, then," Gus said.

"You're not seeing double?"

He shook his head.

"Don't be insulted by what I say next, but you look like . . . shit. Battered shit. Like, I'm surprised you're not dead, level of shit."

Gus didn't argue the point. "Drive on, then."

Maya whipped the rig around. Then they were headed northwest again, with her scanning the roadsides for any indication of a missed road.

"There's a crossroads somewhere along here," she said, mostly to herself, before braking hard, much to Gus's discomfort. "I know it. Passed it enough times. So hard to see with all the snow. Wait. There. Right *there*. That look like a highway to you?"

Gus looked.

Right outside his window, no, he couldn't see it. All he saw was a plowed-up mass of snow along the roadside. But in the distance, there was one of those small forests that sprouted up out of nowhere. That particular forest had a clearing straight down the middle of it. Although the land there was buried, it was wide enough for a highway.

"See the signs?" Maya was pointing, her gloved hand stretched out right before Gus's nose. "Road signs? There and there?"

He sat up a little more. The signs *were* there. Two of them. Small white ones high above the snow, perhaps displaying speed limits. Easy to see when you're looking for them.

"Yeah, I see them."

"Hold on." Maya hit the gas. They surged along the highway to where she thought the highways intersected each other. Then she slowed the rig down and turned, lining up the plow with a snowbank perhaps three feet high.

"Brace yourself," she said, working the joystick controls and lowering the blade.

The pickup charged the snow.

And hit dead on, the impact shoving Gus forward then back. A fine spray freckled the windshield, but the truck plowed through.

"All right," Maya said, bent over the wheel.

The pickup listed to the right, off the paved shoulder and hit crushed stone, which they both knew right away. Maya righted the machine.

"Note to self," she said. "Stay on the road."

"That's a good note," Gus said and checked his side mirror. A black strip trailed behind them, growing longer by the second.

They quieted then. Gus leaned into his door, watching snow shoved aside in the wake of the blade. As for the actual sides of the road, he was unable to see a damn thing.

Ahead, the forest loomed underneath a darkening sky.

19

That same morning, as Maya and Gus were steaming their way for Regina, the Dragon rose, stretched, and went through his morning ritual, like any normal person preparing for another day at work. He washed his face from a shiny bathroom basin, cleaned his armpits, and took a dump (no TP, so he wiped with water and his own bare hands). He ate a bottle of preserved plums for breakfast and washed it down with a glass of sugary purple drink, then donned his work clothes while going over his to-do list.

The second settlement they'd been informed of was short on people but long on comfort. Trunk had embellished the size of the town yet again, which further annoyed the Dragon. The prick had lied, no doubt to squeeze an even greater amount of goods out from the Leather. The Dragon was glad the mercenary was now one of the mindless. Served him right.

As it was, it only took a night raid to subdue the two-dozen inhabitants of the sleepy little strip of cabin country, and by afternoon, they'd all been lowered into the trailer. The Leather kept back two, however, for a session of stern questioning, with the goal of discovering any other hidden pockets of humanity in northern Alberta. Evidently, there were not, based on the amount of physical punishment both prisoners endured. Oh, they were defiant, like some others, but only until the Leather started playing piano with their bare toes. With a hammer. Brutally simple and a hundred percent effective. By the time Leech had completed his sonata on the first victim, the other one was more than ready to answer any questions. A shame the only place they knew about was the one the Leather had already taken. Both prisoners went into the trailer with the others after their interrogations. The mindless could still walk on mashed toes. Didn't bother them.

With two successful raids under his belt and his trailer half filled with roughly sixty new recruits for their mindless forces, Dragon felt a little R&R was due. So when their little convoy sighted a nearby town off the main highway, the inflictor ordered his driver—Slipknot—to head for the little prairie oasis. The town, called Catty River, was a scattering of houses around a gas and service station, a Rosie's Grocery, a medical center, and, apparently, the world-renowned Catty River Bed-and-Breakfast, which could accommodate half a dozen guests.

The Dragon claimed the B and B for himself, while his underlings took up residence in the neighboring homes.

The whole crew stayed in Catty River for a few days, living off the victuals of their recent conquests. The Dragon might've stayed longer, in fact, so comfortable was he, but it had snowed the day before, reminding him that winter was creeping in and that it was getting on time to return to base.

Which was that morning.

Rested, cleaned, and fed, the Dragon pulled on the leather mask with his namesake. He then wrapped a scarf around his throat, checked himself in a mirror, and nodded at the sheer badassness he radiated. Intimidation was half the battle.

Ready to kill the day, he went to the front door.

When the Dragon stepped out of the world-renowned Catty River Bed-and-Breakfast, he stopped and stared.

Snow. Perhaps half a foot of it on the ground.

The Dragon sighed. Vacation time was over.

A wisp of exhaust drifted past him. His minions were already warming up the machines. Three pickups, the Dragon's own semi, the tanker carrying the convoy's fuel, and the mobile stairs taken from an airport hangar, to allow egress and ingress from a plane. The transport truck hauled both the stairs and the trailer filled with mindless, and included a very comfortable sleeper cab, which the Dragon claimed as his own.

With a grunt, he hauled himself up into the passenger side of the cab. He closed the door and squirmed until comfortable. Once situated, he stared ahead with a depressing sigh, spying the snowy road that would eventually take them home. Two of the pickups pulled out ahead of the transport, lowering their plows and clearing the way in a creamy wave that fell upon the shoulders.

"Ten centimeters down, at least," Slipknot quietly reported. "Give or take a notch."

And five hours to get home, the Dragon thought, keeping that one to himself. Instead, he drew in a great deep breath.

"All we need is some Christmas music," Slipknot said.

That earned him a look.

Taking the hint, Slipknot released the airbrakes, shifted, and got the trailer moving.

The Dragon reached down and adjusted his seat, leaning back until he got it where he wanted.

The snowdrifts deepened. The clock showed 4:46 by the time the grey-black crown that was North Battleford came into view. The Dragon eyed the dark city over the pickups clearing the road and honestly looked forward to getting back. Looked forward to showing off the bounty of a successful mission. Looked forward to seeing the Mallet squirm from his successful foray, if only for a little bit, and certainly looked forward to receiving praise from the Dog Tongue.

But most of all, he looked forward to seeing the Chemist. Very much so. Behind his mask, a little smile spread across his face. Thinking of the Chemist did that to him.

Not twenty minutes later, upon much-improved roads, they were rolling up to the makeshift fortress wall. The closer the Dragon got, the more attentive he became, until he moved his seat to an upright position and simply gawked. Disbelief flooded his person.

The gate was wide open and there were no sentries on the wall.

The lead pickups drove into the inner courtyard, while Slipknot did the same, slowing down and steering on through.

The sight of the destroyed entrance stiffened the Dragon. A second later he spotted the dead Leather spattered across the snow-frosted asphalt, fallen in front of the buses. The transport slowed to a stop in a chuff of airbrakes, and the Dragon couldn't get out fast enough, his heavy leather coat swishing around his ankles.

Red and Gold were already moving on the wrecked entrance. The Dragon followed them to the steps and stopped, spying two shotgun casings, dark against the snow. He quickly snatched them up, brooded over their implications, and then hurried into the lobby.

Red and Gold stood over the second Leather, shot dead like the first, lying in his own gore sprayed far and wide across the tiled floor. The smell was strong, stomach-turning, telling the Dragon this was a *recent* killing. One boot tap to the dead Leather, resulting in very little movement, told him rigor mortis had taken over.

Maybe a day at least, but no more.

The rest of the Dragon's crew arrived on scene and beheld the corpse.

"Go," the Dragon commanded.

Weapons already out, the Leather went.

Not sparing another moment, the Dragon marched to the office of the Mallet. He didn't expect to see the man alive, but when he found the door open, he edged inside and stopped in his tracks.

Nothing out of order. Except, there, on the desk, was a bag. A reusable shopping bag, green in color, with one side of the thing drooping, to reveal the dull curvature of what looked like leather. Glancing around the Mallet's office and seeing it empty, the Dragon advanced to the desk. He peeled the edge of the bag down a little further, enough to see what was inside. Once he did, the Dragon froze, the sight shocking. When his disbelief subsided, he reached in and extracted the head of the Dog Tongue.

The skin was a dull blue-grey, but there was no mistaking the face—the lower jawline drizzled with stubble. No mistaking the warlord's executioner's mask either, which he still wore. What was disturbing, besides the decapitated head of the Leather's warlord, and the fact the body was nowhere in sight, was the broad cleft down the center of the Dog Tongue's skull, and the putrid, chalky white pudding dried out inside.

The Dragon placed the head on the desk. There he stared at it for a few seconds longer, his mind spinning with the implications. Then, as if getting a whiff of bad air, he grabbed the head and stuffed the thing back into the shopping bag.

The Dog Tongue was dead. What did that mean?

What *did* it mean?

He whirled in a flourish of leather and headed for the fifth floor.

To the Chemist's room.

There, Red and Gold were already waiting, swords ready. The door to the room had a shredded hole in it the size of a manhole cover. A second door—the Mallet's room—was open just up from the Chemist's. The Dragon, feeling the drop in temperature, dreaded to see what lay inside. The cold air hit him as he entered. There, below a fluttering set of curtains still hanging off the window, was the Mallet. The leader was clearly dead, crumpled in a heap. His one side had been blasted away in a massive bite from a shotgun, further evidenced by more spent casings. The room had been trashed, showing all the signs of a heavyweight fight having gone down. Gone down badly for the Mallet.

A handheld crossbow lay discarded on the floor, between the bed and wall. The Dragon picked it up, recognizing it as belonging to the Chemist. Her only weapon. Discharged. The bolt nowhere in sight. He glanced around, ignoring Red and Gold standing guard at the front door, their swords lowered, their samurai armor gleaming in the sparse light.

Then the Dragon saw the teeth.

In the corner, underneath the window, not too far from the dead Mallet. A meat hook was on a nearby cabinet, which was puzzling. A second meat hook lay before the smashed-out window. The inflictor walked to the spot, picked up the bloody teeth—a pair of molars—and studied their curved roots and golden fillings. He rattled them in his hand while he leaned out the window for a look. The courtyard was far to his left. Directly below, however, splayed out between a row of small trees protected from the weather by cloth sacks, was the unmistakable form of the Hook. The dead inflictor looked like he had caught a rocket with his chest, drenching everything nearby.

Fertilizer, the Dragon thought, and that was the only thought he had for his fellow bodyguard.

He whirled on the Leather behind him and held up the crossbow.

"Find her," he commanded through a set jaw.

They scattered.

An hour later, they reported back to the Dragon, who sat and waited in a sofa chair belonging to the room. He faced the window, holding the crossbow in one hand, while grinding the two discovered molars in the other. On the table was the shopping bag with the Dog Tongue's head, which the Dragon had retrieved from the Mallet's office. The grim trophy was well covered, but the Dragon could lean over for a quick peek if needed.

He glanced up when his minions stopped before him.

"She's not in the hotel," Red reported.

"Everyone else is dead," added Gold.

Grim news indeed. The Dragon squeezed the teeth. "All dead . . ." he repeated with a feigned note of regret. "And the Chemist is missing."

Then it came to him in a flash.

"The refinery," he growled.

They saw the smoke blanketing the sky long before they got there. Not long after, they smelled the smoke. Acrid and harsh enough for them to reach for the ventilation controls of their vehicles.

The refinery's gate was open, but everything beyond that was smouldering. The huge container tanks flashed fire, lost in that gauzy, tar-smelling smoke that withered and waved before drifting to the north. The on-site work and living modules resembled shattered eggshells, cupping still burning fires and well on their way to being razed to the frozen ground. Water pooled in places from melted septic systems. It was a small site, much smaller than some of the ones he'd worked on during his time in the oil patch, but it was invaluable to the Leather. Priceless. Perhaps even their greatest asset. All gone in a fiery ending. As he stood and stared, the harsh chemical smoke clawed at the Dragon's throat. A coughing fit took him, strong enough to bend him over. When he finished, red-eyed and tasting fumes, he retreated to the transport trailer and slammed the door shut.

There, he cleared his pipes again with a mighty effort, composed himself, and stared at the destroyed facility.

A grim Slipknot waited, drawing breath through his breathing tubes, unwilling to say a word. He stared ahead as well, his steampunk mask impassive, while he gripped the steering wheel of the big machine,

Time dragged on.

Which the Dragon eventually became aware of and twirled a finger. "Back to base," he ordered, ending his dismayed silence.

As the convoy's engines revved to life, the Dragon put aside the Chemist's crossbow and cupped the bloody back teeth. He shook them, shook them hard, as if they might reveal the answers he needed.

Who did this? Where are they? Where did they go?

Was she alive? Had they kidnapped her?

And that truly frightened him—she'd been abducted, and been taken far and away from him, never to be seen again.

It wasn't possible. He couldn't believe it.

No, he couldn't believe she was gone. Not the Chemist. She was perhaps the most important of the Leather. She possessed knowledge that rivaled—dare he say exceeded—the Dog Tongue's.

Whoever had killed off the Mallet and the Hook had also destroyed the refinery, striking at the beating heart of the Leather. Perhaps only a day or two ago. The enemy was also armed, with shotguns. That was fine. The Dragon had their shields with them. Police ballistic shields, used for herding the mindless, but more than capable enough of stopping a shotgun slug.

The Dragon realized he had only one place to go.

He leaned toward Slipknot, getting the driver's attention.

"Drive faster," the Dragon advised in a tone not to be debated.

He had to see Vampire Joe. In Regina. Once he did that, he could search for the Chemist and the ones responsible for the destruction of the refinery. And the deaths of the Mallet and the other minions, his Leather companions. For his own sanity, he allowed himself to hope—beyond all hope—that the Chemist was still alive.

On impulse, he squeezed the molars in his hand.

20

Nighttime—the world buried in a moonlit cream, seen over the steel upper lip of the plow fixed to the pickup. A steady deluge of curds fell to the side, pushed out of the way by the machine's momentum, leaving a single cut in the snow. They had passed through the forest perhaps an hour ago. The trees had thinned out in the dying red glow of the truck's taillights, until they disappeared entirely.

Gus hunched forward, his fatigue replaced by nervousness. They were crawling along, listening to the plowing, scrubbing asphalt rather than seeing it. It was the only way they knew they were still on the road, as there was no other point of reference between the speed limit signs. The land remained flat, the pavement a straight strip, so when Maya saw the speed signs, she accelerated just a little. Crushed stone raked the steel edge at times, until she altered course and got back on asphalt. It was loud when the plow made contact with the rocky shoulder, loud enough to alert just about anything that might be lurking on the prairie.

Like what? Gus asked himself, scanning the surrounding void. *People*, came back the answer. Cut off and surviving on their own, and potentially crazier than shithouse rats, with nuts and sprinkles.

"You gettin' tired?" he asked Maya.

She didn't answer. Leaning forward and watching the road, she hadn't said much since driving out into the great and awesome nothing.

"At least we're still on the highway," Gus said, filling that silence. He checked the dashboard clock. 8:04 p.m.

"Mary and Joseph," he muttered, and put a hand to his head.

"How you doing?" she asked, sounding tired.

"Head's not so bad. Not so loopy anymore. Don't need to throw up, either."

"All good," she remarked. "Try and stay back in your seat, will you? I can see better that way."

"You can see?"

"Not much, but everything counts. Unless you want to get out and walk on ahead."

"Think it'll help?"

Maya shrugged. "It'll slow us down even more, but it'll help. Which reminds me."

She lowered her window, flooding the interior with frigid air. She stuck her head out and peered ahead. After tolerating a few seconds, she pulled herself back in and raised the window.

"It's the coat, right?" Gus asked.

"Yeah, it's the coat. At least I *hope* it's the coat."

"I hope so, too." But he still had that buttery feeling between the ass cheeks.

"Just hope . . ." she trailed off, shaking her head. "Just hope we get clear of them."

"You still think they're coming . . ."

"Oh yeah. The Dragon wasn't around when we got the Dog Tongue's head. When he gets back to Battleford he'll go straight to the fort, and we both know what he'll find there. He'll find the Dog Tongue's head, along with the others. He won't find me. He'll order a search, which won't turn up anything. After that . . . he might go to the refinery. And he might not. Eventually he'll head south, to report to Vampire Joe. See where I'm going with this?"

Gus saw.

"He'll see the strip we cleared," Maya continued, "but might not investigate. Not right away. He *will*, though, when he gets to the Four Towers and discovers Vampire Joe dead and gone. Then he'll backtrack to where we turned off. That's a lot of time, however. We can hope for a snowstorm to blow in and cover our tracks."

A hot rock of doubt formed in his guts, but he didn't say anything.

"You killed the Dog Tongue," Maya marveled again, as if convincing herself. "That's amazing. I mean . . . I still can't believe it."

"Wasn't me."

"Still, he's dead."

"There's still a group of them out there," Gus reminded her.

"Yes."

"Couldn't they start another band of savages?"

Maya became pensive. "Without question. But it'll take time. A long time. Who knows what might happen."

Gus didn't like the sound of that. "Look . . . I'm getting better here. If you're so sure they'll be coming after us, then I tell you what. You've . . . obviously been through some serious shit. Why don't you let me out at the first house and drive on? Get away, free and clear? I'll take my guns, and I'll end the whole goddamn bunch of them."

"You're feeling that much better?"

"Oh yeah," he lied. What he'd said a moment ago was true enough, but that was probably because he was sitting in his seat. His head still felt like a piece of puffed rice, and there was pressure around his eyes, which were swollen. One prodding touch informed him of that. He was no longer tasting and spitting blood, so that was a plus.

"They could capture you," Maya said. "You'd tell them where I went."

"Except I won't *know*, because you'll have driven off into the night, right? And we're hoping for snow, correct? We get some of that and you could make your, your escape and . . ."

This time he trailed off. Where would she go? Where *could* she go?

Then again, if she dropped him off, it would no longer be his problem. All he wanted was a chance at finishing off the last of the Leather. Maya was considering it. He could tell just by looking at her. She had nothing to lose. Not really.

"We're square," Gus said, sweetening the idea. "I saved you—or I mean—*you* saved you. And you saved *me* in the process. So in my mind, we're even."

She nodded. "We are."

A row of highway reflectors rose up from the snow. They curved into the night, indicating one of those rare turns found on the prairie highways. Maya kept abreast of them and completed what seemed to be a very long and graceful arc, sloping upwards.

"Must be an overpass," she said, watching the things.

The reflectors streaked by, winking out as the headlights left them. Gus was about to speak when there was a spine-yanking crack up front that shot to the rear, whereupon the truck plunged into the night.

Gus screamed. Maya screamed. Stomachs crammed into throats. Hands flew wide, bracing for the worst. There was a split second of weightlessness, followed by a wall of snow rushing toward the windshield and a compactor crunch of metal. Gus and Maya lurched forward, smashing into airbags magically deploying in an explosive bang of fabric. Seconds of terror-filled grunting then, where their minds buzzed, frazzled by what had just happened. Then a *timber!* moment, as the truck pitched over onto its side, dry tumbling them in their seats for a final vicious cycle.

Neither had bothered wearing a seatbelt.

What was worse, Gus realized in a lightning bolt of terror, was that as they bounced, the unsecured Glock *bounced with them*, rattling, click-clacking off glass and fake wood in a terrifying, roulette table spin of chance. He tried tracking it, but lost sight, only to have the sidearm rebound across his temple and face.

Where, for a microsecond, he stared into the black and empty eye of the muzzle.

The truck fell on the driver's side and everything stopped with it. There they lay, panting, letting off little grunts and moans, wondering if the ride was indeed finally over. A contorted Gus was face deep into Maya's armpit, having slipped out from behind his airbag. He twisted, fighting the deployed cushion of air, shoving it away and squirming onto his back. He landed against the window, crammed against Maya, and pinning her arm underneath. The duffel bag full of supplies rested on top of them both.

She pulled and pushed at him and the bag while trying to free herself.

"*Christ* have mercy," Gus groaned, attempting to hoist himself off of Maya's trapped right arm. They untangled themselves, awkward to do with the inflated airbags. Gus extracted his knife and stabbed those meddlesome sacks, which deflated with flatulent puffs.

"Goddamn things," he swore, fighting the fabric. He relented and sheathed his knife once again. The duffel bag was next, and they shoved the heavy thing through the seats and into the rear. After managing that brief but strenuous feat, they still remained somewhat mashed together, enveloped by darkness.

There they stayed, gathering their thoughts, doing internal checks.

"You okay?" she eventually asked him.

Gus believed he was. He patted himself down, finishing with his boys, and sighed in relief. If anyone was going to get a gearstick shoved into their nuts, if there was even a remote *chance* of it, it would be him. "Yeah. You?"

Maya brought up her legs. "Yeah. Seems like everything is working."

Gus struggled to give her some room and failed miserably. Maya took the initiative and crawled over him, into the back seats. There she popped back into view.

"What the hell happened?" she asked.

"The *fuck* happened?" he corrected. "The pavement went out from under us."

"That's what I saw. I was in line with the reflectors. We had plenty of room."

"I thought we had plenty of room, too. Christ Almighty."

He squirmed a bit more, got one leg up over the armrest, and put a hand down, where the brake was. The cold contact of the Glock greeted his fingers.

"Little shit," he muttered and picked up the weapon. "Bad gun. *Bad* gun. Nearly shot me in the face."

"The thing flew by me, too," Maya said. "I hate guns."

"Yeah, well," Gus held the weapon and looked up. "Right now, I'd say it might be the one thing to get us out of here. Just a minute."

It took a little more contorting, but he wormed his way around the fronts seats until he got his legs underneath him. Then he stood, sort of, hunched over, and reached up and tried the door.

Wouldn't budge.

"Can't get it open?" Maya asked.

"Nope. But that's okay. I got this." He showed her the gun.

"You think that will do the trick? Use the shotgun."

That wasn't a bad idea either. Gus put the handgun aside and searched for the Ramfist. Thankfully, it had jammed itself underneath the glove compartment. He wrestled the weapon free, sized matters up, and regarded the window.

"What are you doing?" Maya asked.

"Checking the magazine. Empty. Wow. Okay, you got the duffel bag back there. Open it up and fish around for one of these."

Gus held up the empty magazine, barely visible in the cab.

A shuffling then, the sound of things being moved around. "Here."

He took the shadowy item and inserted it with a snap. Readied it and shied away from the dangerous end.

"Okay, look away and plug your ears," he told her while aiming at the glass.

Boom.

Glass pebbles rained down, dark glitter that reminded Gus of teeth for some reason. When he looked up, the glass was gone.

"Where's the window?" Maya asked.

"Probably in orbit somewhere. This thing packs a wallop."

"I've noticed."

"All right," he said. "I'll go first."

No easy feat. He got his elbows on the window frame and hoisted himself up and out, the effort taking more out of him than he wanted. Bent over the door, he lay there as snowflakes peppered his face. Took him a moment to realize it was snow, which resulted in a pained smile. Snow would cover their tracks. Well, if it got worse. But if it got worse and they were in the middle of nowhere . . .

"See anything?" Maya asked from below, interrupting his thoughts.

Gus looked around and did indeed see something.

The overpass.

Against the night, he could just make out the gaping hole that swallowed them, at least two truck lengths across. The thickness of the bridge was visible enough, as were the bent ends of rebar stalks, which collectively resembled a sagging net. Chunks of concrete spotted the road underneath, as well as two other vehicles that had previously crashed. One was a van, landed lengthwise, with a dark smudge on the top that might've been the exact width of their pickup.

Something else rested on a slant beside the van, but Gus wasn't sure what it was. A large flat sail of some sort.

"You working on something up there or . . . ?" Maya asked from below.

Gus knelt on the rear passenger window and motioned for Maya to pass up the duffel bag. Then the Ramfist and the HK assault rifle. He dropped everything on the ground below before helping her out of the wreck. Just pulling her out made him dizzy. Moments later, they stood in snow shin deep, examining the overpass and its crater.

"It's practically the whole width of the bridge," Maya said, pointing. "Structurally, these things are built to last years. Much better and cheaper than steel. But something . . . yeah . . . looks like it wasn't neglect. It was blown apart."

"Blown apart?" Gus repeated, struggling with the bag a few paces behind her.

"Yeah, you can see around the edges. Cleanly cut. Well, it's crumbly but not from erosion. This was a onetime punch that blew out a section of the bridge, and then . . . oh wow. Look at this."

Hard to look at anything, but his eyes had adjusted. Everything appeared a little lighter against the snowy backdrop. So when Maya walked over the van, she stooped and held up a wide, nearly square piece of material with one end splintered.

"Plywood," she announced, "Very thin. Certainly unable to take the weight of a vehicle." She dropped the wood and pointed at the bridge. "There are fragments still up there. See them? What is that? Is that . . . is that a support strut of some kind?"

She hurried over to the van, placed a hand against the roof, and kicked away another flimsy sheet of plywood. She then picked up what might've been a thick carpet, which she spread out at arm's length, and let drop.

"Oh my. You know what they did here?" she asked him, half-turning.

"Uh, no."

"Some scheming bastard saw this hole above us and figured, *this is a great place for a trap*, and proceeded to cover up the bridge with plywood and carpeting. Just like tossing a sheet over an open pit. So anyone driving over it . . ." She pointed at herself and Gus. "Would go splat."

"The fuck would they do that?" he bluntly asked, but he already knew.

Maya answered anyway. "Because there are some sick, predatory assholes out there these days, that's why."

Gus thought that a touch hypocritical, if not a little ironic. Or as Toby used to say, *ironical*. He didn't say anything about her being *part* of a small army of sick, predatory assholes, however, remembering her reaction from earlier. Seeing as she saved him, he elected to keep quiet.

Maya motioned for him to catch up while pointing at the rear of the van. The bottom door hung open, and the interior, which was a little harder to make out, appeared gutted.

Gus rooted through the duffel bag, found the heavy-duty flashlight, and was happy to discover it still switched on. He shone the light inside, revealing a pair of rear seats, a shelving unit, and nothing else of interest except for discarded food wrappings and containers.

"They took whatever they could find," she said and pointed at the other crashed rigs. "Bet those are looted as well."

"So, what are you saying?" he asked, waving the light around. "Someone might come looking for us?"

"Maybe. Switch that off. Conserve power. And just in case someone *is* still around."

Gus did so.

Maya shivered as she looked around. She reached into a pocket and pulled out her leather mask, which she then pulled over her face.

Gus watched her do so, a little surprised she'd still kept it.

"What?" she asked. "Oh. My face is cold. It's freezing out here. You don't have anything?"

"Threw mine away."

The mask stared at him, hiding her expression, which was probably one of *well, too bad for you*. On that thought, he hefted the bag over one shoulder, holding the Ramfist in one hand.

"You want me to carry any of that?" she asked.

"I'm good."

"You're walking like a train hit you."

"It's heavy."

"So, at the very least, take the guns out of it and allow me to carry the ammunition. If you don't trust me."

"I . . . said I'm good."

Maya watched him. "I can see you have trust issues."

"No, I don't," Gus said, facing her.

"Might I remind you I shot an inflictor to save you? One charged with protecting me? That's an automatic death sentence to the Leather, I should add. And then there's the fact that I gave the guns back? On your side of the truck? And should I remind you of your episodes of slipping in and out of consciousness *in* the truck? Where I could've pushed you out the door and be done with you? Or just cut your throat? If I was so inclined."

A burning sense of guilt seeped through Gus.

"I mean," Maya summed up, "I guess this could be part of my master plan to lure you into a false sense of security, where I kill you and then take everything you have. Or maybe, stranded out here like we are, I'm actually willing to help carry some of the weight before you collapse?"

Without a word, Gus handed over the duffel bag, feeling as if he'd been through a similar predicament before.

"Was that so bad?' Maya said, adjusting the thing as it hung off her shoulder.

"No. It wasn't."

She hefted the assault rifle, aiming it away from him. "I imagine you feel better, too?"

He nodded. His shoulder was already thanking him. "Why'd you keep the mask?"

She faced him, and didn't answer right away. "I don't know," she admitted. "I tucked it away in a pocket a little after I took it off. I . . . I was going to burn it. Later, when we were someplace safe. Good thing I didn't."

Gus nodded that it was a good thing and didn't say anything more about it.

They turned to their pickup. The plow was off, and the front hood crumpled a good two feet from initial impact. Everything past that looked intact. A strengthening breeze blew a fine sheet of snow past them.

"We better get moving," Maya said. "Before anyone catches up to us. And before this flurry gets any worse. And we freeze."

Gus sighed. "Know where we are?"

"Not a clue. You?"

"Nope."

"Pick a direction, then, except," she glanced around and nodded, "that way. We drove in from that way."

Gus eyed the overpass. There was an open space between the van and the crumpled sedan, which had landed flat on its chassis, but all four tires were flat.

He pointed at that gap, and presumably the road that lay beyond it.

"Après vous," Maya said.

21

Under an increasingly cloudy night sky, the Leather convoy barreled down a two-lane highway, destined for Regina. Light snowflakes moistened the pavement, while more flattened against their windshields. Aboard the transport truck, the exploding spatters thickened enough for Slipknot to switch on the wipers.

The Dragon rode shotgun. The newly crowned warlord of the Leather stared ahead, while his fingers drummed a rucksack bundle in his lap. A mere shopping bag for the head inside was too insulting to the Dog Tongue's memory. Far too beneath him. The rucksack wasn't that much better, but the material was a better quality and design. Granted, the Dragon had been planning on replacing the Dog Tongue when he finally perished, but he still respected the man for everything he'd accomplished during his reign. He'd sculpted the Leather into a formidable force on the brink of greatness, if not empire, and while he was reduced to no more than a desiccated head without a body, the Dragon wasn't about to toss his melon aside like so much garbage. No sir. Not him. He'd give the Dog Tongue a proper send-off when the time was right. Plus, carrying around the man's noggin as a memento would keep the lessers in line.

Vampire Joe might contest his claim to the crown, but the Dragon was confident he would be able to convince the man otherwise.

All the Dragon truly needed . . . was the Chemist.

Ahead, the brake lights of the smaller pickup trucks flared to life. Slipknot did the same, braking, quickly working the controls as the much bigger machine took more effort and energy to stop. Air brakes sang as the great machine slowed down. The Dragon leaned forward and saw the reason for the holdup.

In the deepening night, a side road appeared, a freshly plowed strip carving its way through an avalanche's worth of snow. One lane, going off to the east, leading between the spiked baubles of Skull Road. The sight of it puzzled the Dragon. He wasn't aware of any plans to open a new highway this winter. However, this was Vampire Joe's territory, and he might have opened a new road for whatever reason. The Dragon wondered why Vampire Joe might have green-lit the new strip, all the while drumming his fingers on the head in the bag.

The one called Bonemaker emerged from his ride. He walked, gunslinger style, to the freshly plowed turnoff, the headlights bleaching his imposing figure. At the intersection, he inspected the piles of snow and even kicked a mound. Assessment completed, he walked back to the transport truck.

The Dragon lowered the window and leaned forward.

"Freshly plowed," Bonemaker reported. "The snow hasn't frozen."

That black ribbon of road tantalized the Dragon, who wondered if those responsible for it were the same ones who had killed the Mallet and the Hook. Chances were good. And if so, did they have the Chemist? That thought scorched a hole through his mind and guts, making his decision easier. They would follow the road, considering who the Chemist was and what she could do, any delay would allow this mysterious foe even more time to escape.

Vampire Joe and his minions could wait.

"Back everything up," the Dragon commanded, adjusting himself in the seat. "And follow that road."

A short time later, the two lead pickups turned down the new lane, their plows adding to the chunky wake already marking the sides. Whoever had made the initial cut had come close to the shoulder, making it an easy thing to judge the rest of the pavement. Steel edges scraped the surface, the sound carrying across the open expanse. Thick traceries of bare trees rose on either side, lit up by the headlights.

The Dragon leaned forward, no longer drumming on the skull.

Are you somewhere up ahead, Chemist? he thought. *Are you even alive?*

He hoped so.

Almost an hour later, the brake lights of the lead pickups once again flared to life, slowing as they rumbled up the ramp of an overpass. They eventually slowed to a stop. Slipknot worked his magic, bringing the big machine to a chuffing halt. Ahead, the headlights revealed a section of the road entirely missing, as if a meteor had crashed through it like a flimsy curtain.

Bonemaker and the one called Leech got out of their trucks and cautiously treaded up the ragged edge. They peered below, and in short time, Leech returned to the main transport.

"There's a truck below," he said. "Along with a van. And a car. All smashed. The van's the most recent. Maybe happened a few hours ago."

The Dragon gave orders while he got up to fetch his flashlight stashed away in his private bunk. Within minutes they were beneath the overpass standing around the crash site, inspecting it. As Leech had said, the van was the most recent. Boot tracks, two sets of them, passed underneath the overpass and shuffled off into the night. The Dragon stared in that direction, scanning the darkness beyond the concrete above his head. He didn't wait very long.

Leech returned to his side.

And held out a familiar set of motorcycle goggles.

22

Gus and Maya trudged through snow that would often rise to their knees. The cloud cover had fragmented in the last hour, revealing an endless winter plain that gleamed beneath the night sky. While not quite the brilliance offered by a full moon, they didn't complain, focusing on placing one foot ahead of the other.

They pushed on, at times passing road signs that announced speed limits of eighty or showed stick diagrams that indicated lodgings. *Lodgings* sounded good to them, but damned if they could see anything in the distance. The cold deepened, the winds picked up, and the clouds closed ranks. Ice fléchettes blew into and stung Gus's face. Still wearing his coat, he was the more insulated of the pair, but his exposed features were taking the brunt of the elements. His eyes were dry but his nose was all runny. Maya had her mask, but no winter coat to speak of, and her leather outerwear seemed woefully inadequate against the strengthening weather.

"Must be minus twenty," Gus guessed.

"Just keep walking," she said.

"Just sayin' . . . must be minus twenty."

"Minus twenty, twenty-one, yeah," Maya agreed, sounding cold. "Around there. Just be mindful." And at that point she sniffed hard. "Of any tingling. Or burning sensations. In your face. Your hands. Any exposed skin. That's the first sign . . . you're at risk of frostbite."

"My face is tingling."

"What? Shit. Here." She stopped and turned to him, a black wraith in the night. She pulled off her mask and offered it to him. "I know," she nodded, her hands bare and looking blue. "It's a Leather mask. Put it on anyway. It'll keep the heat in long enough to warm you up. When I start getting chills, I'll take it back. We'll share, okay?"

Gus regarded the mask then her. Her inflamed face didn't seem so red in the dark. And she was right. He really didn't want to wear the mask, but he relented and pulled the thing over his head, discovering it was slick with sweat.

"Better?" she asked.

"You could've wiped it down first."

"What? We're friends now, remember? At the very least a degree of trust has been established. What's a little perspiration between buddies?"

Fuckin' gross is what it is, Gus thought, but kept that to himself. It was warmer than nothing, but tight around the swollen parts of his face. "We'll be in trouble if the temperature keeps dropping."

She started walking once again. "Even more trouble if the wind gets stronger."

Gus fell into step behind her, still thinking about her hands. He wore his gloves, tucked away when he was firing the Ramfist, but he pulled them on while on the march. She had tucked both hands into her armpits the whole time.

"Hey," he called out. "Here. Trade you."

She turned, studied the offered gloves, and took them without comment. They were a little big on her, and she held them up to make that point, but Gus thought she was smiling just a little all the same.

Then they were walking again.

"Christ, it's cold," he muttered, flexing bare fingers on the Ramfist. "Don't you think it's cold? It's cold. Real cold. I think my balls froze a while back."

Ahead, Maya cocked her head and muttered. "Nice. Well. Forgive me if I don't reciprocate that thought. I won't tell you . . . which lady parts of mine have gone numb. But you might notice I'm walking faster."

And she was.

He hurried to catch up, coming within a couple of strides behind her. That short burst of energy fatigued him. A guardrail appeared, the snow tethered to the lower part, and they stayed inside of that.

Gus turned and stared back at the way they came. "No signs of pursuit."

"Good," she said. "That's good. Maybe we . . . we gave them the slip."

"Maybe."

"These gloves are good. And no sweat, either. Thanks."

"This mask is tight. And it was a bugger to pull on."

"But you're warmer, right?"

"Yeah."

"There you go," she said. "Now. You look left. I'll look right. Watch for houses, convenience stores, anything that might give us shelter for the night. Even a bus stop would be something at this point."

"This . . ." Gus sniffed again and rubbed at his nose. "This reminds me of another time I was stranded out in the snow."

"No cold stories, please. If you have stories to tell, let them be about Bermuda. Or Saint Lucia. Anywhere with beaches and hot sand. Or hot rum toddies. Or tanning salons. Getting trapped in a tanning bed. Oh yes, that would be a good one."

That would be fucked-up, Gus thought and realized he was falling behind again. The woman could walk, even while carrying the rest of his gear in the bag. It only reminded him of how smashed he was.

"Cold, cold, cold," she muttered, every footfall leaving a wake which Gus took advantage of, walking in her steps.

After a while, he hurried ahead of her, and took the lead.

"My turn," he said, regretting the burst of energy. "The guy only beat my face in. Not my legs."

"Lucky."

They stopped talking after that, slogging on, searching the absolute edges of what they could see for any signs of civilization. It eluded them, and they continued plugging through the snow, the flurry softening into huge fluffs that took their time falling.

Twice more Gus and Maya switched mask and gloves. The last time, her hands were visibly trembling. And his face definitely felt as if it were burning.

"Temp's dropping," he said, realizing the sweat under his coat and clothing was saturated and cold.

She nodded. "At least . . . minus . . . twenty-five. Twenty-six. I'm gonna be pissed . . . if it hits minus thirty."

Gus smiled in spite of that. "You're funny. For someone who used to work for the Leather."

That stopped her in her tracks. Gus halted as well, sensing, nay, *knowing* full well he'd just put a big old, shitty-assed boot in his mouth.

"I wasn't one of them," she said. "I told you. I only . . . I only made the gas. I never . . ." but then she faltered, and for a second, appeared to be on the brink of falling over. "I just made the gas."

She steadied herself, waited for a reply, a response of any kind. When Gus didn't say anything, she lowered her head and went right back to walking.

Though it hurt him to do so, he struggled to catch up. "Ah, listen," he said, reaching her side. "Look, I'm sorry. I didn't mean to offend."

"You didn't offend," she said without turning, waving a gloved hand. "You reminded."

Snow kicked up as she increased her pace again.

Guess I did, Gus figured and struggled to stay with her. A part of him warned him not to remind her again.

An hour later, perhaps around midnight, the shadow called Maya stopped and pointed an oversized glove. Gus spotted it, a small building dark against the snow, or at least he thought it might be.

"That's either a place, or not," Maya said, her words not sounding quite right.

Gus pulled up beside her and tore off the mask. "Here."

"You keep it."

"Your face is starting to freeze. Wear it."

With tufts of snow still falling, Maya regarded the thing.

"Besides," he said. "I think I'm close to losing a layer of skin off my fingers."

That didn't make her smile, but she took the mask. When it was on, she handed over the gloves.

"Sweet mustard pickles," she said in mild disgust, failing to notice how she stunned Gus a little with her choice of words. "You said *I* left sweat inside this thing? All right. You've had your revenge. You ready?"

"Yeah," he said, still thinking about one of Toby's favorite sayings when Benny was around a job site. He certainly hadn't expected it, but he realized he was glad to hear it.

"Then we go," she said. "And that better not be an oversized billboard out there. I'll be so mad if it is."

Energized by the hope of nearing the end of their march—and hoping it was a little better than a bus stop—they hoofed it toward the mystery structure. His feet were no longer cold but bordered on freezing. He'd been mask-free for only five minutes, but his ears felt weird, perhaps stinging. He wasn't sure.

"Let it . . . be a house," he said, his mouth already stiffened by the cold.

"Be a house," Maya repeated, sounding a little better, her hands tucked into her armpits.

And as they drew closer, they saw that there *was* something there, growing more distinct, gaining height and mass, rising out of the surrounding prairie. It wasn't a house, however, but a large two-story building. It looked abandoned, the windows dark and snow-crusted, but to two half-frozen people on a winter's night, it looked damn fine indeed.

"Oh, my," Maya whispered, but it sounded louder. He was right beside her, in case she stumbled. Or worse, *he* stumbled.

"Motel?" he said, his mouth still not working quite right.

"Motel," she repeated.

They didn't have the gas to rush the place, only enough energy to muster on through, the snow beneath their feet becoming increasingly deeper.

Which was about when Gus fell into a ditch.

At any other time, it would not have been a big deal . . . except he was carrying the Ramfist.

He fell with a startled huff, holding the shotgun before him as he crashed over it. The shotgun fired. Maya dropped to her knees, the duffel bag falling beside her. Gus recovered almost immediately and jerked himself up, snow covered and freezing. He spotted her, saw that she wasn't moving. Leaving the weapon in the snow, he scampered out of the ditch, and hurried to her side.

"You okay? Maya? You okay?"

Slowly nodding, she held out her hands, and Gus released a huge breath of relief. "Oh sweet Jesus," he huffed, placing a hand to his chest. "Thought I gunned you down. Blew a leg off or something."

"I think I'd be over there somewhere if you did."

"True," he said and smiled.

"Help me up."

He did, almost falling a second time.

Maya flexed her hands and fingers. "Cold."

Gus held them in his gloved hands, but she pulled them away, inserting them back into her armpits. Embarrassed and feeling somewhat rejected, he left her to retrieve the Ramfist where it had fallen. Then he inspected the ditch, how it ran alongside the hidden road they walked, and where it ended in a culvert almost hidden in the snow. The pavement Maya had dropped to her knees upon was the turn-off for the motel, it seemed.

Gus had merely wandered a little too far off the trail.

The motel loomed not a hundred feet to their right. A few snow-covered lumps that resembled cars blemished the parking lot. A sign with its glass lettering all smashed out hung above the door. The words could still be read, and they said, in a large, jagged font, Rest A While Inn.

The words *Rest A While* were stacked on top of each other, right next to a larger, emphasized *Inn*. Gus saw that the first letter of each word, in descending order, read *RAW*, and wondered if that was intentional or not.

Duffel bag slung across her back, Maya headed for the front door. He limped after her.

The front walls looked weird at first, until they realized they were looking at redwood logs, with a huge overhang that extended a good fifteen feet or so over the main entrance. Boards covered the windows on the first floor, nailed in place, with snow plugging the crevices. The windows were boarded up on the second floor as well. Thick planks reinforced half of the main entrance, while the other half had a sheet of pig iron drilled over it. No sound came from within the building. No light seeped through any openings. Judging by the unspoiled layer of snow on the parking lot, Gus figured no one had visited the RAW Inn for a very long time.

They slowed to a stop before the boarded-up doors, when Gus held out an arm, drawing a look from Maya.

"I'll go in first," he said. "Check it out."

She nodded. "Be quick, okay?"

He nodded and sized up the doors, seeing no handles. Then he spotted a rope with a hand-sized loop, dangling down from a metal ring nailed into the wood. Stepping aside and aiming the Ramfist, he indicated for Maya to pull the thing open. She did, giving him a good look.

The door swung open, pushing aside snow. A dark, featureless cavern lay beyond the threshold. A dank, musty smell of body odor drifted past, strong enough for Gus to get a whiff. And a smell of something else, not so easily identified.

"Shit," he said. "Someone either died in there or . . ."

"I don't care at this point," Maya whispered, cutting him off.

Neither did he, truth be told. And it was one of those situations where, if it were a movie and they were the characters, the audience would be screaming at them to *not* go in there. To get the fuck out of Dodge while the getting was good.

But there was no getting out of Dodge. There was only the freezing open prairie, which would soon kill them both.

So in he went, boots scuffing bare floor, tracking in snow. He aimed into the lightless depths, the Ramfist heavy in his hands. He got a step inside when he glimpsed a slab of something hurtling at him out of the dark, a split second before it cracked into his forehead, nearly removing the whole enchilada from his shoulders. Gus fell for the second time that night, and the last thing he heard—after the Ramfist clattering off the floor—was the short but disturbing echo of Maya shouting a warning.

Then . . . nothing.

23

The sensation of moving reached Gus in that sludge-filled vat of unconscious blackness, and he might've groaned despite himself. For that involuntary slip, something thundered into his head yet again, and he knew no more. Voices eventually reached him, coarse and buzzing, but also high-pitched and frantic. Both spoke a language he didn't understand, and then he was floating again, pulled one way and then another, an out-of-body participant in a multidirectional tug of war. There was no resistance on his part. None at all. He was merely along for the ride.

The voices returned, a woman's voice, sounding frantic, talking at the end of a very long tunnel. There was an urgency there, a desperate level of energy, and as he came close to waking, another voice shouted, belonging to a man.

"Shut up you Leather bitch or I'll skin your ass here and now."

Gus opened his eyes, distantly aware he was on his back.

"You can't," Maya was yelling. "Stop this right *now*. We just wanted—"

A hard expulsion of air, then. It sounded like Maya had just thrown up and she stopped shouting. Gus twisted his head around until he saw a man stepping back from a chair. Maya was duct-taped to it, her mask gone and her inflamed face contorted. Long threads of drool hung from her lower lip.

"You yak something fierce for a goddamn Leather," the man said before stepping in and smashing a hand across her face. "So shut up you piece of frozen *shit*. Just shut up. And stay shut up. You'll last longer. Maybe even 'til the morning, though I'm pretty sure I'll drive a knife through your eye before sunrise."

"Get away from her," Gus *tried* to say, but it came out like "Guh . . . aaaa . . .", and that depleted him, leaving him woozy from the effort.

The man, a tall, gaunt ghost of an individual with a black beard that flourished greatly, stopped, turned, and assessed. He was frightening. Black of eye and teeth, it seemed, with a hyena's leanness. Then the ghost stomped over to where Gus lay. A mystery object hard as steel flicked across Gus's forehead and stars exploded across his vision while a spike of pain went through him. A second later, blood trickled into one eye.

"Want another, smartass? Huh? Want another?" the angry ghost asked before leaning in close and whispering in Gus's ear. "Say another fuckin' word. Just one fuckin' word. Go on. I'll wait. I'll also take your tongue out faster than you can say it. One twist and scoop. Shut you right up."

The stink of a long-neglected mouth enveloped Gus, threatening to dissolve his nose. A knife loomed before his eyes then, big and gleaming and close enough to see the scratches from repeated sharpening.

"That's better," the angry ghost warned. "Stay that way. You'll fuckin' last longer. And don't try me. Seriously. I'll cut through your cheek to get to that tongue. And once I start in, who knows when I'll stop. I like cuttin', you see. Cuttin's a hobby of mine. Love to cut. Animals. People. Asswipes of allll kinds. Big. Small. Fat. Skinny. I don't discriminate. You name it, I'll slice it to the bloody bone. I'll leave whole swaths of red meat. You'll never guess what happens after that."

Gus winced, still blinking away blood, and didn't dare open his mouth.

"That's right," the ghost noticed. "Smart after all. You keep it shut."

Without warning, the ghost sank the knife deep into the wooden surface Gus was currently splayed out across. The impact alone caused his asshole to clench. A finger snapped off its end and the whole thing quivered.

"You keep it shut too, honey," the angry ghost advised. "See the blades? Lotta them, right? I got fuckin' *tons* to spare. Even hooks and spikes. Needles and cheese grates. You name it, I *got* it, and I'll fuckin' *use* it. So shut the fuck up. Fuckin' Leather *queef*."

A door swung open, sounding like it had been kicked in.

A second voice boomed. "The fuck you have here, Rye?"

"The fuck it look like?"

"I'd say sweet 'n sour ass roasts for the next week or so."

"*I* say garlic goodness in a nice butter sauce if I get my way. For *at least* the next week. Maybe even a few days more. If we diet like we discussed before."

"Fuck that. I ain't fuckin' dietin'. Tell you what I want, I want hot dogs. Big fuckin' wallbangers. The meat grinder hasn't been used in months."

"Oh, I'll do it. Make no mistake. I'm looking forward to some nice patties, myself. The last ones were freezer burned. You could taste it."

"Whose fault is that?"

"... I'm not *sayin'* it's anyone's fault."

Gus's eyes narrowed in horrified disbelief. *What the screaming fuck had we walked into?*

"We caught something?" a new voice asked.

"Rye knocked the shit out of a couple of chicken nuggets trying to break in."

"I didn't. This asshole was like this when he got here. I only hit him once. Twice. Only twice."

"Nothing wrong with a little shit-kicking," the new voice said. "Softens up the meat. They drive up?"

Silence.

"Ryan?"

"Don't think so," Ryan, the angry ghost, reported.

"You don't think so? What about you, Vonn?"

"Hey, I just got here myself, man."

"Fuck, guys, there could be a small *army* of chicken nuggets out there, just waiting."

Receding footsteps then.

"Awww *Chazz*, no one's out there," Ryan bellowed after him. "We wouldn't be talking like this, for one."

Another bout of silence.

"Well, he's gone," Vonn said in a quiet voice.

"I see that, dickhead."

"... Shut up."

"You shut up. And don't get me started. I was already warmed up before you got here. So unless you're looking for an ass-paddling from a spiked bat . . . I mean it—anytime you want to go."

"Fuck off."

"You fuck off."

"Blow me."

"You blow—"

"*Hey you dumb fucks, come here.*"

A third bout of silence, and then the two dipshits, as Gus had already labeled them, stomped out of the place. The whole inn must have hardwood flooring or some such material as they clomped away, heedless of their racket. He listened, listened hard, and heard them talk somewhere in another part of the motel.

"You okay?" Maya asked from nearby.

Gus turned his head, feeling the stiffness there. "No. Not really. You?"

"No."

Some angry yelling from beyond, followed by the slamming of a door. Then another slam.

"Who the fuck are these dipshits?" Gus asked.

"I think . . . they're Norsemen."

That turned Gus's head.

When he'd last met up with Scott, shortly after landing and getting a place to stay on Big Tancook, Gus and his friend caught up on events after Scott had left the house on the mountain. He'd gone into Halifax, met up with Amy and Vic and Buckle, and encountered a group of rabid cannibals calling themselves *Norsemen*, of all things.

Who spoke their own unique language.

Which brought out a talk about where they came from, and how long they'd been cut off from civilization to actually develop their own language. And develop a taste for eating other people. Which, both he and Scott agreed, was exceptionally fucked-up. Scott surmised that it took longer for the language, but in regards to chomping down on someone, not long. Especially if there was nothing to eat. Which sparked the next item of discussion, where could these people have been living if there was nothing to eat? There was always something to eat. Even if a person didn't have some stock of groceries at home, a society could still rediscover their hunting skills through trial and error. Or even develop them, if properly motivated, like starvation was apt to do.

Neither Scott nor Gus had firm answers. The far north, perhaps? The deep woods? Some part of the country, like the Canadian Shield, where survival could have—nay— *must* have been especially brutal? They didn't know.

"Back in the day," Maya said, "when the Dog Tongue was . . . consolidating BC, he waged a small war with a pack of savages calling themselves Norsemen. Long story short: the Leather won. These might be survivors."

"How do you know?" Gus asked.

"Look around the kitchen."

The kitchen?

Gus lifted his head. *Oh . . . shit . . .*

The countertops were the first thing he saw, then the huge table he was strapped down to, spread wide and completely vulnerable. Maya was perhaps ten feet away, sitting before a second table and duct-taped to a chair. Her mask lay on the table before her, near a number of wooden cutting blocks festooned with knives. Then the prepping areas, the grills, and the ovens—on a smaller scale than the kitchens back at the Anchor Bay, but that didn't matter. All that mattered to him were the number of *knives*, hanging from racks, stuck in blocks of wood, or simply lying about on cutting boards.

There were other utensils. Pots and pans and long dull meat skewers that hung from pegs. What truly surprised him, however—and this was where his voice failed him—was the chain saw resting on top of the kitchen counter. Both the chain saw and counter looked filthy. Dried spots, streaky stains, and pieces of unknown matter spattered the backsplash in a wild and unchecked arterial spray. The next thing he noticed, what he zoomed in on, almost laughably so if he wasn't so freaked out of his skull... were the *condiment* bins lined up on another counter. Large lettering spelled out onion powder, garlic, salt, and pepper. He thought he read *Himalayan* sea salt. Even *paprika*, which only mystified and horrified him even more. There were others, but out of his sight.

On some morbid cue, Gus's stomach actually rumbled.

The stink he smelled upon entering the place, though. That god awful brew pent up indoors without ventilation. The body odor had been part of it, but spilled spices was the other. Along with whatever else these three *man-eaters* had toiled and bubbled over and left for the other one to clean up.

There was an audible thump when a bewildered Gus dropped his head onto the table.

"You fought these guys?" he asked weakly.

"No, I was excused from that."

"*Excused?*"

"*I made the gas,*" Maya stressed. "Back then I was deemed too *important* to risk. I provided the juice for their *machines.* There was no one else. If I died, that was it. They would've been put back years until someone figured it out. Or they got ahold of someone who could do the job."

"Oh sweet Jesus," Gus whimpered, and had the unwanted and brief sensation of spinning when he closed his eyes.

"Just don't... don't aggravate them is all," she said.

"*Aggravate them?*" he blurted and immediately checked on the whereabouts of their captors.

"They might not kill us for days, or they might butcher us in seconds. Especially if you give them a reason," Maya said.

Gus wanted to remind her of the conversation they'd both just overheard, where the Norsemen very much sounded like they weren't about to wait days. Instead, he kept quiet and rolled his head on the table—*the oversized cutting board*, he corrected himself. That brought on another sickening realization, one that threatened to turn his stomach. He was a look away from being skinned, gutted, perhaps tenderized, and then... seasoned.

Before literally being put through a meat grinder.

He let his breath out in one long puff.

Then the worst thing, or at least the *next* worst thing, sent a shiver along Gus's taint. The growing sound of boots clomping on the floor, indicating the three cannibals were coming back.

Both Gus and Maya shut up, more tense than ever.

Two of them stopped around Gus, while the third went for Maya. The two looming over Gus resembled male grizzlies. Hair. Great mops of uncut hair and beards. One had his mane tied back, while the other allowed his to flow au naturel. Both could have been crooners in some glam rock band for their hair alone, except both were, unfortunately, ugly as fuck. Red eyes. Bulbous noses. Bad skin blistered with ripe pustules and blackheads that, if squeezed, would not pop, but *launch*. The cannibal diet clearly had its drawbacks. Hygiene aside, both appeared warmly dressed, wearing at least one sweater each. Perhaps two.

As Gus sized up one and then the other, one of them picked his nose.

Gus closed his eyes. Perhaps he could play dead. Maybe then the two bears would lose interest and move off to deeper parts of the forest. He cracked one eye open. *Shit*.

"Did you walk here tonight?" Chazz asked.

"Yeah," Maya answered in a low voice.

"No ride?"

"We . . . lost it. Coming over an overpass. We went through a hole we didn't see."

Ryan broke out in a rotten-toothed smile and slapped Vonn (the one with his hair tied back) across the arm. "A*haa*! Thing's still getting them!"

"Hadn't checked on it in weeks," Vonn said, smiling and nodding. Vonn's remaining teeth appeared *green*. An actual seaweed shade of green.

"You wreck the plywood, Leather bitch?" Ryan asked.

Maya didn't answer.

"Well?" Vonn prodded.

"Best speak up, honey," Chazz advised. "If you want what happens later to be quick and easy. And painless."

She relented. "Yeah. We went through. All the way to the bottom. The rig's still out there if you want to check."

"That sounded like an order," Ryan said. "You ordering me around, Leather bitch?"

"No," Maya sighed.

"Good. All right then. Where'd you get these cannons?"

No reply.

"Those are mine," Gus answered, filling the silence.

A second later, a third head loomed over him. Like Vonn, Chazz also had his hair tied back. Chazz also had the biggest set of lips that Gus had ever seen on a guy. Not even the Wildman beard hanging off his face could hide those things. Gus fought down the impulse to ask if the guy liked sucking off hornet nests.

Chazz bared his teeth, and that caused Gus to swallow.

The crazy, hornet nest–sucking whack job had *filed* everything in his mouth down to broad uneven points.

"Holy shit, Rye," Chazz said in blunt amazement. "You put a little extra pepper on that plank or something?"

"He was like that when he *got* here, Chazz."

Chazz and Vonn exchanged amused looks, before Chazz focused on Gus. "Where'd you get the guns, you Leather *prick*?"

Gus blinked. "I . . ." and he checked himself from correcting the man. "I got them from . . . some crazies back east."

"This, too?" Vonn had a knife in his hand, and he stabbed it into Gus's armored vest. A hard series of sewing machine probes that rattled him. The vest stopped the pointed tip, but didn't stop Gus's ass ring from tightening to the snapping point.

"Got that . . ." he struggled to breathe. Not only were they *fugly*, but their collective breaths *stank*. "Got that from a dead soldier."

"You killed a soldier?" Ryan leaned in. "My *sister* was a soldier."

"I didn't . . . he was already dead. There was a bunch of them. I took the first one that fit."

That took the gas out of Ryan's oven, it seemed. At least they didn't hurt him.

"That's probably true," Vonn said. "Enough dead grunts out there if you go lookin'. 'Specially in the cities."

"How do you know?" Chazz asked.

"I know."

"Where's yours then?" Ryan demanded, cooking with gas once again.

"Couldn't find one big enough," Vonn replied.

"Yeah, right."

"So you two," Chazz resumed, talking over the others. "Walked all the way from the overpass . . . to here?"

"Yeah," Gus said.

"No wonder they're half froze," Vonn noted.

"That's a long-ass walk," Chazz said.

"Long, *frigid*-ass walk," Vonn added.

"Gonna have to rig that drop again in the springtime," Ryan said. "Someone else might drop in. See what I did there?"

"Shut the fuck up, Rye," Chazz told him. "Just shut the fuck up."

And amazingly, Ryan shut up, though he didn't look happy about it.

"Here," Chazz said, and handed over the Glock. Gus's Glock. That brightened Ryan's eyes. "New gun for you. Bullets come out that end. And don't shoot your dick off."

Ryan smirked and inspected the weapon.

"Well," Chazz said for all to hear. "I don't know about you, but I'm fucking beat. Time is it, anyway?"

The other two Norsemen looked away from Gus.

"Three-ten," Vonn reported over Ryan's "Ten after three."

That got them glaring at each other.

"That late?" Chazz declared. "Fuck me. I mean. Glad you two biscuits dropped by and all, but couldn't you have done it earlier? Say, noonish? Well . . . fuck it. Chop 'em up now if you want, Rye. I don't care. I'm not going anywhere tonight or tomorrow for that matter. They look secure to me. But if you do chop 'em up, make sure you clean that shit up. Remember what happened last time?"

Ryan didn't say a word. Obviously, he remembered.

"Don't give me that look," Chazz warned. "You knew what you were doing. I know I got salmonella from that. Shitty work there, head chef. Shitty. Anyway, looks like you got them tied down good there, 'eh?"

"Yeah," Ryan said in a dejected voice.

"Used a whole roll on the bitch," Vonn said.

Chazz gave Ryan a cold look. "A whole roll, Rye?"

Ryan glowered again and kept his mouth shut.

"You know that shit's a finite resource, right? Once it's gone, it's gone."

Ryan nodded.

Chazz shook his head in frustration. "If you chop them up tonight, make sure you get it done *right*. S'all I'm saying. I don't want to be picking tape slivers outta my steak or my teeth. Okay? Okay, then. That's all from me. Good night, children. Oh and Vonn? The thunderstick's yours, okay?"

Vonn gleefully rubbed his hands together.

Chazz walked away.

The other two watched him go, watched for seconds, then they faced each other.

"You going, too?" Ryan asked.

Vonn lowered his brow. "It's after three, Rye."

"I know. Figured I get a head start on things."

"They're not going anywhere. Look." Vonn tugged on something out of sight, and the leather strap keeping Gus's right hand in place tightened significantly around the wrist.

"And you *did* use a full roll on her," Vonn finished.

"So you're going back to bed, too?"

"I am most certainly going back to bed. You did a solid job here tonight, nailing both these pheasants by yourself. So you do whatever floats your fucked-up boat. It's still your watch, though. Keep you awake, I guess. Just remember, if you *do* chop 'em up . . ."

"Yeah, yeah," Ryan waved the remainder of that thought away. "I *could* kill them now," he said, pitching the idea.

That puckered all of Gus's sphincters.

"Do it, I don't care," Vonn mumbled as he turned to leave. "Just don't *do* it, *leave* it, and then go to bed. Not my turn to clean shit up. It's *yours*. And you know they'll shit themselves. And you know what Chazz will say if he walks in here in the morning and gets a whiff of it."

Evidently, Ryan knew.

"My two cents?" Vonn said at the kitchen exit. "Leave them. At least until tomorrow noon. Or whenever you get up. Do them both, then. I'll help out. A little. I'll definitely mix up the seasoning. And I'll do the rub. How's that sound?"

Ryan considered it.

Vonn didn't wait. "You think on it. Do what you want. Just don't say I didn't warn you or offer to help. You get cranky over that shit and then you argue otherwise."

Vonn left, his footsteps drifting off into a deeper section of the motel.

Ryan stood over Gus, considering him, considering him *hard*, when he abruptly stepped out of sight.

Oh thank you God, Gus projected.

Ryan returned with a meat cleaver.

Jesus Christ! Gus thought, eyes on the verge of popping.

Whereupon Ryan chopped the cleaver into the wood not an inch away from Gus's face, leaving him blinking as if he'd just sustained a lightning strike.

"Leave that here," Ryan said. "Keep it handy. If I hear one peep outta either one of you, I'll come back and use it. On you *first*."

'Course, Gus thought. *Why not?* He brought out the worst in the crazies. It was like he oozed pheromones or something. Honestly, it was getting on his nerves.

But he had a potential ace up his sleeve. One he struggled not to give away, even though he could barely suppress his surprise over *still* having it.

Collie's *Sig Sauer*. His hidden backup, tucked into the waistband *of his jeans*. He'd kept that uncomfortable piece of metal at the base of his spine, underneath his vest, the whole time after leaving the Anchor Bay. The barrel gouged his ass cheek, but it was still there. Cannibals they might be, maybe even sleepy ones, but they were thankfully stupid. They hadn't searched him at all, or if they did, they missed the Sig entirely.

Problem was, he had no way of getting *at* the weapon.

"You okay over there," Maya whispered.

Gus nodded. "Don't let them hear you."

"He's gone."

"He's not gone far."

They became quiet then, but Gus could hear Ryan stomping his way through the motel. The man walked heavy, but he was walking away.

"Patrolling," Maya whispered.

Gus softly thumped his head against the table. "You're gonna get my dick chopped off."

Silence, then. "It's just a bird."

"It's *my* bird."

Maya shut up, conceding the point.

"They don't like you," he said in the lowest possible voice.

"No . . . no they don't," she sighed. "Should've thrown the mask away. Then they wouldn't have known I was with the Leather. Even if they saw the rashes on my face, I could deny it."

That hooked something in Gus's head. "How'd the Leather get you, anyway?"

No reply for several seconds, but then Maya took a deep breath. "I . . . was taken by them three years ago. In the spring. I was in my cabin, where I was hiding out from the zombie outbreak. In Alberta. They must have seen the smoke from my chimney and just snuck up on me."

She paused, collecting her thoughts. "I wore the Leather for days. Months even. They dressed me up and shoved a ball gag in my face. Hauled me around wherever they traveled. Everyone suffers the same. They do it to break people. Break their will. Then they reprogram them. Transform regular, everyday people into . . . these broken, twisted things. Where they're fearless. Ready to do things you wouldn't believe, because they've suffered, and don't want to ever suffer like that again. The scary thing, some switched over a lot faster than you would think. Like they read the job description and just signed up. Fanatically obedient killer in a psychotic world that has to wear leather? After the month I just had? Sure. Why not? I can't tell you how many people . . ."

She stopped, and Gus didn't need to look to know why.

"Yeah. I did whatever they told me to." She started again. "Whenever. I . . . killed people. Butchered them. Too many to remember. I had no choice. None. You don't know what it was like. I mean, it's terrifying. *Horrifying.* And not only did I have to do it, I had to *watch* . . . other people do the same. Get converted. Get broken down. Good solid people just . . . well . . . it was just as bad because you have to act like you're *okay* with it. The beatings. The torture. The *murdering* . . . I couldn't do a *thing* because I'd be dead, too. Or worse, I'd have to go through the reconditioning all over, since obviously the first time through didn't do the trick. And if that doesn't work, well, they dump you in with mindless. So I played dead. Drank from the cup and acted like everyone else. There might've been others like me, but . . . who knows. When you wear the leather, only the superiors speak. The lessers, the *minions* didn't—at least not around them. Not even with other minions. You're never certain what the reaction might be. The one you talk to might give you up, just to improve their own lot in the Dog Tongue's eyes. So you stayed quiet and sucked it up. To survive. To avoid punishment or worse. Which is what I did. So, yeah, I'm guilty. Of it all."

Gus turned his head to better see her.

"But, unlike the others," she went on. "I didn't break. Didn't give up. No matter how bad it got. Deep down, I stayed me. To a point. All that horror, that hive mentality, it will change you to a degree. There's no stopping that. But one day, when they were running low on fuel, scavenging the last few drops, I did what was forbidden for a minion. I spoke up. Directly addressed the Dog Tongue. As soon as I opened my mouth there were at least four other minions on me, forcing me facedown to the pavement, where one of them already had a machete to my neck. Didn't happen, obviously. The Dog Tongue waved him off, and I told the Dog Tongue for a second time I could make gas. Told him I'd make fuel for him, if given the chance. For any machine they drove. I'd even bring him to the sites where I worked. That was perhaps the most scared I've ever been, because all the while I was on my knees and pleading my guts out? All he did was watch. With four of his inflictors right there. Men who would butcher people at a glance. You know what that's like? Being watched by someone who . . . *commanded* people to kill for them? On a whim? With no more conscience than swatting a fly?"

Gus knew a little about that, but he didn't say anything.

"So, considering what I'd been through, I pulled off the unimaginable. I got transferred. He put me to work, and I did what I said I could do. Very quickly I was considered too valuable to go on raids, but the Dog Tongue would still make me watch the Leather break people. Convert them into the Leather. Just to keep me in line. You hear what I'm saying?"

"Yeah."

"I'm . . . ashamed of that. So very ashamed. All of it. Even when I was back on an oil patch and in relative safety, they still did things. And I *let* them do it. My inability to act, to do anything, was . . . very bit as deplorable as if I were doing those things myself. I just went along. Just watched . . . just to stay alive . . . Oh good Lord . . ."

A mewling of sadness, then, quickly stifled, but he heard it all the same.

Gus sighed and stared at the kitchen ceiling.

She sniffed. Several times. Choking down whatever bubbled to the top.

"Maya," he said.

"It wasn't until a year ago," she said, ignoring him. "I decided I'd had enough. I had to do something. I was becoming far too indifferent, you see. Desensitized. I was becoming as detached and uncaring as the Leather. Already had, I suppose. I couldn't let myself go any further, because if I did, the part of my psyche I'd hidden for so long would disappear. And I'd become one of them. So I planned. I schemed. I knew the operations. Knew the dangers. Got my hands on some everyday household chemicals and slowly gathered amounts in the right proportions. It took time. A lot of time. But I set up some pretty powerful explosives around the refinery. All I had to do was flick a switch. The leaders watching me didn't know what I was doing. I told them I was just hoarding cleaners. Installing sensors and doing maintenance. Then I'd give them a long technical explanation that would put a person to sleep on their feet. In short time they let me be. They never suspected me because . . . in their eyes I was one of them. And when I finally flicked that switch? To blow everything up? I planned to be right in the middle of it all. There'd be no pain, just a huge explosion. Multiple ones, in fact. Taking me with it. And *him*. That was the plan. When the Dog Tongue came for me . . . I'd set everything off. Blow him up. And as many of them as I could take with me. But most certainly *him*. He was the maestro of it all. The initiator. The *instigator*, even. You got him first, though. Saved me the trouble. After all that work and careful planning. You wanna know something? The one time I was glad to be wearing the mask? Was when that messenger brought us the head of the Dog Tongue. He had to do that because no one would believe him otherwise. When your liege and ruler dies, and you're telling your superiors that he's dead . . . you need proof to back that up. When the Mallet pulled that . . . monster's head from the bag—a shopping bag, no less—it took everything I had *not* to say a word. Not to show *any* of the elation going through me. The *relief*. I think I had a smile on my face, actually, and maybe even tensed up. But they were all shocked. They thought I was, too. If it wasn't for my mask, I'd be dead."

She stopped again. Then, "When you started your attack on the hotel, the Mallet came to my room. We'd all heard the shots. He told me to get in the corner. I had that crossbow I shot you with—sorry, by the way. Little late with that, but . . ."

"S'okay," Gus said quietly. "Didn't hurt."

She choked back a soft chuckle. "When you came into the room, I knew the trap they had set. I knew the Hook was just up the hall. It was going to be either him or the Mallet, you see. If you went into the Hook's room first, the Mallet would come up behind you. But you, well, you took care of that. When the Hook had you, however, I knew you were going to die. I also knew—I *thought*—what if you were responsible for killing the Dog Tongue? Were there others? How many of you? You see what I'm saying? I had only seconds to make a choice. That was the chance I had to take. That's what I meant by saving myself. So I shot the Hook. And he was an inflictor. Not the first person I had to kill, but he was the first to truly deserve it. I had to save you, to finally get away from the Leather. To at least have a *chance* of escaping the Leather."

"And here we are."

Another wet chuckle. "Here we are. I don't care. The Dog Tongue's dead. They're all dead. I still can't believe it."

"Except the one called the Dragon."

That quieted her. "Yes. Except that one."

"The vicious one."

"Yeah."

". . . Yeah," Gus said.

"And he . . ." Maya trailed off. "He'll start over. Without a doubt. Pick up right where the Dog Tongue left off."

Gus lay on that hard table with the cleaver embedded next to his head and stared at the ceiling. "Not if I got anything to do with it."

She didn't say anything to that.

Which was right about when the one called Ryan started screaming.

24

"You got your pecker caught in your zipper again, Rye?" Chazz muttered when he heard the man roaring down below. Then he made out what the guy was saying, and what he was saying sounded bad.

"Someone's comin'! There's a lot of 'em comin'!"

The fuck?

Chazz rolled off his bed and went to his boarded-up window. Yanked back the curtains. One narrow slot between the planks allowed him to see outside, and he pressed his face up against it, glancing right and left before his eyes went wide.

There, coming up the road, and not caring one fuck who saw them, was a convoy of vehicles. Big, bold, and bearing down on their place, plowing up a storm, and not caring one goddamn shit. Pickup trucks, and what looked like a transport truck. At least that's what he thought it was. The angle wasn't completely right and the smoke and spray from all that flying snow made it hard to see. They were lined up, one after the other, with the bigger machine trailing the smaller ones.

Maybe even a few more behind it.

It was the Leather. He knew it. Because he had two of their bitches below.

Bitches who'd led them straight here.

In the dark of his room, glaring like he was, Chazz stepped back from the window. He processed the scene before him, even as the glare from the headlights of the approaching vehicle lit up the eye slot.

"Battle stations!" he yelled, hard enough to hurt. *"Battle stations, shitheads! Battle statiooons!"*

And went to his closet.

Minutes later, he was decked out in his own armor. Like the Leather piece of shit strapped to their cutting board said, body armor was all over the land. Just a matter of finding something that fit, was in decent condition, and required the least amount of effort cleaning zombie shit off it. He even had a police riot helmet with a visor, which he'd decorated with bear fangs glued to the surface.

He whipped open his door and charged down the hallway.

Hollering "*Battlestatiooons!*" all the way.

Aboard the transport truck, the Dragon shifted and leaned forward, trying to see ahead, through the diminishing backwash flung up by the lead trucks. Those rigs were slowing down, forcing Slipknot to apply brakes.

The Dragon was still having a bitch of a time seeing what was going on.

Then he saw—lowered his window and saw even *more*.

A motel. Two stories. Dark and ominous, the picturesque cliché of any horror movie one might see at an ancient drive-in. Only thing missing was a full moon overhead. And corpses outside, hanging off a fence.

The latter was most certainly doable.

The Dragon reached for the rig's air horn.

"Hole-lee *shit*, fatman," Vonn muttered as Chazz, taking three steps at a time on his way down, landed in the ubiquitous superhero crouch. Which he held for a split second before snapping his head up, whipping his hair and man bun back for extra effect. All that was missing was the music.

Both Vonn and Ryan were on opposite sides of the entrance, standing before boarded up windows. Both men regarded their leader (and Chazz would beat the shit out of anyone forgetting it) and turned back to their posts. Carts loaded with crossbows, clubs, axes, and shotguns were next to each man, within easy reach. On the floor next to Vonn was the green duffel bag taken from the two biscuits in the kitchen.

Ryan wore his own armor, complete with Viking horns and green face paint, locked and loaded with the Glock.

An equally armored up Vonn, wearing a serial killer hockey mask, crouched on the other side. The thing did shit for protection, being only a cheap piece of plastic meant for Halloween, but try telling that to a guy who used to watch slasher flicks like a seven-year-old watches Saturday morning cartoons. Vonn hefted the thunder-rod and glanced out a slot in the boards.

"Took you long enough, hoss," Vonn said.

"Fuck off."

Chazz rose from his superhero crouch and strode with purpose toward Ryan, also watching the oncoming convoy through his own personal slot.

"They stopped, Chazz," he reported.

"Looks like three pickups," Vonn added. "Two pups in front of a wiener dog, a gas pig behind that, and the third pup behind that."

Shoulder to shoulder with Ryan, Chazz peered out at the vehicles. "That's a fucking Leather motorcade. I goddamn guarantee it."

"You think?" Ryan asked.

"Fuck yeah, I think," he snapped back. "Fuckers are looking for the two biscuits in the kitchen. The transport truck zips up that body bag. Goddamn thing is probably filled with rotting lips and assholes."

This time, Ryan and Vonn didn't say a word, listening to the assessment and looking forward to the approaching violence.

The transport truck's air horn ripped the air, startling all three of them.

"Little chicken fuckers are eager," Chazz said, recovering first. "Yeah, here they come."

The pickups slowly made the turn, plowing as they entered the parking lot. The transport rolled to a stop in a swirl of exhaust, the rear of the trailer just a little way past the turnoff.

"Pricks are clearing the lot!" Ryan yelled and stuck the Glock's muzzle out the window slot. Vonn did the same.

"Let 'em," Vonn said. "Saves me the trouble."

"Fuck, I don't give a shit," Ryan said. "We already got breakfast in the house. Now we get lunch and dinner."

"Keep them honest," Chazz said, turning for the stairs. "Otherwise, don't shoot until you see the whites of their chicken fuckin' eyes. Fuckin' Leather. Gonna ruin our fuckin' windows, too. I'm headin' back to higher ground."

Ground came out strained as Chazz hauled ass up the stairs.

The boys kept their eyes on the trucks.

It took less than ten seconds for Chazz to reach the room situated right over the motel's front entrance. There, set up and ready, was a desk and chair, and the recently appropriated big gun taken from the Leather pricks they'd captured the night before. The guy didn't have a leather mask but his girlfriend did, which made him a Leather by default.

The small force about to lay siege to the motel proved it.

Also on the table were stacks of spare magazines for the rifle. A very sharp medieval broadsword and shield rested against the wall, both of which were Chazz's close and personal weapons of choice.

His people, the Norsemen, were all dead and gone, but Chazz and his two surviving henchmen had managed to hide themselves in the backroads maze in the big empty of Saskatchewan. Sorta like in plain sight, if a person could see that far across the swells and dips of the prairie. The plan was to rebuild, get back to small army status, and then go after the Leather, who'd wiped out their road clan a couple years back. That was the plan, the *original* plan, but they were experiencing difficulties in the recruitment of qualified personnel. Being cannibals didn't help matters either, so for the last two years, the three of them kept mostly to themselves.

Slowly going insane.

The Leather plowing their driveway were about to learn how insane they'd become. Memories of what the Norsemen once were also gave Chazz a scorching, carpet burn for revenge.

He got into position at the desk, gripped a metal knob, and slammed back the slot in the boarded-up window. The rifle was next, charged with a loud snap and fitted to both shoulder and eye. Chazz shrugged to loosen up and took two quick breaths through his nose. The red dot zigged-zagged over a shadowy plain before he sighted a target. A pickup truck pushing huge swaths of snow before it. Chazz tracked it only for seconds before switching to the transport, but that too wasn't the trophy he wanted to initially bag. He wanted to make a statement. A loud statement.

He lined up the tanker, hiding at the rear of the parked column.

"I'll punch this pig," Chazz vowed.

And opened fire.

Light crackled off the tanker's hide in a ragged line, stretching from the rear to the cab, until flames erupted near the front, dazzling in the night. The Dragon reacted like anyone would. He ducked, but then tried to locate the shooter. There, the window above the entrance to the motel. Fire filled the Dragon's side mirror then, distracting him a second before the tanker erupted in a warplane's afterburner gush of flame and smoke, sending ripples across the snow.

The Dragon's eyes widened with almost theatrical anger.

He clawed at the door handle and opened it. A cold blast of air swarmed the cab and he swung himself out. Landing hard, he straightened and hurried around the front of the rig. All the while, Bonemaker and Leech continued to clear the parking lot.

Slipknot jumped down as the Dragon reached the driver's side. They huddled behind the big machine, near the cargo holds, where Slipknot hauled out a ballistic shield. The Dragon took it while his minion took out another one. Behind them, Red and Gold ran along the burning wreck of the tanker, fortunate they hadn't gone up with the big rig. They rushed to the rear of the transport and continued along its side, keeping under cover. When they reached the cab, Slipknot already had a pair of shields waiting for them.

Which was right about when the Leather minion called Slit pulled his pickup around the burning tanker and drove onto the parking lot. In a huff of V-8 power, he aimed his machine—also equipped with a snowplow—at the motel entrance and gunned the gas pedal.

The truck swept out one of the columns holding up the motel's overhang, causing half to crash as the pickup powered forward, slapping the truck across its box bed. But that didn't slow the machine as it smashed through the reinforced entrance in a loud clap of steel and wood. The truck sank deep inside the motel lobby and stopped in a cloud of destruction, whereupon an angry popping erupted.

The Leather behind the transport stared at the mess of the main entrance, listening to the gunfight within. It only lasted a short time, during which the shooter on the second floor decided to pay attention to the other pickups still plowing his parking lot.

Bullets lit up the frames of the two trucks. Taking the hint, they raced back onto the highway, stopping in a screech of brakes before the burning tanker and its fiery stream pooling on the pavement. A swath of fire flowed into the ditches. The pickups reversed, carefully rolling past the Leather pressed up against the transport trailer.

Pissed off about the tanker, the Dragon straightened in time to hear the pickup stuck in the motel's front do a hard reverse. Slit gunned the machine backwards, heedless of the potential destruction. The rear smashed into the other half of the wilting overhang, ripping it out in a flurry of planks and debris. The pickup raced backwards, away from the punched-in face of the motel and toward the flaming ditch. There it dropped in a heavy clap of shocks, crunching its rear into the embankment. Part of the box bed extended across the pavement in a scream of sparks, while fire flashed up around the smoking machine.

The Dragon signaled his troops to the rear, while he and Slipknot hung back. He flipped open a second cargo hold and hauled out a green container. Ripping the lid off, the Dragon grabbed and held up a slinky piss bag no bigger than his fist.

He passed it off to Slipknot. Once upon a time, the transport driver could easily throw a football the length of a field. It wasn't a football being handed to him, nor was the Leather as young as he used to be, but he could manage one motel parking lot.

Moments earlier, back in the motel lobby, both Ryan and Vonn stopped and stared at the snowplow-mounted pickup charging at the entrance.

"The fuck is he—" was all Ryan got out before he dove for the floor an instant before the doors imploded in a frenzy of wood, glass, and pickup truck. The rig's plow slammed into chairs and tables, mashing them together, and heaving everything over the front desk area.

Before the truck came through, shaking the building down to its foundation.

Vonn and Ryan got to their feet. Seeing the truck in their midst, the pitter patter of falling debris, and the smoky destruction billowing throughout... well... they lost it.

Ryan unloaded several rounds into that dusty, dented carcass of a truck, stabbing holes into the cab and nearby glass. The noise from all that shooting was swallowed up by the ball-shivering blasts coming from the Ramfist as Vonn commenced firing from the other side. A side mirror, a passenger window, and half the windshield blew apart. A jagged cannonball-sized crater ripped through the passenger door. The chrome handle disappeared with an audible twang. The glove compartment blew apart, ripping up a huge section of the dashboard a split second before most of the seat on that side exploded in a burst of white stuffing. In fact, Vonn blasting the truck at close range was the equivalent of a howitzer shelling the shit out of a stuffed pillow.

Which the driver quickly realized.

Somehow, despite all those punishing shots to the metallic body, the driver hunched low, worked the shift, and reversed in a deafening roar of sheer eight-cylinder might. The machine surged back out the way it came, smashing Ryan's side of the entrance and making the hole bigger. Rubble showered the snow-printed tiles as the rig reversed and escaped. Not so far, however, as the boys continued blasting the offender, concentrating on the cab itself. The rest of the windshield blew apart. Headrests, too.

The truck landed in the ditch, sending up a wave of snow, and all fight left it. Then the fires started.

The shooting stopped.

Vonn and Ryan reloaded, spotting a cluster of figures gathering at the rear of the transport truck. Though it had been a while, they knew what was about to happen. They'd seen it once or twice before.

From his second-level perch, Chazz saw it as well. The truck smashing through the motel had rattled him right down to his shitkicker boots. He recovered quickly and reacquired his target. But then the truck reversed and shook the nutty pancake batter out of him a second time.

He recovered faster that time and spotted the activity around the transport's sizeable ass.

"Oh no you don't," he whispered, and sighted one of the figures gathering there, with what looked like riot shields.

Chazz fired.

Pang.

The target ducked behind the upraised shield at the same time Chazz squeezed the trigger, resulting in him plugging the barrier instead of the hated Leather. Then more shields appeared, like a small Roman formation, as the Leather behind the barrier worked to open the doors of the trailer.

Chazz squeezed off three more rounds, sharp well-placed shots that rang off the shields but did no damage other than rattle the owners.

While he searched for a clear shot, one of the Leather stepped back and threw something at the motel.

Chazz adjusted his sights and fired, missing the little bastard as he ducked behind cover much too fast.

That little something landed somewhere below him, but Chazz had no idea where. Not that it mattered. He knew what it was.

"Game's on, shitbags," he turned and roared out, *"Watch for the rush! It's coming our way."*

"Vonn!" he heard Ryan shout from below. "Help me reload this thing!"

"You reload it!"

"I never did one of these before!"

Rolling his eyes, Chazz ignored them and focused on the trailer. The shield wall abruptly fell back and the doors swung open.

"Goddammit," Chazz muttered, and pressed the weapon hard against his shoulder.

First it was three. Then five. Then a dozen, at least. Spilling out of the trailer's rear and falling to the ground. The fresh ones sprang up in a flash, and judging by how fast, it appeared the Leather had a load of fresh ones. The mindless stood and charged the motel, arms swinging like marathon runners on their last fumes with the finish line in sight. There were no visible features, only the frightening outlines emerging from the trailer and bolting across the parking lot.

Chazz opened fire.

He blew one off its feet, a sneaker flying in the air as it flew backwards.

Another shot rang out, spinning one mindless and knocking it down. Three zombies stumbled over the falling corpse and wiped out on the pavement.

A third shot missed but the fourth snipped off the upraised arm of one charging corpse at the shoulder, twisting it off its feet. That target tripped two others when it landed. One of them tried, of all things, to do a stomach crunch to get itself up.

Chazz blew the head clear off.

"That's one," he said, but now a full charge of the undead corksniffers was rushing the motel. Not quite a full trailer load, but enough, maybe five dozen or so, and most of them quite spirited. A few tripped on those fallen few struggling to rise. Two slipped on patches of black ice uncovered by the snow clearing and greased up by not so fresh gore.

By that time, Vonn and Ryan resumed firing down below.

Chazz supported from above, committing the one mistake no one should do when shooting charging zombies.

He got caught up in dishing out destruction.

A short burst ripped up one reanimated runner from sternum to nose, blasting him backwards in a stutter of meat and bone. Another rip of bullets whipped a zombie's head around and hooked him off his feet. A third burst and the magazine emptied, so Chazz reloaded as Vonn and Ryan continued firing below—Ryan apparently figuring out how to reload the Glock on his own.

A fresh magazine loaded and ready, Chazz snarled at how the undead had already crossed the midway point of the parking lot.

One of them exploded in a black burst of sludge, falling in two pieces. Another got launched backward, knocking down a handful more. The runners were moving too fast to get proper head shots in, so Chazz did what he could, spraying whole bodies and delighting in the effects. When they fell, either he or Vonn or Ryan lined up the fallen and blew their skulls apart.

The rifle shuddered comfortably against Chazz's shoulder as he either clipped or nailed zombies full-on. The undead dropped. Heads exploded. Another zombie flew backwards, a wet crater in its torso. Slowly, the charge withered, but didn't falter entirely. Zombies lifted themselves up from the cold, cold ground, leaving stringy matter in their wakes. Some stepped on their own inner hosing which dangled from gunshot wounds, and the pressure yanked even more from the gaping cavities. Others still, no longer able to run or walk, pulled themselves along the ground, one clutching claw after the other.

They were still gunning for the wide-open hole where the entrance used to be.

"Hold the line down there, you cocksicles," Chazz yelled, swapping out the empty magazine for a fresh one and readying it. *"They're getting closer."*

"We got this, Chazz!" Ryan hollered back, in between the cannon blasts that swallowed up the noise of the Glock.

Goddamn straight we got this, Chazz thought with a snarl, screwing his face back into the rifle sights.

Back behind the trailer, while gunfire ripped through the ranks of the unleashed mindless, the Dragon opened up another compartment and started pulling out equipment. With the help of Leech, the Dragon hefted a pair of tanks and strapped them to his back. Velcro buckles were lashed into place at the leader's waist and chest. Fuel lines were opened up and gauges flared to life, their needles somersaulting and showing full loads. The Dragon took an offered safety mask, one that a torch welder would use to protect his face and filter smoke, and fitted that over his regular guise. Then he hauled on fire-retardant gloves that resembled thick oven mittens.

Gunfire continued to crackle and pop. That was fine. No problem at all in fact. The mindless were shock troops, used to overwhelm defenders and force them to waste whatever ammunition they might have. But whoever was in the motel angered the Dragon by destroying a very valuable tanker. One that held all their reserve fuel. Not only did they light up the tanker, but they also lit the pickups and pinged a few rounds off the transport truck.

That twisted the Dragon's balls.

Once he finished gearing up, he held out both hands. Leech handed over the Dragon's most cherished weapon. And the most fun one to operate.

Light from the burning tanker fluttered over the advancing form of Dragon as he strode toward his minions. There, they walked before their leader, protecting him with upraised shields, getting him within striking range of the motel.

Which wasn't very far, really.

Then, the shields parted, and the Dragon aimed his flamethrower from the hip.

Chazz panned left and right, sizing up the transport and its doors left ajar.

No Leather to be seen.

The fuck? Chazz uncorked his eye to locate the leather-wearing sonsabitches and saw their shields right away. At the midway point of the parking lot. Standing ankle-deep in the gunned-down stew of several unmoving zombies.

No sooner did he look when the shields parted, revealing a shadowy outline hefting what might have been a rifle. Except there was something off about the figure, which Chazz didn't have time to puzzle out, as he rushed to get a bead on him.

The figure opened fire first.

Sending a scorching, *blinding* stream of fire at the second level of the motel.

Chazz threw himself back as the flame razed the window he'd been behind. That devastating spray smacked the exterior, shattering glass under the lavalike temperature, charring wood around the edges and, worst of all, sticking. Fire clung to the motel in a broad, raging sheet. Short red licks probed and darted in between gaps, transforming the room into the glowing interior of a kiln. Chazz sat up and stared as that blazing stream washed the motel left to right. Smoke puffed through unseen cracks. The temperature spiked dramatically as the world outside the window resembled the shifting surface of the sun.

Valor nowhere on his mind, Chazz scampered to his feet. Grabbing his rifle and a few remaining magazines, he bolted for the door.

"They're burning down our house!" Ryan yelled and held up his pistol—which he had reloaded himself. He whirled into the gaping hole of the entrance and, holding the Glock two-handed—the left supporting the right—popped off three shots outside.

When a stream of flame enveloped him.

He screamed, a horrifying, short-lived gurgle that sounded like he was drowning in oily phlegm. His clothing charred in a second as he staggered to the right, blindly exiting the gush of fire lancing into the lobby. Ryan stumbled into a wall and moved along it, as if remembering the old rule of stop, drop, and roll, before falling in a flaming heap.

That blinding lance of fire swung right and left, clinging to everything it touched, transforming the ceiling into an upside-down gas burner.

Then the blaze cut off, but Vonn could see it hadn't really. Whoever was directing that fire merely swung too far to the right, away from the entrance, razing the exterior to the far corner and scorching every foot.

Still wearing the slasher hockey mask, Vonn crouched, feeling the heat of the flames spreading across the ceiling. Vonn was perhaps the most realistic of the three men living in the motel. At least in his opinion. He knew the Norsemen as a faction were finished—long finished, in fact—but he listened to Chazz rant about rebuilding and reconquering, and yadda yadda yadda, because the man was a roommate. And there was strength in numbers. Plus it saved him from having to think too hard about things, which made life a lot easier living in the motel.

Didn't take no great amount of thinking to see the motel was well and truly finished, and that if Vonn didn't make a swift retreat *now*, he would perhaps share Ryan's fried chicken fate.

Two shapes hurried through the wrecked entrance, their swinging limbs on fire. *Zombies.* Uninhibited by the growing blaze and the smoke.

Vonn turned and fired, smashing them back outside, through the burning hole in the face of the motel.

More zombies charged through, however.

Rather than let them stumble over the waist-high debris, Vonn shot them as well. Rushed shots that destroyed entire arms or legs, or perforated torsos in big spattering gobs that sprayed out their backs, flinging the victims every which way, including out through the entrance.

Which was right around when the Ramfist clicked empty.

Wide-eyed and horrified, Vonn ran, taking the only route clear to take, since the stairs were cut off by the deluge of destroyed furniture left in the wake of the retreating pickup truck.

He bolted into the kitchen.

Where he swung the door behind him, whirled, and realized the thing was swinging *back*. That swinging door mortified Vonn, who wavered before rushing to a workstation. There he dumped the Ramfist and started dragging the tall table toward the door when a runner burst through, slamming into both table and man and knocking both over. Vonn landed on his back, the impact rattling him hard enough that when he looked up, he was only feet away from a blue-grey face coming for him. Black teeth snapped below eyes that had shriveled in their sockets. Grimacing, Vonn got a forearm across the throat of the thing, catching it in midlunge, but unable to stop its momentum. That gnashing, chomping bear trap of a mouth inched closer, while its hands clamped onto the living.

Vonn realized it was sapping his strength and then remembered his knife. He fumbled for the thing as the mindless pushed itself closer. The Norseman found the handle and yanked the blade free as his arm strength continued to weaken. He squealed as he stabbed the zombie's head twice and failed to penetrate an exceptionally thick skull. With a boyish shriek, he stabbed twice more, slicing undead scalp and releasing a pasty, polluted jelly, spattering his mask and neck.

The mindless lurched forward, close enough to bite down on Vonn's serial killer mask. Several teeth popped free of its rotten gums from the contact, the wicked roots plied into view. Vonn got his knife arm against the zombie's forehead, brought his fists practically together, and angled the blade into one of the zombie's eyes.

Whereupon he shucked that oyster, sinking sharp steel deep into the socket, through the lifeless raisin of an eye.

The mindless collapsed on top of him.

Breathing hard, Vonn pushed the dead thing off.

When three more mindless burst through the door in a puff of smoke.

Vonn squealed again, jumped to his feet, and reached for a butcher knife as all three zombies tackled him to the floor.

The impact knocked his mask askew, blinding him, and Vonn went feral, slashing and stabbing the offensive line on him. Chests, shoulders, throats, each cut releasing a downpour of watery filth.

One of the mindless bore his free arm back and chomped into his wrist, sinking its cracked teeth into the bone. Then it reared back, pinching skin and cloth and releasing a torrent of scarlet. Vonn's feet did a frenetic drum roll as the other zombies clawed at his armor. Blood spritzed the kitchen floor as Vonn screamed and grunted, kicked and flailed, underneath that combined weight.

Gus heard that losing struggle and it didn't sound good.

A shadow fell over him then, and he saw it was Maya, her inflamed face filled with urgency. She hurried to the table Vonn had started moving, and finished shoving it across the swinging door just as bodies slammed into the thing. A rack of long knives hung nearby, over what might have been a prepping table for salads. Maya grabbed one and went for Gus as three blackened hands sprouted from the barricaded doorway.

Vonn screamed again.

One of the zombies atop the cannibal raised its head and noticed Gus. It stood, its chest saturated in maroon, and collapsed when Maya grabbed a shoulder and stabbed up and under its chin. She took a second to grab another knife from the rack.

"I got a gun under me," Gus shouted.

That redirected her. She came for him as a sharp note rang out from the table pressed up against the door. A diseased head poked its way through.

Maya stabbed a second zombie through the ear, and it crumpled onto Vonn, who was still wrestling with the last mindless. With a parting shot, Maya kicked the thing just enough that the Norseman was able to fling the zombie off him. Blood flowed from one sleeve, however, splashing white tiles.

Maya abandoned the exhausted man and stopped by Gus, who thrashed against his bonds.

"Under the table, under the table."

And they were. The knots holding his leather straps in place were all underneath.

Maya sawed through the nearest one in seconds and Gus's arm was free. She scrambled to cut the next strap as the mindless continued to push against the blocked door.

She rounded the table when a bleeding and wheezing Vonn stood, staggered, and glared hate at her. He didn't have time to speak before three more zombies shoved aside the meddlesome table and charged into the room. Vonn spun and didn't have the strength to stop the rush. He embraced the first zombie as it crashed into him, pressing him to the floor. The other two jumped on top.

Another pair of mindless rushed through the doorway—which was on fire.

They went for Gus.

Who sat up, both arms free, and brought up Collie's Sig Sauer. He fired four shots.

Two heads backed up on their shoulders, black matter spewing from grisly entry and exit wounds. They fell as Maya released Gus's first leg. Vonn screamed again. Gus steadied himself, aimed and fired, snapping back a skull and dropping one of the monsters piled on the Norseman.

Maya pulled at Gus's leg, yanking him off kilter and ruining his next shot. More zombies entered the kitchen. Vonn released one last lingering squeal as the mindless tore his mask off. The zombies filtering into the kitchen joined the melee. They sank fingers into Vonn's gagging mouth and orbital cavities for a better grip of their meal. One of the things ripped up a fat length of skin that stretched until snapping. More blood sprayed across the tiles.

"Come on!" Maya roared at Gus, flipping smaller tables over, impeding the rush of more burning zombies staggering into the kitchen.

Gus scooted off the table, got boots on the floor, and brought up the Sig.

Gunfire, but not from Gus—coming from overhead somewhere.

Then Gus saw his shotgun, the discarded Ramfist, on the other side of the kitchen.

"This way!" Maya screamed, standing at a door at the far end of the room.

Charging mindless forced their way into the kitchen, tripping over the fallen and struggling to get clear. Gus wavered, looking from the zombies to the Ramfist, hating to leave such a cannon behind, but then relented. He rushed after Maya, who was already outside in the night. Bracelets of duct tape shivered off her wrists.

She slammed the door behind him as he landed in a snowdrift that reached his knees. Smoke blew past, heavy and harsh on the throat, while a great fiery glow rose from the front of the motel. Another flurry of gunshots, muffled but distinct, from within.

Maya hoofed it for the side entrance of a three-bay garage. Gus followed in her tracks at his top speed. She stopped at the door, tried the knob, and couldn't turn it. Then she got out of Gus's way—who rushed in with a full head of steam—and kicked the door with everything he had.

The door flew open.

Gus stormed inside with Maya behind him.

Both stopped and stared.

Three snowmachines. The racing kind. Sleek, green-and-white hogs with their weight in the nose, with short seats and storage containers in the back. Thick hand muffs covered the steering handles, offering extra warmth while driving. The machines occupied two of the garage bays. The remaining bay had what looked to be a huge still with accompanying tanks. Hoses and a tarnished knot of brass pipes linked the setup together, and Gus thought for a second the Norsemen had pieced together their own little booze station. Then he spotted a gas nozzle hanging from one of the tanks.

Gus went to one, and after a frenzied search saw a key was needed.

"Here!" Maya said.

He turned in time to catch the set of keys she'd tossed at him. Maya stepped away from an empty rack just inside the door. She hurried to one snowmachine, inserted a key and jammed a thumb into the starter button. It roared to life.

Gus placed the Sig on one rig and hurried to the garage door. Working the release rope overhead, he hoisted the thing high enough for the snowmachine to get through.

Maya left the machine she'd started and jumped on the next while Gus opened the door before it. When she got the engine going, she threw the last key out into the snow.

"Follow me," she yelled.

"Where're you going?" Gus yelled back, but the words were lost in the roar of the engine. She powered the sled across the concrete floor, sparks flying in her wake, until she hit snow. Then she was off to the races, buzzing away into the smoky night.

Gus jumped onto the other machine, gripped the handles, and squeezed the throttle. The powerful buck nearly whipped him off the thing's back, shooting him outside. He held on, eased off on the gas, and, when he had control, glanced back at the motel.

A gauzy halo wrapped around the building but flames waved merrily from the front.

Gus squeezed the throttle and blasted after Maya, who had a considerable head start.

And who had left an easy-to-follow trail in the snow.

25

Smoke filled the upstairs hallway, but Chazz didn't let that slow him down. He pushed through the choking clouds and stopped at the top of the stairs. When a handful of zombies clambered into view with all the poise of rabid hunting dogs, he gunned them down in a long burst, blasting apart skulls and bodies, riddling stairways and tiles.

Then he whirled away, his back slamming against the wall, and reloaded.

Hands pounded on a door below him, while the crackling of the fire grew.

The slap and clack signaled the weapon's readiness. Chazz peeked around the corner.

There, at the bottom of the stairs, aiming a gun up at him, was a leather-clad ghost, its outline just visible in the smoky dark.

An orange stream exploded from the gun—the flame*thrower*—coating the walls, stairs, and ceiling in a fiery glaze. The fierce heat forced Chazz to retreat. He raced down the corridor, putting distance between him and the fire, before stopping and searching for a doorknob. He opened a door and plunged through, closing it to just a hand's width behind him. There he waited, fighting for breath.

Dense smoke puffed past him, which he knew was not good.

A faint screaming gave him pause, and the sound ended almost as soon as it started. Chazz waited for more, thinking it was one of his boys. Probably dead. Might've been Ryan, who was always up for violence, but enthusiasm wasn't a replacement for intelligence. And it might have been Vonn, who was more resourceful and smarter. Chazz hoped the Leather hadn't gotten him, but the truth was, it didn't matter. The motel had been breached. The mindless were inside—*Leather*-grown mindless—as well as their handlers. The thought made Chazz's innards coil and fizzle with hate. The Norsemen were batshit crazy, make no mistake, but the Leather? *Insane.*

Chazz crouched and sized up the room. He was in the far wing, away from the garage where their snow sleds waited, fueled and ready. Well, *his* snow sled waited, if his suspicions of being the last one turned out to be true. That thought poisoned his guts. And done in by the Leather at that. If he was the last, he intended to do some serious heavy-handed destruction to the dickheads below.

Path chosen, he considered the hallway and grabbed a towel from the bathroom. He wrapped it around his face, then dropped to his belly and crawled into the hallway, staying below the smoke. He brought up the rifle and aimed at the bonfire lighting up the smoke, back where the Leather lit everything up.

All right, shitpeckers, Chazz projected, struggling to control his breathing. *Stick your faces out. Gobble fuckin' gobble.*

The fire snaked along the walls, rippled along the ceiling, devouring all that combustible goodness. The smoke thickened, impossibly so, reducing the flames to wild flickers wrestling with clouds. A low rumbling perked Chazz's ears, one that threatened to engulf the entire motel.

Not entirely surprising since the whole place was one huge goddamn matchbox. Back in the day, the heavy log and lumber structure seemed like a fortress to a zombie attack. Right now, all things considered, it sucked a rattlesnake's shit hole. Flames grew brighter, creeping along the walls and floor.

He choked out a cough, which became nearly uncontrollable barking where he couldn't get any good air back in. Smoke stung his eyes, adding to his misery. He got in a breath, however, and held it for whatever he was worth.

A figure materialized in that cloudy gloom. A hazy face but then it darted back from sight. A few seconds later, two, perhaps three outlines emerged from the stairwell. Two disappeared almost immediately, but one—with a golden face no less, threaded its way down the smoky corridor, its figure backlit by the flames.

Realizing he'd missed a chance to gun all of them down, Chazz snarled and aimed at the approaching Leather, who held a pair of swords.

Chazz lit him up, a full burst that stitched the Leather across the wall until he crashed to the carpet.

That brought the others.

Chazz let off two short bursts and crawled back on knees and elbows, retreating deeper into the room. He stood and waited, struggling to breathe, fighting a worsening cough.

A deep hiss of dragon fire shot by the open door. One blast. Then another, answering Chazz's initial volleys. The doorway ignited and charred. The carpet went up in a burning patch.

Christ, Chazz thought and retreated to the window, realizing he'd ducked into what was essentially an oven.

With only one way out.

"*Sayonara, fuckers,*" he roared and smashed out the glass with the butt of the rifle. The curtains came away with a good yank and he threw them over the lower frame. Before doing anything else, he stuck his head out the window.

Fresh air, God blessed and nothing sweeter.

An empty plain basking in firelight lay beneath him.

Bootsteps approached, or what he thought were bootsteps, prompting him to move faster. He dropped the gun outside, then heaved himself over the sill, gripping it like it was life itself. His legs dangled, reaching for ground a good six or seven feet below him. He lowered himself to his waist, then his chest—just as that flamethrowing shitbag filled the doorway and aimed.

Chazz let go as a sheet of fire shot out the window, immolating space he'd only just occupied.

Unfortunately, he crash-landed on a narrow metal sign post he'd missed seeing entirely, a sign directing traffic to the rear of the motel.

Steel and upright and positively unmoving, the sign's edge punched him squarely in the small of his back, hyperextending his spine to the point of breaking, paralyzing Chazz at the moment of impact. Breath-stealing pain swallowed him whole. Stunned, he flopped off the sign, which, as a parting gift, hooked his arm on the way to the frozen ground.

Chazz landed in snow, grimacing hard enough to crack his remaining teeth, and reached for his screaming back. Nothing moved below the waist. A rapid code of sputters, hisses, and groans left him as he tried to move his legs without success. His right leg eventually twitched but his left wanted nothing to do with him. Knowing he was in the worst kind of danger, he looked around for the assault rifle and caught a steel-toed boot to the face.

That destroyed the last of his teeth in one devastating explosion.

In addition, the vicious kick also split his maxilla (that bone keeping all his upper teeth in place) while crushing his nose and nasal cavity.

It also knocked him out cold.

Seconds later, hands grabbed him, pulled on the senseless parts, reviving him enough that he felt himself dragged along, head swinging between upraised arms. Everything below his eyes raged white hot while blood and shards of what might've been bone filled his mouth and prodded his throat.

He was dropped on pavement caked with a compressed layer of snow and eventually flipped over.

Smoke polluted the night sky, but he had no trouble seeing the four figures standing over him.

Chazz rolled his eyes, suffering from his many hurts. "Fuck... you," he slurred with a heavy nasal tone, the words coming from his destroyed face.

The gathered figures didn't reply, didn't move, until one stomped on Chazz's hand, crushing at least three fingers against the pavement. Chazz cried out and grabbed his ruined paw—his right one in fact—except the person standing on it ground his boot heel deeper into that tortured appendage.

And worked it, for a good five seconds, until releasing it.

Chazz clutched his broken hand and held it to his chest. When he glanced up, the one with the welder's mask and flamethrower stood over him. The flamethrower drooped in the owner's hand while smoke wafted around him.

"We're looking for someone," the Leather said. "A woman."

"Fuck... you," Chazz repeated wearily, wincing, suffering through the bloody remnants of his mouth.

Someone kicked him again, cracking his head to the right. Chazz only thought he closed his eyes, but he must've lost it for seconds, for when he came to, a set of knives had replaced the flamethrower. Those twin knives extended from the Leather's forearm, up to the main grip, which the Leather held in a fist.

"Did you have a woman here?" he asked.

Chazz nodded in spite of himself.

"She was one of us?"

Against his better judgment, Chazz again nodded and spat gobs onto his chin.

"You have a garage," the Leather stated. "Back there. Two snowmobiles are gone. Did the woman take one?"

Chazz's eyes narrowed. He shook his head. It beat speaking, and speaking was hurting more and more.

"I won't ask again," the Leather warned. "Did she take one of the machines?"

Part of Chazz was glad the assbag wouldn't ask again. He took his time, probing his mouth with his tongue, which ached as if someone had dropped a piano on it. Again, he shook his head.

That didn't seem to please the Leather, who straightened his back. He slowly knelt upon Chazz's arm, pinning it to the pavement and adding to his pain. The Leather wrapped a mitten around the back of the cannibal's head, gripped it hard, and lifted, as if about to give the dying man a sip of water. Instead of water, however, those twin blades moved in until their tips rested against the bags of Chazz's narrowed, watering eyes.

Chazz set his jaw and huffed and puffed, expecting the worst.

And he got it.

Long seconds later, after the screaming and thrashing had ceased, the Dragon rose from his victim. He regarded Slit, who carried a shotgun in one hand, and a duffel bag in the other.

"Spare ammunition," the minion reported.

The Dragon didn't hear him. He removed his claws and sheathed them. He threw back one side of his duster and freed the flamethrower from the long holster extending down his leg. Armed and ready, he walked back around the burning motel, followed by Slipknot and Slit. There, not far away, was the garage, and stemming from it were two sets of them snowmobile tracks, leaving the open bays before becoming one.

He stared at those tracks going off into the night.

It was the Chemist. He knew it. She was alive. But it puzzled him how she couldn't get away from her captors while the fighting was going down. And if she did get away, why was she with them now? She most certainly knew it was the Leather coming for her. Had to know they would come for her. Perhaps she had been forced to leave by her kidnappers?

That bothered the Dragon. She was the Chemist. She'd been with the Leather for *years*—killing, torturing, but later only watching such acts without question. She'd been creating fuel for the Leather all the while, for *years*. She'd even designed, built, and modified the Dragon's *flamethrower*... for which he was eternally thankful.

But now someone was trying to take her away from the Leather. Perhaps even a lowly Norseman who realized who she was. What she could do. Which was priceless. Maybe they would force her to become one of the Norse. Or, if it wasn't the Norse, maybe attempt to win her over to whatever mindset they possessed.

The Dragon inhaled cold winter air and tasted smoke.

No.

The Chemist was one of the Leather. She belonged to them. She belonged to *him*. Whether she knew it or not. Maybe she'd ran, not knowing who was attacking the motel, and her kidnappers went after her. It was as simple as that. The Dragon would find her. He had to. Besides reclaiming her, only she could potentially reveal what happened to the Mallet and the North Battleford crew.

As for whoever drove that second snowmobile... the Dragon glowered behind his mask. He'd find that person as well.

A snowmobile remained in the garage. It would stay there. The Dragon had no intention of using it to follow those tracks in the snow. Assuming the sleds were fully fueled, they would not have a range of any more than five hundred klicks. The Leather still had two functional pickups, somewhat shot up but not badly. The Dragon's transport was intact and mobile. Their fuel supply would be limited, however, with the destruction of the tanker, but the remaining rides had reserves. At the very worst, Regina had reserves as well, in the pit of Vampire Joe's house of horrors. The minion called Gold was dead, gunned down by the piece of shit the Dragon had killed minutes earlier. Besides their shields, they'd all been wearing armored vests, but one of those rounds blew out Gold's relatively unprotected neck, killing him instantly.

The Dragon stared across that dark expanse. The Chemist was alive, of that he was glad.

He would find her.

Or die trying.

26

During the first hour after escaping the motel, Gus would glance back, looking for signs of pursuit. Nothing, except for that long, straight cut left behind them, underneath a hazy quarter moon. They drove deep into the night, buzzing across the freezing plain with the wind gusting into their backs. Maya didn't turn on her headlights, but Gus had no trouble following her. The instrument panel had a gas gauge, which showed a needle indicating almost a full tank. So he settled in, following Maya's lead some fifteen meters ahead of him.

Snow. A world of snow and darkness.

The machines motored across that great expanse until Maya slowed to a stop and waited for him to catch up. A shivering Gus halted his rig beside hers and kept the engine running.

"Thought you weren't ever going to stop," he said, making himself heard over the noise.

"How much fuel do you have?"

Gus checked his gauge. "Three quarters full. You?"

"About the same."

"You cold?" he asked.

"Freezing."

Gus wiped his nose. "Thought we were dead back there."

"We have to press on," Maya said, getting to the point. "Find somewhere warm."

"You know where you're going?"

"No idea. I'm a mountain girl. All this flat land? I'm lost. You?"

"East coast boy. Never been this far west."

Nodding and looking miserable, she scanned the awesome emptiness and wiped a hand across her nose.

"Was that the Dragon back there?" Gus asked.

"We can talk later, okay?" She faced him. "Let's get moving. I'll keep ahead. We've got to get out of this cold. I can barely feel my face."

"Yeah." Gus nodded. "Okay."

With that, she jammed her hands back inside the hand warmers and sped off, the engine buzzing. Gus followed.

Sometime later, she turned into a wide lazy arc that caught his attention. Minutes after that, he saw the reason for the turn.

A house. In the middle of nowhere, encircled by a few trees. As they drew closer, a second building came into view, adjacent to the first. A row of windows materialized slowly, dark as obsidian, as well as several planks leaning against a deck. Maya drove to that landing and stopped at its base. Gus halted feet behind her. He sank to his knees when he got off and frowned at the depth.

Maya was already climbing through a drift on the deck. "Deeper . . . than it looks," she warned, her mouth stiff from the cold.

"Yeah," he muttered, feeling his own chops partially frozen. He trudged onto the deck.

At the door, Maya kicked back the snow. Gus helped, and together they cleared away the base. She tugged at the latch and failed to open it. Releasing a frustrated grunt, she stepped back and folded her arms. "You got . . . that gun?"

Which came out in a chatter of teeth.

"Yeah, but I'd rather not use a bullet," Gus said and kicked the door. It didn't give like the last one, and four good stomps later, he stopped and stared at the thing. "Goddamn," he said. "That's a tough door."

"Nobody home," she said, watching the windows.

"I could break the glass."

Cold as she was, she didn't say anything more. He was feeling it, too, but she was still without a coat and her mask. The window on the door's left looked like a better access point, so he looked in, unable to see a thing.

He pulled out the Sig. Settling in close to the glass, he put his elbow through the pane. It wasn't a clean break. Plenty of jagged teeth lined the frame, but he did what he could to hammer it away. Pocketing the gun, he climbed in, feeling tiny nubs clutch and claw at his vest. A sink caught him, then he tumbled over a countertop and landed hands-first in a kitchen. Gus rose unsteadily, feeling as if he might've pulled something, and lumbered over to the back door.

As he suspected. Two extra sliding locks, top and bottom.

Feeling his latest tumble, he undid everything and pulled the door open.

"Oh, thank you," Maya huffed, sounding frozen as she hurried inside. Gus closed the door, but the cold flowed inside through the smashed window. Not that it mattered much. The house was an ice box, even though it sheltered them from the wind and elements.

Worse, however, was that it was much darker inside than out.

Trembling with arms folded, Maya shuffled into the dining room. Gus flicked nearby switches on the wall. No lights. No surprise. A fridge was behind him, so he opened that, saw a few things stowed inside, and left them.

A whisper of fabric came from the right.

"Oh shit," Maya whimpered from somewhere deeper inside the home.

Gus couldn't see where, though, and rang his knee off a hard corner trying to follow her. The impact hobbled him as he limped through the room.

There, with the night shining through a gap in some heavy curtains, sat Maya in a huge recliner. She had a blanket wrapped around herself, right up to her chin, leaving only her pale face.

"Oh, this is good," she chattered, pulling the material up higher. "This is good."

Gus scanned the rest of the living room. "I'll see if I can find you something better."

She grunted at that, so he left her alone and ventured further into the home. He kept the Sig out and ready, barely seeing where he was going. With the racket he'd made getting into the place, he didn't expect any undead, but he did figure he'd find corpses of people who'd departed the world by their own hand. Would not be the first time he entered an aboveground grave.

His search ended in what appeared to be the master bedroom. A pair of windows with their curtains only half-drawn allowed a feeble after-midnight glare into the room, outlining a huge bed. A thick comforter lay on top. Gus scanned the murky interior and shuddered upon noticing a walk-in closet.

Walk-in closets always creeped him out. Never knew what might lurk in one, or where it might go.

This closet, however, was filled with clothing, extra blankets, and other items he couldn't rightly make out. Didn't matter. He walked back out and nearly collided with Maya, standing in the doorway with the blanket wrapped around her.

"Jesus Christ," Gus fired off. He rubbed his knee where she'd knocked him and sent a glare her way.

Without a word, Maya went around him to the bed. She threw the blanket over the comforter and unzipped the leather vest she was wearing, but it got stuck halfway.

"Help me," she hitched. "With this."

Gus wavered at the request, uncertainty flooding him. In the end, however, he helped her take off the vest. The material peeled away, revealing a thin sweater underneath. Powerful shivers gripped her all the while, and when she reached for the hem of the sweater, she struggled to pull it over her head.

Once again, Gus helped, getting the garment over her head.

There was a T-shirt underneath, and she was going for it.

"Gotta strip," Maya said, voice trembling. "I'm... a block of ice. Here. Help me."

Once again, she could only manage to lift her shirt halfway, exposing a bare midriff with more than a few scars lashing it, unmistakable in that spare light. Gus faltered at the sight, then helped get the T-shirt off over her head. That got tossed onto the sweater.

"Now... now the boots," she said as her shaky hands worked on a belt. "Hur... hurry."

Gus pulled off the boots and chucked them aside. Seeing her fumble with her belt, he helped her, undoing the buckle and unfastening the leather pants. She placed hands on his shoulders so that he could pull them down to her knees.

When it was over, she plopped down on the bed.

Gus got her pants off, her socks, and, when she stood up, the thin leggings she wore underneath. In nothing more than a sports bra and underwear, she pulled back what she could of the bedcovers. Just a little, before she had to let Gus do the rest.

She was thin. Not quite skeletal, but a marathon runner's build. As if days of constant activity had bled away all excess fat. A litany of scars marked her moonlit skin, thick lashes and warped *X*s, from neck to thighs, as if she'd repeatedly dived headfirst into a briar patch. Or had often been dragged through one. When she lay down, she reached for the blankets and failed to pull them over herself. Gus helped with that as well, tucking her in up to her chin, and even pulling the comforter up around her head.

Maya closed her eyes, but didn't stop trembling, on the verge of convulsions.

"What are... you waiting for?" she asked in a quivering voice.

A confused Gus didn't answer.

"Get in," she ordered.

That shot a lightning bolt of fear through him, and though on the precipice of frostbite and even hypothermia, she still sensed his hesitation.

"Strip, first. I need. I need your... body heat. Get in... and get close."

Fear morphed into shock, rooting him in place.

And in that dark place, her eyes beheld him, dark and penetrating. "Please."

That unlocked him.

Gus stripped, tossing the Sig on the bed and dropping the rest of his shit on the floor. His layers came off in a puddle until he got down to his underdrawers, the cold biting at his person the entire time. Leaving his socks on, he was about to get in, when he remembered the blankets in the closet. A frenzied minute later, when the cold really started to bite, he lifted the extra layers he'd heaped on and climbed in beside her, ignoring the ridged spine of her back.

She was shaking. Gus wiggled in close, pressing his chest up against her.

"Put your arm around me," she said.

So he did, whereupon she took his wrist and pulled him closer while she pressed back, completing the spoon. *Cold*, she was cold, but he held on, with her bottom firm against his crotch. Gus realized the predicament and didn't dare move a muscle,

"Let me get a pillow," he said.

"What for?"

"For . . . below. My . . . thing is . . ."

"I'm *freezing* here," she cut him off. "This is survival one-oh-one. Shared . . . body heat. Don't . . . perv it up."

That shamed him for even going there. His other hand was in that neighborhood, however, so he gave himself enough room to cup himself, creating a barrier of sorts down there. He didn't speak of it, and neither did she, so he hugged her closer. With a sigh that set off a much stronger shudder, Maya snuggled down even more, lapping up whatever heat he had in him. She was a dry block of ice and smelled of dried sweat, not entirely unpleasant. It made him wonder how much he stank up the bed.

Arm around her. Chest to back. Skin on skin.

Her breathing slowed and after a while she wasn't shivering so badly. Maybe. The blankets trapped the heat underneath and Gus's breathing slowed. His eyes became heavy and he realized he hadn't slept since the night before. A lot had happened since then. The biggest thing being him . . . cuddling up in bed . . . with one of the Leather.

A *former* member of the Leather.

We all fuck up every now and again, right? Milo's voice whispered in the great silence of the house.

"Yeah," Gus whispered back, and adjusted an arm just a little. His eyes closed, but not before he pressed his forehead against the back of her neck.

Completing the connection.

He woke with a lurch, jerking his arm back and reaching for a gun that wasn't there.

Sitting up in bed, Gus remembered where he was, and stared at the black chasm that was the doorway. It was a lot lighter in the room, as the sun once again nudged back the night.

"What's wrong?" Maya asked, leaning toward him from where she lay on her side. Gus looked at her, then the door. "Thought . . . I heard something."

"I didn't."

He looked back at her. "You okay?"

"Uncertain if I'll ever be okay again . . . but I'm much improved over a few hours ago." She smiled sleepily. "You're one toasty unit."

He wasn't sure what to say to that. "I'll be back in a minute."

With that, he got out of bed and pulled the blankets back up, so none of that precious heat was lost. The house was a freezer and his skin prickled as he looked for the Sig. He located it at the foot of the bed and chastised himself for letting it out of his sight.

Gun in hand, he went through the house, feeling a draft from where they'd smashed the window. Three bedrooms, a dining room, a living room, a den, and an office. Three bathrooms, including one just off the master bedroom. All meticulously kept and not a person or body in sight. Best of all? No basement. That greatly relieved him.

Back at the front door Gus peeked out of the spy hole there. Not a soul in sight. He tiptoed around to the picture window and looked out at the untouched frozen landscape, quaintly framed between two bare maple trees. No vehicle in the driveway. No cleared highways. Best of all, no sign of anyone coming after them.

Standing there, practically bare-assed and in need of a leak, Gus scratched one butt cheek and freed his underwear from his crack. He located a bathroom and took care of matters there. Leak finished and patrol done, he went back to the bedroom, and placed the Sig on the nearby night table.

"Well?" Maya asked.

"Nothing. Place is clear. No sign of your Dragon."

A noticeable pause at that. "He's not my Dragon."

"Sorry."

She wasn't so sleepy anymore. "No offense taken. Believe me. Now get back in here."

Gus did so, and without any lingering hesitation like before. He didn't cuddle up to her, however, as that depression he left was still comfortably warm.

She rolled onto her back, blankets up her face, and stared at the ceiling.

They stayed that way for seconds, not speaking, just absorbing the warmth of a shared bed.

"We have to get moving," she eventually said.

"Yeah," Gus agreed.

"He won't give up."

"He wants you that bad, eh?"

"Yeah," she replied. "That bad. The motel? He torched it. With his flamethrower."

"A flamethrower?"

"Mm-hm."

"You guys were, ah, friends?"

"No. Although I pretended to be when he was in the same room. I never let myself be alone with him. It was tricky, ensuring there was someone around when he was around, and when he didn't want anyone around."

"Oh."

"I mean . . . he didn't make any advances . . . but he was working up to it. He was definitely . . . attracted. I mean, I'm nothing to look at, but considering what's out there? I look pretty damn good. I wore extra layers to frump myself up, so I didn't get any attention. From anyone."

"And that worked?"

"Yes and no. Like I said, I was getting my share. And that was in spite of everything—even wearing the mask. Really, the only thing that . . . saved me . . . was the Dog Tongue. He made it a rule. No screwing around. It clouded judgment, in his opinion. Diverted energy from the one driving objective, to take control of everything."

Gus made side-eyes at her.

"I think," Maya continued, "the Dragon was working himself up in the ranks to a position where, when the Dog Tongue reached his goals, he could . . . make his move. On me. It was coming. Like maybe put in a request for me. Once the Leather took down everything. Everyone. Procreation would have to be addressed."

Gus knew what that meant. "Sorry."

"That's all over now. Mostly. Hey, you took care of that."

"Some of it, yeah. I had a lot of help."

"You awake then?"

He was. "Yeah."

"All right. Let's get dressed here and search the house."

"The place looks good. Whoever lived here wasn't around when shit went down. As far as I could tell."

"Take a look for something to eat then. Canned goods, especially. Just make sure that the cans aren't rusty or dented or anything. Nothing else. Okay?"

"Cans? After all this time?"

"As long as the cans themselves aren't damaged and are in a cool place, like a cupboard. We should be good. Go take a look and I'll search for some extra clothes for us. Especially me. I nearly froze my butt off last night."

Gus smiled. He rolled out of bed and got dressed. His clothes were damp, cold, and felt unclean. His coat still smelled faintly of piss, as a quick sniff check confirmed.

"Stinky?" she asked from the other side of the bed, one lip hitched up, showing missing teeth.

"Yeah. Just wondering why the zombies didn't come for me when I was strapped to the kitchen table."

"Fresh blood," Maya replied. "The Leather discovered urine attracted them, but fresh blood trumps it. Thankfully so. Can you imagine what that would look like if they were filling up bags of blood? Sick."

Sick indeed, but Gus didn't think it was beyond the Leather.

"Where'd he get that flamethrower?" he asked.

"The Dragon? That's on me. I built it for him."

"You built a flamethrower?"

Maya looked at him. "I didn't have a choice. He knew my background and asked if I could do it. I said I could. Had to. They knew I tinkered with various independent pressurized fuel systems, so . . . yeah. Anything less and they'd be suspicious. You . . . don't last in the Leather if they suspect you."

"So you gave in," Gus said.

"Yeah, I gave in. You understand why, though."

"I understand he has a goddamn *flamethrower* that he uses on people."

"Mostly undead, but yeah. A few people."

They locked gazes then, and Gus was no longer thinking about the shared warmth and all that shit from the night before.

"I'll go look for that food," he said and walked off.

Feeling conflicted, Gus made his way through the house. She wasn't a Leather. Not no more. She saved him and herself when the opportunity presented itself. Even blew up the refinery, and that took preparation, so he believed her. The scars on her convinced him as well, but the reality was she could have gotten those from anywhere, anytime.

Still, he didn't like the idea of anyone intentionally building weapons for the Leather. Not after what he'd seen. Even if her story made sense to him.

She didn't have a choice, dummy, his brain barked at him.

*

A waiting bathroom door reminded him of a second, even more necessary morning pit stop. So he did that, thankful for the distraction. Once done and flushing (lifting his spirits greatly), he stopped before the mirror. Which was the first time he had had a chance to look at himself since North Battleford.

Whoa.

The sight stunned him. He blinked, as if that might improve the picture. It did not. His face looked tenderized. Brutalized. Splotchy with purple and blue and that sickly sepia that reminded him of jungle rivers. Both eyes were black and swollen, his left worse than the right. A mass of flesh drooped over his eyelid, which explained the nagging pressure there. A lump on his forehead looked to be receding. He opened his mouth, saw the remaining teeth and the two new holes in the back.

"Oh man," he whispered at the reflection, feeling his guts turn and his anxiety rise. A face like his needed medical attention and there was none to be had.

Needing a distraction from his distraction, he wandered into the kitchen, located the pantry, and opened the doors. It wasn't full, but there were canned goods. He grabbed a couple and turned them around. Beans and wieners. Corn. Carrots and peas. Beans in tomato sauce. Even two cans of corned beef. There were others as well, all in good condition and without any of the defects Maya told him to watch for. In addition to the food, there was the usual assortment of boxed pasta and things well past their expiry date.

"You better have a can opener around here," he said, and started going through the nearby drawers.

He found one next to the sink and held it aloft like he'd just found Excalibur.

On impulse, he pulled open the cupboard right above that.

There, staring back at him, was a bottle of rum.

Captain Morgan White, in fact. The dashing decal smiled broadly at him.

The sight of his old friend caught him completely off guard, but he reached out and took the bottle down, marveling at it, mouth puckered into an *O*.

"How you doin', buddy?" Gus asked quietly and didn't get a reply. Not that he expected one, but, you know, given the history, it would not have surprised him. Still, the bottle remained just a bottle, and nothing more.

"You are the right kind of drink I need, but . . ." Gus let that word hang, and, eventually, placed the bottle with the buccaneer face back in the cupboard, just the way he'd found it.

"You stay here," he said to the bottle. "Safer, I think . . . Good to see you, though. Real good. Hope . . . hope you're doing well."

With a final nod, Gus closed the cupboard and smoothed the wooden surface. On impulse, he opened it again. There was the captain, still smiling.

Gus smiled back and gently closed the door.

Just around the corner was a cloth bag hanging off a coat hanger. Stuffed into that bag were a bunch of other bags. Gus extracted one and put the cans inside, along with the opener.

He checked on things in the living room, looking out the windows for any signs of the Dragon and his minions. There were none, so he went back to the bedroom and stopped halfway.

"You decent in there?" he called out.

As an answer, Maya stepped into view with her arms outstretched. A sweater covered her torso, and she wore a pair of jeans.

"Jackpot," she said. "Guy had plenty of sweaters. I'm wearing three. And he had four pairs of long johns. I'm warmer than . . . well, I'm warm."

"You almost had a joke there," Gus said.

"Almost. You find anything?"

"Except my face. What's left of it."

"Yeah, you took a beating."

"Where I come from, we'd call it a shit-kicking."

"You might have a broken cheekbone or something."

"What?" Gus asked. "You think?"

"Look, not to change subjects to detract from or diminish your facial hematomas, but did you find anything else?"

Remembering, he held up the bag and rattled it.

"All look good?" she asked.

"To me it does," he said, "but you best check."

"I laid out some clothes for you, too. Double them up if you want. Underwear included."

Gus nodded and they passed each other in the hall. He held out the bag of grub and she took it.

"We good?" she asked.

"Yeah. We're good."

"Because I don't want you to go on thinking I was happy doing what I did for the Dragon. I wasn't. Not then and not ever. With him or any of the Leather. I did what I did to survive. You have to understand that."

Gus nodded. He understood, dismissing his earlier thoughts.

"Good," she brightened a little. "Do whatever you have to do in there. I'll be in the kitchen when you're finished."

Nodding he would, he went on into the bedroom.

As promised, clothing awaited. Everything she said and even a few pairs of thick socks. Gus stripped down and pulled on the fresh clothes, smelling a hint of wood on them. The Sig went down the back of his pants, though he wished he had a proper holster. Last thing was the pissy coat, and after getting into some clean clothes, he loathed putting it on. He took it by the collar.

"There you are," Maya said as he entered a kitchen much better seen in daylight. "All spruced up. Feel better?"

"Yeah. As long as I don't think about my face. You?"

She wiggled all ten fingers, then moved away from the counter, and what she had hidden behind her back. Two bowls filled with beans and wieners. Approximately a can in each.

"This is yours," she said and handed him the bowl and a spoon.

Not hiding his surprise, Gus nodded thanks and dug in, his face souring just a little, at both the taste and discomfort of chewing.

"Yeah, I know," Maya said. "Texture's a little off, and I'm not sure about the nutritional value of the wieners. But the beans should be good. And we need the calories."

"Tastes like a tin can," Gus said.

"Can't be helped. No power to heat it up. It was this or nothing." She started eating, and for minutes, the only sound was that of them chowing down. She ate daintily, if not quickly, using a dish towel to wipe her mouth at times. Gus used his hands and sleeves. When they finished, they left the bowls in the sink. Then they found the coat closet and dug out four coats of various sizes. Two were smaller, fuchsia and white, while the others were larger and darker.

"Weird," Maya said. "These are women's coats but . . . there were no women's clothes in that bedroom."

"Maybe the other rooms."

"Didn't look like it to me. They looked more like guest bedrooms."

Minor mystery aside, they took the coats, which were bulky but with the extra layers underneath filled out perfectly. There were boots for a guy, but two sizes too large for Gus. Multiple sets of gloves, as well as ski masks and hats.

"Oh my," Maya said and pulled on one, then another. "Oh, *my*."

Gus had to admit, two would be better than one. And they stretched. He did the same, doubling up on the winter hats.

They left the house shortly thereafter, with the bag of food swinging in Maya's hand. Not a lot, but enough for a few days if they stretched it out. Nothing to drink, but Maya suggested they melt the snow—which would have to make do until they found something better.

The garage was next.

Two bays, one empty. Gardening supplies as well as a ride-on mower. Skis. A modest selection of hand tools, nothing of particular interest. A hockey net with a cardboard goalie inserted. Hockey sticks nearby, their edges frayed from use. A set of helmets were there as well, but neither Gus nor Maya wanted to wear them, not with the doubled-up winter hats.

"No gas," Gus said after a quick search.

"No." Maya looked around. "All right, let's get out of here."

"Where?" Gus asked. "I mean . . ." and he waved an arm, "out there is . . . the flattest part of the country."

"Suggestions?"

"Well . . . no."

"This is how I see it. We won't get very far on snowmobiles."

"Snowmachines."

"Whatever. We only have the gas in the tanks. And they will be after us. After the flamethrower incident you still want to make a stand?"

"Not right now, no."

"Then we go west. Maybe dipsy doodle here and there. Hope for snow to cover our tracks, and—what's wrong?"

"Dipsy doodle?"

"My mom would say that all the time. Long been a part of my lexicon. I'm sure you have your favorites."

"I just swear."

"Well," Maya granted. "All right. That's you. I'll shut up now. You might have noticed I tend to blab a lot. Maybe even more these days. You don't get to talk much when you're one of the Leather. When they speak to you, okay, but otherwise, no. Not out in the open, anyway."

"You're right," Gus said, getting her attention. "You do blab a lot."

She fixed him with a look.

"Tell me to fuck off anytime," he said.

She didn't, though.

So they got on their snowmachines—which was part of Gus's lexicon, but he kept that to himself. And he suspected lexicon meant dictionary, but he would keep that to himself as well. Maya was smart. Real smart, and, without question, smarter than him.

"Got your pistol?" she said as they approached the side entrance to the garage, which was unlocked.

"Yeah. You not taking any of those tools?"

"Like what?"

"I dunno. The hammer, maybe? That would work in a fix. Or even a knife? From the kitchen?"

She reached into her coat pocket and pulled out a kitchen knife, sheathed in a plastic grip.

"I tucked this away while you were trying on clothes," she said.

Gus nodded warily, wondering what else she might have on her. "How'd you get out of that chair back in the motel kitchen, anyway?"

Another tight-lipped smile. "I pulled a Houdini."

"Yeah, I saw that. Mind sharing? In case I'm ever strapped to a table again."

"Wouldn't have worked for you anyway. They tied you down with leather straps. They had my hands lashed to the chair with duct tape. Thankfully, they used the cheap kind, which can tear if you know how to work it. I saw a video online once when I was a teenager. Done by a CIA instructor talking about escape techniques—specifically if you're strapped down by duct tape. So I tried it out and it worked."

"You tried it out?" Gus asked.

"Yeah, my sister taped me to a chair."

"Jesus."

"I know, right? Dysfunctional family. Other teenagers are out and about in their free time, but we're studying so we can apply for scholarships and doing escape tricks in the garage. Oh, I'd tape her to the chair, too. It worked, but only with the cheap tape. The more expensive stuff, not so much. Their mistake."

Gus supposed it was.

"Time to ride," she informed him. "My danger sense is tingling."

"You got one of those too, huh?"

"Danger sense? If you don't have one these days, you're already dead."

A short time later, dressed in their newly acquired winter clothing and with their meagre rations tucked away on the snowmachines, they mounted their rides, and drove off toward the horizon.

27

Wind cut across their faces as they powered across the unending open expanse of Saskatchewan. Maya took the lead and Gus followed, watching her streak ahead in short pulsing bursts, slowing to allow him to catch up. At times, instead of moving in a straight path, she would drive in wavy lines. He didn't know what to make of those, and he followed her example, wondering about the need for evasive driving. The sky and land were clear, however. No signs of danger in any direction. Not even a traffic sign for that matter, which made him wonder if they were anywhere near a highway.

After perhaps an hour of such antics, it struck him that there was no reason for her erratic weaving—other than she was free from her Leather overlords. And loving it.

He eventually decided to take the lead and buzzed by her in a blast of speed. When he eased off the gas in favor of conserving it, Maya whipped by in a spray of snow, and gunned it for the figurative border. Gus maintained his conservative pace, but he smiled underneath his ski mask.

She was enjoying herself. Probably the first time in years.

Around noon, they stopped in a small, wooded area, where the trees provided ample cover. Gus pulled up alongside her and gave her a look.

"You're having a good time," he said, as she stood next to her machine in knee-deep snow.

"Sorry, got carried away there," she said. "Been a while since I've been on one of these things. We had them when we were kids. I, ah, wanted to see how well she handled, in case we needed to make a run for it."

"Did she pass?"

"Oh yeah," Maya replied. "Flying colors. Might've used up a little more fuel but we're closer to where we're going. Wherever that is."

Gus got off his machine for a stretch, sinking to midshin. It was a good ride, but his ass was numb from sitting, and his knees weren't the happiest either, despite droning along on relatively flat land. He looked while Maya munched on snow.

"Don't eat the yellow stuff," she warned him.

"You kiddin'?" He frowned. "We learned that in grade one."

"I didn't see any, just so you know. But there could be moose around here."

"Moose?" Gus asked, looking around. "Seems kinda . . . flat."

"Herds were migrating, but they do seem to like more wooded areas around ponds and lakes, where there's abundant plant life. We'd get them all over Alberta. They'd be strolling through our backyard all the time."

"Lucky you," Gus said, a little off-kilter in the snow.

"You okay?" she asked.

"Just stiff."

Maya nodded and pointed at some nearby stumps. "Someone's been cutting wood around here. See that one there? I cleared the snow off it. The stump's still light colored, which means it's a fresh cut. No tracks, though, so it was done before this last snowfall."

Gus looked around. "Way out here? Long way to travel."

"No choice. But, realistically, if you don't have alternative sources of power, you go back to burning wood for heat. And anyone with the time, know-how, and available biomaterial could produce ethanol on a small scale. Enough to power their motors. To get around and do things."

"The Leather haven't rounded everyone up?"

"Not yet, and maybe not ever. It's a big country. Lotsa places to hide. Lotsa places off-grid."

"How would you find them?" Gus asked and cringed. "'They,' I mean."

She smiled. "Smoke."

"Smoke."

"Folks have to heat their homes in the winter. Where there's smoke, there's people."

Gus supposed so and decided to change topics. "So where we going, again?"

"No clue. What I'd *like* to do is circle back to Alberta. But that's not going to happen considering our fuel and food."

"I have a suggestion."

"Okay."

"We head back to Regina. Back to the Anchor Bay."

That stiffened her. "You still want to fight the Leather."

"Oh I want to kill every last one of the shitty-assed bastards," Gus replied. "And the Anchor Bay . . . well, I spent time there. Searching the place. Patrolling it. I know the corridors and the rooms. We could ambush them. If we go back and wait."

"They would go back there, eventually. As far as I know, they don't know Vampire Joe is dead. Or the Dog Tongue, for that matter. Unless . . ."

Gus waited.

Maya relented. "Unless they found the Dog Tongue's head at the motel."

"Dog Dick's head?"

That made her smile again. "Yeah. The Mallet had it. Proof of death, you see. If the Dragon found that, he'd know Dog Dick—that's so great. I'm using it from now on—he'd know Dog Dick is dead. Some alliteration for you."

Gus wasn't sure what alliteration was. "The main reason for heading back to the Anchor Bay is supplies."

Maya pointed at him. "You're right. That place is loaded."

"Food, water, power, and tankers in the garage."

"Right, it was one of those autonomous, independent off-the-grid setups. Not many of those around."

"So . . . sound like a plan?"

"It'll be dangerous."

"I'll take care of that. You can . . ."

"Watch your back?"

That took him off guard. "Yeah."

"I saw that hesitation. I'm not offended. Trust is hard to come by these days. Just remember, I saved you from an inflictor. To the Leather, that's like . . . that's like shooting a prince."

"Thought you said they were more like bodyguards."

"They're fucked-in-the-head sadists is what they are," Maya said with a trace of heat. "Sorry. Anyway, come to think of it, it was only a few hours ago we were literally in bed together. So . . . we're really going back and forth here with helping each other out?"

"All right, I trust you."

"You don't sound like it."

"I do."

"It's okay. A lot has happened within the last day or so. And you have your trust issues. Hard not to these days. No doubt you've had experiences to justify that."

"Really, I do."

Maya held up a hand. "I believe you."

An awkward silence followed.

"So, your idea is to go back to Regina?" she asked.

"Uh . . . yeah."

"Cool. Just one thing, though."

"Okay."

"I can understand your desire to kill off every last one of the bastards."

"Shitty-assed bastards," Gus corrected.

"Shitty-assed bastards," she repeated. "Sure. And I appreciate you helping me when you did. And I will reciprocate when and where I can. But . . . if I'm being completely honest here . . ."

Gus knew he wasn't going to like the next part.

"As much as I appreciate everything you've done, I need you to understand I'm not going to be taken by them. Not after everything I've been through. I'm not going to risk being captured. I'm just not. So if you're . . . about to die, and I can't save you . . . If the odds look too much in their favor and I risk being taken . . . I will leave you. In a heartbeat."

He was right. He didn't like that part at all. Not as much as he expected, however, and considering everything she'd been through up to this point, he understood completely. As weird as that might sound. There was no budding romance between them. Not even close. This was survival, of two people with different goals, but currently aligned and traveling on the same path. Until those paths deviated from each other.

"You okay?" she asked.

"Yeah."

"You understand what I said?"

Gus nodded.

"And we're good?" Maya fished. "Even with your trust issues and all?"

"You've been very clear."

"Good. Just so we understand each other."

He nodded again.

"So, Regina," she straightened. "Okay. Sounds like a plan."

"You know how to get there?" Gus asked.

Maya shook her head. "I don't know where we *are*. But the sun came up that way, so if we head *that* way . . . maybe . . . we'll intersect with Skull Road. You remember that one."

Gus did.

"We hit that and turn right . . . it should take us back to Regina. Maybe. And the Anchor Bay. If we have the gas to get there."

"I'm not so sure we do."

"I'm not sure, either. Guess we'll find out. You good to go?"

"Yeah," Gus said. "Just need a minute to take a leak."

"Not a bad idea. I need to do that myself."

"Try not to get stuck in the snow, then," Gus warned her as she turned to leave.

Maya didn't comment. And after the conversation they just had, with her revealing she would leave him if his death was nigh . . . he figured . . . if the situation was reversed, and she was going to be captured, or about to die, and there was nothing he could do . . . maybe he would leave her as well.

On that note, his bladder demanded release, so he trudged off to take care of business.

Not long after, they were on the move again, heading south and looking for some indication of a road. Even a house or two. Something belonging to civilization that would provide a hint as to which direction to go. Once they left the wooded area, it was back to the white and far-reaching stretch of prairie, which simply befuddled the hell out of Gus.

So much open land. And nothing on it.

He could see how a person needed a car in such a place. Or a horse. Something to get around on.

Maya cruised ahead, taking the lead once again, and Gus watched her every now and again in between scanning the horizon.

If the odds look too much in their favor and I risk being taken . . . I will leave you. In a heartbeat.

Cold words, but she was being completely honest, if not practical. Gus wondered if that was Maya talking or some residual mindset from being part of the Leather. Maybe both.

She certainly was enjoying the snowmachine, streaking across the flat land well ahead of him. Gus opened up the throttle to gain some ground, not wanting her to get too far ahead. He didn't think she would leave him on the plain, but a part of him wondered if she would. If she was really that hardcore against being captured, she might decide the Anchor Bay wasn't the best play, and she just might run. Leave him to his revenge fantasy.

Not a fantasy, he told that inner voice. *Fuck you for going there.*

His grip tightened on the snowmachine's handles.

Which was right about when Maya, some thirty or forty meters ahead of him, became airborne in a shocking flip of her snowmachine, where the front smashed into some unseen obstacle. Maya flew from her ditched ride, which flipped once before crash-landing on its seat, bottom-up. She continued sailing, arms pinwheeling, legs kicking, as she tumbled head over ass through space and time and landed in a puff of white.

Gus gunned his machine and sped up, only to brake hard as he approached the crash site.

A ditch. Or rather, a cavity of some length and depth, where the snow hadn't completely filled and that Maya hadn't seen. A ditch deep enough for the front of her ride to plunge into, momentum doing its thing, and crash-land after a spectacular somersault. The machine lay a few feet beyond the drop, its front end mashed like a cheap beer can.

Gus glanced around for other pitfalls and saw none, so he increased his speed until he reached Maya's side.

She was lying on her back, splayed out like a snow angel. The grimace around her eyes said it all.

"Maya," Gus yelled, jumping off the rig and freezing before touching her, fearful of broken bones. *"Maya."*

He slapped her cheeks.

"Owww," she moaned and squinted at him. "You again?"

That put a smile on his face. "Me again. Yeah."

"What's your name, anyway?"

"Gus."

"Give me a minute." Her eyes closed, so he waited.

"I don't think anything's broken," she finally said, sounding shaken from the crash.

"Well, that's good. Can you move?"

That got a nod, and she gently flexed one arm, then the other. She did the same for her legs, and Gus helped her to her feet.

"Ow," she released, and clung to his arm until her legs granted her a little more stability. "What happened? Did I hit a moose?"

"Not quite. This way."

Gus led her over to his rig. He sat her down first, then squeezed in before her. She wrapped her arms around his midsection and held on, but not quite as tight as he would have liked. So he took it slow and a moment later they were stopped at the crash site of Maya's ride. And the hole she'd sunk into.

"Whoa," she whispered close to Gus's ear. "And I thought . . . potholes in Alberta were bad."

"I'm not sure that was a pothole."

"Some settling happened there," she said, still sounding dazed. "A sinkhole. Maybe. Anymore around?"

"Hopefully not."

"Oh . . ."

She locked onto her wrecked snowmachine. "Oh my."

Oh my indeed.

The front pretty much had its teeth kicked in, with the nose mashed into the engine block, and the engine block bursting the plastic and fiberglass housing surrounding it. Both skis were buckled back onto themselves. Then there was the smell of leaking Dog Piss Premium, turning the snow a greenish blue.

"And I liked that thing, too," Maya moaned.

"You sure you're okay?" Gus asked.

"Just a little woozy, is all. I flew thirty feet, you know."

"You were cruisin'. Good thing there's snow down."

"Except the ground's frozen underneath."

Gus shrugged his eyebrows in a *suppose so* sorta way. "So much for that," he said. "You stay here. I'll salvage what I can from your ride."

There wasn't much to take except the meagre stores of food tucked away in the back. They wore most of the clothes they'd found, so that was fine. Gus took the few cans she had in the storage compartment—which wasn't damaged at all—and transferred everything over to his machine.

When he was done, he got back on, and Maya wrapped her arms around him.

"Sorry," she said.

"Don't worry about it. With that sun and everything in white? If I was ahead of you, I would've been the one doing the flip."

"Not that. I mean earlier, when I said I'd leave you. When I did."

"Oh. That."

"You didn't leave me after that."

He felt a moment's guilt. "'Course not. If it were me, you wouldn't have left me behind, either, right?"

"Yeah."

"See? We good?"

"Yeah. We're good. Gus?"

"Yeah?"

"Thank you."

He nodded at that, and she must have seen it, because her arms tightened around him all the more.

"I'll drive," he told her. "Until you get your marbles back."

"I'll be fine."

So they drove south, continuing across the plains, searching for a reference point to get to the Anchor Bay as soon as possible. And wait for the Dragon. If he wasn't already there. The thought crossed Gus's mind.

The other thought, which wasn't nearly as dark but every bit as dire, was the fuel gauge on the snowmachine. How far had they traveled on one tank of gas? A long way. How much farther did they need to go? No idea, but they might not make Regina according to the needle, which was sinking to the halfway point of the last quarter in the tank.

The sun eventually started to sink, and dark clouds gathered for a suspicious meeting. If Gus and Maya didn't find a place for the night soon, he doubted they would have to worry about the Dragon or his remaining Leather. Because they would run out of gas and be stranded in the middle of nowhere. And with the temperature dropping, he didn't think their extra clothing would keep them alive until the next day.

Maya pressed her cheek against his lower neck, holding on tight. After a while, she turned the other way, which felt like her regaining her senses enough to be on the lookout. And with perhaps an hour or so of daylight remaining, with long streaks of purple and pink coloring the sky, Maya tapped his shoulder and pointed.

There, in the distance, were the outlines of several buildings, rising from the prairie like forgotten tombstones.

Gus checked the gas gauge.

Maybe, he thought. *Just maybe*. At the very worst, they could walk the last few kliks to the place. *Any* place. As long as they could keep warm until the morning, when they could figure out their next move.

He steered for the buildings, keeping an eye on potential pitfalls ahead and the gas gauge.

In time, the buildings thickened. Became more numerous.

And slowly evolved into a city.

28

The motel burned brightly, spewing smoke that enveloped the blaze in a polluted halo. Corpses burned in front of the building, splayed out around the entrance, where the flames raged. Ravaged timbers collapsed from within, and the harsh sounds carried across the winter wasteland. The truck in the ditch continued to burn, as did the stricken tanker, which would continue to cook well into the morning.

Not that the Leather would wait around for it.

The Dragon and his minions left the motel to burn, and burn it did, long into the night, until the distance became too great to see the flames and its glow became the dawn's light.

Sitting in the passenger seat of the transport, the Dragon glowered and stewed. He wasn't pleased. Not in the least.

He'd missed reclaiming the Chemist by the barest of margins. That it *was* the Chemist, he had no doubt. He could sense her, knew she had been at the motel. The Norse had confessed as much and the Dragon killed him for it, and for gunning down one of his chosen minions. Gold would be missed. It took time to create a Leather, especially one as devoted to the cause as Gold had been. In addition to that, all of their mindless had been destroyed. Either by gunfire or by the motel blaze. Those would take time to replace as well, as raw material was increasingly harder to find. Then there was the tanker and most of their fuel reserves blasted to hell.

Heavy losses indeed.

There were some gains too, though. Meagre but definitely useful. Before the motel fire grew too hot to bear, they'd managed to recover an assortment of weapons. A pistol, an assault rifle, and a shotgun, all with spare ammunition. Not a lot, as the Norse had spent most of their rounds spraying down the attacking mindless.

The guns now belonged to the Leather, however, and they would make use of them.

Staring out at the featureless country passing by, the Dragon drummed his fingers on the bag with the Dog Tongue's head, the hard cadence dimpling the material.

The Chemist had taken a snowmobile east, but there were no roads behind the motel, and the snow crust looked flat but uneven, suggesting dips in the land. They couldn't drive their rigs over that. One bad bounce, one missed ditch, and disaster would certainly find them. So the Dragon ordered his minions back into the remaining pickups, clearing the road for the transport truck. It took time. Snow covered the highway, and they proceeded at a crawl, going north, until they discovered a more easterly route.

All through the night, they searched for signs of passing snowmobiles. The Dragon hoped they would cross a highway sooner or later. He also hoped the weather held and no snow would fall.

Any other time, the vibe in the cab would be a subdued one. This day, with the strengthening dawn, the vibe became increasingly intense. Sunlight set the frozen land a twinkling, and not a track in sight for kilometers.

You lost her. The Dog Tongue whispered from the bag.

That roused the leader from his morning stare. He ceased tapping on the head and withdrew his hand. He stared at it, the thing resting on the nearby cup holder. The big truck rolled along, gently rocking him in his seat as he waited for more. He was very much aware of what he'd heard. When the head didn't speak again, he made subtle side-eyes at Slipknot, checking for a reaction of any kind. Slipknot appeared totally absorbed in his driving, gripping the wheel with both hands, concentrating on the plowed road left in the wake of the pickups.

So the Dragon waited a little longer, and when it became clear the head was not about to speak again, he decided the voice was obviously imagined . . . but then the head spoke.

You lost her.

That locked down the Dragon's attention.

You . . . fool.

And *that* shot stiffened the Dragon's posture. He shifted uncomfortably, from one cheek to the other. Another not-so-subtle glance at his driver, who remained oblivious.

She was there, the head whispered, in a voice that came from a very deep place. *Who else could it be? And there was another. She's with him.*

The Dragon gripped edges and corners he didn't see and pressed himself back into his seat as if cornered with no escape. He stared at the bag. Stared hard. And slowly, he reached out and pulled down one flap, exposing that dusty executioner's mask split right down the middle. With furtive little jerks he peeled away the material, uncovering dead and cloudy eyes that stared. At that point, he waited for those eyes to fix on him. They did not, so a few seconds later, he uncovered a snarling mouth, the blue-grey lips slightly parted.

The Dragon watched the dead head, waiting for more.

He didn't wait long.

She betrayed us. For him.

The Dragon slowly shook his head.

She's with him.

"She's one of us," the Dragon said in a low but firm voice. "One of the Leather."

No longer, answered the head. *She's made her choice. To run. When we are at our weakest.*

"She's one of us," the Dragon repeated, a little more force in his tone.

From the other side, Slipknot gave a not-so-subtle glance over at his leader.

She's betrayed *us. Betrayed the Leather. Left us all for* dead.

"No, she has not."

When you find her, kill her. The most agonizing way known to you. As punishment for her treachery.

A bump in the road caused the head to rattle, prompting the Dragon to steady it with a hand. He held it in place, his thumb at the corner of one dead eye.

This is my will, the head continued, and now the eyes seemed to glare at him. *My command. Don't dare defy me.*

"She's too valuable. I'll . . . recondition her."

Fool. She's beyond reconditioning. She's been longing to be free of us for years, biding her time, waiting for her moment. That moment is now.

"She's loyal . . ." the Dragon trailed off and glanced over at Slipknot, who quickly turned his attention back to the road. "I'll recondition her," he resumed. "I'll break her will. Completely, this time. I'll leave only what we need."

What you *need. I know what you want her for.*

Heat spread across the Dragon's face, scalding underneath his mask. He tightened his grip on the head. Edged his thumb closer to the moldy surface of the Dog Tongue's eye.

Anyone can see your lust for her. I would have given her to you. As a prize. A reward. For your loyalty. My Dragon.

"I'm still loyal," he rumbled back, pressing his thumb against the eye.

Then prove it. Find her. Kill her. The most painful way possible. Nail her to a plank and drag her in your wake. Let Skull Road eat her alive, until there's nothing left but a bloody framework of bones and sinew.

"No," the Dragon whispered, and sank his thumb into the head's eye. Colorless jelly spurted, shivered, and oozed down a cheek, displaced by the invading digit.

Yes, the head persisted, heedless of the wound. *Nail her to a plank and let her drag in your wake. Let the asphalt scrub the skin from her face and head. Until there's nothing left. Do as I say, or suffer my wrath.*

"I will *not*," the Dragon said, unable to control himself, shaking the head and thumping it on the armrest.

The transport suddenly slowed down as Slipknot worked the shift, bringing the massive rig to a crawl. Out in front, the remaining brake lights belonging to the pickups flared to life. With fell purpose the Dragon glanced at his driver, who pointed at the windshield.

There. Far off but easily visible in the cold morning light.

A pillar of smoke.

The Dragon blinked at that telltale wisp in the sky.

"Sound the horns," he said.

It was all over in less than an hour.

The Leather could have done it in any of their usual ways. Pollute the water supply with the plague-ridden body of a mindless. Chemical cloud to suffocate the settlement. Infiltration, either with a mercenary or an unmasked Leather. Even a straight-up siege—if walls were present.

But any of those methods would take time. And patience. And in the case of poisoning the water supply, the carcass of a mindless was also needed.

The Dragon currently had none of those things.

So the signal was to ride into town and overwhelm whoever was there. Shock and awe.

It would be quick. Brutal. And, sometimes, not without casualties.

The Dragon was in a mood for killing, however, or even inflicting serious pain. Interestingly enough, just after he tooted the signals for an all-out attack, the Dog Tongue's head went silent. The Dragon appreciated that. He took a few seconds to inspect his jelly-coated thumb before wiping it off on his leg.

As it was, the smoke rose from the chimney of a single-story house, with a reinforced gate set into a brick-and-mortar wall that spanned several hundred meters around the property. Planks boarded up the windows. A barn stood out back, surrounded by tractors and combines and other farming equipment. Located as they were, literally in the middle of nowhere (in the Dragon's mind, anyway), in hindsight it was easy to see how they were unprepared for what happened next.

The lead pickup bashed through the gate, ripping it off its hinges and carrying it right up to the front door of the dwelling, where it dropped onto a modest deck. The other pickup circled around back, plow blades lifted so as not to dig into anything hidden under the snow. The transport truck barged through next, barely fitting through the destroyed gateway. One pickup continued circling the dwelling, while some minions broke down the front door. Gunshots rang out. Screams cut the morning air.

The Dragon fitted his claws to his hands and forearms and swished the blades together in a flourish.

A man wearing sweatpants and a T-shirt jumped from one of the house's windows with a shotgun in hand. He ran for the barn. The circling pickup looped the corner and clipped him as he dove to escape the uplifted plow and he lost the shotgun.

More screams from inside. Women. Children. Even a few shouted curses from menfolk. Within minutes of breaking in the door, the Leather marched the people living there out into the front yard. The minions forced them to their knees and watched them.

The Dragon got out of the transport truck. Took his time walking over to the line of prisoners, his great leather coat swishing at his ankles.

Three men. One in his fifties, the others younger, perhaps in their thirties or late twenties. Three women around the same age. Four children. Two girls, two boys. All red-faced, shivering and sniveling. Bonemaker stood guard at their backs, his fancy new automatic rifle held at the ready. Red stood in front with his swords drawn and ready, a little out of place without Gold nearby.

Slit stood with his battle axe held across his pelvis.

Leech emerged from the house, his boots hard on the deck. He signaled all clear.

The Dragon studied each of the prisoners in turn, and when he turned his terrible attention upon the children, they did indeed start to cry.

The men glared at him, the palpable, smoky hatred of those knowing they'd been caught napping. The Dragon didn't appreciate the looks or the attitude, so he stepped into the old man without warning, and killed him with one punch to the throat.

The screaming started again. The crying became a terrified bawling.

The Dragon pulled his claws free of the old man, letting the corpse fall.

One of the young men lurched for the Dragon, but the Dragon slapped him down with a backswing. The minions sprang into action then, securing the prisoners, leaving the Dragon to land on his attacker, sinking his knees into the young man's chest.

Whereupon he pistoned a set of claws into his victim's face.

More screams, of an even higher pitch.

One of the women sprang upon Slit, grappled with him, and hip-tossed the minion to the ground with surprising ease.

Red cut her down from behind with a two-handed slash of his katana, slicing her across the back in a spurt of scarlet.

The children jumped to their feet and ran, shrieking all the way,

The Dragon rose from the dead man and looked for trouble, and flinched when Leech fired a shotgun blast into the air. That froze the works of them, long enough for Slipknot to shove the remaining adults facedown into the snowy ground.

There they stayed, the last-ditch effort quelled.

Slit stood, using his axe as a crutch to do so, and the Dragon reprimanded him with a long glare.

Leech went after the children.

The Dragon let him. He studied the prisoners, ignoring their moans for mercy. He kicked the last living man—a hard, breath-stealing boot to the guts that doubled him up. When the woman next to him started screaming, the Dragon kicked her as well, robbing her of air. To make a point, the Dragon kicked the man again, even stomped on a hand, crunching fingers into a blue and purple mess.

Slipknot appeared, ball gags and zip cords dangling from his fists.

The Dragon stopped him with a hand. The leader rolled his shoulders and studied the home. Moments passed until he gave permission to Slipknot, allowing the minion to bind the new meat.

While Slipknot worked, the Dragon indicated his other minions to get the prisoners into the trailer. Commands dispensed, he took his time walking back to his truck, motioning Slit to follow. The bloodlust wasn't entirely sated, but he wanted to start a new batch of mindless. He decided on making do with plain old destruction.

He pulled on the welder's mask and strapped on his tanks, then fired up the flamethrower.

And lit up the house.

Then he strode around the back of the burning dwelling and beheld the barn out back. Old and wooden and cold.

He lit that up as well.

Several snow-covered lumps as tall as a man lay nearby the barn, and since the Dragon was in the mood, he lashed a fiery burst across one, which erupted into flame. Impressed by the combustion, he lit up the rest, razing them all with liquid fire until they caught and spewed smoke and strands of hay into the early morning sky.

Then he heard the cries of terrified livestock trapped inside the barn.

That gave him pause, only long enough to understand that there were animals inside the structure. Cows and horses by their baying. Not that it made any difference to him. Let them burn. Everything was meat to the Leather.

The Dragon watched the blaze until the timbers cracked and the roof crumbled and the frenzied animal noises long stopped. He watched until great black clouds of mayhem rolled off the fire and blew eastward. At some point, he reached inside a pocket, mindful of his claws, and gathered up the bloody molars like they were dice.

He squeezed them for luck. Squeezed them *hard*.

When he walked back to the truck, his Leather had herded the new meat into the rear. The Leather didn't have any extra corpses to toss in on top of them, but that was fine. They'd find something. Some slab of infected gristle to steep in their drinking water. Change the whole lot. Or not. He'd think on it later.

Smoke continued to spread across the sky, thick and acrid and terrible to behold. Flames consumed the house, the barn, and had already ravaged the hay bales. Flames consumed it all and waved at the Dragon, giving thanks for the feast. He breathed in the smoke, tasted it, and suppressed a cough, scolding himself for taking in too much. The scene of the burning property, however, lifted his spirits, just a little.

Needed that, the Dragon exhaled and allowed Slit to pack away the flamethrower.

A little welcome diversion from his present problem. A little demonstration of power, to show that the Leather were still ruthless. Still as dangerous as ever. Despite their numbers.

Now, he thought blackly, *we find the Chemist*.

29

The snowmachine carrying two people motored down avenues tethered in shadow and blanketed in snow. They traveled through long lots of an industrial nature. Parked semis filled some. Motor homes filled others. Lengthy buildings of corrugated steel with fleets of vehicles parked outside. Tractor equipment. Fabrication shops. The lots got smaller, but the buildings grew tall enough that the sun went missing and the sky darkened. Apartment buildings towered above it all in the distance, rising above a snowbound cityscape.

Maya held on to Gus as he steered through white knobs of traffic, where the snow started at midtire in places to full-on embankments that swallowed cars whole. In the denser areas, Gus had to slow down and plot the best course through the tangles. Some of those traffic knots weren't just stopped in the middle of the street, but rather smashed together, telling the usual backstories of mass hysteria during the outbreak of the zombie plague. Twice, he and Maya had to stop, dismount, and physically turn the snowmachine around as streets became whole junkyards, where collided vehicles barred them from going any further.

After backtracking a couple of times, Gus applied the brakes at an intersection offering yet another route to take.

"See any signs?" he asked.

"Only street signs. Nothing about the city."

Which was the same for him and it was driving him nuts. They had no clue what city they were exploring. The place felt bigger than Annapolis but not quite on the scale of Halifax. Or Regina, for that matter. After those places, his experience in cities was done and over, as he hadn't visited that many outside of Nova Scotia.

"Maybe it's another part of Regina?" Gus asked.

Maya, now recovered from her snowmachine incident, looked around. "I don't think so. I've been to Regina plenty of times in the last year, delivering tankers to Vampire Joe. Even took the scenic route around a couple of times. None of this looks familiar."

"None at all?"

She shook her head. "I think we're still farther north and nowhere near Skull Road. Which is supposed to be the main highway for the Leather."

Gus sighed, scanning for some kind of clue as to where they were.

"Does it matter?" Maya asked. "I mean, really? Let's just find a place for the night."

"I'm lookin' for that too. A hotel, if I can find it. One like the Anchor Bay."

"If we're lucky," Maya said. "Not all those high-class places are self-sufficient like the Anchor Bay. I only know of two others with their own independent power grid, and one of them is in Banff. Which is a long way back that way."

Gus turned, peering over her head in the direction they just traveled.

"How's the gas looking?" she asked.

"Lookin' pretty low."

"Like how low?"

"Low. The needle's touching the E."

"So we'll be walking soon."

"Yeah," he let out in a sigh. "Definitely walkin' soon. One way or the other. All right. I'm headin' this way."

Which was south, judging by the dying sun.

So they went that way, with Gus standing in the seat, doing his best to find a hotel for the night.

Then he saw it, some fifty meters down a street, a sign on the side of a short but stout brick-and-mortar building resembling an old train station. THE JONA something appeared on the side of an overhang jutting over a parking area.

"Think I see something," Gus said.

"What?"

"A hotel. Maybe. Hold on."

They motored through a four-lane street nearly overwhelmed with all manner of vehicles. Gus steered the machine off the road and onto a white rollercoaster of a sidewalk, riding an assortment of drifts toward the broad overhang.

Stamped across the side of the structure was an elegant font, which spelled out THE JONATHAN INN.

It was an older building, historic, aged and dignified. Three or four levels at least, primarily brick. A series of opaque windows on every level faced the street, capped off by a series of white arches that crenated the top. Grey faces carved from white stone featured prominently throughout, their bemused expressions gazing down upon trespassers entering the hotel. Cables drooped from the front of the building to the massive overhang, and the tatters of what might have been flags of all nations fluttered in a breeze.

They climbed one last white hill before leveling out and entering the shade of the hotel's overhang, where the snow wasn't nearly so deep. Gus stopped the machine right before the main entrance. Narrow bars twisted into intricate patterns protected the ground-floor windows the entire length of the building. Some windows had beige faces at their centers, while others had suns, but a design of some manner adorned them all. Flowerpots awaiting spring hung between the windows. Elaborate fractal designs resembling wild vines spanned the brick separating the floors. Gus suspected that in the summertime some serious greenery clung to and flourished all along the exterior.

He switched off the engine and studied the Jonathan's stylistic choices.

"Art Nouveau," Maya said.

"Huh?"

She pointed. "The design. Distinctly Art Nouveau. See those bars? The long, curvy, organic lines? All the iron and glass and brick? Those floral touches? Right there, see? Those curls that resemble waves? Classic features. Art Nouveau all the way."

Gus was just glad he didn't have to paint the place.

"This place is *posh*," Maya said. "I can smell the money. Can you smell the money?"

Sizing up the windows and the dark entrance, Gus smelled something, and it wasn't money. *Art Nouveau?* If Maya said so then it must be. To him, however, it looked like a creepy old hotel from some '70s horror movie, where secret societies might hold meetings on the upper floors after midnight. Or a bald, grey-skinned vampire would make his lair. One of the faces caught his attention. Where the others were relatively intact, this one had a huge diagonal crack splitting it. And the eyes were missing, as if scooped out.

Gus scowled at it all. "You're good here, then?" he asked.

"Yeah, I'm good," Maya said, getting off the machine. "Going to be night soon, so this is it."

"This is it. You think it might have power like the Anchor Bay?"

"Possible. We'll see shortly."

Eyeing the windows stained by the elements, Gus pulled out the Sig as he rounded the rear of the machine. He got out the bag of food and handed it over to Maya.

They walked up to the entrance.

Brass lettering above the door. THE JONATHAN INN. THE DISTINGUISHED CHOICE SINCE 1989.

The distinguished choice, Gus mused, tapping his thigh with the Sig. He pulled on the handle. Then pushed.

It opened.

"Easy enough," Maya said.

"Yeah, it was." Gus glanced back at the snowmachine. It was parked underneath the overhang, but what concerned him was the glaring track left behind in the snow.

"You looking at the tracks?" Maya asked.

"Yeah."

"Can't really be helped. Unless it snows."

"You still think this Dragon fuckwit will be after you?"

Maya nodded.

"All right. Well," Gus pushed his way inside, "this'll be our killing ground."

Red carpet underfoot continued to a second inner door, where they entered the lobby, and walked into a smell of road-killed skunk.

"Oof," Gus gasped and screwed up his face. "Nice."

"I've smelled worse."

"You personally?"

That got him a wry look.

"Kidding of course," he smiled. "I kid."

"S'okay," Maya said. "You fired the first shot. Just don't pout when I start firing back is all. But look at this place."

He already was.

Opulent. Decadent, even. The lobby, draped in shadows, projected an air of corrupt wealth. Dull wood-paneled walls one might see in some 1800s adventurers' club, where the members sat around in a cloud of cigar smoke and discussed recent expeditions to Amazonian jungles. A front desk area built of the same fine material, darkly prestigious, with a dusty silver bell resting upon its surface. What looked to be a gift and duty-free shop was to the left of the entrance, situated behind a large sitting area. Finely carved chairs and tables populated the floor, as well as a pair of sofas. Half of the chairs were either knocked over or pulled away from their tables, as if all the guests had decided to vacate the premises in one mad rush. The sofas looked like they'd been vandalized, their pillows shredded and stuffing strewn across the floor. The carpeting inside the lobby was ravaged to tatters. The exposed pitted wood underneath hinted at an ant or termite infestation.

It appeared the Jonathan was due for repairs.

Hanging over it all were three huge chandeliers, their diamond-shaped crystals twinkling in the dying daylight.

"Place looks trashed," Maya said.

"Not the first," Gus replied, Sig pressed against his thigh. "And I've seen worse."

They walked to the front desk, their footfalls echoing in that grand space, and Gus was glad to see that they had an old-fashioned cubbyhole cabinet for their room keys, just like the Anchor Bay. Thick dust glazed the desk surface, as well as the sign-in books, the four computers, and a collection of stationery. A little ceramic gold cat, sitting on its ass with one paw raised in greeting, sat right next to the desk phone.

Gus went behind the desk. "Rooms?"

Maya nodded.

"Third floor, okay?"

"We'll have to climb stairs."

"I prefer high ground," he said. Something behind the front desk caught his eye—an elaborate key with a dark-striped gold bar at the tip. He took that, as well as a pair of keys marked 313 and 314. A quick search produced a flashlight underneath the counter as well, but the batteries were long dead.

He handed Maya a key. "We'll be neighbors," he said.

"Look over there," she pointed.

At the far end of the lobby, past a European-styled coffee shop, was a glass toll booth. A sign reading SUBWAY hung above a metal barrier lowered a quarter of the way down.

"They have a subway line here," she said in a low voice.

"A train?"

"Apparently."

They left the subway alone and walked toward a row of elevators and the stairwell. Fading daylight from the many windows stretched across the floor, and, like the lobby, the carpet had been ravaged. The boards underneath, pitted and scarred. Potted trees, bare and long dead, decorated the hallway. Little signs hung above glass doors, the nearest one saying ST. MARTIN'S.

Gus stopped and studied the area, spying for signs of life.

Maya continued on for a little while more, leaning in to see what exactly St. Martin's was.

"Fusion restaurant," she said. "Styled like a bistro from 1900s France. Bet it was popular back in the day."

Gus shrugged his eyebrows and glanced back the way they came.

"The next one is for a cigar shop," Maya said. "And the other signs are . . . looks like little boutiques. Clothing and such. Nice."

"Think there's anything to eat in the restaurant?" Gus asked.

"We can check it out."

So they did. The double doors to St. Martin's were unlocked, so they pushed their way inside, right into that dead skunk stink, made even more potent by the lack of ventilation.

"Holy shit," Gus muttered, and covered his mouth.

Maya did the same.

He wandered past a bar area, stopped, and quickly checked what they had in stock. There was a cooler which he opened and pulled out bottled water.

"Mineral water," he said, holding it up.

"Plastic or glass?" Maya asked.

"Plastic."

"Don't drink it then. The chemicals in the plastic will have leached into the water by now."

"But it's in the shade."

"In a powerless environment for over, what? Four or five summers? Where the temperatures can hit the high thirties? Go ahead and drink it. You'll have your own toilet to barf in later."

Gus frowned and put it down.

The freezer contained meats, as well as a stink that prompted them to shut the door and leave everything where it was. Shriveled vegetables filled the coolers. There were unopened bottles of condiments, and cans of pasta sauce and stewed tomatoes in a pantry, but oddly enough nothing else. Maya put a few cans away in her bag. She also tried the gas range, which produced fumes, so she switched the burners off. Gus found a couple of boxes of long wooden matches in a drawer and left one on the counter next to the range.

Upon leaving the place, Gus picked up a pair of glass pitchers. "Snow water?"

Maya approved.

Gus headed out the front entrance to fetch snow for his pitchers. When he returned, the two resumed their search of the hotel. They walked past the cigar shop just after St. Martin's, keen on reaching the upper floors before nightfall. They tried the elevators, but continual mashing of buttons did nothing to revive them. Not a gig of life. Frowning, Gus moved to the nearby stairwell, pulled open the door, and held it.

Maya walked on through with a nod of thanks.

They hiked up a spiraling staircase, holding onto a brass railing caked in dust. Gus noticed the carpeting was in much better condition than the lobby's, but didn't think much of it. Three stories later, they pulled open the door to the third floor.

And stepped out into a dream. Dark rugs, pristine and untouched, covered the floor every ten paces. In between them peeked hardwood stained a deep, luxurious brown. Long flowing lines reminiscent of warm summer winds blowing off tropical waters decorated sunny walls. Ocean-green pillars curved upward at several intervals, holding up a ceiling spotted with clouds. The chandeliers were smaller than the lobby's, resembling medieval candleholders. Light fixtures adorned the walls as well, but the main light source came from tall, narrow windows that shone through fading rectangles along the corridor.

They walked along, gawking at surreal paintings. The doors to the rooms were the same green as the pillars, with old-fashioned keyholes set in a brass plate.

"All this money on decorating and not a dime on a backup power source," Gus grumped, his foot bothering him.

"Only the newer hotels had that," Maya said. "If they had the initial capital to invest. These older buildings? The marketing strategy probably focused on selling the old-world charm."

"Those stairs were an old-world pain in the ass."

"You're funny. Sometimes."

Gus stopped, drawing a look from Maya.

"Just listening," he said, prompting her to do the same.

Nothing. Not a sound of anything. Just the solemn creaks of old wood when they shifted from one foot to the other.

"You seeing this?" Maya marveled. "I bet these rooms cost a fortune."

Gus didn't comment, though it did look nice. He glanced up and down the corridor, noticing that most of the doors were closed. Choosing one, he tried the knob and discovered it locked. Checking his flanks, Gus fished out the potential master key and inserted it.

And with a soft clatter the door opened.

Gus went in, gun-first.

Another upscale room, with all the fixings. Four distinct areas consisting of an entry space with a closet for coats, a sitting area with a round table and chairs, an adjacent kitchenette, and the bedroom itself. Lavish furniture, long dark curtains over silky drapes. Hardwood floors coated in a fine film of dust, and a king-sized bed the size of a cropped bouncy castle, with dreamy duvets and sheets, waiting for whoever laid the money down. The bathroom was again from the past, the chrome dimmed somewhat, but the tub was deep and magnificent with a tall backrest. A glass partition for the shower. Toilet and bidet, along with a roll of toilet paper—which Gus pinched and confirmed as two-ply.

Très bon, he said to himself.

Nothing but the best for the Jonathan's guests.

"This my room?" Maya asked.

"If you want it."

"Let's see the rooms you picked out."

"I know not what it is, mind you," Gus said. "This is my first time here, too. Let's work our way up, checking the rooms as we go. I'd like to make sure we're alone."

"Each room?" Maya said, her mouth twisted with disbelief. "That could be dozens of rooms. Out of hundreds. I mean, we'll be walking around in the dark."

She had a point. Daylight was fading fast, as what was coming in through the drapes wasn't much. Gus went over to the window and took a quick peek.

"Holy shit," he said, and motioned for Maya to join him.

"Holy *shit,*" she said, but more impressed.

The window didn't face the city street but rather looked out upon an inner courtyard, consisting of an old-fashioned playground surrounded by a green racetrack. Slides, ceramic clowns, a merry-go-round with creepy horses, and even a dark, burnt-out looking crater of a swimming pool, complete with artificial palm trees. All under an aquatic blue light that stemmed from the ceiling, which took their breath away.

It wasn't a ceiling, but rather a blue-tinted dome, ribbed by girders that resembled whalebones, converging on a massive centerpiece of a chandelier that dangled and twinkled with otherworldly brilliance. Whatever daylight shone down on the inner courtyard was steeped in that all-encompassing stratosphere blue.

From where they gawked, they could see the other side of the hotel, a hundred meters away at least, where each level had windows overlooking the same courtyard.

The sheer scale of all that ingenuity and willpower demanded Gus to take a moment to suck it all in.

The Jonathan Inn was *huge.*

"Oh my," Maya whispered. "This place is the cat's pajamas."

That stirred a memory. "Two kinds of people in the world," Gus said, peering out over everything. "The ones that go 'that's the cat's pajamas,' and the ones who go 'who the fuck puts pajamas on a cat?'"

That earned him another mildly amused look from Maya.

"Something a buddy once said," Gus said, clearing his throat. "On a job site."

"House painting, was it?"

Gus nodded and stepped away from the window. "You're right about searching this place. Maybe tomorrow. For now, let's just get to these rooms. Before we're left in the dark."

So they did.

A short time later, as daylight steadily retreated and the floor creaks grew louder, they entered room 313 . . . and discovered it was identical to the first room they had checked out—except a ten-minute walk later. Like that first room, it had a glorious view of the inner courtyard.

"All right," Gus said, handing over her key. "This is yours. Lock the thing from the inside. Fluff up the pillows there and sleep with one eye open."

Maya looked around. "Those are summer sheets."

"Oh. Well. I'll strip out the other beds and bring them over. How's that sound?"

"And you'll be next door?"

"Right next door. With this." He held up the sidearm. "I'll keep the master key with me, if you don't mind. I'll need it to open the other rooms, to get those extra blankets."

"Duvets."

"Whatever."

"Mind if I come along?"

"Uh, no, not at all."

So they spent the next hour stripping the comforters and sheets from a half-dozen other beds, lugging them all back to Maya's room. Gus helped out with tucking in the loose ends. When they finished, they traveled a little farther down the hall and pulled extra blankets from two more bedrooms.

"I'll sleep with my clothes on," Gus explained. "Won't be so cold that way."

It was dark by the time they got settled away in their rooms, with an eerie alien light seeping through the windows overlooking the courtyard. Once they added the extra bedding, Gus walked Maya back to her door, a little wary of the vastness of the corridor. The stylistic design of the Jonathan might have been a love note to a time gone by, but at night, without power, where the floorboards creaked and shadows grew . . .

The place was creepy as all fuck.

"So, ah," Maya said, standing on the threshold to her room. "What's the plan?"

"Well," Gus said. "We sleep on it. One eye and one ear open. Tomorrow morning, we check on the front for tracks. See if anyone followed us here."

"And if there's none?"

Gus faced her and noticed that she looked much better in the shadows. *He* probably looked much better in the shadows, for that matter. "I'll be honest. I hope they find us, because I don't want a new pack of Leather fuckwits running around the country. I remember what you said earlier, so you do what you want, but me? I'll . . . take care of them."

"Kill off the shitty-assed bastards? That what you said?"

"Something like that. Can't remember the exact phrasing, but yeah."

"Yeah."

They stood there, in that three-story tomb of a hotel, wavering on what to do next. Gus glanced in her room and then both ways down the hall, where the farthest ends faded into starless voids. Any moment he expected some leftovers of the mindless, crawling along the carpet, dragging, stretching things ripped from body cavities, all intent on the fresh meat staying at the hotel.

He saw nothing of the sort, however... but he still expected it. And creeped himself out in doing so.

"Ah... you... ah..." he faltered and scratched the back of his head. "You got room in there?"

"In here? Yeah, sure. Oh you mean you want to sleep over?"

"Yeah, I can sleep on the floor."

"After sleeping together the night before? We can do it again. I mean the bed's huge. And if it gets too warm we can lose one of the comforters."

"Might still be warm, though," Gus said innocently enough. "And I snore."

"You fart, too," Maya said. "And mumble. But I think I can handle it."

"I fart? In my sleep?"

"Constantly. And mumble. Wouldn't be bad if I could understand what you were saying. Just *maw maw maw*," she reported, with one eye open.

"Oh yeah," Gus smiled sheepishly. "I've been told that before. Yeah. Sorry."

A smiling Maya bade him enter. Which he did. They closed the door, locked it, and placed a clothes chest up against it, just in case. The night deepened, the temperature dropped, and without any light they became thick silhouettes shuffling about the room.

"Christ I can barely see a thing," Gus muttered at one point.

"The bathroom's worse," Maya said. "There's no water, but there's one flush in the box."

"Go ahead. I took care of business back in 316, I think it was."

So she did.

Gus sat on the bedside closest to the door. He placed the Sig on the night table, next to a pitcher filled with melting snow. Like before, a nervousness creeped in, and he knew why. Running a hand over the top comforter, he remembered another time. When he and Collie and the folks from that summer camp were on the run and hiding out in Lazy Lou's bedroom furniture place. A lifetime ago. Even longer ago were the nights Tammy would come over to his place and crash. Or he would go over to hers.

Toilet flushed. One and done. The door cracked open and Maya, nothing more than a faceless wraith, came out with outstretched arms.

"Not so bad when you come out of the bathroom," she whispered. "It's almost sunny out here now."

"I bet."

She rounded the bed and sat down on the other side.

Taking off her coat, she got in on her side. Gus removed his vest and coat and got in on his. It was a big bed. Huge, really. You could fit two more people between them.

"Listen," she whispered.

Lying there on his back, he did.

Nothing. Not a damn thing.

Then, the very last thing either one of them expected, Gus's stomach growled.

"Sorry," he said in a very low tone. "Been a long day. Should've eaten something before bed, I guess."

"Don't worry about it."

"I'll wait until morning."

"Don't want to head down to St. Martin's there?"

"Now?" Gus asked. "You crazy? It's scary out there, man." He sniffed and scratched at his man bits, confident she couldn't see what he was doing.

"Gus?"

"Yeah?"

"How many bullets you got in the gun?"

"I dunno. Maybe five or six."

"This is going to sound bad, but . . . if the Dragon finds us. And . . . if he's about to capture us. Well . . . shoot me. Please. I . . . can't go back to living like that. *Existing* like that. Not after finally getting away. You understand?"

"Yeah. I understand."

"Thanks again."

"For what?"

"Showing up when you did."

"Thank you again for shooting the meat hook."

"Just 'the Hook.' Not 'Meat Hook.' I mean, yes, he *used* meat hooks but . . . yeah. You get it. Goodnight, Gus."

"Goodnight, Maya."

And they went to sleep.

30

A blue-tinged morning found them still in bed, this time with Maya spooning Gus, one arm draped across his belly. Gus opened his eyes, did a self-assessment, and wondered for a moment who was clinging to him. Then his eyes widened and he turned to check matters out. Part of Maya's squished face came into view, little snores ripping.

Feeling the urge, he reached down to lift her arm and she came awake instantly.

"What is it?" she asked with sleepy urgency, head coming off the pillow.

"Nothing. It's morning. I'm getting up."

"Oh."

Gus got out of bed, felt the mattress moving more than necessary, and saw Maya getting up with him.

"You don't have to get up," he told her.

"Need to. We got things to do, right?"

"Well, yeah, we do."

"Okay, then. Good talk." She shuffled to the bathroom.

"I'll go next door and meet you in the hall, okay?" Gus said, picking up the Sig from the night table.

"Sure."

He pulled away the chest and opened the door. One quick peek, and he was gone for the crapper. A long time later, he emerged from his chosen room and saw Maya waiting for him in the hall. When she saw him, she shook her head with a hint of frustration.

"Didn't think you'd be gone so long," she said.

"My morning moment," Gus said, closing the door behind him. "I get a lot of thinking done. Fair warning, don't go in there."

"Wasn't planning to. You hungry?"

"Yeah."

There were plates and eating utensils back in their room, so they prepped the table and laid out what they had. Maya opened some cans, and they shared a breakfast of corned beef, peas, and carrots, topped off with beans in tomato sauce. The beans and sauce went over the corned beef, making it a little more palatable—but not much. They finished eating in short time, washed it all down with melted snow water from the night before. They closed the door but left it unlocked, eager to explore the hotel.

Minutes later, they reached the ground floor and entered a lobby lanced by sunbeams. Gus and Maya went outside where a clear sky greeted them. The snow sparkled, and there were no other tracks besides those they made the day before.

Satisfied, they went back inside, and walked past St. Martin's, where that dead meat smell lingered.

"How much food we got left, again?" Gus asked.

"Another meal, split between us. Then it's pasta sauce and stewed tomatoes."

"Yum," Gus said. "Well, bound to be cans of something stashed in here."

"In here?" Maya asked. "Maybe. Out there? I'm sure we will. What are we doing this morning?"

He stopped and scratched his beard. "We explore this place. See what the layout is. Maybe find something we can use as weapons. Plenty of knives in St. Martin's kitchen. If we have time, maybe we fortify some places. For when our guests get here."

Maya nodded.

"You can stay here and keep a lookout if you want," he offered, pointing a thumb back at the lobby.

She shook her head. "I think I'd rather tag along with you. Strength in numbers and all that. We always check on the front from the windows."

"Good point."

"Okay. Let's get busy."

They searched the cigar shop. There were plenty of butane refills, including stainless-steel lighters, of which they took a pair each. A nearby gift shop had a number of delicate crystal vases for flowers, which would shatter much easier than glass bottles when thrown. Gus and Maya then hunted for the laundry facilities and located them down a short hallway off the main corridor. The laundry room also contained a good supply of chemical cleaners, which, as Maya explained, would, in the right amounts, produce a bigger burn than the butane. She also found several rolls of paper towels. So, over the next two hours, they set up an assembly line across a couple of tables, and with Maya doing the measurements with spoons taken from St. Martin's kitchen, she concocted a dozen highly flammable firebombs. She added a finishing touch of paper towel fuses, hand-rolled into fat wicks and plugged into the vases.

The laundry room also had several garbage bins that contained old refuse, including lint.

"Highly flammable," Maya informed him. "Goes right up."

Under her supervision, Gus rolled the bins back to the lobby and started dragging furniture to the main entrance, where he heaped everything into a makeshift barricade shaped like a horseshoe. Once they'd built up a decent wall of tables and chairs, he dumped the contents of the garbage bin over everything. They also tossed bedding onto the heap—sheets, blankets, even curtains. Topped everything off with leftover lint from the dryers' uncleaned filters.

Perhaps three hours later, tired and sweating, they stood back and studied the setup.

"Not bad," Maya said.

"Think it'll make a difference?"

She shrugged. "It's an obstacle. It'll slow them down a little. We'll be lucky if we burn their feet. Just so you know, those firebombs? There's the risk of burning down the hotel."

"You're the one who doesn't want to get caught."

She smiled at him.

"Then fuck it," Gus said, sizing up the barricade.

Fire extinguishers abounded, housed in small cabinets. Maya clipped the bindings, removed the safety pins, and lay them in a ready position. Kitchen knives were placed on windowsills or stuck blade-first inside large flowerpots.

The electrical room wasn't far from the laundry, and there they confirmed the worst. The hotel took its power from the city power grid, and since the grid no longer functioned, they were without juice. In among two workstations and several dead computers, someone had left behind a hand-powered rechargeable flashlight. Gus took that for later. None of the elevators worked, but there were four fairy-tale staircases that climbed to the top floor, with carefully fashioned robust spindles, and broad sweeping steps carpeted in red. Those were separate from the less alluring stairwells that were enclosed behind doors and spiraled straight up.

The enclosed staircases interested Maya, as rubber strips lined the doorframes, essentially becoming contained silos when shut.

"What are you thinking?" Gus asked while she inspected one, running her fingers along the door frame.

"I'm thinking . . . if I had enough cleaner, in the right proportions, I could, in theory, whip up a functional tear gas."

"Tear gas? Jesus, Maya. Do it."

"Thought that would put a smile on your face. Thing is, it would be pretty crude. We'd have to disperse it from the top floor so that it would drift down, and we have to use it within a day or two at most. Because it would start dissolving to a point where it wouldn't be effective."

"Ah . . . what does it do, exactly? Like, burn your eyes or something?"

She rubbed her face. "Irritates the eyes. Blurs the vision. Inhaling it would be no fun as it would screw up your sinus cavities for a couple of hours. It would feel like . . . someone poured pepper straight into your head. Soldiers can handle the stuff to a point, but us regular, uninitiated folk? One whiff and it would be debilitating. For us and them."

"If we inhaled it?"

"Or it leaked out."

"What about keeping it in a bucket?" he asked. "And we keep the bucket at the top of the stairs—like the third floor—ready to be chucked if we were chased up there."

Maya cocked an eyebrow.

They returned to the laundry room and covered their faces with disposable face masks. For the next hour, Maya measured out chemical cleaners into a plastic bucket. Only enough for one charge, but it was one they didn't have before. She then secured the bucket with a wide strip of plastic and a single layer of tape, fetched from the nearby kitchen.

"Okay," Maya said. "This is how it works. In theory. If they're in the stairwell and we're at the top, we shake this thing up and throw it at a wall. Throw it *hard*, okay? So that everything spills out, by which I mean *gushes*. That's it. Dirty but effective."

"Which stairwell?"

"The first one we used. We'll lead them up it."

By the time they had it in place, it was late afternoon. Not about to quit, however, they checked the front entrance and saw that the coast remained clear. So they continued exploring the ground floor, discovering a wine and cocktail bar in the rear, along with a formal cigar room and a coffee shop. There were no guest rooms on the lower floor, but there were maintenance rooms, unfortunately filled with nothing helpful, except a selection of disinfectant spray cans. Maya placed two in her coat pockets.

By then, the day was nearly done, and the halls were getting dark.

Three clear glass entrances led to the inner courtyard, the area bathed in blue by that overhead dome. Hotel room windows encircled the upper sections, overlooking the playground amusements. A white gazebo stood amongst several fake trees near the center. The pool they'd spotted from their room was to the south, at the center of an artificial tropical oasis.

Two of the doors—the one in the rear and the one nearest the subway entrance with the partially lowered gate—had been smashed. The door close to the subway entrance drew Gus's attention, as tatters of grey hair lined the floor.

"Something wrong?" Maya asked.

"Mindless came through here," he said, pointing.

"Doesn't surprise me."

He peered into the courtyard. Besides a few trampled plants long dead, there was nothing of interest.

"Anything wrong?"

He sniffed, still getting that faint but noticeable scent of dead skunk, which had carried a long way from the restaurant.

"No, I don't think so," he said warily. "I *hope* not. Sun's going down. Let's get something to eat before dark."

Supper was another can of corn beef, with another can of mixed vegetables thrown on the side, and everything covered in tomato sauce from the St. Martin's kitchen. It wasn't much going down, especially cold like it was, and the vegetables tasted like tin and left Gus's lips tingly, but everything stayed down. When they'd finished, they settled back in their chairs and regarded each other quietly.

"Well," Maya said with a little smile. "I don't remember eating this much corn beef ever in my life. I'll probably pass a brick in the morning."

Gus chuckled. "I liked corn beef and hash way back when, but like this? I'll probably pass a brick myself, but maybe two or three days from now."

"Well, I hope we're still around for you to take that dump."

"Yeah, me too."

Maya turned her attention to the window and the early night sky.

"Something on your mind?" Gus asked.

She looked back at him. "We're . . . not going to make it. I mean, it's going to be difficult. We don't have much food left. Certainly not enough fuel. And as far as I know, we're nowhere near a Leather outpost where we can resupply ourselves. That's if the Dragon doesn't find us. Which he'll do."

"I'll end him when he does," Gus said.

An uncertain Maya turned back to the window.

Gus picked up the pitcher and poured the last of the water into their glasses. He drank his and shook the pitcher. "We're out of water."

"So I see."

Gus sighed and glanced outside. "Should've remembered to fill these earlier. Mind if I borrow the flashlight for a while? I'll head downstairs and get some snow. For the morning. Or later tonight if we want it."

"You want to go back down there?" Maya asked in disbelief. "In the dark? Seriously?"

"They did it in the old days."

"That was well water and I bet it wasn't after dark in a deserted city."

"So that's a no?"

Maya studied him. "Can't say we won't need the water. You know you'll be climbing over that barricade, right? I better come with you."

"No, no need. Just lock the door and stay put until I get back. I won't be long."

"You'll be at least three-quarters of an hour."

"Then I'll try to make it back faster."

"Another earlier bedtime?"

"I'll stay up for a bit. Keep watch."

She paused, then, "Are we sleeping together again tonight?"

Gus hesitated. "Up to you. I was comfortable last night."

"I was too."

She bit her upper lip then and glanced out the window in a thoughtful way, leaving him with the question *is she flirting with me*?

"Almost hot," he said before he could put the brakes on his brain. "Temperature-wise. I mean under the blankets. I mean . . . you know what I mean."

They shared a smile at the self-inflicted word trap he'd screwed himself into.

"Well," she said after a moment. "We'll figure something out."

"Yeah. Guess we will. Uh, yeah. I'll go get that snow."

He took the pitchers. She followed him to the door, unlocked it, and watched him step outside.

Gus checked left and right before facing her. "Won't be long," he said.

"Don't kick the bucket," she warned him. "You'll be sorry if you do."

"I won't kick the bucket."

"Say it like you mean it."

"I won't kick the bucket."

"That's better." She held his gaze for a little longer and then closed the door.

Gus stared, suspecting she might be looking out the peephole at him, which he surprisingly didn't mind. Pitchers in hand, he made his way to the stairwell, mindful of the loaded bucket containing Maya's improvised gas bomb. *Maya*, he thought as he descended the stairs. Nice name. Different. Rolled off the tongue. *Maya*. He remembered last night, when they were sleeping more out of comfort than survival. Then he thought of Tammy and Collie and frowned.

"Yeah," he said and sighed, the sadness rising. Before it got out of hand, however, he found himself in the trashed mausoleum that was the Jonathan's main lobby. The barricade stopped him, so he put the pitchers down and proceeded to pull things aside, just enough that he could get through. It took longer than expected, and he worked up a sweat doing it, but he made a gap wide enough, and slipped through with the pitchers.

Outside, the snowmachine waited, parked underneath the overhang.

"How you doin'?" he asked it, and thankfully didn't get a reply. "You good? Good."

The snow remained unspoiled, except for their one track, and no sign of any visitors from beyond. A gathered drift to the right looked like a good place for clean snow, so he got busy. Two packed pitchers later, he deemed the mission complete. He strolled back to the entrance, where he stopped and looked back at the city.

The night was clear and the stars were just beginning to show themselves. Snow glowed in the streets, promising to sparkle once the moon came out to play. A couple of planted trees nestled into one street corner, bare and crooked but holding on for the spring. The nearby buildings brooded like monuments, their windows lightless and gloomy.

And not a soul in sight.

Gus exhaled a puff of steam and watched it dissipate. He huffed out a second cloud just for fun. The cold pinched his cheeks, looking to leave a bruise. One last look and listen of the city, the mysterious and unknown city, and he moseyed back inside. A few quick minutes later, with a little more elbow grease and some swearing, he restored the barricade and inspected it.

Might slow them down, he thought. *Enough to put a bullet into at least one. Maybe two.*

Then it would get tricky, as he only had a few rounds remaining in the Sig. He could shoot, but he wasn't that good against moving targets trying *not* to get shot.

The Leather. The Dragon.

A terrible heat flared within him, and for a few seconds, he stood and simply let the hatred flow. Maya entered his thoughts then, and that hatred dissipated like smoke in a breeze. Time was getting on, and she might be wondering what happened to him. That's what he told himself. The truth was, Gus was starting to like her company.

One last look at the barricade before he heard it. Or thought he heard it, enough for him to stop and really listen. To really focus on what he heard, or wonder if he'd simply imagined it.

Then he heard it again. Faint . . . but there. And getting louder.

The rumbling of a dull edge upon pavement.

31

Though he tried his best to hide it, hope spiked within the Dragon, like a needle on a seismograph signaling one mother of an earthquake. His posture also gave himself away, as he leaned forward in his seat, watching the two pickups ahead as they slowly pushed away snow from the highway.

It seemed like only hours since they left the farm with their small but fresh load of fodder, but of course it had been much longer than that. All sense of time seemed to warp for the Dragon afterward, until, in an open landscape blanketed in white, they found a single set of snowmobile tracks. One that sped across the same highway they traveled upon, intersected it, and continued to the east.

Only a tanker leaking black paint could have been more noticeable.

It took time to follow the tracks, as the snowmobile had traveled in a straight, unbroken line. Their shrunken convoy had to use the highways, and the highways on the prairies were usually straight runways between towns and cities. The Dragon didn't care, however. They had the scent. Only one set of tracks but no matter. He knew who drove the machine. Who it *had* to be.

A city crept into view, a subtle line of featureless blocks on a purpling horizon. There were road signs, but ice and frost hid their words. None of that mattered. The snowmobile tracks led to the city and eventually merged onto the highway the Leather drove upon.

Straight into the downtown core.

Ahead, the brake lights glared as the trucks slowed to a stop. Slipknot brought the hissing semi to a halt behind the smaller machines. The Dragon craned his neck, seeking a reason for the delay, and only saw a knot of stranded traffic. Traffic that would require time to clear for their convoy to proceed. It didn't impede the smaller and much nimbler snowmobile. Its tracks weaved in and out of the tangle until they were gone from sight, lost in the gloomy spires of the city.

The remaining Leather were getting out of their rides.

The Dragon grabbed the Glock from a cup holder and reached for the door.

She's here, the Dog Tongue seethed from the bag. *I can smell her.*

"I know," the Dragon agreed.

She is very important to the Leather, the Dog Tongue said, changing his tune from earlier. *To you. Make sure you bring her back to us. To* me.

The Dragon considered the head, its snarl of a mouth, its ruined eye, the color of its dead skin. And the smell. Honestly, he was growing tired of the thing. The Dog Tongue didn't seem to realize he was dead and gone, that his time had passed, and that the day of the Dragon was finally breaking. Even worse, he was continually droning on about future plans for conquest.

In the driver's seat, Slipknot did not move.

And for those who took her, the Dog Tongue continued, *show them no mercy. None, my Dragon.*

That thought wasn't a bad one. Not in the least. Though the Dragon had suffered with the Dog Tongue's company while on this hunt, he had to admit the decomposing piece of meat did have its moments. Perhaps he would keep it around afterward, when he was finally reunited with the Chemist. That image captivated him for seconds, where she was at his side. As a queen. And in time, the mother of his children.

"No mercy," the Dragon whispered, and glared at Slipknot. "Wait for us."

The driver nodded.

The Dragon exited the transport, the cold biting, his boots thudding on compressed snow. The deserted streets held his attention while he waited for his minions to gather. Seconds later they appeared, wearing their armored vests, weapons bared and ready.

"No way through?" the Dragon asked, motioning Slit and Red to help strap on his flamethrower tanks.

"Not with the machines," Bonemaker replied, holding the automatic rifle.

The Dragon cocked his head.

"Too much hardware," the minion reported. "Buried under an avalanche's worth of snow."

"Then we walk," the Dragon said. "Until we find her. And whoever is with her."

With that, he held up his war mask and realized it was too dark for the thing. With a sigh, he placed it back in the storage hold of the big rig and closed the lid.

He pointed at Slit and flicked a finger at the path to take.

The man in the plague mask nodded and hefted his battle axe. He turned, the shoulders of his leather duster collecting a few flakes, prompting the Dragon to look heavenwards. The sky scintillated with starry brilliance, but a black mass crept in at the edges.

The Dragon approved.

He did his best work in the stormy dark.

Gus waited, sitting on a chair he'd hauled away from the front desk. The mechanical sounds he had heard earlier had ceased, so he hunkered down low in the lobby, watching the streets, his nose practically resting on the windowsill. The snowmachine was still out there, not that it mattered. The trail they left would lead whoever was out there straight to the hotel.

The Leather. No question in his mind. His guts rolled with the knowledge. He awaited their arrival with all the enthusiasm of someone about to have hot dogshit dumped on their front lawn.

How much time had passed since he left Maya? He wasn't sure. Maybe an hour, at least. Maybe she would come looking for him. That troubled him a little, although if she did show up, he hoped she brought her firebombs. Just in case.

The deserted streets resembled frozen half-pipes, right up to where icy crusts flowed down the sides of the nearby buildings. Nothing moved within the deepening shadows. The night sky grew darker, prompting him to look up. That darkness slid over the mounds of snow, dimming their nighttime radiance.

Gus leaned back, stretched, and glanced behind him.

And did a double take at what he saw. What he *thought* he saw, a trick of the sparse light and heavy shadow, a flicker of movement along the floor. He stared, waiting for more. He focused on the entrance to the subway across the hotel lobby, where the metal grate hung at not quite half-mast. His heart thumped and his pulse quickened in his ears, but nothing stirred in the dark. So he gave up and went back to watching the streets.

There.

Lumbering along and not making any effort to hide themselves. At least two. *No,* he squinted, spotting a third figure materializing between the snowed-in vehicles. Three of them. But then a *fourth* shape came into sight. Gus stooped lower behind the windowsill, practically snorting dust with every intake. He readied the Sig and held it against his thigh. Six shots. That was all he had. And despite making a promise to Maya, he intended to use a shell on each Leather shitbag until he ran dry.

Five of them, dark outlines lumbering against the frozen cityscape, approaching like a string of executioners. Weapons gleamed as they got closer. One in particular caught his eye.

Holy shit, Gus thought, recognizing the HK assault rifle. Odds were that was his. And if they had that, they probably had the ammunition as well. He sighed through his nose and thumped his forehead against the windowsill.

Things had just gotten a little more dangerous.

The five stopped in the street. One of them might have turned back to the others, but then they were moving again. Toward the Jonathan Inn. They had spotted the snowmachine.

Gus gripped his sidearm just a little tighter.

One of the figures carried an axe, and sometimes used the thing like a cane as he trudged through the snow. That one's mask had a long caricature of a nose, its profile caught in the dim light as the man checked his flanks.

Gus retreated from the window. He crept back to the front desk, where the thicker darkness would hide him until the shooting started. There would be plenty of it in the next few minutes.

The space behind the front desk wasn't so cluttered, so he stayed low and peeked out to watch the five killers approach the entrance, their shapes growing more distinct with every step.

The shade of the overhang darkened the group, but four of the five stayed back while one continued toward the entrance. Gus tracked him, losing him until he reached the front doors. There, the Leather disappeared behind the outer wall. For seconds he didn't move, until slowly, cautiously, a sliver of his head and upper body edged into sight and stopped. Without question he spotted the briar patch of overturned furniture.

Daring not to breathe, Gus slowly brought up the Sig in both hands.

The other shadows drifted in and out of sight as they inched closer to the windows. The one with the battle axe eased through the doorway with nary a sound. He gripped the fearsome axe with both hands, ready do some hacking. Over the threshold he slunk, hunched at the shoulders, looking to clear the first section of the barricade.

Oh no you don't, Gus thought and aimed.

Two shots cracked, shattering the pent-up silence. The Leather staggered as if stepping on a live wire. He fell, the battle axe landing with a single dull *clack*.

The figures outside the hotel scattered, taking cover.

Gus ducked himself, swearing at his total disregard for his ammunition, but it was hard *not* to shoot round after round into those fucksticks.

A groan and a scuffling perked his ears, sounds of limbs being dragged across the tiles. Gus peeked over the desk and nearly lost his head when the Leather returned fire, blowing out windows in a spray of glass. Bullets screamed overhead, plugging the wall behind him and raining splinters and fragments. Bullets punched holes in the desk, spraying particles and forcing Gus to flatten himself. A round clipped a dead computer monitor, slapping the piece of hardware off the surface where it crashed across his shoulders. Baring missing teeth under the barrage, Gus tried to become one with the floor.

The shooting abruptly stopped.

Cringing, glancing up at the sudden silence, Gus listened as debris pattered the tiles all around him. On hands and knees, he wormed his way to the end of the desk and peeked around it.

There, the guy he just shot, staggering away from the entrance like a vampire staked through the chest. That caused Gus to do a double take. He'd put two in the Leather's chest. There was no way . . . then it hit him. *Body armor.*

Those sly-assed, rat-fuck *bastards.*

Right, he vowed. *Head shots from now on.* Not a problem. He had plenty of practice targeting skulls. He swore at himself, however, for not anticipating the Leather to be wearing some sort of protection.

It got quiet, then. Real quiet. The kind of quiet where you knew a bad moon was rising, where you stayed low and out of sight for fear of losing your head. He wasn't squaring off against mindless anymore, he was squaring off against ruthless sonsabitches who had made hunting humans their life for the past few years.

Gus strained to see but the Leather had all disappeared, taken cover.

"We want the woman," someone called out, sounding both fatigued and pissed off. "Send her out. Do that . . . and we'll kill you quick."

To some, that might have sounded like a real bargain.

Gus, however, wasn't about to bargain with a bunch of dicks.

"Chemist!" the voice shouted, louder this time. "You in there?"

Gus refused to say anything, to give himself away. They were fishing, probing, knowing he was in here, but unsure of where. Or his condition. Not yet, anyway.

But he had to see. Had to keep an eye on them. On where they were moving.

Joints cracked loud enough to cause him to freeze and wince when he rose to a crouch behind the desk. Then, he inched his head out until he could see around the corner.

There.

Standing outside the front doors, carrying what looked like a rifle, was a thick-bodied Leather—feet planted wide and wearing the commonplace coat that went to the ankles. No features were visible, just an indistinct caul of a mask. What looked like the tips of wings peeked over the Leather's shoulders, puzzling Gus.

"I can see *youuuu*," the Leather sang in a creepy voice.

Gus stopped breathing, easing the Sig up his side.

"I don't . . . offer deals," the Leather said. "At all. So consider it. Seriously. Send out the Chemist . . . and I'll kill you quick."

"Go fuck yourself," Gus yelled back and aimed—but did not fire as the speaker whirled out of sight.

"No . . ." the Leather countered in an utterly chilling tone. "I'll fuck *you*."

That venomous promise silenced Gus for a few seconds, until a subtle rustling hooked his attention, coming from his left. A skittering, perhaps from a fist of crumpled paper blowing across the floor, or a dried leaf. The sound turned him, and he wondered if the Leather was distracting him while attempting entry from another quarter.

"Come in here and I'll shoot your dick off!" Gus shouted back, a touch too desperate for his own liking. *"And, yeah, I'm that good a shot."*

Staying low, he snuck along behind the desk until he reached the far corner. There, without sticking his head out, he scanned the dark, seeing only the furniture belonging to the coffee shop area. Then the raised gate to the subway. A corner cut off his view beyond that, and Gus cursed at his failure to anticipate the Leather's plan to flank him. That little blunder reminded him he wasn't a tactician. He'd spent too much time shooting up dead things to anticipate the moves of a living opponent.

"You wanna hear about it?" the Leather asked, just outside the door. "How we'll kill you, if you don't turn over the Chemist?"

The question distracted Gus. He then gauged the angles of the lobby, fearful of exposing himself, his danger sense thrumming like a pair of divining rods detecting water underfoot. Another soft scraping, jerking his head in the very direction he heard it from. He scanned the foreboding dark, his grip tightening on his gun. Someone had their boots off, perhaps, but were accidentally kicking debris along on the floor. Just enough to torture him and divide his attention.

"We strip a person down," the Leather explained. "Tie their ankles and wrists to a couple of two-by-fours. Usually with wire. Nice and tight."

"You know you're fucked in the head, right?" Gus fired back, unable to help himself. "The whole, 'It's Halloween every fuckin' day' bunch of you."

That quieted the Leather.

The skittering again, maddening, closer than before. Gus focused on one point, straining to pick up movement.

"I changed my mind," the Leather said. "No deal. I'll kill you slow. Torture you first, of course. Make you sing. *Scream.* Hit those high notes you never thought possible."

A frustrated Gus rolled his eyes. He couldn't hear *shit* over all the yakking. A sick feeling swelled in his guts, knowing the worst was coming. He considered chancing a retreat, across open ground to the stairwell, where Maya's bucket of fun waited to be used on the third.

Another telltale scratching, freezing him as he glimpsed the source—just as a bead of sweat dribbled into his eye. Furious, Gus scrubbed the moisture away, sighting an out-of-focus ink blot against the unlit cavern of the corridor, scurrying across the tiles in a drunken, herky-jerky locomotion. Gus's mouth hung open, and a prehistoric chill stropped his spine and crystalized his balls.

Oh no, he thought.

His side vision picked up everything, how it moved left. Right. Then full stop. Left. Left again, then around the corner, out of sight. Only to be replaced by *another* coming from the same direction.

Gus had no trouble seeing that one scratching its way along, one much bigger than the first. The same sick, off-kilter motion, as if pulled by a string.

It couldn't be.

Not here. Not now.

"We'll hammer your toes into a pulp," the Leather droned on from beyond. "And leave them on you. Do the same to your fingers. Ever get your fingers caught in a car door? It'll be like that. Worse, because we'll smash *everything*. Hard enough to make things spatter. One by one. Leave it all looking like squashed raspberries on a sidewalk. And when we run out of fingers and toes, well . . ."

Eyes wide and holding his breath, Gus lowered himself just a little, watching the floor.

Many things were moving there.

"We have a pair of tongs," the Leather continued. "For stretching out tongues. Ever see a person have their tongue pulled out of their head? By the root? Think about that."

Gus barely heard him, unable to tear his attention away from the rats scurrying across the coffee shop floor. A *lot* of rats. Not ten strides away from him. He didn't know if they were the undead kind that he'd faced in Annapolis, but something told him they were. That short-circuiting way they moved. This city, this *entire* city, had a rat problem, just like Annapolis. Like Halifax. And those rats, left alone all this time, with a near infinite supply of rotting meat, had gorged themselves.

In doing so, they had clearly become infected.

And multiplied.

Fuck the Leather outside, blathering on and on. Gus had bigger problems.

One of those problems bumbled along the tiles, resembling a stuffed sock that might've just pulled itself free from a cauldron of oily, industrial sludge. It was the first of a string of them.

All headed right for Gus.

A frantic Gus backed away, bumping a shoulder into a cabinet behind the desk. The fallen computer monitor crackled underfoot and he slipped, falling to a knee while catching the countertop with a hand. A shard stabbed his knee, stinging it, and he yanked it away while glancing back.

Jesus!

A baker's dozen of the diseased little creatures came behind the desk, claws clicking, their sickly little tails trailing. Gus blurted a shocked gasp and stood and *ran*, exploding from his hiding spot, and bolted for the stairwell door just up the corridor.

Some forty feet away at least.

Gus heard a harsh gurgling from somewhere behind him, and a fiery stream lit up the entire lobby in his wake, swinging after his fleeing back and heels and igniting everything it touched. A terrible orange hue swept over the floors and walls. The temperature spiked. The corridor and stairwell door, near invisible before, became a livid mural of light and shadows—his own growing along the right wall.

A door which he would have to pull open.

The heat singed the back of his head and ears, all the way down to his boots.

Gus screamed and dove past the corner, into a heap of chairs—one leg spearing his cheek and drawing a stinging line to his ear. He shoved the thing away and drew up his legs just as the fire stream lasering across the lobby abruptly stopped. He heard the gurgling again—like someone clearing their throat right in front an overly sensitive microphone—and the opposite wall became a blazing, gas range ring of fire for seconds before ceasing.

Gus stood, cheek and knee stinging. He looked toward the lobby, expecting pursuers, and saw the burning carcasses of rats once pursuing him out there in the open. Cooked dead in their tracks.

Not waiting around for more, he turned and ran.

32

The Dragon released the long trigger of the flamethrower, and with a flick of his head, sent his minions into the hotel. They hurried inside, becoming wraiths in the billowing smoke. Furniture got kicked aside. Chairs tossed and tables were flipped out of the way. Fire crackled around the front desk area, giving off plenty of light. Bonemaker shoved his way through the barricade first, and he darted to the corner where his little rabbit had gone. There, he slammed his shoulder against the wall, prepared himself, and flipped around it, rifle aimed and ready to fire. The minion called Leech stopped behind him.

When the Dragon entered, Red and Slit had already widened the breach in the crude barricade. He waded into the burning lobby, the smoke bothering him, sparking coughs. That prompted him to reach under his mask and lift his scarf over his mouth.

Slit, slowed somewhat from taking a couple of bullets to his armored chest, retrieved a fire extinguisher and went about dousing the flames.

Which weren't easily put out.

"Get this shit under control," the Dragon rumbled as he strode by it all. "Leech—help him. Bonemaker. Red. With me."

The word given, the three of them hurried down the corridor, leaving the others to combat the flames. They sprayed the place with foam, grey smothering gobs of it. A chalky mist rose from the discharge, mixing with the smoke and spawning a palatable cloud. Neither Slit nor Leech paid any attention to the burning little lumps resembling bunched-up socks. Red even stomped on a pair, to put out the flames, before he located a second fire extinguisher. He grabbed it, readied the device, and stopped to examine one of the little frying bodies.

His eyes narrowed at what he was seeing. Not that it bothered him.

It was an old hotel.

Place was probably infested with the things.

Some two city blocks away from the Jonathan, where the abandoned city traffic had halted the Leather convoy, the minion called Slipknot scratched an itch under his steampunk mask. He listened, certain he heard a couple of shots echoing off the snow-swamped streets and avenues. He quickly lowered his window and heard the savage, full-auto reply from Bonemaker's assault rifle. The sound of that great gun made Slipknot a little envious. He would love to fire that thing. Gripping the steering wheel, he extracted a nearby machete hanging over his doorframe and got out of the truck.

The gunfire stopped when he hit the ground, and the only thing he heard then was his own raspy breathing. There was ice underfoot, made slick with the snow, and he slipped and grabbed the door for support. He righted himself and took a moment to listen to that deep smothering silence, waiting for more gunfire. Everything wore a white cap, as fine as cake frosting. He shivered, but it was still good to get out of the cab. Stretch the legs. Wasn't healthy to be sitting for longer than an hour. Not too many knew that. Not even the Dragon. And trying to tell the Dragon about *anything* was like talking to the Dog Tongue. You just didn't do it, unless given permission first.

So Slipknot stood alongside the semi, shin-deep in white shit, and closed the truck's door. Flakes fell, a little steadier now. Shouts, distant and dreamy, sounded from up ahead. The scouting party hadn't gone far, but Slipknot couldn't tell what they were saying. He took a firmer grip on the machete, even swung a few practice chops, and waited. The surrounding buildings were a respectable height, their fronts caked with ice and snow, the frosted windows dark and gloomy. Slipknot glanced at the trailer, wondering if the prisoners inside had heard the shooting. They probably had. He didn't give them another thought.

Movement in the snow attracted his eye, crawling along the truck's big wheels, toward him. Dark lumps breached the drifts, churning through. Several in fact, until he realized what he was looking at, easily seen against all that stark greyness of the snow.

Rats. There were rats underfoot. Not that rats bothered him. Back in the day, his downtown apartment in Saskatoon had a rat problem. Whole nest of them had taken up residence in a vacant studio apartment downstairs, and the scratching and resulting stink eventually alerted the tenants next door. Those people informed the lazy-ass landlord, and word was the rats had chewed their way through the walls, into the kitchen cupboards of the apartment next door. Slipknot wasn't around when the exterminators arrived on site. Nor was he around for the mayhem that followed, but they apparently took care of the rat problem.

Two of the little devils were presently coming right at him.

Brave little shits, he thought, the deep snow slowing them down. When the first one got close enough, he stomped on it, squashing it with two strikes. Then he backed up a step, sniffed, and waited for the next one. He crushed that one as well, using more force than intended and perhaps bruising his heel. When he finished, he inspected the kills and checked around him. No more rats, so he planted a hand on the nearby fender for balance and dragged his boot heel along the pavement, hoping to clean off any furry shit and guts potentially sticking to it. Once done, he rolled his shoulders, brandished his machete, and looked in the direction where the shooting had come from.

Rats, he thought, shivering again.

In the end, only them and the cockroaches would inherit the earth.

33

Halfway up the fairy-tale stairs leading to the third floor, sprinting like a prince in desperate need of a shitter, Gus tripped and fell, clacking his face on the edge of a carpeted step. Grimacing as he turned over, he cupped his lower jaw and realized an inch more and he could have seriously fucked up his nose.

Footsteps below, urging him to get his ass in gear. Gus stood and continued climbing, but slower than before. The staircase opened onto the third floor, a ways down from where Maya was. Gus banked, didn't bother checking on his pursuers, and charged down the hallway.

Rats were on his mind.

They were only the regular kind, he told himself.

No, that treacherous part of his brain countered. *Those are the infected kind. The fuckin' zombie kind.*

Yeah, they were, remembering how they came at him. Maybe the Leather burned them all. Maybe there weren't any more. His brain didn't say a word to that, but the silence was as good as a *yeah, right* scoff.

Yeah, Gus agreed unhappily.

A ghost stepped into the hallway ahead of him.

He waved her back inside, and Maya did just that.

"Get the bombs," he whispered out of breath, stopping inside the room.

"Is it them?" she asked.

"Yeah. And something worse."

That stumped her, and Gus didn't have time to explain. He closed the door to just a crack, watching for pursuers while Maya gathered up the firebombs.

"I heard the gunshots," she said, placing the homemade explosives into the bag. "I knew then. I'm sorry. I didn't want to come down—"

"Don't worry about it," Gus told her. "Leave everything else. We gotta get out of here."

"What?"

"CHEM-*MIST!*" came the distant roar, thundering along the corridor. That blast surprised Gus and Maya, who faced each other for a split second before she joined him at the door.

"That's the Dragon," she said, mortified.

Gus peeked out of the room and couldn't see anything. They were close, however.

"We're here, Chemist," the Dragon boomed. *"We're heeeere. We'll have you back in a few minutes. After I fry one little shit . . ."*

Gus glanced at Maya—who frantically rattled her head *no*.

He brought up the gun.

Maya stopped him and opened up the cloth bag. She handed him a firebomb.

"You got your lighter?" she asked.

"Goddamn right, I do."

"We won't have much time."

Gus supposed they wouldn't. "You ready?"

"We're running?"

"As far and as long as we can. I wasn't shittin' you earlier. We gotta get out of here and not because of these fuckers."

"There's someone else?"

"Some*thing* else, yeah. You ready?"

"Yeah."

Gus checked the hallway and opened the door just enough to get through. Maya was on his heels. They stayed close to the wall and, glancing often over their shoulders, hurried from that booming voice.

"CHEMIST."

That ruffled Gus's feathers, and he turned to see three shadows far down the corridor. Without thinking, he brought up the gun and fired twice.

Two of the Leather scattered.

The one in the middle stood his ground, and, literally, returned fire.

A great gout of flame rushed up the corridor, illuminating its Art Nouveau decor and gloriously ribbed support beams, and surged past Gus as Maya hauled him back against the wall. That scorching lance of fire raged past them and then swung inwards . . .

A face-melting tendril nearly cooked Gus's head as Maya pulled him through the doorway she'd just opened. Fire engulfed the entrance until she slammed the door shut.

"The fuck was *that?*" he wanted to know.

"His flamethrower," Maya answered.

"How can it reach that far?"

"I did some work on it. Look, we can't stay here."

Angry and bewildered, Gus produced his lighter. "Get ready to open that thing," He nodded at the door. "And get ready to run."

Maya nodded back.

He lit the firebomb's fuse, which lit up brightly. "Open it!"

Maya did and Gus swung himself outside to throw the bomb down the corridor. It smashed against one of the beams and sprayed fire across the width of the passageway.

Maya and Gus ran in the other direction.

A second later, the Dragon released another blast, waving it behind them, zigzagging the stream left and right, up, and down. Everything combustible exploded with crackling delight, producing life-stealing smoke that billowed and coiled within the confines of the hallway.

Through the flames, the Dragon saw them run before the smoke swallowed them whole. He released the flamethrower's trigger, which chuffed into silence. A fiery slash raged across a wide carpet, stretching some fifteen feet ahead of them—the result of the thrown Molotov cocktail. The blaze cut off the hallway, stopping all pursuit.

Confusion filled the leader as he lowered the nozzle and processed what he saw. Before the smoke thickened, he was certain he saw the Chemist running on the heels of whoever was *ahead* of her.

He wondered why the Chemist was running away.

And feared the worst.

Gus and Maya rounded a corner and pounded past a crook in the corridor, heading for an inner set of windows that overlooked the courtyard. They charged past the glass, running toward the rear of the hotel. An emergency stairwell came into view, the white diagram with bold lettering just barely visible, and they slammed on the brakes.

"Here," Maya gasped and opened the door. Gus followed without question.

They pounded down the steps, firebombs clinking all the way.

Second floor. Maya pulled open the door and directed Gus through, who entered gun-first. How many shots did he have left? One? Two? None?

He'd find out soon enough.

"Looks clear," he said, swinging one way and then the other. "This way."

Maya hurried to Gus's side. "I saw three of them up there," she said.

"Yeah, I did too. There's about a half-dozen of them."

"That's about right."

"We need to leave this place," Gus panted, slowing to a brisk march.

"You said that. What's this thing you were talking about? Mindless?"

"No—well, yes. But not like you think—zombie rats."

Maya stopped in her tracks, which prompted Gus to stop in his.

"Really," he nodded. "Trust me on this. I don't how many of them there are, but once upon a time, I torched a whole fuckin' city full of the little monsters, and I *still* didn't get them all. Blew up my house on a mountain and I doubt *that* got them all—*but* I sure as fuck left a mark."

"Rats?"

"*Rats*. And don't *not* believe me until we're free and clear of this place."

The corridor gracefully turned and they continued at a brisk walk while checking over their shoulders. Gus scanned the shadows and every pocket of darkness ahead, fearful of what might be lurking. After a hurried march which turned them south, or what he thought was south, he veered for the nearest hotel doors. Locked, which forced him to fumble for the master key.

"Keep a lookout," Gus said as he searched his pockets.

"Of course."

"And watch for rats," he added. "All that scuffing along the walls downstairs? The shredded carpeting? They did that."

Her features crunched in disbelief. "But . . . how many would—"

Gus stuck the key into the lock. "A lot," he said and opened the door.

Inside they went, closed the door, and locked it. Gus huffed it over to the window and looked at the streets below. A breadbox-sized cabinet next to the air conditioner had lettering on it. Gus stooped to read it.

EMERGENCY LADDER. USE IN CASE OF FIRE.

"Holy shit this place is ancient," he said, opening the cabinet. A folded rope ladder waited inside, bolted into the wall. Strategically placed so that all one had to do was open the window, open the box, and flip the rope ladder up and over the sill.

"God love ya," Gus said and examined the window. Two locks—the simple lever kind where you flip up and done. He did so, top and bottom, and pushed on the frame. A blast of freezing air stunned him, and a smattering of snowflakes caused him to look up. The night had clouded over. The snow they hoped would cover their tracks had finally arrived, hours too late.

"All right." He hauled out the ladder, flipped it over the sill, and let it tumble to street level.

"You go first," he said. "I'll hold on up here."

Maya climbed out with a helping hand. "Oh it's cold."

Gus knew. "Hold on tight. You ever use one of these before?"

"No. You?"

"No."

"Great," she said. Taking hold of the rope, she met his eyes for a second and started down. Gus held on to her coat for extra support. She struggled to get her feet into the warping, stubborn loops of the ladder, which fluttered in a building wind. Unspoiled snow cushioned the sidewalk below, along with a row of parked cars with white tops.

Maya lowered herself three feet and Gus had to let her go. She swayed, grunted, pushing off the wall at times, but continued climbing down. He checked on the locked door to the room and then the street. Dark storefronts were visible across a four-lane avenue. Maybe a couple of restaurants. Planted trees and raised flower beds along the curb. A growing line of ink emerging from a storm drain caught his eye, paralyzing him, and he stared in dawning horror at what was coming.

He glanced down at Maya.

"Oh Jesus," he whispered.

She was kicking and shoving herself away from the wall, creating room to dig in a foot. She had descended another two feet, leaving another seven or so before her feet touched sidewalk—right where a dozen or so rats waited, swarming over each other. Another, thicker stream of vermin spilled forth from up some unseen storm drain, while more ragged lines slunk into sight, emerging from dark crevices along the avenue. They crawled through the snow and converged on the descending Maya, who was oblivious to the gathering danger. Worse still, those ravenous lines of rats were thickening, going from dozens strong to potentially hundreds.

"*Maya!*" Gus whispered urgently. "*Stop! Climb back up.*"

She lifted her contorted face.

"Don't go any further. Get back up here."

"You're joking."

"No, I'm not, just—oh shit, *don't*—"

But she did. She checked on how far she was to the bottom. Only a second, but that waiting pool of infected death snapped her head up, and when she looked at Gus, he saw the fright on her rash-covered face.

Energized by what was below, she started climbing back up. Hand over hand, boots skidding against the wall, little grunts leaving her all the way.

"That's it, come on," he said, reaching for her.

From his point of view, the hotel wall was suddenly a frozen plain of brick, and at its center, Maya bounced along on her belly. Lines of rats fed into a growing, seething black hole directly below her, growing bigger with every passing second.

Gus glanced down and his face went slack.

Rats filled the streets in droves, blotting out the white purity of the snow. Rats clambered over the slower bodies of those beneath them, creating a shifting, stumbling strata, merging at the base of the hotel, where they piled atop each other. The vermin pool thickened, widened, as more and more of the undead rodents amassed beneath Maya.

She slipped, one boot skidding down the brick wall, her body slapping the surface. Gus reached out, fingers splayed, but she was a good foot away. She didn't drop, didn't lose composure, and was able to hoist herself up. Gus got a hand on her and pulled. He grabbed her upper arm. Her lower back. Until he dragged her through the window and dumped her onto the floor, both gasping all the way. She collapsed, curled up in a heap, while Gus leaned against the air conditioner.

"Gimme a minute," she said, struggling for breath. "That . . . was a workout."

Gus glanced out the window.

Holy *shit*.

Rats. Thicker than before, impossibly so. Stemming from places he didn't know existed. A floodplain's worth, pouring into the street from both directions, from the farthest ends. They were coming from everywhere. From the drainage systems. From the alleyways. From the buildings across the streets. They spewed forth from unseen holes at the bottoms of doors. *Rats*. Collectively gathering below, crawling over each other to scale the wall.

And, thankfully, failing in droves.

Gus hauled the window shut.

"We got a bigger problem," he said in a low voice.

Maya stood and went to the window. She covered her mouth at what she saw. "God Almighty," she said.

"This way," he said.

"There's so many."

Gus knew. He rushed to the door and checked the peephole.

"What do we do?" she asked him, right behind him.

Gus opened the door and a Leather with a red demon mask and a pair of swords bashed inside the room.

34

Back in the street, the Leather called Slipknot studied the night sky. Clouds had moved in, bringing great fluffy chunks that fell lazily upon the world. The temperature dropped, piercing his leather duster and the layers underneath, but not enough to bother him. Slipknot moved around the front of the big rig, listening for any more shooting. All had gone quiet, so he assumed the Dragon had matters under control. There was no doubt otherwise, knowing the quiet but positively vicious disposition of the leader. One didn't start talking to severed heads in bowling bags just because one enjoyed it. That latest sidenote bothered Slipknot, bothered him a whole lot more than he let on in the Dragon's presence. And though he considered this little group a tight-knit one of similar minds, there was no one he dared talk to about the Dragon's most recent... pastime. As disturbing as it was, the others probably wouldn't give a damn who the Dragon talked to, or, worse, they would wonder why Slipknot did. Which would quickly get back to the Dragon himself and lead to Slipknot getting taped down and roasted in some hotel bunk one evening.

No thank you.

Deciding to keep his mouth shut, Slipknot placed a hand on the nearby fender, to steady himself on the hidden patches of ice. The urge to pee took him, and he wandered toward the rear of the truck, walking past the unmoving rats he'd stomped into the snow.

No sound from the prisoners inside the trailer, which was a good thing. They were probably freezing to death or had decided to finally break down and drink the water tossed in for them. The water had been steeped with mindless blood. One sip was all it took to sprout new mindless two to twenty-four hours later. And they would drink. They all did, in the end.

He pinned his machete under an armpit, then assumed the stance while pinching at a hidden zipper. Got his lad freed—colder than he thought as evident by what he had to work with—and cut loose near the very last tire.

Piss. Even the word sounded fine, especially when you had to go. Some soft sibilant Zen shit right there. That hot stream hit the snow underneath the rig, opening a fissure right down to the bare pavement. Peein' in the snow. Nothin' better. He swiveled his hips a little, lasering in a figure eight.

Something nudged his ankle, getting Slipknot's attention. More to the point, it nearly scared the shit out of him. He turned, still holding his one-eye wiener, and gawked at the rats scurrying around his boots. One even darted up his instep, which he kicked away with a frenzied jig, sending the little furry runt flying across the street.

Which was right about when Slipknot stopped and stared, his mind a crackling white screen of disbelief.

Rats filled the street, flowing from the storefronts. An undulating field of arched backs, white tails, and bobbing snouts that stretched to a point where he couldn't see any road at all. Rats blanketed *everything*, swarming along the rear of the trailer, blackening the snow with their unholy numbers. They zeroed in on him, rubbing their greasy little bodies together, producing a frightening—nay, shit *liquifying*—hiss of motion that was oddly amplified by the snow-choked avenues.

All Slipknot had time for was to grab his machete (his lad had already ducked inside) while performing another quick and dirty jig along the side of the truck. The rats closed in from all directions. With every footfall, he stomped on heads and bodies on his way back to the safety of the cab.

Holy shit.

Only halfway to the cab, but the sight shocked him to his core. *Rats.* Everywhere. Black streaks of them flowed from alleys. From snowed-in storm drains where they dug free with evil vigor. From underneath vehicles. The surrounding white rapidly disappeared under their numbers, as if some gigantic container of chunky coffee grounds had toppled, spilling its soupy contents into the city in one sustained gush. And some of the rats were huge. *As big as wiener dog pups,* Slipknot realized. The faces drawn and pinched and snapping as their deepening numbers encircled the big rig.

Waves of them lapped around the cab.

Slipknot headed for the short steps because of their proximity. His long legs carried him along in great strides—until his boot hit a patch of hidden ice underneath the snow. Not fifteen feet away from the door.

Night flashed between feet and ankles before he slammed down, cracking his skull off the pavement.

Dazed and baring teeth, Slipknot rolled onto his belly, hands gripping the impact point on his head. Things crawled over his lower legs. Between his legs. Pressed against his side and over his back. Then his arms.

All within seconds.

Sensing the not so feathery weight, Slipknot lifted his face just as a black sea's worth of rats washed over him. They snapped at his face, his forehead and eyebrows, his eyes, nose, and lips. They latched onto everything, sinking yellow teeth into soft yielding flesh. Slipknot screamed, batting the tide away, spraying black arcs as the rats kept stealing little bites. He pushed himself to his knees, the rats feasting on fingers and wrists. His forearms and elbows. Rats raced up his inseam, gnashing at his thighs and crotch, getting his attention there while others swarmed over his legs. Slipknot smashed one hand against a big wheel, then the other, shaking several vermin free. He tore fistfuls from his chest before they could reach his throat. Slapped more from his thighs and stomped on others gnawing at his boots, only to slip on one of the larger ones, and down he went, on his hands and knees again.

Again the rats swarmed over him, inflicting dozens of rabid bites about his bare and bleeding hands. Screaming, Slipknot slammed them against the lower edge of the trailer, while dozens—*hundreds*—wanted a taste of him, surging up his thighs to his waist. Slipknot fastened a hand around a pipe underneath the trailer and used that to stand, rats falling as he planted his back against the side wall.

The street was livid with the little monsters.

Panting and whimpering, Slipknot forged ahead, rats clinging to him every foot of the way. They became so thick underfoot that every step threatened to bring him down.

Ten feet.

Their ranks became a snapping morass nearly shin-deep, their combined weight significant. They clamped down on his outer layers, striving for penetration. Slipknot continually slapped them away or tore them off. He stopped at times to stomp with a frenzied energy, crushing several until he chanced another step, trailing blood in his wake.

Five feet, and he was at the fuel tanks, the footsteps to the cab right there.

He slipped on the shifting, greasy mat of countless bodies, but managed to grab the truck as he landed on a knee. A deluge of rats swept over his lower legs and thighs. Rats clung to his coat, swung from his elbows, and drooped from his waist. Slipknot pulled himself upright, but his hands didn't have a firm grip anymore.

The door was right there.

But there were *thousands* of the evil things trying to bring him down for the final time.

Ignoring the rising, thrashing depths that reached his waist, Slipknot lunged for the door—but the masses pressing up against his lower self smothered his launch, his fingernails painfully glancing off the metal step.

He landed, face-down in that dreadful tide.

Rats bit at his arms, ribs, face, and neck. They clicked black teeth off the lenses of his steampunk mask, rooted up the ends around his Adam's apple and shoved invasive snouts against his skin.

Just before the dreadful bites.

They chewed away Slipknot's throat in seconds.

The dying minion disappeared under the swarm.

And did not rise again.

35

One of those swords flashed down for Gus's wrist—attached to the hand holding his gun. Gus jerked it back and only had the weapon knocked from his grip. A fist backhanded him, square across the jaw, torquing his head to the left.

His legs became boneless, and he slumped backwards.

"They're in here!" the red-faced demon shouted down the hall. *"They're—"*

Which was when Maya barged forward and drove her not insignificant mass into the armored Leather, knocking him past Gus, into the bathroom. Rage-fueled grunts peppered the air as the minion and Maya grappled, until the demon face pushed her head back at arm's length, a hand clamped about her throat.

The smiling red mask tilted one way then the other and walked her out of the bathroom. Maya hammered and clawed at the hand holding her throat. Until Gus sprang from the floor, crashing into the Leather's legs and taking him down.

There was a mad scramble then. A flurry of failed punches and effective blocks. Hands pawed at Gus's face. A palm heel pushed up his chin. A finger spiked one nostril. The other sword-wielding hand sought to stab him. Gus kept that hand at bay while trying to pry the other off his face. They rolled, coming up at the edge of a queen-sized bed. Gus punched the mask—three hard blows that skewered the red demon face aside, effectively blinding him. The Leather punched back, narrowly missing Gus's exposed throat and clipping his chin. The blow staggered him, enough for the Leather to draw back his sword. Maya appeared, stomping on the sword arm, then the wrist. The Leather released the weapon with a squeal and smashed her knee, toppling her.

As Gus scrambled to get on his feet, a set of arms looped around his neck. A powerful strength sought to choke the life from him. It was a move he'd had plenty of training for, courtesy of one Collie Jones. So when those arms clinched his vulnerable neck, Gus's muscle memory kicked in.

He shifted his hips and snapped a fist back into the Leather's balls.

The Leather wore armor, armor that extended to his crotch, but a hammerfist to the nutsack still carries some weight, and the armor wasn't made of metal. Gus's fist smashed into the Leather's pickle and beans, buckling the brute and forcing him to release him almost instantly.

A gasping Gus turned, somewhat off-kilter, and stood, driving his knee into his attacker's face as he did so. The connection rocked the mask, dropping the minion to the floor. Breathing hard, Gus stepped back from the fight.

The Leather rose to his elbows and knees, red mask twisted to one side, cupping himself with one hand.

Which was right about when Maya—with an angry peal of effort—hacked the minion's head half off with one of his own swords.

The cut wasn't clean. A high collar stopped the blade from taking his head clean off, but the result was still the same. He clutched at his neck, a red torrent pouring between his fingers. The Leather collapsed without a sound, sprawled across the carpet, half-decapitated.

Maya dropped the blade and helped Gus to his feet.

"I'm good," he said, sparing a glance at the dead man.

"That's Red," she said. "One of the Dragon's boys."

Gus nodded and sought out the dropped gun. He found it near the open doorway. When he turned back, he saw the full picture of the dead man in the room.

"You okay?" Maya asked him.

He nodded. "Let's get out of here."

They checked the corridor before entering it, and then fled past a series of columns, support beams, and doors.

"Chemist!" the Dragon's shout echoed behind them, and this time, he sounded livid.

Gus and Maya spotted another emergency stairwell door. They rushed through the portal and let the door swing closed behind them. Gus considered going up, but elected down, hoping they might reach the snowmachine below and escape into the plains. They hurried to the ground level, nearly dizzy from their rapid descent. When Gus yanked open the door he nearly shit himself because the floor was teeming with rats.

He couldn't close the door fast enough because of the traitorous hydraulics overhead, designed to prevent slamming. Rats came through and Gus kicked them back.

Maya stood nearby, plunging a hand into the cloth bag.

"CHEMIST!" the Dragon roared from above, the acoustics shivering Gus to the bone. He kicked back the rats, but they plugged the opening, preventing the door from completely closing.

"Come on," Gus said and did the last thing he thought he would do.

He yanked the door open and fled into the hallway.

It was darker than before, but they had no trouble seeing how the rats covered everything in a seething, rumbling carpet. Hundreds skittered forth from around a corner, which Gus recognized as the entrance to the subway. Maya lit and threw one of the firebombs in that direction, where it exploded in a blinding flash. Fire lashed the vermin, igniting several, and lighting up the way to the main entrance.

Gus and Maya halted.

Rats flooded the entire lobby floor.

Some of which were already clawing their way up Gus's boots.

He kicked them away as Maya lurched to one side, dealing with her own attackers.

"This way," she yelled, and mashed her away across the rat-infested lobby. Gus followed, mindful of where he stepped, landing on rats squirming under his heel. Though wobbling at times, they managed to stay upright, but they would not for long.

Ahead was a smashed glass door.

Maya hurried through and Gus followed.

Onto a rubbery mat cushioned for serious walking, and momentarily clear of rats. That spectacular ribbed dome lay overhead, high above the inner courtyard. The gazebo and playground once viewed from above looked much grander on ground level. All that was needed to complete the fairy-tale scene were falling snowflakes.

Maya whirled, another firebomb in hand. She lit the fuse.

Gus got out of the way as she threw the thing, lobbing it through the smashed doorway and exploding it off the wall. Fire washed across the threshold and floor, transforming their pursuers into a shifting, burning mat.

Gus almost cheered. Almost. Until the rats poured through the breach, scurrying over the flames and their immolating brethren in an unending flow. That mass of bodies *trampled* the flames underneath, threatening to douse them completely.

Maya was already lighting another firebomb. She baseball-pitched it at the rats pushing through the burning doorway. The ceramic burst apart in a less-than-impressive ball of flame. She smashed a third bomb before the advancing rats, setting off a much larger pool of her lethal concoction.

The advancing vermin crawled through the flames, igniting, and slowing to a stop. From the hall, firelight fluttered, dying under a horrific rush of bodies.

Maya pulled on Gus's shoulder and they ran, across that shadowy interior beneath the lightless dome, flames rippling behind them. They charged past the playground and open areas with lines of patio furniture. The pool came into sight, and as they ran past, a solid wedge of rats scuttled up the slope from the deep end.

They slowed, spotting a fissure in the murky deep end, where the pool ended in a frothy blackness.

"Come *on*!" Maya urged, breaking Gus's paralysis.

They raced across that expanse, quickly outpacing the undead vermin. A glass door came into view. Maya got there first and pulled it open, ushering Gus through.

He glanced over his shoulder once more, in time to see the fire—the same one Maya unleashed only seconds earlier—burning much brighter on the far side of the courtyard, as if it were receiving a spilled barrel's worth of crude.

36

The Dragon didn't think dividing his forces was an issue. Not with the firepower they had between them. Not with the level of viciousness they possessed. He had no issue sending Bonemaker—still armed with the assault rifle—to the left and sending Red to the right, while he stood guard at the stairwell. And, on impulse, he actually decided to check on the floor below, to ensure they didn't slip by through some devious witchery.

Red's distant shout of *They're in here!* reached him just as he was reaching for the door latch of the second floor. The Dragon hurried back up, grunting from the weight he carried. He rushed through the hotel until he stood in the open doorway of one room. There he found Red splayed out on thick carpet, his head half-detached from his body, his bloody swords nearby. Two wet steps into the room and he stopped, shock morphing into rage. He spun back to the entrance and looked around, glimpsing a pair of ghosts fleeing farther down the corridor, vanishing around a corner.

"*Chemist!*" he roared and gave chase, his anger powering him forward. His infatuation with the Chemist was starting to bleed over the lines into hatred, one stemming from a growing suspicion that she no longer wanted to be a part of the Leather. That was unacceptable. There was no going back once you wore the leather. None. The Dog Tongue himself preached that very law.

A closed door to another stairwell. The Dragon slowed to a stop and pulled it open, letting it swing closed behind him.

Downwards he thundered, every footfall echoing off the walls.

Nearing the bottom, the sight of a half-open door greeted him. A plague's mat of rats scurried about the base, preventing the door from closing. Smoke wafted through, reminding him that things were burning nearby, which he assumed he'd started earlier.

Fires his minions had failed to extinguish. The Dragon stopped on the fifth step from the bottom, where he watched the little animals.

A *lot* of little animals.

In fact, there were more rats milling about the doorway than he cared to see.

Sensing him, the rats scrambled to the staircase and clawed their way upwards, hoisting themselves up one step at a time.

That feral charge perplexed the Dragon, and the dead skunk stink radiating from them seeped through his mask. There was something wrong with these creatures. Something off. The numbers alone were worrying. And they made no sound—other than the clicking of claws upon the floor, and a weird swishing.

They certainly had no fear of him.

Which was a mistake.

The Dragon squashed the first rat to come within range, grinding the creature into the metal edge. He didn't stop there. Descending the stairs with his size thirteen workman's boots, where the insulated rubber reached his midshins, he monster-mashed his way down, kicking and squashing everything underfoot. That attracted more rats into the stairwell, inciting them into a frenzy. They attacked his lower bits, clawing, nipping at his ankles, failing to breach the rubber. The Dragon felt them down there, pressing, squirming. He mashed dozens into the floor and ignored the rest, marching right out the door.

Into an unchecked *river* of the little bastards.

Rats attacked his lower bits as he stomped his displeasure, flattening dozens more without pause. The blazing doorway drew his attention, fire he immediately knew was the work of the Chemist. She was a burner at heart just like he was, part of the reason he liked her.

That rising tide of biting, gnashing pestilence continued to foam about his ankles, some standing on their haunches like unwanted puppies. The Dragon kicked them all down and waded through their ranks, crushing more underfoot. There were so *many*, eager to bring him down, and therein he sensed danger. Glancing around, he realized he was near the lobby. The fires he'd started seemed to be put out, however, but smoke still lingered, making it near impossible to see. No sign of his minions, and if he was walking in vermin, no doubt they were as well.

He coughed, breathing in the bothersome smoke, its heavy curls scratching at his throat despite his mask and scarf.

Weight around his knees distracted him. *Rats*, actually up underneath his ankle-length duster, nipping at his leather pants. The pants were actually a secondary layer, covering an ordinary pair of jeans. He didn't think the rats could pierce the outer material, but he wasn't about to give them a chance.

He reached down and swatted them underneath the coat, clearing them off. He circled, stomping, doing a storm dance upon their frail little bodies. Another bout of coughing, but it didn't slow him. He squashed so many it threatened to turn his stomach, whereupon he straightened and glanced around. They crawled for him, an endless flow of reinforcements, filling the hallway as far back until their numbers disappeared in the smoke.

A chill went up the Leather's spine.

"Dragon?" Bonemaker called out from the stairwell.

"*Go back,*" the Dragon yelled, coughing as he did so. "*The way you came! Cut them off from the other side if you can. I'll follow from here.*"

With that, Bonemaker left, leaving the Dragon alone with the rats. The Leather leader slogged through their waves, squashing bodies as he went, deeming the creatures a plague. A troublesome, meddlesome plague. Risen from dark ages both recent and ancient and ultimately beneath him.

But they were only rats, after all. And he, well . . .

He was a dragon.

And he was about to get medieval.

With a death metal roar, he leveled the flamethrower at the masses skittering over the floor charging him and squeezed the trigger.

As soon as Gus and Maya entered the western corridor of the hotel, dribbles of rats sputtered from the dark. Certainly not like the numbers they'd just seen, but Gus knew there would be more. Many, many more. And if they were gaining access to the hotel through the hole in the pool and the subway entrance, he didn't want to think about what might ultimately be lurking beneath their feet.

Maya took the lead, running for the smoke-filled lobby. Rats materialized from the haze but were easily avoided.

"The snowmachine?" Gus asked, catching an unpleasant whiff of bad air and burnt meat.

"*Snowmobile,*" she corrected and lurched to a stop. Gus halted beside her.

Rats infested the lobby. A knobby, heaving weave of rodents both large and small, prodding the air with snouts, where those on the bottom strove to climb above the rest. Their filthy slick forms hopped and skittered over each over, scampered and charged, creating a loathsome slurry tide that scrubbed against and rose above the baseboards. Worse, rats infested the remains of the makeshift barricade, exploring every little crook and cranny. They overran the front desk, dragging along bloated, putrescent bodies the size of cats, trailing white tails and, at times, pushed off the top by other rats. Those that fell landed on that mattress of madness below, where they struggled to stay atop the surface.

That densely packed mass of undead mayhem noticed the living and shifted toward them. A breath-stealing wall of decomposing flesh, musculature, and rotting fluids shifted with that tide, blowing toward Gus and Maya, polluting their eyes and sinuses, coating the insides of their mouths.

Clutching at her nose and mouth, Maya stumbled a retreat from that oncoming deluge of zombie might. Gus barely suppressed his own olfactory urge to barf.

They staggered back to the stairwell, outpacing the debilitating stink pursuing them. Gus opened the door and pushed Maya through, and only got through himself before the foremost ranks reached the base. Leaving the door, they hiked back up the stairs, hearing the rats struggle through the bottleneck.

Halfway up that spiraling helix of steps, Gus grabbed the railing and stopped to glance back.

One deep breath. Two. *Three.*

Holy *shit.*

A loamy spearhead of rats clambered up over the last step he could see, as if the hotel was a stricken luxury liner, sinking in a sea of matted fur. The rats clambered up to the next step, little claws seeking purchase, only as long as it took for the following waves to catch up. When they did, the lead rats would step on them to gain the few extra centimeters needed to haul themselves up and attack the next step.

"*Come on,*" a tired Maya said, hauling on his shoulder.

Equally tired and perhaps more in pain, Gus chugged after her, his legs burning.

She reached the landing to the second floor, opened the door, and leaned halfway in—only to jerk herself back out.

"*They're in there,*" she whispered harshly and proceeded up the steps.

Whirling after her, Gus freed his gun and got halfway to the third floor when the second-floor door barged open. A Leather aiming a shotgun stepped out and Gus fired, punching out chunks of the wall next to the minion's head. The Leather flinched and ducked back inside, hampering another figure behind him.

Gus fired at that fat target when the chamber clicked empty.

That sound signaling a spent magazine practically *boomed* within the confines of the stairwell, catching the attention of the Leather, who stuck their heads out.

Gus bolted after Maya, tapping into that special tank of energy reserved for when he was about to have his ass shot off.

Boots clicked on tiles as the Leather stepped into the open and fired that hip cannon. The blast shook the interior, the noise powerful enough to start ear bleeds. The wall exploded a foot behind Gus, showering him in chalky fragments.

Ramfist.

He'd know that thunderstick anywhere.

That knowledge nearly turned Gus's shit to mustard. Panting, calves hurting, he scampered up the final few steps to the third floor, where Maya waited with the open door.

"Get in here," she whispered-screamed at him, shaking a strip of plastic from her fingers.

She held a bucket. The one filled with her homemade tear gas. Which she lobbed into the stairwell, banging part of the container off the door as it went through. The plastic lid flew off like an oversized saucer, and that final knock tilted the now open missile. It spiraled wildly off a rail and then a wall, releasing a cloud as it fell.

Maya pulled Gus back, just as the door finished closing. They splayed themselves to the right and left of it, catching their breaths, not knowing what exactly to expect.

Seconds later, the screaming began.

Gus looked at Maya, whose wide eyes mirrored his own.

The door opened.

Two Leather, heads shaking as if freshly blinded, attempted to push their way through. Whether they could see or not was of no consequence. One of them held a battle axe. The other one—

Gus shoved the gunman into the axeman and they stumbled against the doorframe. Gus punched the axeman's throat and kicked out a knee, dropping him to the landing outside. The gunman whipped the Ramfist around and fired, close enough for Gus's eardrums to flatline. Screaming, he shoved the gunman's head back, clacking it off the doorframe, and yanked the shotgun free of the Leather's grasp.

Then he tackled the stunned gunman, heaving his person up under the minion's arm, going for a move Collie had versed him in—which, oddly enough, wasn't a dick-punch. The Leather unleashed a weak elbow, which failed to do damage. Gus tightened his hold against the Leather's back, wrapped his arm around the man's neck in a V, and initiated a choke hold with every ounce of strength he had left.

If you knew what was coming, maybe you had a second or two to react, to attempt an escape.

If you knew what was coming.

Gus banked on what Collie preached was true—these days, most people *didn't* know such lethal offensive moves. And anyone who *did* know had an extreme advantage over others.

Gus clamped down on that meaty neck trapped in his V-shaped arm and squeezed. Squeezed for juice, trying to burst that tomato in one all-out show of brute force. The Leather, having never had his carotid's flow of blood cut off to his brain, blurted a gasp before instinctively grabbing at the arms wrapped around his gullet. Wrong move, as he failed to budge them. Then he clawed at Gus's face, raking fingers down his forehead and drawing blood. Gus arched his back to avoid more damage, and fell back, scooting down the doorframe, until his upper body landed in the corridor of the third floor.

By that time, the hand clawing at him weakened. The tiniest strained grunt popped from the Leather's lips, and his hands went back to the strangling arm. Much weaker than before, all strength bleeding away.

Gus held on, kept crushing that neck, feeling the man go limp.

Which was right about when the *other* Leather, the one with the battle axe, swung that godforsaken weapon up and down, splitting apart the instep of Gus's planted right foot in a ringing connection of steel on wood.

That blunt smack was immediately drowned out by the discharge of the Ramfist, fired by Maya. The shot nailed the axeman point blank, flinging him back and bouncing him off the wall, where he tumbled out of sight down the stairwell.

Howling in pain, a wide-eyed Gus writhed on his back. The Leather whom he had in a choke hold rolled over onto his stomach, which was enough for Maya. She aimed and fired, brutally bucking the minion across the doorframe, his spine hyperextending while ink spattered the whole area.

Then she was at Gus's twisting, rolling side.

"Let me see," she whispered at his ear. "Let me see."

Grimacing, nearly wild with the pain, Gus released his double-clutched leg, and lay there as still as possible.

Maya bent over him . . . then she was turning for the door.

A suffering Gus looked as well.

The tear gas was drifting back into the corridor.

"Oh no," Maya said and scrambled, hauling Gus to a sitting position. "Get up, *now*. I know it hurts, but get *up*."

He got up, limping, his sinuses already stinging as if he'd taken a snort of pepper. Seconds later his eyes burned and watered.

"Oh shit, oh shit," Maya intoned, experiencing the same while slinging his arm around her shoulders.

They staggered away, leaving a bloody track behind them.

Maya stopped them at a door. She tried it and it mercifully opened. They lurched into a room, with Maya slamming the door behind them. A short hopping shuffle later, she dropped Gus on a bed and went for the bathroom. She returned, grimacing all the way.

"*Ooooh*, this is bad," she said, holding a dry face cloth at her eyes. "This is bad. All right. I gotta take your boot off, okay? Give it here."

Gus did, stretching out his tortured leg.

She undid the laces and pulled without warning, ripping a cry of pain from him, sending a searing flutter up the entirety of his foot. Which was parted, about two inches into the instep, between the second and third toe. He chanced a look and saw the blood oozing from the cut.

"Oh *Christ*," Gus moaned as she applied a cloth to the wound, then wrapped everything in with a roll of Scotch tape.

"Crude, I know," she said, stopping for seconds to squeeze her eyes shut before wiping them. "Can you walk on it?"

Gus pushed himself to the edge of the bed. He tried to stand and did so, but limped a step after that.

"Best I can do."

"All right."

"Where's that light coming from?" he asked.

They both turned toward a window, which, to their burning eyes, periodically resembled a flickering orange smear. The view of the inner courtyard drew them over, and they peered below.

Things burned.

Through the smoke, a blackness surged across the landscape, sprouting from the broken pool.

And from the west side, from the area they could not see, shot forth sheets of flame.

37

With grim determination, the Dragon strode across the inner courtyard, pausing at times to scorch clear the way before him. The rats were everywhere, crawling straight for him. He would plant his feet and blaze the vermin with the flamethrower, sometimes in a straight line, sometimes in a circle. He'd leave a thirty-foot smouldering strip of burning bodies, and march as far as he could before repeating for another section. That created space, but it didn't deter the little shits, which was about when the Dragon suspected a greater menace afoot, one that would garner closer examination at a later point.

Now, however, he just wanted to find the Chemist.

And deep fry the one who had taken her.

His path took him past the empty pool, where he stopped and stared in pure awe.

Rats channeled up the slope, bubbling forth from a wide thunderbolt of a fissure located in the deep end. And from the looks of it, he'd just discovered the uncorked well from which they were spewing.

The Dragon hosed down the rush in one bright fan of flame, transforming them into an orange lick of molten bodies. The advance disintegrated. He unleashed another torrent into the deep end, burning the source. Columns of smoke flared up, greatly reducing his already limited sight. A harsh coughing fit gripped him, harder than before, his shoulders heaving enough that he released the trigger. His mask had an additional inner lining to lessen smoke inhalation, but it was seeping through despite the wide-open space of the courtyard. The Dragon knew he should *not* be using the flamethrower inside the hotel.

But as his old man would say on quiet evenings while sitting on a back deck ... *Fuck it.*

Flames crackled madly in his wake as he left the pool behind. After that mass extermination, the tide of rats lessened. Across the courtyard he strode, in an unwavering line, glancing at the clouds of trapped smoke filling the place. A wall appeared before him, so he turned, choking back a cough, and gazed upon the destruction he'd wrought. The doorway at the far end was nothing more than a hazy rectangle of flames. The fire in the pool still burned, but the flames flickered as if somehow smothered.

Movement distracted him as more vermin appeared, scurrying along the floor headed right for him.

Incredible.

He wondered where they were coming from, and if their extraordinary numbers could actually douse the fires. Depriving the flames of oxygen through sheer mass attack alone? If so, then he wasn't dealing with ordinary rats. He was indeed dealing with infected vermin. *Mindless* vermin.

Another bout of coughing seized him, but the Dragon still managed to find an exit and pull the door open. More of the little devils, swarming the corridor beyond. The hotel was livid with them.

The nearest ones overran his feet, biting, clawing at his ankles.

The Dragon stomped before opening up with the flamethrower, burning a swath across the floor and up the opposite wall, immolating a pair of artificial trees. He stepped into the hall and razed a forty-foot cone of fire in the direction of the lobby, letting the door at his back close before the courtyard rats could overtake him.

The smell of burning hair and meat polluted the air. Smoke teared up his eyes. His frame hitched and trembled from the fumes. Through the resulting haze, the Dragon ceased firing and again crushed the bodies mobbing his boots. After a few seconds of heavy footwork, he stooped and picked up one half-crushed attacker by its bare, eight-inch tail.

Cocking his flamethrower at the hip, he took a moment to examine the dead thing. Protrusions of internal matter gleamed in the firelight, spilling forth from the creature's orifices upon being crushed. The Dragon ignored that. The face of the rat mesmerized him. A tumor of gut hung from the thing's mouth, trembling as the thing twisted in his grip. Sooty bone peeked through missing patches of hair and skin. The rat's jawbone was missing, as was its right ear, and both eyes. All the while he examined the creature, its emaciated four-fingered claws dog-paddled with a twitchy gait—unaffected by its condition or the thickening smoke. The motion twirled the creature around, where its empty eye cavities shone against the firelight. Black, scorched things as offensive as cigarette burns.

A rare mix of fascination and horror filled the Dragon, until a fit of hacking caused him to drop the dead thing. It landed at his feet, on top of dozens of undead crawling about down there.

The Dragon mashed them all into the tiles. A soft thumping and scratching turned his attention back to the courtyard, where a growing pile of claws and teeth worked upon the door.

The smoke triggered more coughing. He adjusted his mask and sized up the battleground through watering eyes. He could barely see *shit*.

With mounting frustration, the Dragon hefted the nozzle and whirled, firing all the way around. Flames engulfed the corridor. Furniture and rats burned. Smoke gathered. He released the trigger, snarling at the latest swaths, and was just about to say some glorious one-liner when he froze.

At the farthest points of the corridor, through the dreary haze, the flames were wilting, flickering out. A new sound perked his ears, matching that of the crackling fires, threatening to surpass it. A rampant clicking, a harsh hail upon tiles. Growing closer and easily heard over the creaking of the dying hotel.

Then he saw them, materializing out of the smoke. The sight eroded his once formidable resolve and he realized what he was hearing were thousands of claws upon the floor.

The Dragon elected to escape. To the right of one burning wall was an open, fairy-tale staircase, curling to the upper floors. Shuddering from another fit of coughs, he trudged through the smoldering dead at his feet, firing blistering streams at the approaching hordes. He flashed the flamethrower one way then the other. Holding his mask tight to his face, he climbed the stairs, pausing halfway to glance back.

Within that haze of death, under flames that devoured wall paintings and other decorations, the rats pushed through, a gloomy black rug under the thickening smoke. Rats crawled over rats, pressing their brethren down, pressing them into the floor and flames and smothering everything. Layers upon layers rushed into sight, drawn to that lone tower of living meat. They didn't squeak. Didn't squeal, but merely scurried forward with whispery determination. Burning debris fell upon some, lighting up puddles eventually extinguished by sheer rabid numbers.

Shoulders hitching, the Dragon sprayed a parting shot across their ranks as they met the challenge of the lower stairs. He counted off the seconds, searing entire waves, incinerating them down to unmoving husks of charcoal matter. The smoke got him barking again, forcing him to release the trigger. The flamethrower's killer breath ceased. He grabbed the nearby railing and hauled himself up, to the next floor, where the air seemed just a touch less oppressive. The steps and walls continued to burn beneath him, foreboding badly for the structural integrity of the hotel.

There wasn't much time before the whole place came down.

He had to find the Chemist before then. She was above him. Somewhere. His minions were afoot as well. They might have already found her.

That thought alone powered him up the steps and through the smoke.

Until the tinkle of shattering ceramic stopped him.

Fire exploded at the halfway point, erupting in a long sheet that even clung to the nearby walls. The Dragon stopped and glared at the unexpected blaze.

Then he looked up to the murky third-floor heights.

"CHEMIST!"

38

Back in the room, with their arms around each other, Gus and Maya staggered away from the window overlooking the courtyard. The Dragon was down there, blazing away. They couldn't see him, but they saw the incinerating pulses of his flamethrower.

Ramfist was back in Gus's possession. They hobbled over to the doorway and checked the corridor. Smoke laced the air, harsh and acrid and stinging their eyes, adding more misery to the teargas Maya had concocted in a bucket. She went into the bathroom and came back out with towels, one of which she tied around Gus's head, covering his face below the eyes. Then she did her own.

"We need to move," Gus said.

"The snowmobile?"

"If we can get to it."

"Wait here," she said and left him against the wall. She ran over to the Leather she'd shot and quickly patted him down, extracting items while the smoke billowed through the open portal. She stopped once, bent over as if in worship, her frame rocking from deep, lung-clearing barks. When her coughing subsided—but didn't really stop—she rummaged through her bag and pulled forth a pair of firebombs.

Which she immediately lit and tossed down the stairs.

She stumbled back to him, her outline backlit by a fiery glare.

"Oh shit," she labored. "This stuff is hard on the eyes."

"Yeah," he said, wiping at his own. "What'd you bring me?"

"Shells," she said, stifling a choke. She pushed a magazine into his hand. "And this."

She jingled a key fob, getting Gus's attention.

"They drove here," she said.

Finishing off a cough, Gus looped an arm around her. "I'm startin' to like you."

They hobbled along at best speed, Gus's nerve-damaged left foot singing, while the split right stamped the floor with wet blots. Each limping step stabbed his chopped foot. Worse, it was hard to breathe, even with the towel, and the coughing came more often. His eyes and nasal cavity burned and suffered from that nasty combination of smoke and mustard gas.

Maya pulled him along, taking the terrible mix much better than him.

The fanciful stairs materialized in the gloom, and she guided him toward them.

"Wait," he hissed, his right foot torturing him. "What about that Dragon dickhead?"

That gave her pause before she again propped him against the nearby wall. She pulled forth the bag with the firebombs, pulled out a pair, and clutched them in one hand while she searched for her lighter.

"We'll have to find another way down," Gus said, fishing out his stainless-steel lighter and snapping its lid back. A ready flame sprang forth.

Nodding, suppressing a cough, Maya lit the wicks. She chucked both down the stairs, smashing them off a wall. It burned wildly, throwing a ravenous orange hue over the depths of the elegant walkway.

"CHEMIST!"

That livid accusation jerked up both their heads, and they stared at each other for seconds. Without thinking, Maya leaned over the railing and looked down.

There he was, easily visible through the smoke, leaning against the wall. An evil keeper of flame himself. Mask upraised and flamethrower in one arm.

And for seconds, neither said anything more, until Maya found her voice.

"Fuck off, Dragon!"

That hit the masked man, perhaps harder than a mallet to the balls. He froze, visibly shocked by the outburst, and then whipped up the flamethrower.

Maya threw herself back from the livid geyser spraying up the stairwell. The jet of flame clung to and torched several paintings on the wall. Even the carpet went up. The brass railing glowed under the onslaught for a good three seconds before ending. The Dragon bellowed something that was probably supposed to sound like rage, but ended in a harsh, chain-smoker fit of hacking.

Which was right about when Gus turned the corner, balanced on one leg, and fired the Ramfist.

Missed, but the shot blasted out a section of wall, driving the Dragon for cover.

"You'll burn, Chemist!" the Leather shouted from below. *"You'll burn! I'll light you up myself. I'll light you up!"*

The words lessened in volume, signaling the Dragon was on the move.

"You got any more of those?" Gus asked through clenched teeth.

She checked. "Yeah, a bunch."

"Smoke's gettin' worse. This place is gonna burn to the ground."

She nodded.

"We'll choke to death before that, though," Gus said, swiping at his watering eyes. "We gotta get to the roof. Before that nutsack does."

With that, he swung his left arm across her shoulders, and again they limped away, suffering from their many hurts and stifling coughs all the way. They reached the next emergency stairwell and pushed open the door. Steps spiraled up and down.

No sign of the Dragon.

Which would surely change.

Gus unhooked himself from Maya and leaned against the wall. The Ramfist came up, aimed at the lower stairs, and he waited for a target to appear.

"Light it up," he said.

So she did. Three firebombs that time, all down the throat of the stairwell. The last one she threw with a parting, "Fuck you."

Fire exploded and raged through the lower levels.

Draping Gus's arm back across her shoulders, they climbed the stairs, one painful step at a time. A killer cottony fog enveloped them as they went, round and round, each bleeding, agonizing step. The effects of the teargas clung to them, punishing them. Their breathing grew more labored, bordering on choking.

Until they nearly slammed into a door, one with a sign that read:

RESTRICTED ACCESS. HOTEL PERSONNEL ONLY.

They stumbled into the safety bar, and the door swung open.

Glorious nighttime air smacked their faces. They collapsed upon the snowy mattress cushioning the concrete roof. There they lay, ripping away their towels, coughing, retching, tongues protruding and eyes squeezed shut, purging themselves of the foul gunk while smoke belched from the open doorway.

"Oh sweet Jesus," Gus choked out weakly. He rolled onto his back, the snow creaking. "Oh that tastes good."

"Sweeter . . . than chocolate," Maya gasped nearby and barked a few last parting shots. That got Gus going, great whooping yelps powerful enough to summon tears. Seconds later he got himself under control and managed to look around. Falling snow smacked his face. He palm-wiped his stinging eyes and only succeeded in partially clearing them. The gas was still torturing his vision, rending everything beyond ten feet or so a surreal backdrop of featureless blocks. The door they'd used had closed, but they were on the roof, surrounded by the city and all its sinister lines and edges.

Maya was still unloading, bent over and spitting into the snow. Gus pushed himself to his elbows, getting his knees under him. He placed a hand on her back as if that might steady her. Her coughing intensified for seconds before tapering off and she lifted a wet face to his.

"You okay?" she asked weakly, her voice wrecked.

He could have laughed. "No. Not at all."

Maya smiled back and glanced around, spotting something important enough to prompt her to stand. She hurried away, leaving the impression of a snow angel that might've been gunned down from behind. Gus heard her stumbling through the drifts gathered on the roof. He stood, hands raw and near freezing, realizing his bootless foot only had a cloth and a sock on it. Amazed at his stupidity, he limped not two steps before dropping to a knee. It occurred to him that the snow might temper the pain a bit, so he rubbed some into his eyes. *Nope.* Didn't do a goddamn thing. He faced the closed doorway and leaned on the Ramfist, keeping the dangerous end away from his face. All he needed was to slip and blow his own head off.

Behind him, Maya strained to lift a snow-covered block.

"What are you doin' back there?" he asked.

"Fire escape," she said. "Won't lower. It's *frozen.*"

Frozen in place or too stubborn to move from years of neglect and disuse, the thing would not budge. That caused her to scream in frustration, and she slammed a hand on the thing. Not smart. She recoiled, livid with pain, and shook out her hurting fist.

Wary of the door and the tendrils of smoke fizzing from it, Gus rose and hobbled after her, using the shotgun as a deadly cane. "Must be another," he said, reaching a low parapet wall encircling the roof. He blinked several times, glanced around, and thought he was seeing a little better.

"How are your eyes?" he asked.

"Better."

"The gas is wearing off."

"Seems like it," she said, rubbing at her face. "Sucking in my own gas. Can't believe it." She glanced around before leaning over and peering into the alley below. What she saw straightened her.

Gus leaned in. "Holy shit."

The alley below resembled a drained medieval moat, where the filth-encrusted brick and pipework dissolved into an indistinct mass of black things. There, rats swarmed, covering the alley floor. They rustled and wavered, rising and falling as if stoked by a tempest. Vermin surged from one end of the hotel to the other. A frothing, churning tar eager to devour a person down to their bones. The rats poured into the alley from both ends, channeled by the foundations of the Jonathan Inn and the nearby building across the way. There was no break in their numbers, no discernable depth, and from Gus and Maya's vantage point, it appeared the rats' numbers were even thicker out front.

"We couldn't make it to the snowmachine anyway," a defeated Gus muttered, watching the horror below. "Even if we could lower the ladder, the rats would eat us alive."

Maya didn't comment, mesmerized by the sight.

Gus staggered around, studying the roof. A series of snowcapped blocks, peaks, and roofs, structures identical to the one they exited only minutes ago. Rows of dead, industrial-sized vents and air conditioners studded the Jonathan Inn's roof as well. At the center rose the ribbed dome of the inner courtyard's artificial sky. The dome towered over the smaller shapes and hid the other side of the hotel.

"Look around," he said. "Maybe . . . maybe there's a ladder or something around here. Something we can use."

Maya trudged off, her boots punching through the snow's soft crust. Gus leaned into the wall, trying to judge the distance to the ground. Three stories. Maybe four. Maybe not high enough to kill but certainly enough to break bones. There were other fire escapes along the wall, three of them—metal stairways positioned at even intervals and scaling the exterior all the way to street level . . . right where the rats gathered and waited.

"Gus!"

He whipped around.

There, emerging from behind the small shack housing the emergency door they'd come through, was Maya.

And she pulled an aluminium ladder behind her.

39

When the Chemist doused the stairwell in flame, cutting him off, well, that seriously pissed off the Dragon.

Has that bitch lost her mind? Or, and this part bothered him even more, maybe she'd had a change of heart? Maybe she was no longer a trusted part of the apparatus known as the Leather. Maybe she, like the Dragon, had longed for the death of the Dog Tongue, and now that that had come to pass, perhaps she had plans of her own. Maybe part of that plan was leaving the Leather—what remained of the Leather—behind. *Including* the Dragon. Maybe the Dog Tongue was right after all.

And maybe, just maybe, she didn't want to be with him.

That thought mortified the Dragon . . . and for a moment a heavy wave of grief and a burden of loneliness pressed down on him. Pain cut around his heart, not physical, but the worst kind of emotional.

Rejection.

Then the betrayal kicked in, burning as only betrayal could burn.

Rats scurried along the second-floor landing and he stomped over them, entering the corridor where thinner groups of the little creatures crawled along the carpet. The Dragon crushed a few, got his bearings, and raced north, knowing there had to be another way upstairs.

In short order, he found one of the many emergency stairwells and pulled the door open.

Smoke enveloped him, gauzy and blinding and clawing at his throat.

Coughing, sputtering, he backed away, letting the door close. When he glanced over his shoulder, what he saw rooted him to the spot. The rats had found him, filling the smoky hallway with their numbers. They rumbled along the carpet, pursuing him with single-minded determination.

The Dragon hefted the flamethrower and hesitated about squeezing the trigger. The hotel was burning. Any more fire would only accelerate its inevitable destruction.

Once again, he remembered the words of his departed dad.

The rats were within ten feet when he sprayed a blazing line across the width of the corridor, some five feet thick.

Utterly fearless, the rats charged across that volcanic hot patch. The first rank charred and stopped. As did the second and third ranks. The fourth got a little closer, however, as did the stink of cooking hair, meat, and synthetic polyester fibers. They pressed on, rumbling across that blistering finish line, each wave gaining a little more ground before they burned to a crisp,

There were so many. So very, very many.

The fire happily feasted on their combustible carcasses as they continued to steam ahead, feeding the blaze. Flames along the sides rose higher, finding new sustenance in the nearby walls and gnawing greedily away at them. A painting practically imploded, its surface going up as if he'd flashed a stream directly across it.

The Dragon backed away. Time was wasting. He turned and ran, hearing the sizzle and pop of burning bodies.

The corridor gracefully turned in a wide curve, until he slowed to a dismayed stop.

Rats.

Crawling over the carpet up ahead, from baseboard to baseboard. A high, thin table with a vase upon it shook and tumbled over when the mindless vermin swept past it.

The Dragon could not believe what he was seeing.

Then he saw the emergency exit. A short sprint before the approaching swarm.

The Dragon scorched a swath across the mindless rodents, from one end to the other, and then he pounded across the floor, reaching the door and slamming into it. He pushed through and, after so many stairs, was surprised to see a short hallway ending in a door. Leaving the rats behind, he hurried to the end of the hall where a sign warned the door was for emergencies. He ignored it, throwing his hip into the push-down bar.

A gush of chilling winter air blew over him, and he stood there, facing a wall of metal mesh. Above him was the night sky, and the fire escape landing granting access to the roof. Below him, rats swarmed the streets, surrounding the base of the hotel, lapping against a foundation partly submerged under their numbers. Huge, misshapen things, as if the surface air had somehow mutated them. They churned and crawled over each other below, as if smelling him far above.

The Dragon believed they probably could.

A scrabbling upon metal reached his ears. The rats he'd left behind were trying to bypass the fire escape door. The Dragon looked to the streets again. Going down the metal staircase fixed to the hotel wall was not an option.

That only left the roof.

No sooner did he consider it when he heard the not-so-distant shout of *"Gus!"*

Grabbing the railing, the Dragon started to climb.

40

Gus's freezing, bleeding right foot became the screeching violin to the fucked-up accordion of his left, and together, they crippled him. Still, when Maya lugged that aluminum ladder—a forty-foot extendable one—away from the shadows, that familiar flare of hope energized him. Enough for him to take the pain and stumble over to help her carry the thing to the wall.

Where they stopped and sized up the gap from one building to the other.

"Butt it against here," Gus said, indicating the parapet. "We'll walk it up and let it fall across."

Maya regarded him. "But it'll bounce and fall."

"It might, but this is a forty-footer. That's a twenty-foot alley. We do it right, all we got to worry about is the kickback."

That convinced her.

Gus extended the ladder ten feet or so, for that extra length, and jammed his legs against the base of the parapet wall. They got under the ladder, pushed the thing over their heads, and gripped each rung hand-over-hand while lumbering forward. They raised the ladder with each step, until the thing was standing straight like an upraised drawbridge.

"Let go and get back," Gus said.

Maya did so, and he pushed the ladder.

It fell, with all the grace of an elderly cedar, and landed with a bounce and a rattle that sent snow falling into the alley. Gus held on, hands stinging upon the final crash down, but managing to keep it from falling into the alley.

"Get across," he said.

"What?"

"Shimmy across like your ass is on fire. Don't look down. Get across and hold it for me. Take the shotgun. Use it like this."

He held it by the barrel and stock, meaning to slide the thing along the ladder.

She stared at him and, for a second, he thought she might argue the point.

Instead, she took the shotgun and clambered onto the ladder.

She started shuffling across, using the Ramfist like a cranky slide that she pushed before her, driving each knee into a metal rung. She looked small on the ladder's length, and vulnerable, considering it was all between her and an awful death.

Five feet across. Ten. Gus held on to the aluminum ends, feeling every vibration, knowing the ladder was good for at least three hundred pounds. That was when the thing was up against a house, however, he reminded himself, and not spanning an alley.

A freezing wind gusted into his face, and he glanced back at the way they'd come. Nothing. No sign of anyone.

She was halfway across. Every movement a clinky slide of metal on metal. Another gust of wind and Maya froze, which caused Gus to seize up in fear.

But then she got moving again.

And swung herself over on the other side, where she disappeared for seconds before popping back into sight.

"Okay!" she called out. "Come on!"

Gus grabbed the ladder and pulled himself onto the thing. It was like a dear old friend. A dear old *cantankerous* friend with an evil streak, which shook and trembled with every movement as if disagreeing with being mounted so and remembered a time when Gus—or someone like Gus—might have treated it badly.

"It wasn't me," he whispered, and made the mistake of looking down.

His balls drew up in terror. It wasn't the height. Heights didn't bother him at all. It was the rats. Enough to strip a person down to the bare wet bone in minutes. Or he figured minutes, since he only saw the end result of their voracious appetite and thankfully not a live victim. They swarmed in murky, oily ripples over the alley floor, where glints of light flickered across the surface. He realized those were multitudes of tails. Goddamn rat tails. That summoned mental pictures of their undead faces, upturned, smelling his slimmed down ass somewhere overhead. Hoping—*praying*—for that one fatal slip. The one where he would fall screaming through space and time, all the way down. Only three floors up so if he *did* fall, he would be lucky to break his neck. Luckier still to die instantly. Based on his past record with accidents, he did not think he would be that fortunate.

"Don't look down," Maya yelled at him.

Don't look down. It was impossible *not* to look down. He was crawling along on a goddamn aluminum ladder that seemed to have all the strength of a tissue in a shitstorm. In all his years, *never* had a ladder felt so flimsy beneath him. But he did as ordered and looked up, seeing a ghostly sheet of smoke blowing across Maya's encouraging shape.

He slid his hands along the sides of the ladder, but his knees suffered the most. The hard edges dug into him as he moved while the entire length trembled with every foot traveled.

Something swung underneath the ladder. A long pendulum that shivered in the dark, distracting him. A rope. One used to bind the ladder to whatever. Right now, it looked like a hangman's unraveled noose. Gus saw Maya holding onto the ladder, holding on tight, glancing down every so often for him, and urging him onward.

He reached out and his knee slipped, and he plunged through the empty space. One foot came up and got shoved against his butt cheek while his pelvis slammed against the rung. Worse, the abrupt halt sent a shockwave through the ladder's length, one where Gus instinctively held on for dear, dear life, riding that terrifying quiver and praying it would stay in place.

A gale force blast of wind slammed into him from the north, fluttering everything again and causing him to clench ever harder. His foot—the bleeding one—felt freezing cold. Snow peppered his face. It took effort, but he extracted his leg, grating it against the rung, and got his knee firmly underneath him.

No sweat. Didn't even shit himself.

Maya held onto the ladder, but she looked like someone who'd just dropped their newborn baby.

Baring teeth, his face numb, Gus pulled himself along, taking that extra second to ensure his knees were in place before moving forward.

Ten feet along. Only ten fucking feet. At this rate the rats would be on the roof. Or the building would be totally on fire. Or the Dragon would find his way up and squeal in delight at the little piggy on the spit before him, all set for the luau. Another powerful gust of wind, just as strong as before, rattling that length of metal stretched out between the buildings, stopping Gus until it lessened. *Don't look down*, he repeated and concentrated on grabbing the next rung. Then the next, feeling as if he was crawling along a vibrating railway track, and the train was gaining ground.

"That's it," Maya coached him, closer now. Most certainly past the halfway point. Which meant he was directly over that death pit below.

"*Stop looking down!*" she yelled at him. "Why are you *doing* that to yourself?"

Gus looked up, didn't bother answering because he didn't know why. The ladder continued to flex and shake underneath. *Oh Lord*, he thought, his treacherous brain finally on board and urging him on, but not too fast.

Even Maya was into it, nodding encouragement, and even smiling at times.

Five feet left. No more.

He permitted himself a feeble smile.

"You got it," she said. "You'll be over here in less than a minute. That's—"

Something crashed behind Gus, the slap and bang of someone kicking open a door.

He didn't have to look, because Maya saw everything for him, and she ducked out of sight.

Which was right about when he heard someone shout, "*Stop right there!*"

And the angry crack and note of what might have been an electric guitar string lick seared the air over his head.

Gus seized up on the ladder, getting as low as he could. Only once before had he felt so helpless, and that was when he was strung up from a tow-truck boom, facing down a single zombie, seconds before a withered Wallace instructed him to start screaming. Such a memory filled his head as his eyes, wide and darting, flicked left and right, up and down, then straight across.

Where Maya popped back up, holding the Ramfist.

She fired. Two blasts that pounded past Gus like battleship shells. There was a brief silence, but then the first shooter returned fire, driving Maya for cover, sending up plumes of snow where the bullets hit and ricocheted into the night.

Squawking a note of terror, Gus moved ahead one rung.

An explosive line ripped across the top of the wall where Maya once was. One round panged the aluminum ladder in a flareup of sparks, and a terrifying shudder and shake.

Gus held on, despite wanting to bury his head.

Maya sprung into view again and fired, one echoing boom, but it seemed to stop the shooter.

Then Gus heard it. *Felt* it.

The distinctive quiver of a once firm foundation about to give.

Oh shit, he thought.

Shooter behind him, no doubt about to spray him dead with the next burst. Rats below, jumping, snapping, cheering the shooter on. Maya on the other side, behind a wall, trying to cover him.

And what looked like the shredded left end of the ladder, where it rested on a weakened section of brick.

The ladder lurched again, the only warning it was going to give him. All the warning he needed, really.

Panting, whimpering like a child fearing the monster in the darkened closet, Gus did the only thing he could.

He bunched his legs up and *launched* himself at the parapet, pushing off on his nerve-damaged foot, causing the whole ladder to vibrate like a trampoline going lopsided.

For an instant, he was airborne.

Then the shooting *really* started.

41

One round drew a sizzling line that exploded blood up the length of his left arm.

Another skimmed along his back, off his body armor.

And that was it. The other bullets split the air around him, shrieking obscenities all the way, but missed.

Gus crashed-landed on top of the parapet, on his belly, with his ass and legs left dangling in the wind. Maya grabbed his arm and the lower end of his vest and hauled him over. More bullets zinged by, and one hit and pitched Maya back three steps, ripping a pained grunt from her at the moment of impact. Her arms pinwheeled until she landed flat on her back in a deep drift.

Where she didn't move.

Leaving Gus to look up from where he'd fallen, realizing with dawning horror what had just happened. If he was terrified before, he was fucking *petrified* now, and he crawled over to her on four limbs energized by adrenaline-spiked fright, heedless to his wounds and the grief they were giving. He landed next to her and didn't know where to put his hands, so he lifted her head. Saw the dewy hole in her shoulder, and the deep, deep soak of blood in the snow.

"*Maya,*" he whispered in panicked fright. "*Maya!*"

Her head rolled, eyes closed, her mouth ajar.

And Gus lost it.

42

Hurried by the gunfight just out of sight, the Dragon rounded the corner of one shack-sized structure and stopped in his tracks.

There stood Bonemaker, not twenty feet away from him, standing in an open doorway and firing the automatic rifle. Light lasered across the open space between one building to the next, where someone launched themselves off a ladder and landed halfway over a wall. Legs kicking.

A figure sprang up and pulled the struggling person over.

The Dragon lifted his flamethrower, looking to support Bonemaker, but held off. At that distance, he would lose accuracy but gain a wider spread, which wasn't something he was ready to do until the Chemist was in the clear. Sure, he might've threatened to light her up himself, but the reality was, that was just talk. Meaning to frighten her. The truth was, he would do no such thing.

The standing figure pulled the other over the wall when Bonemaker unleashed another burst. The shots connected, and the standing person lurched backwards, grunting, sounding like . . .

The Dragon tensed, staring at the spot where the gunned victim had just fallen.

Bonemaker came into sight as well, stepping away from an open doorway, rifle firm against his shoulder and looking to finish the job if the opportunity presented itself.

When a stricken cry of anger and grief tore across the rooftops.

"*You fuckin . . . piece . . . of shit!*" A pause to draw breath. "*You* shot *her!*"

Bonemaker stood poised and ready, waiting for the speaker to show himself, to at least lift his head into sight.

Those stricken words, however, paralyzed the Dragon, nearly robbing him of all strength.

You shot her.

You shot her.

Who *she* was, there was no doubt. Not in the Dragon's mind.

But Bonemaker had.

It took seconds, long fuse-flickering seconds where the rage caught up with that realization and judgment was passed.

Bonemaker cocked his head toward his leader and lowered the rifle just a little when the Dragon lit him up with one pull of the flamethrower trigger. Bonemaker didn't even have time to scream. The blast, from a distance, enveloped the minion in a fireball equal to the sun. The Dragon didn't stop blasting his henchman, not even when the Bonemaker's fiery silhouette collapsed onto the roof, stamping his outline into the melting snowdrifts. Another blast, just to dispel the surrounding snow, to get down to the charred carcass underneath. The Dragon then took two steps closer and unleashed a firestorm upon the corpse.

Two seconds. Five. The flame lighting up the roofs of both buildings.

Then the mixture in the tanks—devised by the Chemist herself—ran dry, and the prolonged afterburner of flame sputtered, choked, and died.

The Dragon drew back, realized what had happened, and threw the flamethrower down, the nozzle still connected to the tanks on his back. He walked over to the blazing remains of Bonemaker, and then turned to the building across the way.

There stood a man.

With what looked like a shotgun.

Who fired.

Missed, but the force of that very close shot drove the Dragon to his knees.

"You goddamn sonsabitches!" the man bellowed from across the way. "You fuckin' *fucks*."

Then a roar of frustration, because he'd fired his last remaining shot.

The Dragon heard the telltale clicks of an empty chamber. All the while, his hand drifted to the *other* sidearm he'd only recently taken from the Norse.

43

On the verge of screaming himself mute, Gus shook the Ramfist before whipping it away, where it clattered against brickwork. He hoofed it to the ladder and shoved the end off the ledge. It fell off the buildings, scraping the walls most of the way down before crashing into the alley floor.

With one last, furious, vengeful look at the Jonathan Inn, Gus limped back to Maya's side, at a complete loss for what to do. He saw the bloody wreckage of her shoulder, that she was unconscious, and he feared the worst. He tore his winter cap from his head, plugged the hole in her shoulder, and held it there.

"Oh," he said, his whole throat contracting to the width of a straw. "Oh. Don't you dare. Don't you dare. You . . . you're free now. You hear me? They can't get over. All we gotta do, we . . . we just gotta get down from here. Get down from here and find some rides. That's all we gotta do. Just . . . oh God, Maya. Don't do this to me. If you didn't know before, I'm not in a very good place mentally. If you go there, if you *go*, I mean, I'll—"

Then the surprise of her opening her eyes. She looked positively wasted, as if drunk beyond all recognition, but she reached for and weakly clutched Gus's forearms.

"What . . ." she said, barely getting the word out.

That robbed him of the ability to speak.

"What happened?" she finished.

He lowered his head until he made contact with hers, where her acne was as red as springtime posies, and couldn't bring himself to answer. Couldn't make a sound, anyway, without his voice utterly failing him.

"Is she alive?" yelled a voice from the other side.

The Dragon.

Gus squeezed his eyes shut, barely feeling what ran down his face.

The Dragon's voice boomed again. "Is she—"

"*YES, FUCK YOU, YES, SHE'S ALIVE!*" Gus screamed back, the blast shaking him.

Maya blinked, as if very, very sleepy.

"I can't get across," the Dragon yelled back, softer than before, and with a note of defeat.

Miserable with grief, Gus lifted his head.

There stood the Dragon, the last of the Leather, at the parapet of the Jonathan Inn. His arms hung by his sides, while dying firelight backlit his bulky mass.

"It's a good goddamn thing you can't," Gus swore. "Because I'd fuck you up every day from here to Christmas."

The Dragon didn't respond to that.

"Is it bad?" the Leather finally asked. "The bullet wound?"

Gus rolled his head at the stupidity of the question. *"Yes,"* he grated. "She's bleeding. Bleeding out."

That caused Maya's eyes to flutter open, and she tucked her chin in to examine herself. What she saw clearly didn't impress her, and she closed her eyes again. Gus wasn't sure if it was on purpose or from succumbing to shock.

"You . . . you need to save her," the Dragon said.

That stopped Gus cold.

"Put pressure on the wound," the Leather continued. "If you can. Plug it. Get her off the roof. Here . . ."

Seconds later, something landed in the snow, not two feet away from Gus.

"In case you need it. I don't."

Gus sniffed, smelling smoke. He studied the Dragon, still standing on the roof across the way.

"Get it," the Dragon said. "It's my scarf. Use that as a bandage for now."

Gus lowered Maya's head and lurched over to where the scarf had landed. A quick pawing through the snow and he realized it was indeed a scarf. Wrapped around what looked like his missing Glock.

"There's . . . there's a first-aid kit in the semi," the Leather said. "If you can get to it. That's if you can get off the building. There might be something there, I don't know. I can't help her. Can't save her. Not over here. But maybe, maybe you can."

Gus couldn't believe what he was hearing. A veil of smoke drifted over then, followed by a flurry of snow. But then more smoke. The Jonathan was burning, from the bottom up. From the inside out. Continued to burn from the firebombs and from the razings of the Leather himself.

"You have the gun," the Dragon continued. "My tanks are empty. Get moving. Before you do, just one thing. Did she really want to leave the Leather?"

The absurdity of the question was agonizingly solemn, and even in the precious seconds that followed, Gus found himself nodding. "Yeah, she did. She was waiting for her chance."

The Dragon fell silent, then, "Get pressure on that wound."

That unlocked Gus. He hurried back to Maya's side, opened up her coat as much as he dared. He inspected her winter cap, and tore it from her head. Without pause, he swapped out his saturated cap for hers, and plugged the soft cotton material into the wound. Then he looped the scarf underneath her armpit and shoulder and tied it off as tight as he dared.

"You do it?" he Dragon asked.

The smoke was thicker now, but the fire consuming the corpse on the Jonathan's roof had all but burned out. The Dragon was still there, tall and menacing, and not budging.

"Yeah," Gus replied.

"Then get off the roof. Do what I said. It's all on you now."

Gus stared at the killer.

"Tell her . . ." the Dragon started, "I had thoughts of leaving. Once. Long ago. Then I gave up." He faltered then, sifting through memories. "Get moving. While you still can."

Oh I will, Gus projected. *Don't you worry.* He staggered to his feet, taking terrible pain. He lifted Maya, nearly fell from her weight, and limped toward a dark portal that would lead downstairs. Every step was agony.

The Dragon watched them.

Gus drew closer, seeing the door already wide open, cemented in place by a large snowdrift. He stopped to angle Maya through and caught sight of the Dragon, a dark shape in the thickening smoke.

That narrowed Gus's eyes, the last second he would spare on him. With Maya in his arms, he wobbled through the doorway at his best speed, leaning heavily against the wall.

The Dragon watched him every step of the way.

When they were gone, the last of the Leather took in a great, mind-clearing breath through his nose. Smoke scratched his throat, and he squinted back the burn around his eyes. He glanced over at the smoldering remains of Bonemaker, then at the open door behind him. Not surprising, rats were spilling over the threshold, falling into the trampled drifts. There they puddled, before forging through the powder in an ever-expanding wave.

The Dragon set his attention on the now empty doorway of the next building over. *She was waiting for her chance*, the man had said. The Dragon couldn't believe it, couldn't believe that she had so expertly hid her intentions from them all, including him, for so long. She was truly one of a kind, and it only strengthened his attraction for her.

Gone now, he mused finally. *Gone* . . .

He missed her already, but didn't question her wisdom in such matters. As much as he wanted to rule in the Dog Tongue's stead, without her, he discovered he didn't give a damn about it anymore. Not if she wasn't by his side. Weird. Not that he would dwell on it. The rats behind him would see to that. Already he could hear them.

Vermin. A crawling pestilence, slinking forth from the darkest night. All beneath him.

For he was a Dragon.

Exhaling through his nose, he fumbled at his coat ends until he pulled forth his custom-made claws, one for each hand. As the snow fell and the smoke thickened, he pulled on the weapons, turning them over one way then the other with a sad fondness. His shoulders shuddered as he fought back a cough, then he checked on the ledge before him.

The notion of crossing that chasm was nowhere in his mind.

One last glance behind him. Even more rats now falling from the doorway. A knobby landslide of decomposing bodies, crawling for his ankles.

The smoke didn't affect them at all.

"I'm a Dragon," he whispered to the death at his back, and he hoisted himself, tanks and all, onto the ledge. Ice-coated and crunchy with the snow, he fumbled for balance and slowly straightened. Claws scraped the inner surface of the parapet, reaching for him. He didn't look at the masses flooding the alley. Instead, he faced the open doorway the Chemist had been carried through. He extended his arms, claws dull and gleaming in the night, and took one last breath.

"I'm a *Dragon*," he repeated, his voice brimming with power—and a touch of pride.

He brought his claws in, tucking their tips directly under his mask, under his chin, so that there would be no mistake.

"And Dragons can *fly*, bitches."

Without so much as a tremble, the last of the Leather leaned forward like a stony monument about to topple . . . and topple he did, falling without a sound, headfirst into the alley.

To disappear from sight.

44

Down Gus went, plodding through a vat of darkness, with only the walls to guide him. His tortured feet screamed at him the whole way. The flashlight was gone, dropped somewhere and lost forever. Maya's boots scuffed along a smooth plastered surface, while her head hung from the crook of his arm. Warm blood covered his fingers, but he didn't think about that.

He couldn't save Tammy.

Couldn't save Collie.

But God as his witness, he sure as fuck was going to save Maya.

Or die trying.

"Oh Lord," Gus huffed, pausing to adjust his grip and her weight in his arms. "Oh..."

It was cold inside the building. Uncomfortably so. Winter had invaded this refuge and claimed it as its own. There was no wind, but with every descending step he felt he was going deeper into a nearly bottomless Arctic crevasse where there was no light. And perhaps even no escape. If he'd had light to see, he wouldn't have been surprised if frost coated the walls.

He went down one level, shoulder rubbing against the wall until he hit a landing. There, he felt around for a door handle and located one. Panting, groaning, he pulled it open. A gush of icy, stale air hit him, but it was free of the stink of rats and things long decayed.

The fuck are we? he mentally intoned, looking around. A feeble light crept in through a series of windows ahead, dimly revealing a maze of office cubicles. His boots scuffed over spilled paper, and Maya's boots tapped the edge of a nearby partition. Wanting no part of stumbling through all that, he moved along the wall, toward the light. Office of some sort, obviously, but he could not care less. All he cared about was Maya, and the limp deadweight she was becoming. If he didn't get her somewhere safe soon, she would undoubtedly die, and his arms would permanently be two inches longer.

The rows of cubicles ended and a huge table came into view, the top littered with items. Gus muscled Maya's unconscious form over to the table and used her to clear a section with one clumsy swipe.

Just before his strength left him and he dropped her on the surface.

With no time to spare, he swiped the table clear around her head, discovering a heavy pair of scissors as well as discarded pens and paper. He put all that aside and pulled her legs up onto the surface.

"All right, all right, next . . ." Gus muttered, hands quivering in that dark place.

"Stop the bleeding," Maya said weakly, stopping him cold.

"Stop the bleeding?" he repeated, diving for her head and placing an ear to her mouth. "You say stop the bleeding?"

"Caw . . ."

"What?"

"Caw . . . ter."

"Cauterize?" Gus asked, but she was gone again. Make no mistake, that's what she said. Burn the wound. Stop the bleeding. He could do that. They did it all the time in the movies. All the time. That led to him pawing at his coat pockets until he produced his lighter.

Needed something to burn, and lo and behold, he was in an office. He grabbed all the nearby combustible material he could find—paper and flyers—and heaped it into one corner of the table. He lit it, not two feet away from her head. A ghoulish hue fell across her features.

What next? His mind raced, and he turned around.

There, hooked over the back of a chair parked in one of the cubicles, was a sweater. Gus grabbed it and dumped it next to Maya.

Several magazines lay about as well, and he took every one, feeding the fire periodically, mindful of it burning low.

Back to Maya. He unzipped her coat and snipped through the Dragon's scarf and clothing with a pair of discarded scissors. He tore and tossed away the saturated wad of a winter hat, exposing an ugly hole where the bullet had entered. Muscle and gristle gleamed. Gus saw the bone was still there, shattered, within a bleeding mesh of meat.

"All right," he whispered, and hurried with the next step, rolling up one magazine. There was nothing to cover Maya's face, so he stood at her head, pressing one forearm over her brow to keep her still.

Then he lit the lighter. The tall flame offered no assurance about the next part.

With a shaking hand, he put the rolled-up magazine to the flame and created a torch—one that would quickly burn to the quick.

"Here we go," he said, and applied the makeshift torch to that grisly wound.

Maya bucked, but he leaned in and held her down. She squirmed, but he kept her in place and kept the flame away from her face. Finally, she succumbed, either to the pain or blood loss, and went still.

That scared him the most.

Breathing in the fumes of cooking musculature and ignoring the sizzle of skin and juices best left inside the human body, Gus burned her until the bleeding seemed to stop. Around the same time the little fire on the table died away. The torch he held burned low, closing in on his fingers, until he dropped the thing on the floor and immediately rolled up another. When that one was ready, he lit it from the dying torch.

Then he went back to work.

There wasn't much left, so it didn't take long, and Maya didn't regain consciousness. He didn't care, because when he had cauterized all he could, beholding the grisly work he'd done, he placed a wet finger under her nose and felt her breathe. That tiny, deep sleep breeze greatly relieved him.

"Thank you, baby Jesus," he whispered. "Thank you."

He rolled up another magazine, stuffed the top with loose leaf paper, and lit that. The world had light once again, and it showed a deathly pale Maya and her angry rash. She was out, sleeping or unconscious or whatever, but as far as he could tell, the gunshot wound was sealed, down to a watery, charcoal dribble. And she was still alive. The temperature in the office was near zero, if not below it, so he zipped up her coat and laid a hand on her forehead. A great and powerful weariness seized him then, as well as a desire for a much-deserved drink. He pushed himself to search the office space ... where every pained step produced a bark of *fuck*, or *goddammit*.

He found only the usual assortment of useless desk clutter. Hanging off one chair was a sports jacket, which he took. In a closet he grabbed a pair of light coats. One of the offices had curtains made of a thick cotton and smelled of dust. Gus yanked down the whole works, rooted out the rods, and gathered them into his arms. When he came out of the office, light from the left caught his attention. Windows faced what he assumed was the Jonathan Inn, and the hotel was on fire. On fire and well on its way to becoming a massive conflagration in the night. Smoke and flames raged through the hotel's windows, melting glass and charring curtains. Moisture clung to the brickwork, as if the building were gripped in the throes of a worsening fever. Gus watched it burn for a while, the firelight casting a glow within that part of the office. After a while he returned to Maya's side.

"You'll be all right," he said, more for himself, perhaps.

The jacket he rolled up into a pillow and placed under her head. The curtains he laid on top of her. He transferred his torch into a metal bucket and heaped in more stationery. It smoked but it also pushed back the cold a little. Grunting, he cleared the other part of the table and laid his hurting self down next to her, under the curtains. He didn't cuddle her for fear of waking her up. After a while, he turned on his side to face her and pressed himself against her as much as he dared.

"You'll be all right," he whispered, but feared the worst.

As the Jonathan burned in the background, Gus watched Maya's peaceful expression, and the rise and fall of her chest.

45

When he woke, it was dawn, and sunlight, not firelight, brightened the office interior. He drew back from Maya, examined her up close, and hovered a hand over her mouth and nose. Then he waited for what seemed like a very long time.

Until he felt it.

The barest expulsion of breath.

She was alive and breathing.

Relief flooded Gus then, and he settled down. Only for a moment, as he realized he had cuddled up to Maya during the night, spooning her side while draping a leg across her. Grimacing, he withdrew and rolled onto his back. She continued to sleep, so he got off the table with a limp and a bolt of agony, followed by a whispery *fuck*.

He glanced around. Alone. They were still alone. Nothing and no one had found them during the night.

Needing to see outside, he shuffled off toward the windows again, using partitions and chairs to help himself along. He stopped in the same spot as the night before, where he'd watched the hotel burn, where the sunlight was presently strongest.

The Dragon's fire—as well as Maya's firebombs—had gutted the Jonathan Inn. Deep oily stains marked the brick exterior. Smoky wisps sailed away from melted windows while the charred remains of once fancy curtains fluttered in the morning's soft breeze. Ice glinted at points of the brickwork, tips aimed at the ground below.

Gus hobbled closer to the office windows, placing his hands on a waist-high heater, and peered down into the alley.

Nothing. Not a thing. The snow had melted away from the concrete down there, but there was no sign of the millions-strong rat swarm that had hunted them throughout the night. He remembered Annapolis years ago and quickly dismissed the hope that the fire might have burned them all. Maybe it had taken a terrible toll on the horde's numbers, driving them below ground, but to have burned them all? Doubtful. And yet, he was hopeful.

A minute later, he was back at Maya's side, reluctant to wake her and wondering if she would. He placed a hand on her good shoulder, then her forehead, and her eyes cracked open.

"Breakfast ready?" she asked weakly.

That left him momentarily speechless. "Almost. You want coffee?"

"Green tea, please."

"Figures," he said, a smile spreading across his face. She offered a pained one back.

"Think you can walk?" he asked.

"What?"

"Walk. Think you can do it?"

She thought about it, and as an answer, pain contorted her face as she turned onto her side. She immediately clutched at her wrecked arm. Gus leaned in and held her by her good arm, providing whatever support he could.

"Oh man," a pale-looking Maya groaned as she got to her feet. "Think I'm gonna puke."

Despite the warning, Gus held onto her.

Maya leaned forward and a moment later nodded that the moment had passed.

"What's the plan?" she asked.

It was a good question. As an answer, he smiled back at her.

Almost an hour later, after a few wrong turns, they reached the ground floor. Maya's arm was in a crude sling, made from the sweater he'd found in the office. He left her at a security desk while he ventured outside. Cold, but calm, and without much of a wind. The snow covering the streets had been trampled under the swarming vermin, all gone in the light of day.

He cautiously made his way to the burned Jonathan Inn, and the snowmachine, the same one they had left underneath the overhang, was still there. Still in one piece, although Gus didn't want to think about how many rats had dragged their undead ball sacks over the thing. That was almost enough for him to *not* get on the machine.

But he did anyway and tried to start it. The engine flared to life with a soft roar, and Gus smiled thanks. His fuel gauge was next to empty, but he hoped it would be enough to find the semi the Dragon spoke of the night before. The ride back to Maya wasn't pleasant, but he made it, and had her sit behind him. She draped one arm around his waist and laid her head against his neck.

They left the Jonathan behind and did not look back.

They eventually found the transport truck, as well as two pickups abandoned in the street two blocks away. Gus and Maya left the snowmachine on a sidewalk, and together they checked out the cab of the transport. Empty, but with keys in the ignition, and the fuel tanks half-full, so he helped Maya into the passenger side.

A rucksack took up most of the floorspace. Grunting annoyance, Gus leaned over Maya and picked the thing up by a handle, which caused it to partially open.

Maya noticed him stiffen, his face wooden. "What is it?"

"You don't wanna know."

She smiled weakly. "Now I *have* to know."

Standing over her, Gus reluctantly opened the bag.

There, well along in its decomposition, was the decapitated head of Dog Tongue, partially concealed in the depths of the bag. There was no mistaking the dead Leather warlord. His head was split down the middle, and one eye had been squished into a grisly pudding.

Maya averted her gaze, and that was enough for Gus.

He wrapped up the bag and chucked it into the street.

"Sorry," he said.

"My fault. I wanted to know."

"Why the hell was *that* in there?" he asked.

Maya had no answer.

"Sick fucks." Gus nodded at the grisly discovery lying in the snow. "The rats will take care of that. Come nighttime."

"Will they?"

"Oh yeah. No worries there. You okay?"

"I'm good. Get in."

It took some effort on his part to haul himself up into the driver's side, but he got it done. He started the machine—the sound of the engine almost too sweet to his ears—and cranked up the heat.

"Nice," Maya whispered when the warmth began to flow.

"It is," Gus agreed.

There was food in a small fridge—a collection of homemade bread, cured meats, and bottled jams. The same fare left at the Anchor Bay. Savages they might be, but the Leather had people that knew how to feed the rest. He located the paltry first-aid kit, consisting mostly of bandages and a bottle of painkillers, of which they each took two. After helping Maya and himself to water, and quick beef sandwiches, a question popped into his head. "Ah . . . can you drive this thing?"

She finished sipping from a water bottle. "All day long, if I have to."

With her wrecked shoulder, he wasn't so sure, but what he said was, "There's a bunk in back there."

Maya shook her head. "This is good. I can watch you check out the pickups."

She placed her bottle between her knees and held out a key fob.

Gus took the device and got out, closing the door behind him. He sized up the transport truck and frowned. It was going to be a nightmare trying to drive the thing back to Regina, and even then, there was no way the pickups would handle the snow blocking the city's streets.

He held up the fob, pressed a button, and the nearest rig started up without a hitch. Two for two. His luck was improving. He returned to the cab.

"We good to go?" Maya whispered when he opened the big truck's door.

"Yeah."

"Something on your mind?"

Gus thought about it. "I'll be right back." And closed the door.

He limped along one side of the transport, stopped, and took a leak. The piss helped him think. Regina. Could they make Regina? It seemed a long way off.

And as he neared the end of his morning pee, he thought he heard a child crying.

That backed Gus up a wobbly step as he examined the length of the trailer.

No. I mean . . . no. Jesus Christ, no.

He shuffled down the length of the truck until he faced the back doors. He quickly unlocked them and he gripped a bar with both hands . . . and pulled. The door yawned open, the hinges creaking all the way.

Gus stopped and stared, his mouth dropping open.

There, in a huddle, looking both freezing and miserable, and staring at him with wide-eyed fear . . . was a family. A man, two women (one of whom was older than the other two), and four children. The kids looked to be between nine and eleven, all red-faced, sniveling, and shivering from the cold. They wore sweaters, jeans, and socks, but even then, the temperature in the trailer was next to zero, and it stank. One little boy with a pair of filthy fists pressed against his mouth looked to his mom, then his dad.

Gus stared at them for horrified seconds.

Then he lifted his hand, tried to look friendly, and offered a feeble wave of a hand.

First thing he did was get them out and load them all into the warm cab of the semi. The details came during that time. They were the last of two separate families who had survived the past few years by isolating themselves on their farm. Tom was the father of two children; Sara, the mother of two more; and her mother-in-law,

Barbara. The Leather took them all without a real fight, much to Tom's tearful chagrin, and killed his wife. Sara lost her husband as well as her father-in-law. Other than Tom's brutally squished hand, they had suffered through forty-eight hours or so imprisoned in the cold trailer, on the brink of dehydration and huddled together to share body warmth. The Leather had given them water, but Sara suspected it was poisoned, and dumped the bottle near the door to remove the temptation. Without hope, freezing, famished, and parched, they had just about given up. They thought they would die in each other's arms in that lightless trailer.

Whatever food and water Gus had in the cab was doled out and quickly consumed. Though weakened from her ordeal, Sara was the only one who had all her working limbs, and eventually helped with transporting the extra fuel from one pickup to the other. Tom could operate the semi, despite his wrecked left hand, thus relieving Maya of that duty, while Sara offered to drive ahead in the pickup, plowing the way ahead.

Then they came to the biggest question: Where were they going?

They pondered on that while they were crammed into the transport's warm living quarters.

Regina was close, but buried under snow it would be difficult to reach. And since they all needed medical attention, the only place Gus knew of, the only place *close* where they might have a chance to recover in peace . . . was Whitecap.

It was a risk. Winter had set in, so there was a chance the roads might be impassable, but weather patterns were unpredictable. If they could link up with some back roads where the signage was still in place, Gus knew he could get them back to the hidden base. He knew he was supposed to interview these people, as Collie had once done. Considering the meat grinder they'd all been through, however, and looking at the dirty faces of each child and their surviving family, well . . . he'd just have to take his chances.

"I know a place," Gus said.

46

Snow fell in great cottony fluffs, sticking to an assorted wreckage of trailers and ordinary rooftops, adding another layer to what had previously fallen. It wasn't a heavy snowfall, perhaps only half a finger's worth, but it landed on the thirty-plus centimeters already down, overwhelming the countryside in a vast rolling blanket of creamy white. A deep grey haze hid the surrounding hills, and only offered a glimpse of a distant treeline. The prevailing silence was a deep and peaceful one, the setting grand, and the company . . . just the one.

Which suited Rich Trinidad just fine.

A native of Windsor, Ontario, he very much enjoyed the winter. The solitude. The cold didn't bother him one bit, and he relished being outside. So when they needed people for sentry duty, Rich traded in his bandito sombrero for a white woolly cap. He kept his sidearms holstered at his hips, but his main weapon these days was a winter-camouflaged sniper rifle—a bolt action beast, capable of firing fifty caliber shells from a ten-round magazine, with an effective range of just under two thousand meters. That was far and beyond the distance to the destroyed army compound at the base of Whitecap. If Rich needed to make a long-distance shot, he was confident of his rifle, and its stopping power.

He leaned back in a beige easy chair, fluttered his arms, and lifted the white covering that hid him from the chin down. The rifle rested on a firing platform right in front of him, and at times he would lean forward, settle the weapon against his shoulder, and utilize its scope to scan the fringes surrounding Whitecap. Sandbags surrounded Rich's covered nest, all situated just to the right of the entrance to the underground bunker. Snow effectively concealed the guard post, making Rich damn near invisible to anyone from a distance. He would see them long before being seen himself, something that he very much appreciated. And if it was something he couldn't handle himself, he could call for reinforcements on one of Whitecap's off-the-grid cell phones, or just turn and hurry along a snow-shoveled trench some fifteen meters long. An electric vehicle waited at the end of that pathway, ready and waiting to zip through the access tunnel. Underneath his camos, he wore all the gear needed to keep him warm—cap, gloves, extra layers, and thermal long johns, and he had several thick blankets draped over him. Rich considered himself to be many things, but being cold currently wasn't one of them. He figured he looked like a prairie dog with just its head showing. One armed with some serious firepower.

He yawned, quietly, stretching his bearded jaws to the max, and letting the moment pass. When he finished, he rubbed an eye and squinted out at the majesty of the still countryside. The time was a little after three in the afternoon, and the dark would soon seep down from the mountains and swallow the whole of the valley. His cooler of cold sandwiches was empty as was his water, and his coffee was long gone. One of the new guys would relieve him in an hour, whereupon Rich felt like taking his supper in his underground quarters—the safest place he'd known in a very long time. There was a proper cooked dinner on the menu—made with garden fresh vegetables and deer, shot a couple of weeks back before the snow became too deep. He looked forward to a quiet evening of watching old game shows from the '70s and '80s. *Match Game* was currently his favorite.

A noise got his attention, distracting him. The sound of dragging metal, from beyond the trees.

Figures, Rich thought, and leaned forward for the rifle. He screwed his face into the rifle's scope and watched the very edge of Whitecap's plain, where a pair of abandoned checkpoint buildings stood, guarding the one road to the base.

Though still far away, the noise grew in volume. Rich waited for something to appear on the road, turning the rifle a few degrees right or left, only to bring it back to the unmanned checkpoints. No one from Whitecap occupied those buildings, or any other spread across the vast field. Everyone preferred the warm, safe depths of the bunker. Rich was one of them.

A flurry hid the guard posts for a few seconds, and when the wind dropped out a vehicle materialized between the structures, stopped in the road. A pickup truck with a plow shoving a sizeable amount of snow before it. Exhaust spewed from its rear as the machine idled, as if unsure what to do next. Then the doors popped open and figures stumbled forth, stiff from a much too long drive.

Crosshairs centered on the truck. At no time did Rich move his finger for the trigger, content to keep it against the guard. He waited, calmly, patiently, for whoever was getting out of the vehicle to show their faces.

Four children appeared, staying close to their ride. Two adults stepped before them. One walking with a limp. There were others, but they stayed inside the truck.

A stoic Rich Trinidad tracked them with the scope, the crosshairs dead center on one stranger. He shifted his sights on the other, whose lowered head bobbed with every step. No visible weapons.

Lift your face, Rich thought. *Come on. Show it.*

The head came up.

Rich blinked in recognition. *Holy shit*, he thought. The *last* guy he expected to see, assuming he was long dead.

Rich eased his finger off the trigger guard and reached for his phone.

"You ready?" Tom asked.

Gus shook his head. His foot, his poor butchered foot, was a hot and swollen thing that buzzed with a low intensity unwellness. The unpleasant sensation scared him. Walking was no longer a chore, but crippling torture, where every step was a butcher's knife to his instep when he placed pressure on it.

"Yeah," Gus said.

He held on as he hobbled the next pace, reflexively grabbing Tom's coat and failing to contain the squawk of agony that burst from his lips.

"That bad?" the farmer asked.

Gus nodded.

Tom was a good person. Or so Gus thought, based solely on sharing the man's company for the last two days of travel. Sara was good as well. So were Barb (as she insisted people call her) and the kids. They were hurting, emotionally and physically, from the ordeal of the last few days. Gus hoped they would make a full recovery. The semi had run out of fuel the day before, and instead of splitting up the remainder between the two trucks, they piled everything and everyone into the last remaining pickup. A quick stop at a deserted house for blankets, and one oversized boot for his mauled foot, and they were on the road again.

Until the last of the fuel was gone, and the truck rolled to a stop.

Right at Whitecap's doorstep.

Barb called it a miracle. Gus didn't agree. They would still have to walk across a plain crusted over with deep snow, roughly two soccer fields in length. Maybe even farther. It *looked* farther, but that was only because he was a breath away from hacking his foot off himself. The thing was swollen, ballooning around the toes and that awful gash left by the battle axe. A battle axe whose edge was coated in filth and bacteria and God only knew what else.

The thing would have to come off. He knew it. It would have to, before the infection claimed the rest of his leg.

Another step, one where Gus used Tom's mass like a living crutch to swing his hurting foot ahead of him. It still hurt like fuck when he set it back down.

"How about I piggyback you?" Tom asked.

"You can do that?"

"Don't know if I can make it all the way, but I'll try. We can stop for rests."

Gus glanced back at the pickup. Maya was back there, sick and suffering from her own wounds. They were all hurting. And hungry. Tired. Exhausted, really, racing for the finish line of Whitecap before either a winter storm caught them or they ran out of fuel.

"Okay, let's try—" *that* Gus was about to say, but Tom cut him off by pointing at the mountain.

"Those people your friends?"

There, coming down the icy slope which led up to the tunnel mouth, were two snowmachines, pulling sleighs behind them. They made lines down the slope and buzzed across the open plain toward the two men.

"Yeah," Gus said, clutching at Tom's shoulder. "I think so, anyway."

"Guess we'll find out then," the other man said, watching the slow approach of the machines.

A short time later, the snowmachines stopped beside the pair, and three men got off. Rifles were slung across their backs, but the one that got Gus's attention was the guy with the one-of-a kind pirate's stocking cap, long and warm and wrapped around the owner's neck. A trimmed tumbleweed of a beard graced his chin, along with a wide pair of sunglasses.

The smile on Bruno's face died when he saw Gus.

"You okay there, buddy?" he asked.

"Not really, no," Gus answered before brightening. "But I'm sure as shit happy to see you again, Bruno."

"Never would've thought," the man from Bridgewater said. "Well, let's get you onto the sled there. Along with your friends. Get you all in out of the cold."

They loaded him onto the sled, where he laid back in a heap, staring at the odd boot fitted to his chopped-up foot. The rest of them were loaded onto the two sleds, with Maya being laid out beside Gus.

"Brought us back some strays, I see," Bruno remarked.

"Yeah. They're . . ." He studied the profile of Maya, who was awake and staying very quiet. "They're good people."

She turned her head to consider him.

"Never a question in my mind," Bruno said and smiled. "You all relax, now, you're home. So don't worry about a thing."

For the first time in days, Gus did just that.

Less than an hour later, they were all in Whitecap's infirmary.

Tom, Sara, Barb, and the kids were bundled in blankets, given quick checkups, and then fed hot tea and fresh-made buns lathered in strawberry jam. They laid Gus back into a hospital bed and stripped off both boots, with the swollen foot giving them the most trouble. A woman in her forties, with sun-bleached hair and lovely blue eyes, fussed over him, enough for him to look over at a nearby Bruno.

Who studied Gus's considerable injuries with a frown. "Still fightin' guys bigger than you?"

A weary Gus nodded. *Yes he was. Still.*

"Well, you're in luck," Bruno informed him. "Nancy here was part of the group Collie sent back here from Fort Jay. She has over twenty years' experience as an ER nurse."

"Oh," Gus said, nodding when she offered a brief smile over the mess of his foot. "Ah, well, maybe you could look at Maya's gunshot wound there."

Nancy frowned, peeling back maroon bandages. "In a minute. You managed to clean this?"

". . . Only in a snowdrift."

"So what happened?"

Gus told her.

She touched his toes, setting off a stab of pain that he couldn't hide.

"All right," Nancy said. "I've got work to do. I'll see to your friend there after I get you hooked up to an IV."

"Am I going to lose the foot?" Gus asked.

Nancy hesitated. "I'm going to try *very* hard not to let that happen, but ultimately, it'll depend on how far the infection has progressed. And right now, it looks like it's gone pretty far."

Gus lay back while Bruno hovered nearby. "Ah . . . I'm sorta scared to ask, but . . . what happened to Collie?"

"... She didn't make it."

Taking the news like bad medicine, Bruno frowned.

"She saved me," Gus added in a moment of numb reflection. "Wouldn't be here without her. That's a fact."

"Sorry," Bruno said in a low voice. "She was something else. I liked her. Even when she was choking me out."

"And the dick-punching," Gus reminded him.

"And the dick-punching."

They shared a little smile at that.

"Milo make it back?" Gus asked after a bit.

"Milo? Yeah, he did. Matter of fact . . ."

"Look at you," Milo greeted, stopping at Gus's bedside in an electric wheelchair. The soldier smiled, revealing the brutal dental work performed by Vampire Joe's henchwoman. Teeth were missing. So was one ear. And the tips of his fingers seemed a little misshapen, and some a little longer than others.

"Don't mind any of this," Milo reassured him. "I've had worse."

"You made it back," Gus said weakly, very glad to see the soldier.

"More or less." That spotty smile again, but there was genuine warmth behind it. "Ran into some trouble here and there, but we got through it. I tell you one thing. Those kids? Tough as nails. Remember the tall one? Little Chrissy? She drove half the time. Yeah. She did. And when I passed out? She kept driving until she hit an intersection, where she stopped and waited for me to come to. Anyway, we got back. I've been doing therapy ever since."

"Therapy?"

"Yeah. Learning how to walk again. They busted up my toes too much. Had to cut them off. Well, Nancy did. Did a good job, too. You're in good hands here. Ah . . ." he glanced around and leaned in a little closer. "Collie . . . ?"

Gus didn't flinch. "She's gone."

Taking a moment to absorb that, Milo leaned back and nodded solemnly. "She was something else."

She was, indeed, Gus thought and held out his hand.

Milo grasped it, revealing how Nancy had removed a few fingertips as well, down to the first or second knuckle.

"Good to see you, Milo."

"Good to see you, Gus."

"I'm going to ask you to back it up there, cowboy," Nancy said to him. "You can reminisce when I'm done with him. And this one."

"Who's your friend?" Milo asked.

That caught Gus off guard, enough that he chose his next few words very carefully. "That's Maya. She saved my life. More than a couple of times."

Milo's eyes narrowed as he studied her in the next bed over. He nodded at her and Maya returned it with one of her own.

"Get out of here, Milo," Nancy said with heat in her tone. "You too, B."

Bruno exchanged looks with the soldier and laid a hand on his shoulder.

"We're being kicked out," Milo said. "We'll be back. See how you're doing. Welcome home, Gus."

That struck a chord. *Home.* But was it?

"Thanks, man," he said all the same. "I'm glad you made it back."

"We'll talk later." Electric motor whirling, Milo departed with Bruno right behind him.

"Alone at last," Nancy said, rolling an IV bag over to Gus's bedside. She straightened out the tubing and then his arm. "You're a little dehydrated, so I'm going to pump a liter of fluid into you. Along with a bag of antibiotics and some morphine. While all that's going in you, I'm going to open that cut, clean all the infected tissue I can find, and see if I can save the foot. With a little luck, we just might. Sound good?"

"Yeah."

"You just relax then, and let me work my magic."

Which Gus did, with a look in Maya's direction. She was on her own bed, propped up with pillows, and a number of clear fluid bags hanging nearby. A clear jelly had been applied to her face, causing her rash to gleam.

She reached out for him.

Gus clasped her hand and held it.

Not long after, Gus learned from Nancy that the resident research assistant and Whitecap custodian Josh Rogan had passed away. Shortly after she had arrived at the secret government base. That news hit Gus a little harder than he expected, but thinking of the twitchy Josh and his mad scientist way of speech, he remembered the man saying he believed his time was near. Gus hoped he passed without pain, and that he was in a better place. Hopefully with whoever Josh held dear.

Over the next few days, people came and went. The surprise being, of all things, little Monica—real name now known to all as Sandy—and her reunited aunt, Collette. They spoke for a little bit, and Gus marveled at how the little girl, who didn't talk at all when he first met her, was able to carry on a conversation. When they left, with promises to visit, Gus waved and felt a lump rise in his throat.

Milo visited often and chatted for about an hour at a time before leaving. At no time did Gus have the urge to tell the soldier to fuck off, which was a good thing.

One day, Milo glanced over at where Maya was sleeping. Nancy had sedated her with morphine, while she tried to work on the wreckage of her shoulder. She didn't make any promises, as she wasn't a surgeon. At best, she warned, she might be able to restore at least partial movement of the arm.

"So where did you find Maya?" Milo asked.

"Maya?" Gus asked.

"Yeah."

Gus tried to keep a poker face, and in doing so, probably gave himself away. Beeps and chirps of medical equipment became louder in that moment of awkward silence. Gus checked on Nancy, who sat at a small workstation, going over charts and minding a computer.

"She was with the Leather," he finally said, under his breath.

"With the Leather."

"Yeah."

"You mean a meat puppet?"

"Ah, yeah. A meat puppet."

Milo nodded, studying Gus's face, and making him squirm enough to reach down and scratch at his nuts.

Which wasn't lost on the soldier. "You look like you're trying to start a chain saw when you do that. You know that, right?"

"I . . . did not."

"Scratch away. You earned it. Getting back to Maya . . ."

Gus stopped fiddling with his meat and potatoes.

Milo continued. "Ever tell you about one time, I saw a Leather with his mask off?"

Blinking, Gus shook his head.

"Doesn't happen often. Not out in public, I mean. I guess they take the masks off at night so they can sleep. But during the day? Or when they're out and on the march for the Leather? They're always in full freak mode. Masks on, I mean. Always on. It's their uniform, right?"

"Right," Gus said, trying hard to keep his expression neutral.

"Anyway," Milo said. "There was this one time I saw one with his mask off. It was summer. Hot. Guess he figured no one was around. He was behind an old convenience store having a smoke, leaning up against an ice cooler. Mask in his lap. As soon as he saw me, he froze, right? Like, maybe thinking I was going to say something. But then he saw who I was, which is to say, *not* one of the Leather. Still, it was enough for him to wipe his head off, put out the smoke, and pull the mask on again. But for a few seconds, I saw what it was like to be wearing one of those things all day long, all *week* long."

"Must, ah . . . have been rough," Gus allowed, and scratched at his neck to hide his overwhelming urge to swallow.

"Had to be," Milo agreed. "And this guy? Had his hair buzzed down to the quick. I mean he was *shorn*. No hair at all. Maybe some facial hair, I guess, but what really got my attention was the rash all over the guy's face and head. I mean, he was red and blistering. It was bad. Surface of the sun bad, you know? Surface of *Mars*, even."

"A rash."

"Big time rash. Raging. Exploding. Just by wearing a mask. Skin couldn't breathe, I suppose. Anyway, I walked away. Just made like I didn't see a damn thing. That was a tense five seconds, I tell you. But I'm still here, so the guy didn't do anything about it."

Using his lower teeth, Gus scratched at his upper lip and checked on Nancy's whereabouts. Still at her work terminal.

He leaned toward Milo. "She saved my life. More times than I can care to think about."

That narrowed Milo's eyes.

"I'd be dead if it wasn't for her," Gus continued. "Dead."

Milo's gaze flickered from Gus to Maya's prone form, then back again.

"Without knowing who I was, or where I was from, she saved me. Least I could do is . . . is return the gesture, right? Right? I mean, remember what you said to me? Back at the hotel there that time?"

That put a little smile on the soldier's face.

"We all fuck up," Gus finished, daring him to say otherwise, *pleading* for understanding.

For seconds, Milo didn't say anything. Then he leaned back and exhaled through his nose. "Just saying . . . I imagine that stuff Nancy got on her face will clear that rash up. Or at least improve it. She'll be looking like her regular self in a few days."

"Yeah," Gus said, breathing again and suddenly very grateful. "In a few days. It'll be better. She's a good person. She is."

"I'm sure she is."

Silence then, relaxed and understanding.

"Well," Milo started, glancing at a nearby clock. "Must head on back home. The place they gave me is nice. I'll have you over sometime. When you're able. Anyway, the day's getting on. You want anything?"

"No."

"Well, if you do, just say the word."

"Thanks, Milo. Thank you."

That drew a look. "For what? Just being neighborly."

But it was there, unspoken. He was giving Maya a chance. For that, Gus would owe him one.

"Seeya later, chuggernuts," the soldier said.

"Later butterballs."

That crunched Milo's face in amusement. Chuckling, he wheeled about his ride and rode on out of the infirmary, waving over his shoulder as he passed through the doors.

Gus watched him leave.

And that was that. No one else asked him about her. She was with him, and that was good enough for the folks of Whitecap.

So they stayed in the infirmary, on the mend.

Tom, Sara, mom-in-law Barb, and the kids were the first to leave, only after a couple of hours after first being admitted. Nancy checked on them when she had the chance, and after deeming them shaken but by no means stirred, she let them go with instructions into the care of Jane Wong. Jane had taken on the task of introducing the bunker to new arrivals, and was also taking them to their newly assigned homes. Gus didn't know all the details, but he assumed no one would be leaving Whitecap during the winter. He hoped they liked it here, enough to consider staying and becoming part of the growing community. And if not, well, they could leave in the spring.

Gus was the next person to be released, up and moving two days later. Nancy provided him with a wheelchair and a bottle of antibiotics, which she assured him were safe to ingest but to return if he had any feelings of nausea, dizziness, or migraines. He steered the wheelchair back to his room, but once inside, with the door closed behind him, the space seemed more like a well-furnished cell. Worse, a deep and aching loneliness filled his chest, hollowing him out and leaving him longing for company.

He spoke with Milo again, when he came to visit. They talked of what had happened since they parted ways in Regina. Even talked of their lives before the zombie outbreak.

While he was speaking with the soldier, however, Gus's thoughts were elsewhere.

In the days that followed, Gus left the chair behind and opted for crutches. He caught up with Bruno and Cory Shale, and it was good to see them both. He was even glad to see Sarah Burton and mechanic Carson from Camp Red Wolf, who informed him that the people from the summer camp had made a new home at Whitecap, and were very thankful to Gus and Collie for bringing them to the bunker. They lamented over the loss of Collie and Josh Rogan, but were happy with the new additions to the little community, and the possibilities of the coming spring. There was a lot of cleared land around the bunker, and while it was safe to remain inside, people were eager to return to the surface to see what they could do. Not leave the bunker entirely, but keep it at their backs as an option while they stepped outside.

All the while Gus listened and got caught up on past events and future plans. His mind drifted at times, however. To the point where, when the conversations were done, and they'd all parted ways, he would wander back to the infirmary and check in on Maya. He was the first to learn from Nancy that Maya's shoulder was indeed a mess, and that it was beyond her capability. Gus knew Maggie back in Big Tancook might be able to do something, but that was several days away, and traveling was out of the question. Nancy had reset what bones she could, but she doubted Maya would regain full range of motion with her arm.

Nodding quietly, Gus absorbed the news while sitting at Maya's bedside, staring yet not seeing the collection of medical devices hooked up to the sleeping woman.

One morning, when he returned to the infirmary, Nancy gestured for him to go right on in. Maya was awake and fiddling with the IV tubes attached to the valley of her arm. Her forehead and cheeks gleamed under the fluorescent lighting, from where a topical ointment had been applied to her facial rash. A rash that had all but disappeared.

"Hey you," she greeted him in a weary tone.

"Hey. Mornin'. How you doin'?"

"Not bad, same old. Trouble with my shoulder."

"Sorry."

"Oh, it's okay," she said. "I'm not bothered too much. Only really hurts when I try to lift it. Nancy said it'll be like that for the remainder of my days. All things considered, it's a small price to pay. I'll take it."

"A good attitude to have," Gus noted.

"Things have certainly improved for me, especially morally," she added. "Spiritually. Nancy's very good. They all seem like very good people. The way a community should be. Or is trying to be, after all these years. It's . . . weird. No one's been . . . this good to me in a very long time."

He nodded at that.

"Ah . . . I have a favor to ask."

Interested, Gus leaned in.

"Could you . . ." at this point she lowered her voice to a whisper, ". . . not tell people I was . . . with the Leather? I think that would be best."

". . . I can do that."

A little smile crept across her medicated features. "I mean, that's behind me now. I'll be forever guilty, but there might be some people here who . . . if they knew." She shrugged. "You understand what I'm saying here."

"Yeah, I do."

"Thank you, Gus."

"Thank you," he said.

"For what?"

"Saving me."

She smiled. "You saved me first."

Gus wasn't so sure of that, but he didn't argue the point.

47

One month later.

They sat on the warm sand of an artificial beach some hundred feet wide, under palm trees and amongst unmoving grass. Clumps of plastic flowers, arranged in broad, thick bands, crowned tall dunes behind them, granting a little privacy from passersby. The water was calm, smelling mildly of chlorine, and stretched out some forty feet where the view became a perfect sky blue, and a dimmed sun hung between distant mountains. The sound of birds and surf filled the background, playing from hidden speakers. Warm air seeped through hidden heating vents, keeping the temperature at a comfortable but balmy twenty-nine degrees Celsius.

Gus wore a T-shirt, along with an exceptionally reserved pair of blue beach shorts. It was the best he could do with the local shopping options. Maya was the same, but her clothes were much looser on her, giving her a frumpy appearance. She had her arm out of its sling, to exercise it just a little as Nancy had instructed. As warned, Maya did not have the full range of motion with her shoulder, as she could no longer bring her arm above her head, nor could she reach around to her back. Both movements brought her sharp pain. She didn't talk about it unless asked, whereupon she would briefly answer before subtly moving on to other subjects.

There was a little table between their beach chairs. On it, a bottle of Captain Morgan Orange Vanilla Twist, alongside a bottle of Jack Daniel's Tennessee Honey. Both were exceptional with a mixer of ginger ale and ice.

Uncle Jack never visited him again, and Gus did feel regret over his handling of things. The old guy was only looking out for him, after all, warning him not to become that which he most despised. Gus would have explained that as well but had never gotten the chance. Thing was, maybe it didn't matter. Because of the bottle they had beachside—and its label which included a picture of the distinguished gentleman himself. A hint of a smile disarmed his usually stern face as if, despite all his warnings, he approved of how things turned out in the end. Gus didn't become a flat-out savage like the Leather . . . at least not permanently. Even better, not only was Gus still alive, but he was in much better spirits despite his most recent wounds.

Gus hoped the old gentleman approved. He could never stay angry at Uncle Jack. The guy was practically family. And the Tennessee Honey was a damn fine drink.

After what they'd been through, Gus felt a little reward was in order. And he promised himself he would drink responsibly after inviting Maya to the beach . . . for a smile.

Which she did, after sampling her drink.

"See?" Gus asked. "Did I lie?"

"You did not. Tasty."

"Not too strong?"

She shook her head. The leather-blighted rash plaguing her complexion had cleared completely, leaving scars and dents but nothing like before. Also, over the last few weeks, her hair was growing out and was currently at a very chic length. Stealing looks at her every so often, or just while they talked, Gus realized he had to scale it back a little, as it was becoming obvious.

Not that she seemed to mind. "This is nice," she said, eased back into her chair, uncrossing then crossing her legs. "Think we'll get a burn?"

Gus let off a contemplative sigh. "Be surprised if we do. Might get a buzz, though."

"I don't drink at all."

"Well, just nurse that one and we'll go from there. I'm not a drinker myself. Not no more, anyway."

But the occasion justified one.

"I could fall asleep here," she said.

"Well," Gus glanced around. "Go ahead. Even snore if you want. We got the place to ourselves."

Maya smiled, still hiding her missing teeth, which he didn't mind at all. Perhaps one day they would meet a dentist. Get some work done on both of them.

"It's nice here," she said, looking across the water.

"You know it's minus twenty-three on the surface?" Gus informed her. "That's with the wind chill. And four or five feet of snow on the ground."

"No way."

"Way. Rich told me. Before he went for his shift."

She shivered. "This is paradise."

"In comparison? Yeah, it is. Well, serves the purpose. We'll see what happens in the spring."

"What happens in the spring?"

Gus half-shrugged and studied his glass. "The boys—that's Bruno and Cory—will be heading back to the coast. Meet up with the folks on Big Tancook. See how they're doing."

"Are you going?"

"Haven't decided yet. Maybe. Got some friends back there. I should. Maybe you could come along."

Maya considered it, and he sensed he'd just entered into dangerous territory, of a matter he wasn't going to like.

"Gus, I have to talk to you about something."

Well, shit. "Okay . . ."

"How should I say this . . . Look. I believe the people here to be exceptionally nice. Perfect, to be honest. And I've enjoyed my stay . . . but . . ."

Gus's stomach lurched at the cliff-hanger of a word.

"As much as I like this place, come spring I won't be able to stay."

Birdsong and the rustling surf filled the gap of silence.

"What?" Gus barely managed to get out.

"Part of it is who I was," she explained. "I've recognized that I want . . . I need . . . time with fewer people around. I've always been something of an introvert. And while I don't mind living under a mountain in the short term, it's not my home. And that's where I want to be."

"Oh . . ." Gus muttered, disappointed and barely concealing his dismay. "Home."

"Yes."

"Well, this . . . is home for a lot of people."

"I'm sure it is, but it's not for me."

He cleared his throat and shifted. "Where's home, then?"

"Well . . ." she glanced away for a few seconds. "I'm a mountain girl at heart. Grew up in Banff. That's where my family's buried. Before all this started, that is. I know the town. The area. The Rockies. Most beautiful spot in the country, I'll have you know. The mountains. The lakes. Sunrises and sunsets. The alpine air in the summertime. You know the Four Towers? There's a place in Banff like that. Just like that one. Called the Gail and Marcus. Huge place. Twenty stories high. Royalty would be impressed."

"You'd leave all this for that place?" Gus joked weakly, sweeping his hand.

"To go home? Oh yes."

That stunned him, like a plank to the face.

She saw his reaction. "I mean I know you like it here. You have friends. And obviously you're closer to your friends back east. The hotel I'm talking about is entirely green powered, like the Four Towers. It has its own conservatory, so food can be grown there. With a little love, it'll be able to produce fruits and vegetables. It has water. Heat. All the amenities you could want. It was one of the many bases of the Leather, chosen not only for its features but because it's also easily defendable. There's no one there now, of course. Totally deserted. Dog Shit pulled everyone away from there for the push east. An all-inclusive tower situated in the middle of the Rockies, ready for me or anyone to move into. It's an ideal place to start a new community. And, well, it's aboveground."

Still dazed, Gus nodded.

"Geographically, it's out of the way, but . . . it's home. It's an exceptional place, outstanding, really. Offering the means for a very comfortable life. An ideal starting place for anyone, really."

"Well," he said, looking over at her. "Those are . . . all good points."

"Don't worry about the points," she said, and took a deep, death-defying breath. "What I'd like you to consider, if you're so inclined, is to come with me."

Now Gus stared. Stunned again, by the offer. Her choice of words sent a weird tingling through him, a fierce sense of déjà vu.

"We go there and check the place out," she continued in a rush. "Do a little systems check. Ensure all is still functioning the way it should be. We can ask others to come along if they're inclined. I'm an introvert but by no means a hermit. We'll need other people. Without question. Once we've secured the hotel and reestablished a system of transportation and infrastructure. One that doesn't include Skull Road."

She met his gaze and took another breath. "Anyway, that's all for the spring. We have plenty of time to prepare for that between now and then. But the main thing you should consider, about going, if you decide to go, that is . . . is that you'll be with me."

Gus stared at her, in mute amazement. She'd kept a decidedly warm poker face over the last few weeks, but this . . .

"You want me to go with you?" he asked.

She shrugged. "Well, yes."

"Can I ask you something?"

Now she looked uncertain. "Sure."

He put his glass on the table, next to the smiling Captain, and the warm glow of Uncle Jack's Tennessee Honey. He stood, straightened, and without warning, stepped over to where a suddenly uncertain Maya sat in her chair. Gus leaned over, paused for a considering second, and then kissed her, on her cheek.

She blinked, surprised at the contact, the hint of a smile playing about her lips as she rubbed her face. "I'm still using the ointment Nanc—"

He kissed her mouth then, twice, leaving her speechless, her eyes huge and questioning. Then she reached up, gripped the back of his head, and kissed him back.

On that artificial beach, underneath the fake shade, and in the face of a simulated sun . . .

Nothing was more real.

One year later.

Gus rose from bed, rubbed the sleep from his face, and glanced over at the still sleeping form of Maya, curled under the comforters. The air was warm, as was the floor, but the scene outside the penthouse window, which was, in fact, the whole wall, showed a fairy-tale valley, the mountains white-capped and blowing winds colored with snow, all backlit by a sun wrapped in cloudy silk.

Maya mumbled something, still mostly asleep.

"I got it," he told her, smiling faintly. "You stay in bed."

As an answer, she snored.

I got it, Gus reflected, gazing out the window onto that magnificent view that was, in his life anyway, unmatched. He'd only seen pictures of it before in travel magazines. Now, he woke up to it every morning.

I most certainly do got it, he decided. *Boy, do I ever.*

Life hadn't just improved . . . it had become . . . fucking awesome.

He stood, dressed in silk pajamas. The pajamas took some getting used to in the beginning, because when he wore them he was constantly feeling himself up. In bed was another matter, because then he felt like an egg sliding across a nonstick pan. Until Maya held onto him, frequently, in fact, which gave him a newfound appreciation for the things. And having someone in bed with him on a regular basis.

He scratched at his chest, and his eyes fell upon the night table and the letter resting there, once considered an ancient means of communication, but now restored and valued. Scott had written him, sending word from Big Tancook. All was good back there. Amy and kids were fine and growing. Hope to visit one day.

Gus hoped his friend and his family would.

Yawning again, he opened the little fridge near the bed, because it was that kind of room. Inside were half a dozen bottles of breast milk. Rubbing a finger underneath his nose, scratching an itch there, Gus took one out, readied it, and wandered over to the crib. Two cribs in fact. Not five feet away from their bed. Lammy was in one crib, peeking up over discarded blankets. On the way out to Banff in the spring, Gus insisted on making a detour to Regina, to stop at the Anchor Bay. The little stuffed lamb was still in the lobby, waiting for someone to pick him up. Which Gus did and then took him along.

Then he checked on the gravesite. Paid his respects. Held a moment of reflective silence. And left. One day . . . he'd probably return. Maybe.

Inside the cribs lay twins, two months old.

A girl and a boy.

Maya had surprised him when she came up with the names, because, obviously, she'd been talking to people. Not that Gus minded. In fact, he very much liked her choices. Felt good. Felt like a full circle. Where only good things lay ahead.

The boy was Wallace.

And the girl . . . Collette. Affectionately referred to as Collie.

Wallace was still sleeping. That was good. Little Collie was the one fussing, her pink blanket halfway down her front, spit bubbles on her tongue. When Collie saw him, she kicked and waved her pudgy little arms.

Gus straightened Lammy lying next to her. Then he gathered her up in a blanket and fed her the bottle. He stood and turned, watching her watch him while she drank, until her eyes closed, and one hand rested against her cheek. She reached up once and touched hair as fine as a doll's.

That one gesture put a content smile on an old face.

Every day he wondered if he deserved any of this. And every day he was thankful.

There, in the warm room overlooking a winter valley, where a crown of mountains wore white-tipped hats, Gus held his daughter, listened to her eating, and gazed out at the new world.

Acknowledgments

There were many hands involved in the production of this work after it left my desk. I'd like to thank Peter Gaskin, for his time and patience while working on the developmental edit of *Skull Road*. I'd also like to thank Victoria Gerken, Nicole Passage, and the rest of the fine folks at Podium Publishing for editing, proofreading, and marketing the whole Mountain Man series.

And thank you, dear reader, for taking a chance on the stories.

About the Author

Keith C. Blackmore is the author of the Mountain Man, 131 Days, and Breeds series, among other horror, heroic fantasy, and crime novels. He lives on the island of Newfoundland in Canada. Visit his website at www. keithcblackmore. com.

Podium

DISCOVER
STORIES UNBOUND

PodiumAudio.com